# The
# NOONDAY
# CEMETERY

### and Other Stories

# The
# N O O N D A Y
# C E M E T E R Y

## and Other Stories

## G U S T A W   H E R L I N G

*Translated from the Polish by* BILL JOHNSTON

A New Directions Book

The stories in this edition originally appeared in *Opowiadania zebrane* (Collected Stories, vols. 1 and 2), published 1999 by Czytelnik of Warsaw.

Further acknowledgments are found on page 282.

Manufactured in the United States of America
First published clothbound by New Directions in 2003
Published simultaneously in Canada by Penguin Books Canada Limited
New Directions Books are printed on acid-free paper.

Library of Congress Cataloging-in-Publication Data

Herling-Grudzinski, Gustaw, 1919-2000
  [Short stories. English. Selections]
  The noonday cemetery and other stories / Gustaw Herling ; translated from the Polish by Bill Johnston.
     p. cm.
  ISBN 0-8112-1529-6 (alk. paper)
  1. Herling-Grudzinski, Gustaw, 1919---Translations into English. I. Johnston, Bill. II. Title.
  PG7158.H446A25 2003
  891.8'537--dc21                      2003000358

New Directions Books are published for James Laughlin
by New Directions Publishing Corporation,
80 Eighth Avenue, New York 10011

# TABLE OF CONTENTS

# The
# NOONDAY
# CEMETERY

## and Other Stories

# THE NOONDAY CEMETERY

## An open story

*Certain authors, when they speak of their works, say*
*"My book, my commentary, my history, etc." . . .*
*They would do better to say: "our book, our commen-*
*tary, our history, etc.," seeing that usually there is*
*more of other people's work than their own therein.*

—Pascal: *Pensées*

*The dead concealed lie easy in this earth*
*That keeps them warm, drying their mystery.*
*And Noon up there, Noon the motionless . . .*

—Paul Valéry: *The Graveyard by the Sea*

## I

THE PLACE WHICH I immediately dubbed in my mind the Noonday Cemetery is situated one kilometer—maybe one and a half—
from the poor village of Albino in the Salerno region. I visited it
for the first time toward the end of the fifties, without any particular reason or purpose; I was simply impressed and attracted by its
singular location. It lay not so much beyond the village as above
it—an extremely rare circumstance if only for purely practical con-
siderations: The climb up to the cemetery gates required a large
effort from the elderly on their Sunday visits, and from funeral
processions by one- or two-horse cart (the steep and bumpy road
made use of a truck impossible). And never mind the front of the
cemetery with its gate! The cemetery's back was enclosed by a wall

of medium height, and literally hung over a precipice; it could be seen clearly from the main road that led to Salerno. The wall was built on a rock overgrown with bushes, immediately beneath which the hill fell almost vertically to the bottom of a deep wooded ravine. By straining one's eyes, in the ravine one could discern a small house amid deciduous trees. At one time the keeper of the cemetery lived there: in the morning he rode a mule to work up the only path, and in the evening he walked back down to his home, leading the mule carefully, as it slipped frequently on the trail. The keeper's house was known as *la casa al fondo della gola*, "the house at the bottom of the ravine," and the name has survived till today, though now the house is only a memory.

Before I finally made up my mind, despite the burning August sky, to climb sweating and breathless up to the gates of the cemetery, I had been in Albino twice on successive years, visiting a friend of mine who for many years had spent his summer vacations alone in a room with a small terrace that he rented from a farmer.

Renato, my friend, a man of few words, was a librarian and bookworm from Rome. Sickly and convinced that he did not have long to live, he came to Albino in the summers for the "mountain air" and for the thin strip of sea that could be seen on the horizon from his terrace. He was indifferent to everything else. His meals were prepared by the farmer's wife. He himself never left the house to go on walks but was capable of spending the livelong day sitting in a deck chair with his nose in a book. During my second visit, when I asked him about the curiously situated cemetery, he shrugged and with a note of boredom in his voice muttered that the villagers had probably been trying to protect the graves of their loved ones from the floods that were frequent here in the late autumn—the streams of water that flowed down from the nearby mountains (hence the "mountain air") and burst upon the village down in the valley. His explanation was ridiculous, as was that "mountain air," which allegedly came from two extraordinary-looking, almost biblical cliffs a short distance from Albino; these cliffs truly were beautiful, but detailed maps of the region showed them to rise only 300 meters above sea level. I put my own interpretation to my friend, though I am not certain that he took it in, since his nose remained buried in the book he was reading at the time. In my view, the cemetery had been placed high up so that the dead should be properly kept warm, and could dry their bones and their secrets in the noonday summer sun, while at the same time they could watch their sea from the best vantage point in Albino (for the majority of the dead were probably fishermen and sailors). I suspect that Renato was not paying any attention to me. On the other hand, I realized after I had spoken that his old landlord Bartolo had been listening from his chair outside the front door of the house. He stood up at once and said, "Pardon me for butting in, *dottore*, but your guest is right."

In the afternoon Bartolo accompanied me to the bus, which came to Albino twice a day. It was he who told me on the way, rather vaguely and reservedly, about the "house at the bottom of the ravine" behind the cemetery. "Since the death of Fasano, the cemetery keeper," he said, "we haven't wanted a replacement. Now no one tends the graves; no one apart from the families. The house at the bottom of the ravine is empty; they say that at night it's haunted. But it's a long story, *ma è una lunga storia*."

## II

I TRULY WAS sweating and gasping for breath when I reached the cemetery gates; my eyes were soaked in perspiration, and red spots chased beneath my lowered eyelids. The entrance was open; all one had to do was press down on the cracked handle of a wicket-gate in the right-hand corner. I had barely passed inside when the sun seemed to begin burning with redoubled force. I smiled as I thought of the accuracy of my "interpretation": the dead were being warmed and were drying their bones (and their secrets, as Valéry would have it); and as for the sea, from the plateau of the cemetery there extended what was probably the fullest view of the bay. Waves marked by white streaks of foam moved towards the fishing harbor with an even motion, while the sun ignited a multitude of sparks in the greenish-blue water. Far away on the horizon a huge liner was sailing along, so slowly that it seemed to be at anchor. Nearer the shore, several boats had cast their nets into the water. The shouts of the fishermen could be heard, and even the subdued lament of some melancholy southern song.

Most of the graves in the cemetery were marked by crosses that were made of wood and so already rotten; their inscriptions were almost illegible, though they bore oval-shaped likenesses of the dead. A few had crosses or small pyramids of stone where some wealthier family of the deceased had wanted a lengthy (and usually florid) epitaph. In the middle of the cemetery, there stood a partially polished boulder, which I recognized at once as a block from one of those "biblical" cliffs near Albino. I shall say a few words about them here, because it is not often in Italy that one encounters such specimens. The cliffs are stratified and veined, like immense petrified trees hewn down in a tempest by the ax of a lightning bolt. Those conversant in geology could perhaps calculate their age on the basis of the stone veins and the glistening black patches upon them. I called them "biblical," thinking of the rare illustrations in luxury editions of the Bible—the fruit of the illustrators' imaginations. Also biblical in its way, due to its dramatic terseness, was the inscription on the large stone block in the center of the cemetery: six names with the dates of their births and deaths, after which the short phrase: *sconfitti e inghiottiti dal Mare*, "defeated and swallowed up by the Sea." The grave, then, was empty; over the years the fish had eaten all that was left of the six fishermen of Albino.

I leaned against the wall enclosing the back of the cemetery. From a sky that was ashen, or rather by now entirely colorless, the dry flame of the sun descended to the earth without a breath of wind. It was around three o'clock. One had to lift oneself up slightly in order to place one's arms on top of the wall and take in at a single glance the ravine and the bay. The ravine was filled with a swirl of vegetation, dense and wild, overwhelming and choking the barely visible house at the bottom. And yet the mass of greenery did not prevent the play of reflections of light, which at times gave the impression of living beings, human or animal, flitting rapidly amongst the trees and bushes, creeping towards the house and then immediately fleeing from it. The heat was doubtless playing pranks on my eyes, which had misted over. The effect was even stronger as I watched the surface of the sea in the bay, where the sparks struck by the sun formed themselves into strange figures of people and of great fish arching out of the water at a bound. I once read that seeing such things is the first symptom of sunstroke. I lacked the strength to drag myself as quickly as possible to the gate and to stagger back down the steep road to the village, so I looked around in search of the tiniest bit of shade. In the corner of the cemetery there grew a fairly broad bush with large leaves. There I could lie down on the short dry grass.

This corner was ringed by a semicircle of rocks, as if excluded from the rest of the cemetery. Three low graves—one older, two more recent—were marked by three wooden crosses that lacked enameled photographs of those buried there, or even the simplest words of farewell. They had nothing but names and dates. The oldest cross was marked Manfred Weinert, born May 2, 1911, died October 25, 1943. On the two newer graves: Vincenzo Fasano, born Albino, January 6, 1914, died August 16, 1949; and Inge Weinert, *geboren* Mander, born March 23, 1918, died August 16, 1949.

**III**

OLD BARTOLO WORE the expression of a person who has said far too much in the first conversation, and so in the second intends like a good gardener to prune overgrown branches. He nodded his head thoughtfully.

"Yes, yes, *è una lunga storia*, but a man's memory evaporates when he's got the burden of eighty years to carry. Like a puddle in the sunshine, only holes in the ground are left . . . After they landed at Salerno, *gli alleati*, the Allies, headed inland. The ravine on the far side of Albino blocked their way, locking up the road like a great key. They had to displace a German unit that was entrenched in the house at the bottom of the ravine, and in a few pockets amongst the trees. They achieved their goal, wiping out every last defender of the ravine—with the exception of the commanding officer, who, sticking his pistol in Fasano's back, followed him up the path to the cemetery. There he set up a machine gun in the corner by the wall, and fired on the Allies from above in such an effective manner that the entire column was immobilized. The Americans brought the cemetery under fire, though they tried not to destroy it with mortar shells. The exchange of fire lasted all day. Towards evening a shot, either well-aimed or stray, hit the German officer. He fell, or rather, sat down dead, right there in the corner of the cemetery. And that was where he was buried by Fasano, who told the Americans that the German officer had fallen down the hillside towards the bottom of the ravine. I don't know why he did this; some reckoned that during the day-long shooting, as he remained right by the officer's side he had grown to like him and to regard him as the defender of the cemetery; others said he wished to give him a Christian burial. In any case, he brought the frightened priest from Albino, who, seeing the dog-tag around the dead man's neck with his name and date of birth, breathed a sigh of relief, reassured that the man had been a Roman Catholic. The inscription on the cross was added later with the information from the dog-tag. This is all that by some miracle hasn't evaporated from my memory."

"And the two other graves? The grave of Fasano, and of the woman who must have been the wife or sister of the dead officer? Why are the dates of their deaths the same?"

Old Bartolo flushed slightly and scratched his head.

"I don't remember, *dottore*, I really don't remember. People said something or other, they said a lot of things, and the papers wrote about the cemetery in Albino; but it's all evaporated from my memory, it's all dried up. I remember Vincenzo Fasano; he was a good guy. He took care of our cemetery. He left no family—he was an orphan and a bachelor—but I hear he had a distant cousin in Salerno who was a lot older than he. That cousin was a journalist. Apparently he came here often, asking people questions, but then he stopped. God alone knows if he's still alive. His name? I don't know his name."

What was old Bartolo afraid of? What had caused his memory to "evaporate"? It was exactly the same with the other inhabitants of Albino whom I tried to sound out. In the best case they would repeat, almost word for word, the wartime episode from October 1943. In the worst I was turned away with silence, a shrug of the shoulders, and a reluctant *non ricordo*. It took me some time to discover the source of their fear: The house at the bottom of the ravine was considered to be bewitched, cursed. Twice people had

tried to buy it, at a ridiculously low price—the municipal fee, set in
Salerno by the local authorities in the absence of inheritors. And
twice a trial night spent in the house prompted the would-be purchasers to withdraw their offer. The second time a young English
couple from Naples had intended to buy the house. Both worked as
lecturers at the University, and so it was easy for me to make their
acquaintance. It was unbelievable! Emphatically, even rudely, these
educated, intelligent people refused point blank to talk about the
house at the bottom of the ravine. The one sentence that I managed to extract from them was the brief: *It is ghastly*. In fact, they
ought really to have said: *It is ghostly*, since a quiet, a very quiet
rumor amongst the people declared that ghosts were present in the
house at the bottom of the ravine.

At the beginning of September, the weather turned sharply
cooler and I was better able to satisfy my curiosity. I arrived in Albino on the first bus, in the early morning, and walked through the
sleeping village straight to the cemetery. From there, I began a
cautious descent towards the bottom of the ravine, down the path
from the back wall. I say cautious, because in all my life I have
never walked a path so strewn with fallen trees, sudden dips and
loose rocks; I continually asked myself how Fasano could have
come down here with his mule in the evening, when it often must
have been dark; and then in the morning ridden up to the cemetery
on the creature's back. Especially dangerous were the branches extending over the path from the dense woods; they were springy and
needed to be pushed aside slowly and carefully, to prevent them
from striking back like a rod at one's chest or head. Once an adder
flashed across the path; more often, though, I would see a *biscia*, a
harmless grass snake. As I descended the path, the silence seemed
to grow denser along with the vegetation. I began to feel unsure of
myself, regretting the common curiosity that had driven me to undertake this expedition. From the top, the journey to the bottom of
the ravine had looked shorter; now, as often happens, feelings of
uncertainty drew the trip out. Finally I arrived, scratched and cut,
in a small meadow or clearing at whose edge the house could be
seen. But looking behind me I saw, not without a certain irrational
fear, that from here the cemetery on the hill was no longer visible. I
felt as if I had fallen into a deep well.

The house was of modest proportions. The handle on the front
door had been broken and was fastened with a loop of wire. Inside
was one room with a sizeable kitchen where, aside from a large
heating stove, there stood in the corner a low, primitive cooker
with two rings. A broad bed knocked together from planks took up
much of the room; on it there was a tattered mattress, blackened by
age, with stains of an indefinable color, and tufts of oakum poking
out of holes. There were no floorboards in the house; their place
was taken by an evenly packed earth floor, now green with patches
of fresh grass. On the wall hung a dirty, fly-specked reproduction
of the Black Madonna from the Piedmont Sanctuary in Oropa—
how had it come to be in these parts? The general impression of
decay and rot was not accompanied by any stench or stuffiness,
since both of the barred windows were missing their glass. In the
large sty that had been built onto the house I found a trough filled
with rancid water, and on the wall of the house a pair of goat's
horns nailed to a beam. The one unfilthy thing in the whole place
was a bench in front of the house, which had quite simply been
thoroughly washed by the rain.

I lay down on it wearily. Or rather, I was not weary so much as
strangely languid and dizzy all of a sudden. Does there exist an atmosphere of mystery suspended in the air, something invisible that
can be seen only with the different gaze of the initiated? Certainly
so. I know this from writers who are peculiarly sensitive to that
"different gaze" and have attempted to describe it—writers such as
Henry James in *The Turn of the Screw*. And it was this mystery
hanging in the air that I sensed clearly—all too clearly, for it was
mixed with my own disquiet as I lay on the bench. But God or fate
did not give me that "different gaze"; or rather, it has been given to
me at times, very rarely, in dreams. Falling into a deep sleep on the
bench, I saw several times fleetingly (though who can measure
what is fleeting in dreams, where rich and complex events can
sometimes last but a minute, while trifling details can continue for
hours, fading away and returning?), I saw, then, a man and a
woman: now lying on the bed in the main room of the house, now
kneeling at the cooker, now slowly climbing the path towards the
cemetery.

My sleep on the bench in front of the house must have had

something of the quality of a long swoon: Despite the fact that I
had descended to the bottom of the ravine in the early morning (I
had arrived in Albino rested), I woke up at dusk, as exhausted as if
I had fallen asleep after a whole day's walk. I was seized by a slight
panic: I was reluctant to climb back up in the dark. I set off, however, placing my feet carefully, my heart in my mouth, still dizzy
and mortally weary, taking every rustle in the trees and bushes
along the path for a sign of someone lurking there. Halfway up, the
crimson of the sunset died away, and a pale moon sailed into the
sky over the still-pink horizon of the sea. Soon afterwards I was reassured to see the wall of the cemetery, and a little higher a small
flame amongst the dark crosses. It was a mortuary candle, lit on an-
niversaries at the boulder commemorating the six fishermen. At
the base of the memorial sat old Bartolo; he had lost his younger
brother in the tragedy of those "defeated and swallowed up by the
Sea."


## IV


SEVERAL YEARS PASSED, and the Noonday Cemetery slowly
faded from my memory and my imagination, the more so because
my summer visits to Albino came to an end: My friend Renato fell
seriously ill, and was moved from Rome to his family in Padua,
where he spent his time between home and a private clinic under
constant medical supervision (with poor prospects for recovery). I
went to see him only once, sitting at his bedside for an hour. Now
that he could scarcely even read, having been rendered half-blind
by his illness, he recalled Albino (at least with me). But not the
cemetery, which incidentally he had never visited; he just remembered his favorite village, and how he would lie on the terrace,
breathing the "mountain air" and gazing over his book at the thin
strip of sea. How little is needed for that which precedes the
shadow of death to be turned into a paradise lost!

As I said, the Noonday Cemetery had gradually faded in my
memory and my imagination; but I knew that it would never disappear entirely. From year to year the wicket gate at the entrance was
closing more and more; and yet its narrowing gap never ceased to

be open. Why was this? I was conscious of having come into contact with a puzzle which, despite my inquiries, had remained unsolved. We do not like such situations, and not at all because—or at least not exclusively because—we are tormented by our unsated curiosity. Somewhere in the depths of our being, despite all the mechanisms of rationality, there is lit, extinguished, then lit again the tiny light of an innate sense of mystery, which draws us instinctively and irresistibly toward any enigmas that we encounter in life. Nabokov wisely wrote in *The Gift*: "I know more about God than I am able to express in words, and the little that I can express in words would never have been expressed if I did not know more." We pass through life gathering, consciously or unconsciously, reflections of this little divine light, gathering evidence of the fact that as we know more and more, we are less and less able to express it in words.

I remember the date. On June 14, 1962, some friends of mine in Naples persuaded me to go with them to Salerno to a meeting of *Italia Nostra*, the Society for the Protection of the Countryside. The meeting took place in a small room in the local museum, and was attended by about fifty people. To begin with I found it tedious; the noble lament over the systematic disfigurement of the Italian landscape by developers did not move beyond generalizations. I was about to slip out the side door and go for a coffee in the handsome old quarter of that otherwise very ugly city, when a new speaker caught my flagging attention. Like the others before him he introduced himself: He was Vito Licola, a retired journalist from the local Salerno newspaper. He began to speak with uncommon ardor about the danger threatening the beautiful, wild ravine near the village of Albino. "Yes, yes," he added, as if anticipating objections from the floor, "the ravine with the empty house at its bottom is *malfamato*, it has a bad reputation, but that's no reason to destroy it. There's no sight like it in our parts. Shall we allow them to build a big hotel there, with two approach roads, one from Albino and the other from the scenic coast road? There's not much time left to block the plans of the Milan hotel consortium." He was asked questions. Amongst other things, those who had come from Naples wanted to know why the ravine was *malfamato*; but he did not seem eager to give an explanation. "We have to do something, we have to do something," he kept repeating with the obduracy of an old man. "My old newspaper refuses to get involved." Someone in the audience shouted: "Milan's already greased the right palms." The old journalist nodded and sat down.

That evening I invited the man to dinner in a restaurant overlooking the sea. We sat in a glass-walled veranda; before us the lighted pier of Salerno cut the dark night like a knife. At first Vito resisted, dismissing my questions with the expression *acqua passata*, water under the bridge, but with my insistence, I must have convinced him that I was not a hunter of cases from the criminal reports, and that my interest in learning the whole story was genuine and arose from serious motives. I will not shorten or summarize his account. After I returned to Naples I stayed up almost till dawn writing it down as accurately as I could, and here I copy it out from my notebook without any deletions or changes.

## V

"He was my distant cousin, it's true, but we rarely even met, though it's only twenty-five kilometers from Salerno to Albino. He inherited the house at the bottom of the ravine from his parents; old Fasano had once run a pretty decent farm there. The son was illiterate; he didn't even attend elementary school, couldn't sign his own name, and grew up to be wild, uncommunicative and eccentric. He couldn't stand farm work. Apparently he got drunk for joy on wine when he was offered the job of keeper or watchman at the cemetery. Shortly before the war his parents had died—first old Fasano, then six months later his wife—and the twenty-year-old Vincenzo had tended their graves with such solicitude, such filial piety, that the notion arose in the community of turning the whole cemetery over to his care. The pay was low, not to say paltry, but he hadn't accepted it for the money. He could live off what was left of the farm at the bottom of the ravine, whereas the cemetery simply *drew* him. I can't think of any other way to put it: It had been his eccentricity since his youth, maybe even his early childhood, to roam silently around the cemeteries of the region; he'd been seen at virtually every burial within a radius of fifteen kilome-

ters. Only once did I ever visit him in his house at the bottom of
the ravine; I think it was in 1942. At that time I was still spry
enough to undertake the descent, and I was counting on him taking
me back to Albino on his mule, which he did. But I doubt he uttered ten words during my visit. Every so often he would walk out
of the house and stare at the cemetery above. It was thoroughly
bizarre, that almost necrophilic obsession with the graveyard, in a
handsome, well-built man of almost thirty. In any case, that was
our third and last meeting. The two previous times had been at the
funerals of his parents in Albino—in the South you are obliged to
convey condolences to even the most distant kinship after a death.

    "'But it's a long story,' as old Bartolo said in Albino when he
wormed his way out of telling it to you. He might at least have
added: 'A tragic one too.' This was when I took it on. And not for
personal reasons, not because Vincenzo Fasano was a distant
cousin of mine. The fact that we were related only played a minor
role—that was why the editor of the Salerno newspaper had assigned me to the story, to "cover" it as they say in journalistic slang.
What was I to do? And how could I set about it? The only point of
departure was Albino. I traveled there daily, spending many hours
in conversation with the villagers. At that time, immediately after
the tragedy, Albino was talkative, too much so even—no comparison with the wall of silence you ran up against ten years later.

    "You know the tale of the German officer, Lieutenant Weinert:
how he held the Allied forces at bay in the ravine with a single machine gun in the corner of the cemetery, and did so for almost an
entire day. Even now the villagers are happy to recount Albino's
participation in the war; it's all the same which side they were on.
Whereas they rarely mention one important detail in their stories:
That Vincenzo Fasano regarded the German officer as the defender of the cemetery—as a hero—and that he venerated him,
decorating his grave with flowers brought from the bottom of the
ravine."

    "That I heard about."

    "But I doubt you heard how he deceived the German commis-
sion that came after the war to transfer the individual remains of
the war dead to the German military cemetery in Italy, or to return
them home if the families requested it. Fasano insisted that the

grave was empty: The German officer had been hit by the Americans and had tumbled down the hillside into the ravine. It had proved impossible to transport the body back to the top. Fasano had been able only to remove the dog-tag from his neck, referring to it later for the inscription on the cross. The Germans believed his lies, even offering him a reward for that memorial cross over the grave, but he refused to accept any money. *Sono un cristiano* (I'm a Christian), he said.

"It was, and still is, unclear how the officer's widow in Regensburg found out about her husband's grave in Albino. Most likely from that German commission; though if this were the case, she would have been forewarned that she was coming to an empty grave. According to the accounts of those who were present, however, in July 1948 she behaved like a woman who has arrived from far away to visit her husband's actual grave. She kneeled by the cross and prayed for a long time; when she rose she used a kerchief to wipe her face, which was wet from crying. How then did she know that her husband, Manfred Weinert, really was buried in the cemetery? Vincenzo Fasano waited for her patiently the whole time, leaning against the cemetery wall. Before the two of them went down the path to the bottom of the ravine, he too kneeled at the grave, crossed himself and said a short prayer. The widow had arrived in Albino with a suitcase by taxi directly from Salerno, and from the village had been led to the cemetery, where Fasano was at work, but they gave the impression of having known each other before. She didn't speak a word of Italian, and explained the purpose of her visit using gestures. Vincenzo, of course, knew no German at all. Without a word he strapped her suitcase to the saddle of his mule. Without a word she followed him down the path. No one in Albino knew how it could have happened, how that pair of strangers struck up a silent acquaintance, such that—as one of the inhabitants of Albino put it—it seemed as if 'she had come to him at last, and he had long been waiting for her arrival.'

"You should know, sir, that this point was discussed and debated endlessly during the inquiry, but the investigating magistrate eventually excluded it in the absence of any evidence whatsoever. The whole business was, and remains, so mysterious that any additional point here or there cannot have any real significance or change anything. For the investigating authorities in Salerno the case was a classic 'circumstantial' one; the 'circumstances,' moreover, were few in number and revealed little. For the inhabitants of Albino *everything*—from beginning to end—was enveloped in a combination of mystery and dread.

"No, I never saw Inge Weinert. To be more precise: I never saw her alive; about her appearance when she was dead I'd rather not speak. In Albino it was said that she was short, and neither attractive nor ugly; that she was energetic in her movements; and taciturn and gruff, like Vincenzo Fasano. Her gaze was somehow striking: She seemed not to see people standing in front of her, but rather to be looking through them into the distance. She had the gray-green eyes of a cat.

"And so the moment she arrived she went down to the house at the bottom of the ravine and lived there for almost a year. Were they lovers? I think it would be naive to even pose such a question. Every few days she rode with him up to the cemetery. She mostly busied herself around her husband's grave, which makes me suspect that Vincenzo had somehow given her to understand the truth, that the grave wasn't empty after all. I've racked my brains trying to figure out what they had in common, the more so because they couldn't communicate like normal human beings. They could sleep together and together take care of Lieutenant Manfred Weinert's grave. Fasano made no attempt to conceal his happiness; his usual gloom was now often brightened by a smile. But she didn't change, remaining exactly the way she was the day she arrived in Albino. Sometimes she went to a nearby village to visit a woman she'd met—a German Jew and a potter by profession. During the war this woman had been in hiding with her future husband in Salerno, and afterwards had settled with him and their young son in this village, which was known for its pottery industry. The woman was questioned during the investigation following the tragedy. She was unable (or unwilling) to say much. She kept repeating that Inge had been in love with two men, her dead husband and his gravedigger.

"In this way we've arrived at the catastrophe. People die in August too; but it had been agreed when Fasano was first employed at the cemetery, that that would be his month off. So no one was surprised in August 1949 when Vincenzo and Inge stopped appearing in Albino. On August 28th, a local shepherd was driving his herd of goats down the hillside and along the bottom of the ravine. From the closed-up house (even the shutters had been latched shut from inside) there came a fearful stench. The doors were broken down; both corpses were found on the bed in an advanced state of decomposition. A revolver lay in a dried pool of blood in the wide space between the bodies. According to the forensic doctors, the couple had died around August 15th. The rest you'll find in my articles in the Salerno newspaper; I'd be happy to lend them to you. If you wish, I can also arrange for you to have access to the records of the investigation in the public prosecutor's office in Salerno. I can't imagine there'd be any obstacles; it's been quite some time since the case was *archiviata*."

## VI

Two days later I received a registered express package of cuttings from the Salerno newspaper that were all signed at the end, Vito Licola or V. L. The first two were from the last days of August, and all the rest were from September 1949. Evidently, by October the readers had already had enough of the case the press had immediately labeled *l'affare dei due amanti di Albino* (the case of the two lovers of Albino).

It must be said that Vito steered clear of any shrill or sensational tone in his articles. Only in the first one, accompanied by photographs of the bodies found in the house at the bottom of the ravine, did he permit himself some "purple passages" in his description; these were unsavory coming from someone who was after all a cousin of the cemetery keeper, though a distant one. Subsequent articles showed clearly that his main source of information—interviews with the inhabitants of Albino—quickly began to run dry. There was even a certain journalistic accomplishment in the way he made readers aware of how the village closed up gradually like an oyster, in an atmosphere imbued with irrational fear. With every day the "case of the two lovers," which had been "spicy" in its own way to begin with, became more of an *affare demoniaco*, from which it was best to keep oneself at a distance; every word spoken aloud could turn against the speaker. Silence seemed the only security against "the diabolic fluids" that had flowed from the house at the bottom of the ravine.

The modest Salerno newspaper decided to spare no expense and sent its reporter to Regensburg. He spent three days there, but did not even find the family of the German officer. Weinert had been from Dresden; he had only moved to Regensburg before the war to take a job in a chemical company (he had been a recent chemistry graduate), so his family had probably perished in Dresden's notorious Allied bombing. On the other hand, Vito did find Inge's widowed father, a war cripple who had lost not just his legs but his senses and lived alone, looked after by an old woman with a sullen disposition. She had obviously not been fond of Inge, for upon hearing of her death in Italy she brightened up, displaying a barely concealed satisfaction; while Inge's old, bedridden father could not even comprehend the news of his daughter's tragic death. He heard what was said to him, but he had only one response in his repertoire: an inane, mawkish grin.

The police dossier which was made available to me thanks to Vito Licola contained a mass of "personal" inquiries, in other words cross-examinations of the villagers of Albino. These were even less informative than the interviews conducted by the Salerno journalist: The villagers' additional fear of the investigating magistrate had its own consequences. What was important, however, was the core of the dossier, which revolved ceaselessly around the question of whether Inge Weinert and Vincenzo Fasano had made a suicide pact, or whether it was a matter of murder, followed by the suicide of the murderer or murderess. In either case it was impossible to avoid questions about the motive; but a thorough search of the house at the bottom of the ravine had not turned up any letter—which could only have been written by Inge, since Vincenzo was illiterate. The revolver belonged to Fasano—amongst his papers was found a permit to possess a weapon, "in view of his living in complete isolation."

The central question, as I mentioned above—whether the deaths were suicide pact or murder—was the subject of extensive (to my mind, too extensive) medical examinations. The doctors flung themselves on the two bodies, performing endless autopsies, but even to a layman like myself, it was clear that their learned depositions had something of the nature of sand poured through splayed fingers. Two weeks had passed since the deaths; in our climate—in August!—that would be a long time for any productive autopsy. It was a matter of establishing the fine details: the positions of the bodies, the muscles, the expression of the face after death; this would presumably be different for a woman who had voluntarily committed suicide than for one who had been shot to death, awake or in her sleep (for the murder theory pointed to Vincenzo Fasano as the guilty party). The revolver, soaked in blood, could not be analyzed for fingerprints, at least using the investigative technology of the time. In any case, the whole mass of too-smart deductions swung between the two hypotheses; and while the proponents of the suicide pact theory were in the majority (reiterating the argument of the fastened shutters), to the very end a minority view held that Inge was the murderer. One of the doctors asserted categorically that the beginnings of pregnancy could be discerned in the woman's body. And yet, their final conclusion was as follows: "Despite numerous autopsies and analyses, the condition of the bodies makes it impossible to reconstruct with any certainty the circumstances of the deaths." On the cover of the dossier, there was an inscription confirmed by the stamp of the public prosecutor's office and the signature of the investigating magistrate: *Il caso della morte*, it said, with the names and dates, *viene archiviato*. (The case of the deaths has been entered into the archives.)

### VII

THE COMPETITION BETWEEN the two hypotheses was unavoidable, and I will not deny that it made my head spin. What? How? Why? When it came down to it, *some* kind of sensible and plausible hypothesis was the only serious thing that I myself could contribute—in a story to be called "The Noonday Cemetery." Everything else had been provided by others, as conveyed in Pascal's cautionary thought: "Writers would do better to say: 'Our story' seeing that usually there is more of other people's work than their own therein." In fact, shouldn't my subtitle be "Our collective story" rather than "An open story"? I shall return to this in the final chapter. At that time I will attempt to justify my original subtitle.

I truly was dizzy from the different theories; I wanted to put my own authorial mark clearly on the story. At the same time— spurred by his frequent meetings and conversations with me—Vito Licola had decided to upgrade himself to "writer" (a chronic malady of the majority of journalists), and developed at a gallop a taste for his own hypotheses. Some of these were rough, even slightly vulgar (they mostly revolved around the beginnings of pregnancy that had allegedly been discovered in Inge Weinert); and so I received his ideas with what was evidently such an expression of disgust that my acquaintance from Salerno immediately reined in the rushing steed—or rather the lolloping nag—of his imagination. Only one of his hypotheses seemed, as the expression goes, to hold water. Amongst the statements that Vito had collected in Albino, there was one from a person who had happened to be paying his respects at the cemetery one day, and had seen at a distance an altercation between Inge and Vincenzo (conveyed with gestures, and incomprehensible half-words and snarls) at Manfred Weinert's grave. The quarrel was so heated that at a certain point Vincenzo struck Inge in the face; that evening she did not go down with him to the house at the bottom of the ravine, but took the bus to the potters' village. Vito built his theory on this episode: Perhaps Inge had suddenly wanted to return to Regensburg and to take her husband's remains? For Vincenzo Fasano the latter would have been more painful than the former, added Vito, never forgetting his distant cousin's necrophilic preoccupation with the graveyard. Perhaps. But what evidence was there? The altercation observed at the cemetery could have concerned some trivial matter from their life together at the bottom of the ravine. Besides, there was a fundamental problem with the Salerno journalist's general conception. For Vito was an advocate of the suicide pact theory, while his hypothesis pointed to a murder, never mind who committed it, followed immediately by the suicide of the murderer or murderess when faced with the specter of arrest, trial, and prison. My interlocutor fell silent and let his gesticulating hand fall helplessly onto his lap.

After some time a change began to take place in me, slowly at first, then gathering speed. I was losing interest in all the conjectures and hypotheses regarding the mysterious "affair of the two lovers of Albino"; furthermore, I felt a need to enclose the entire story in a chalk circle of untouchability. Things even went so far as to affect my reading of various novels and short stories: I came to see the psychological interpretations of the events and persons described as authorial excess, and I was sickened by the writers' inquiring disposition for which they were renowned and which previously I had valued so highly. No, it was not only a matter of demanding of the writers some restraint—artistic discretion, even—in their attempts to peer into the depths of the human soul. I quite simply came to regard this process, even in cases of apparent virtuosity, as vapid and leading to nothing that might actually move us towards the truth about humankind. Let us take the classic case of Proust. His allegedly groundbreaking psychological inquiry is no more than a brilliantly executed showpiece for the theatrical affectation of the salon, which has only as much to say about human feelings and thoughts as a patient reader is capable of extracting from the endless refined conversation (which is often mere society prattle). In other words, virtually nothing at all. A truly profound author respects the puzzle, the mystery, of every heart, knowing that in it there exist inaccessible and unfathomed hiding places which may be mentioned, but should never, in a prideful reflex, be illuminated by the light of "psychological analysis." Good Lord, to "see clearly in rapture!" How much ink has been used up raising to the heavens that motto of Proust's, which in practice meant an orgy of conventional (if elegant), superficial observation!

It reached the point where I consciously avoided the dying embers of the "case" from the press; for instance, I refused to read an article from an illustrated magazine with rich and extensive photographs, including pictures of Vincenzo Fasano and Inge Weinert that had probably come from the police archives. I preferred to use the eyes of my imagination, forming my own image of the couple from the house at the bottom of the ravine. I visited Albino once again, but I did not engage any of the villagers in conversation, fearful that they would suddenly regain the gift of speech. At the edge of the village I sat on a bench in front of the church and stared in silence at the Noonday Cemetery, splashed with the fresh light of morning. How extraordinary it was up on its plateau above the precipice, with its memorial rock commemorating the six fishermen "swallowed up by the sea"! How it spoke to me now in its own wordless language! It was a phenomenon that wished to remain so, evading the dimensions of reality. I walked up the hill at a slow pace, pushed open the wicket in the entrance gate and stood over the three graves set apart in the right-hand corner. Then I rose up on tiptoe at the wall. I had an excellent view of the ravine, washed clean by the early hour; I would have sworn that the house at the bottom stood out with exceptional clarity, like a picture etched in glass. If I had persisted longer, focusing my gaze intently on the bench in front of the house, I might have seen two specters sitting next to each other, as apparently had been reported at times by shepherds obliged to lead their sheep and goats through the ravine. Were they the victims of hallucinations, phantasms in the sharp noonday light? Would I follow in their footsteps, rewarded for that persistence of mine? Had the governess from Henry James' *The Turn of the Screw* fallen victim to similar phantasms and hallucinations? Naive, pointless questions. In this dimension too it is necessary to consider Proust's motto: to see clearly . . . not in rapture, though, but in bewilderment and terror. The governess from the James story saw the spirits of Evil, victorious specters from beyond the grave. I, from the heights of the Noonday Cemetery, might have seen specters born of the seeds of Death and Love.

### VIII

IF I HAD WRITTEN "The Noonday Cemetery" in the era in which the events it describes took place—a time between the first years after the war and the years 1959-1960—at this point I should have added the final period. But I wrote it in August of this year, 1991, influenced by a seemingly accidental—yet for me meaningful—event.

In July I received an unexpected visit from Hugh, an English writer (he is already too well known for me to introduce him here under his real name). I met him quite a long time ago in Rome at a cocktail party given by some Italian friends of mine. I took a liking to him. We struck up a correspondence, and I had lunch with him twice in London during my short visits to that city (which I find so awful). He was ten years my junior. After graduating from Oxford he had developed a talent for writing, a modest ability, yet one that was sufficient to set up his own little factory for the production of novels. This was especially possible in England, where novel-writing is a learned trade, and a novel every year (so as to stay in circulation), impeccably constructed, neither striking nor utterly hopeless, two or three reasonable reviews, and a decent print run will guarantee the publisher and the author a profit at a reasonable level. Hugh would always send me his novels, and I would read them with a sense of tedium, but not without admiring his ever more capable craftsmanship.

Hugh, then, drove down to visit me in July, virtually unannounced. In an effort to make his stay more enjoyable (Hugh showed little interest in the places recommended in the guidebooks), I persuaded him to go on a trip to my favorite "biblical" cliffs. They did indeed make a considerable impression on him, but I felt intuitively that as usual, he was probably looking for something that would be the seed of a new story. So I took him to Albino.

For many years past my travels had not taken me back there. And, truth be told, I had not wanted to go, deliberately avoiding the place. The well-conserved image of the Noonday Cemetery was enough for me; that and, perhaps above all, the image of the two people on the bench in front of the house at the bottom of the ravine, now living, now as ghosts. In Salerno I had attended a funeral mass for the departed soul of Vito Licola in the beautiful Romanesque Cathedral of St. Matthew the Evangelist; and I learned by chance of the death of old Bartolo in Albino. The threads linking me to the drama were breaking one by one.

At my suggestion, then, Hugh drove me to the place I had purposely been shunning. On the way, as we approached Albino I had a foretaste of massive changes. On both sides of the road, in the ditches, were colorful advertisements mounted on poles: *Albergo Ristorante La Gola* (*gola* means both "ravine" and "gluttony"). A large parking lot had been built at the entrance to the village, from which a new road led through, rounding the cemetery wall. The wall was also new. The old path had proved too narrow to be widened, so now the road hugged the cemetery so closely that it almost swallowed the three graves in the right-hand corner. Then it looped round several bends into the bottom of the ravine. In place of the cemetery keeper's house there was a four-story hotel surrounded by a garden, with a second, smaller parking lot at its entrance.

I could not look calmly upon all this. We sat on the bench in front of the church. And it was there that I told my English friend the story of the cemetery and the ravine. He listened intently. "What a wonderful, exceptional story," he muttered to himself. It was only then that I realized my blunder. Hugh was already sharpening his teeth on his next novel: He would replace the German woman with an English tourist and produce something in the spirit and style of E. M. Forster, a book for English readers with a taste for Italy. I could not allow this to happen.

"Listen, Hugh, I read in some of the reviews of your novels that you're a master of the epilogue; one reviewer actually used that very phrase. You're considered to be a disciple of the novelists of the last century, who generally tried to resolve the plot at the end, and saw the epilogue as indispensable, showing, as if from the window of a departing coach, a smaller and smaller column of smoke on the horizon, in the place where the action of the story was concluded. But this tale does not and cannot have any resolution; it has to remain *open*. Open, I'd say, on all sides, depending on the sensibilities and imagination of the reader. Otherwise it's no more than an accumulation of bizarre trivialities. You, a virtual countryman of James, ought to understand that. The ever-so-young hero of *The Turn of the Screw* dies in his governess's arms, it's true, but that isn't the epilogue of the tale. Something remains which cannot (and should not) be defined, something unfinished, that will stay forever unclosed. In a word, there exists an open story; that's the kind of story I would attempt if I were to write something about this myself. Besides, if you think about it, most of the events in human life possess precisely that quality of openness, of not being closed; they're suspended above us without any resolution."

"I see that you're tactfully asserting your copyright."

I did not reply. But as we drove back to Naples in silence, at a certain point the Noonday Cemetery appeared in the distance on its hilltop, swathed in a whiteish mist, and I admitted that he was right. Yes I would write an open story about it.

> *The dead concealed lie easy in this earth*
> *That keeps them warm, drying their mystery.*
> *And Noon up there, Noon the motionless . . .*

*August 1991*

# A HOT BREATH FROM
# THE DESERT

## I

A FEW DAYS AFTER my heart attack, in the cardiology wing of the San Paolo hospital, I began to take an interest in my fellow patients. The ward contained about a dozen beds. To my right was a priest whose response to his own heart attack was perpetual slumber: He slept day and night, waking only to reach for the glass of water on his bedstand and for his morning meal. After breakfast, like the rest of us he had an EKG taken. The nurse did not disturb him for lunch or dinner, but slipped the prescribed tablets into his mouth herself, without interrupting his sleep or profound doze. During his afternoon rounds the doctor skipped his bed, merely glancing at his EKG and his blood pressure chart. This probably meant that sleep was his principal medicine; such a tired face, puffed with exhaustion, is rarely to be seen—perhaps only on hobos (*barboni* in Italian). Actually, in appearance he did resemble a pious *barbone*, with a metal cross held tight in his clasped hands. His heart attack had apparently struck while he was in the confessional; the alarm had been raised by an elderly woman concerned by the silence from the other side of the grille and the quiet sounds of what seemed to be moaning.

Across from me, in the row of beds on the other side of the room, my attention was caught by a young patient of perhaps twenty-five lying motionless, the top half of his body resting on the raised head of the bed, his gaze fixed on the ceiling. From time to time he lowered his eyes, and at such moments we exchanged glances. How sorrowful was his look, how full of fear, and of some-

thing that I would want to describe as surprise! From the silver cup
on his bedstand I guessed he was a sportsman, whose wings had unexpectedly been clipped by a heart attack. Visiting hours were at
dusk, before the early dinnertime. Every day he was visited by a
beautiful young woman; paying no attention to the other patients,
she virtually lay down on the bed next to him, covering his face,
neck, and hands with kisses. Afterwards, on her way out, outside
the swinging glass doors of the ward she would stop for a moment
to cry into a handkerchief, unseen by her beloved but clearly visible
to me.

Why am I writing this, since the central role in my story is
played by someone else, my neighbor to my left? I suspect it
is because from the beginning I would like to create an atmosphere
of sickness. Everything to come will to a significant degree—
predominantly even—take place within that sphere of human life
which the sick experience with what is left of their instincts, or feel
subconsciously, as a sudden, violent darkening before a slow or
rapid descent. Illness—serious illness of course—has many faces,
but every one of them bears a grimace presaging departure.

My left-hand neighbor was neither silent nor especially talkative. Yet when even just a short conversation opened up between
us, I was able to admire the quick-witted intelligence evident in the
people of the south—their ability to answer questions that have not
yet been asked but are already hanging in the air, as if the whole
time their minds were focusing on the "true" underpinnings of the
matter discussed. I shall call him Ludovico. For many years he had
been an investigating magistrate in Vallo della Lucania, the capital
of the Cilento region; his jurisdiction also included Agropoli and
nearby Paestum. Widowed for some time, he had an only son, an
architect in Naples. In the last years of his father's life the son, who
seemed to be a confirmed bachelor, brought him to Naples, to his
apartment in Santa Lucia. The judge had already been retired for
several years, and a solitary life in Vallo della Lucania could not be
numbered amongst life's pleasures. His son was in much demand as
an architect; he was so busy all the time that he rarely took advantage of the visiting times at the hospital; though every day he sent
one of his draftsmen with a bag of fruit. Judge Ludovico was recov-
ering from his second heart attack; the first, a relatively mild one,

had struck during his last court case in Vallo, for which he had been preparing materials, including transcripts of the hearings. The second heart attack, in Naples, had been classified (like mine) as *acuto*; fortunately his son had happened to be at home and had him taken by ambulance to the San Paolo hospital, where a friend of his was a cardiologist.

At last the day came for the priest to be permanently woken. Never letting go of the cross clutched in his hands, he kept moving his lips in a whispered prayer. I did not even attempt to talk to him, so engrossed was he in his prayers; with his half-shut eyes, he closely resembled someone who has almost drowned and has just been dragged onto the shore. During the afternoon rounds he gave short, almost inaudible answers to the doctor's questions. But at least his swollen gray face was brightened by a good-hearted smile.

Rather crowded hospital wards favor friendships with one's neighbors. Thus, when we were allowed to go on half-hour walks along the corridor, without any prior agreement we formed a threesome: Judge Ludovico, the priest (whom I shall call Zeno), and myself. We walked slowly, bearing our hearts gingerly like balls of fragile glass, from the doctor's duty room to the large window at the other end of the corridor with a view of a dirty, weed-infested field where boys played soccer. Father Zeno kept up with us, pausing when we paused to catch our breath, and listening to our conversation without saying a word. I was not even certain whether he heard what we were saying, or whether instead he was entirely absorbed in his own thoughts. Appearances to the contrary, he was in fact listening. One afternoon, when the judge and I were discussing what were the most serious illnesses of old age—heart disease of course went alongside cancer—Father Zeno all of a sudden quietly whispered: "Amnesia"; and even more quietly he added: "A hot breath from the desert"—*un respiro caldo del deserto*. The judge looked at him with undisguised astonishment.

■

IN THE NIGHT after one of these walks, which seemed to be a deposit on a discharge from the hospital, at around two o'clock—that night I was unable to get to sleep after my last dose of tablets—I heard a rasping sound on my right side. It was very quiet, muffled, as if, despite the pain, Father Zeno was trying not to wake those sleeping. Yet in the faint glow from the nightlight it was obvious that this was more than passing discomfort, as I had first supposed. His face was bathed in perspiration, with large droplets trickling down into his eyes and beyond. And the pain must have been terrible, since I noticed that Father Zeno had let go of the cross and was desperately gripping the iron frame of the bed. I was in no doubt: That was what my own heart attack had looked like. I pressed the button to summon help. The sleepy male nurse roused himself immediately when he took a look at the sick man. Two minutes later a whole team was at the priest's bedside and had screened it off from the rest of the room. I heard quiet conversation; a drip was set up, and the only word that reached my ears was *tardi*. Once the doctor's voice rose dramatically, and she said clearly and almost aloud *troppo tardi*, too late. I lay still, with my eyes open, while the other patients slept. At three o'clock the crowd behind the screen disappeared. Leaning from my bed, I stretched my arm out full length and drew the screen slightly aside. But I only managed to see the dead man's head covered with a sheet. It appeared that out of fear of making a commotion in the night, they had left the body. Its removal had been postponed till the early morning.

Just before dawn I fell into a deep sleep. I dreamed not of any scenes or images, but of a word. The word was "amnesia." It rang out with such force that it seemed to have been repeated by a swinging bell. When I was woken by the nurse who brought me breakfast along with my first dose of medicine, to my right I saw a freshly made bed. My neighbor to the left said: "A sick heart is like a thief in the night. Death creeps in on tiptoe."

Our doctor was the sister of a Neapolitan friend of mine, and so I was considered a "recommended" patient (in Italy a sure mark of better treatment). Sometimes, usually in the afternoons, she would sit on my bed for a chat. From her I learned that Father Zeno had been the priest in a poor, working-class parish on the outskirts of the city with more than its share of criminals and prostitutes. She compared him to a thoroughly worn-out shoe and added: "It's a miracle that he made it to seventy." It was even more miraculous because for the last few years, every so often he would disappear somewhere for a long time; he would be brought home by the police, not so much gone astray as lost, barely remembering his own name and his job, and recognizing his parishioners with difficulty. He should have been put into a home for old and ailing clergy, but who would have agreed to take his place in that accursed neighborhood by the sea, black from the smoke of the nearby steel-works? It was entirely possible that his fourth heart attack (which usually sets off alarm bells) had struck him in the confessional as he grappled with his ever-weakening flashes of memory. No, there was no hope for him; being in hospital could only postpone for a short time his fifth and fatal attack. He was allowed to walk along the corridor so that before his death he should have at least the illusion of being up and about. Though it was not clear that this was something he had wanted; it was possible that he had wished only for a long sleep, ending when he fell asleep for good.

The doctor's explanations were rather vague, and at times gave the impression that she was trying to make excuses for something. But the facts sounded genuine. I recalled the appearance of the infinitely tired priest in the bed next to mine.

I was discharged from the hospital shortly before Christmas. Judge Ludovico did not conceal his envy. When we said our goodbyes he gave me his address in Santa Lucia.

### III

IT IS GENERALLY thought that hospitals, the army, and prison bind people together, creating a community that lasts for a long time "outside," after the enforced isolation has been left. This commonplace view may be justified in many cases, but in mine it is erroneous. I do not like to encounter my former comrades in arms or prison companions, and my recent illness convinced me that this extended to my fellow-patients from the hospital ward. I suspect that this may be a purely personal phobia (perhaps some kind of claustrophobia) connected with some aspect of an exuberant, excessive individualism. It is typical that I forget quickly the names of people with whom fate brought me together in communal living places.

I did not, then, do anything with the address that Judge Ludovico gave me. If I had, and had called his apartment in Santa
Lucia, I would have learned that after a sudden third heart attack in
the hospital Ludovico had been removed to a rest home in Switzerland. He spent a whole year there. We met by chance one mild day
on the promenade near the Piazza Vittoria. It was from this point
that I used to begin the level walk to the fishing port of Mergellina;
my cardiologist had recommended this as good for my health. Ludovico had chosen the same route, in accordance with the same instructions from his doctor, descending to the Piazza Vittoria from
nearby Santa Lucia.

We made a rather curious pair. Young boys swept past us on bi-
cycles (on a sidewalk supposedly meant for pedestrians); on the low
wall separating the walkway from the massive boulders of the
breakwater sat lovers completely shut off from the outside world by
their kisses and caresses; in the inlets and spaces between the boulders there bobbed the floats of the anglers leaning against the wall.
We walked slowly along, stopping every so often for reasons that
seemed to have been established in advance once and for all: to sur-
vey the bay; on a sunny day when the air was clear, to stare for a
moment at Capri on the horizon, or to greet the tiny offshore islands covered with white blankets of seagulls; halfway along the
route, to take in the sight of the fish and octopuses displayed in
tubs in the sidewalk market; and, close to our end point, to stand at
the jetties "checking out" the speedboats and yachts.

There is no sense in concealing the fact that these were long
and monotonous walks, though from their description they may
sound very attractive. Also rather tedious and monotonous—
though pleasant, intelligent, and kindly—was my companion. It
seemed as if his long convalescence in Switzerland had somewhat
dulled his once-sharp intellect. He was enjoying being alive; these
walks, he confessed to me, were his main source of that enjoyment.
At home he led the existence of a retiree ensnared in his little
habits; he played solitaire and occasionally (rarely) was a fourth at
bridge. He had entirely lost his former enthusiasm for reading
books, and would only peruse the local newspaper from cover to
cover; in the evenings he dozed in front of the television. Though
in certain small ways we were alike, I was in a better situation than

he, since for me the morning walk was nothing more than medicine prescribed by my doctor. But after a couple of months passed I grew accustomed to Ludovico. When it happened that he did not appear at our meeting place, I would march at a brisk pace towards Mergellina, not pausing on the way, with a keen sense that something was missing. I imagine that he too felt the same on the days when I was unable to join him.

## IV

ONE DAY WE WENT further—all the way to the jetty beyond the fishing harbor. On the way we passed by a glass-sided chapel which the fishermen had erected in honor of their patron saint. To the best of my knowledge, no services or prayers were ever held there; the most that happened was that wreaths of flowers were placed before the altar. But this time our attention was caught by a sheet of paper stuck to the glass on the promenade side and bearing a clumsy hand-written inscription: "To *Padre Zeno*, guardian of the poor, on the first anniversary of his death, from the grateful fishermen of Mergellina." So he had made it here in his priestly duties, all the way from dark and distant Bagnoli to this jetty washed by the blue-green sea? How was this possible? Why? An old fisherman mending his nets on a patch of sand on the other side of the wall was generous with his information: "Yes, he would come down here, sometimes on foot, and though only once a month, he aroused the ill will of the priest from the local churches of Our Lady of the Snows and Our Lady With Child. He visited up until a certain point; it was said then that he had fallen ill, that God had disturbed his senses. But while he still came, there was no better person, always so willing to help. It's hard to say why he came here, since Mergellina has its own priest, and it's such a long way from Bagnoli. He had a good heart; but we knew that he wished to refresh himself here. Often, when the weather was good he would go down to the sea, roll his sleeves up and spend a long time washing his face and hands. He would also get some fish and mussels from us. Apparently he would give them away to others as soon as he returned to Bagnoli."

We exchanged glances in silence. We were probably both re-membering the ward in the San Paolo hospital, the empty bed on which Father Zeno had slept so voraciously before his fifth heart attack killed him. "Do you remember when the three of us took a walk together down the corridor?" asked Ludovico. "I do. I also re-member how astonished you were at Father Zeno's remark about amnesia." "I had my reasons. The last case I had in Vallo della Lu-cania, before my illness, involved a severe case of amnesia."

From this point on our walks took on a different character. The Judge told his story and I listened, interrupting infrequently with questions. The opportunity to cast off this "burden" (his own ex-pression) in such a way evidently brought him relief, even a hidden pleasure. My interest grew from day to day; I was doubly vexed whenever I had to stay home because of bad weather. And I was de-lighted to see Judge Ludovico return to his former condition: He recovered his mental faculties and was sharp-witted and shrewd.

I have been wondering how his story can be conveyed in in-stallments (it occupied us for two weeks). Though after each walk I made fairly detailed notes which are now lying on my desk, in the end I abandoned the idea of re-creating the story in the first person and dividing it into chapters to coincide with our walks. I deter-mined instead to introduce my own order: to condense the tale as much as possible, have the narrator speak in the third person, and to organize the chapters according to the chronology and logic of events.

**V**

JUDGE LUDOVICO WAS six months from retirement when the case of Mr. and Mrs. Porter suddenly came up in Agropoli. It was immediately given to him; with it he wished to draw his career to a close.

The Porters, Derek and Violet (her Italian friends called her Violetta), were archeologists by education. In the 1920's, soon after graduating from Oxford, they arrived in Paestum as volunteers on an archeological dig. They could afford to work without pay, since they came from wealthy families. They bought and renovated a small house in Agropoli near the ruins of the famous castle, on a low cliff overlooking the sea. They were exactly the same age as the twentieth century; and they were a couple of whom it was frequently said: "it's less and less often that you meet people so much in love." They came to Italy with a good knowledge of the language acquired during their studies, and so in Agropoli they were soon accepted as "locals." Not even the anti-English leanings of fascism affected this relationship, and the authorities in Agropoli and in the Vallo della Lucania region let them be.

Their archeological work in Paestum, on the other hand, did not go so well; the team conducting the dig was ill-disposed towards them. After a few months they were led to understand that the Italian group preferred not to take on foreigners, even unpaid ones. The Porters bore this affront with good grace, the more so because they were in the process of leaving the field of archeology. Violet began to paint, and Derek to sculpt. With great passion, as Judge Ludovico explained, suffice it to say, they became attached to Agropoli and the surrounding area, taking very rare trips to places where they could feast their eyes on the masterpieces of Italian art. "All this was verified during the inquiry," added Judge Ludovico, not without a hint of pride. "Why?" I blurted out. "Did it have some bearing on the case?" "No, but we decided to re-create in detail the whole of the Porters' long stay in Italy. A judicial investigation is often like a series of hundreds of x-rays. The hope is that all at once some hidden shadow will be discovered. Don't forget that it was a question of a puzzling, incomprehensible murder. At least in the first stages of the inquiry."

In their painting and sculpting the Porters had no ambitions to exhibit their work. They sold their pictures and miniature sculptures for a pittance (not for an income, which they did not need), on market day on the square in Vallo della Lucania. Judge Ludovico had often seen them before the tragedy, surrounded by the rich peasants of the Cilento region; the weekly market was a treasure trove of every kind of goods from groceries to clothing and furniture. With an amused smile, to keep up appearances they would haggle over the price of their "masterpieces" (the phrase that they used: *i nostri capovalori*). The peasants who bought the works liked the Porters and never begrudged them the money;

sometimes they would pay in kind with a pat of butter, eggs, a chicken, or a rabbit. Ludovico, then, had seen their "masterpieces" as he passed between the stalls on his way to work. Violet specialized in landscapes; over time she gradually began to turn them into illustrations for fairy tales. Derek sculpted, or molded in clay, tiny, bizarre figures of men, women, and children which were clearly modeled after pieces in the display cabinets of Paestum's museum.

In this way the years went by, and the Porters became part of the landscape of Agropoli and Vallo. The inhabitants of both places grew fond of the "nice English couple," and were touched as they approvingly observed their continual displays of affection in public places. They held only one thing against the Porters: their lack of children. In southern Italy a child is the crowning proof of God's blessing and of its parents' mutual love. Childless couples give rise to so-called "mixed feelings." But even that did not change the attitude to "our Porters," *i nostri Porter* as they finally began to be known.

In May 1939, as dark and terrible clouds hung over Europe, the Porters left for England. They spent the whole war in London, he as a clerk in the War Office (he was of poor health and physically frail), she as a nursing auxiliary in a military hospital.

## VI

IMMEDIATELY AFTER THE war they wrote twice to their neighbors in Agropoli to say that they would soon be returning. In fact, it is inaccurate to say that "they" wrote. The sole author of the two letters was Derek; Violet's signature seemed strangely clumsy and unsteady, as if scratched by a chicken's foot. In one sentence Derek mentioned that "my wife's wartime experiences have weakened her mental strength."

Those words—an old-fashioned expression of concern—Judge Ludovico cited exactly, since he considered it to be the first indication of Violet's "health problems."

The announcement of a quick return to Agropoli turned out to be premature. They did not come back till the mid-1950's. At the beginning the inhabitants of Agropoli were struck only by Violet's appearance. She was pale and gaunt (the word "emaciated" occurred to some people), almost transparent. On their first stroll to say hello to everyone, at every few steps she sought something to lean on or a place where she could at least perch for a moment. She greeted everyone she met on the way, but in such a bland and conventional manner that they were justified in wondering whether she really remembered them. Derek went with her, giving out smiles and pleasantries left and right; yet no observant person could fail to notice the dark glint in his eye.

In subsequent statements and testimonies gathered by Judge Ludovico, Violet's appearance was matched by her behavior. With every day it became more obvious, more glaring even, that from behind her misty veil she did not recognize people she had known for many years. The pharmacist in Agropoli put it like this: *E assente, immersa nel suo sogno di cui non riesce a svegliarse* ("She's absent, immersed in a dream from which she's unable to wake up"). But this was still bearable; Violet's behavior was put down to her "artistic imagination." For as before, every morning when the weather was pleasant she painted. And her landscapes bore no resemblance to what she was looking at; she really was moving amongst mysterious imaginings or visions, in which sea and sky melded into a vast, desert-like space in yellows and reds. One day she failed to leave her house at all. Judge Ludovico clearly remembered the date, September 14, 1958. It marked Violet's complete withdrawal from the life of Agropoli and the beginning of her "illness," as Derek called it, referring to the fact that she shut herself up in her home.

From this moment, for the inhabitants of Agropoli, Derek's face became the reflection of his condition. If one can speak of an expression of concern that grows gradually and unchecked, with increasing shades of anxiety and perhaps even panic, that was exactly how Derek Porter seemed to the people of the town. He took ever more frequent trips to Vallo and to Naples, first locking the door of the little house by the castle. More and more frequently, "visitors from the big cities" (both from Italy and abroad) came to Agropoli. And Hopelessness spread its dark wings ever wider, and more visibly. People wondered why Derek Porter did not urge his wife to lie on the veranda, or why he did not take her out for a walk from time to time. No answer was found to these questions (he himself avoided the subject of Violet in conversation), for no one knew what kind of "illness" she had. And did Derek himself know, pronouncing as he did the word "illness" as though it were in quotation marks? Or the "visitors from the big cities," who were taken for doctors, did they know?

We had come to the fishermen's chapel in Mergellina. The sheet of paper with the inscription about the anniversary of Father Zeno's death, faded now by the sun, was still stuck on the thick plate-glass wall. Judge Ludovico stood before it, lost in thought.

## VII

FROM PORTER'S LATER statements in the inquiry, it was evident that Violet's "illness" eventually became a real illness for him. It was no longer possible to pretend: She had amnesia in a virulent, fulminating form. It advanced so rapidly that it seemed every day to consume, or destroy, a whole new portion of her memory. The doctors no longer had any doubts about the diagnosis, but they shrugged their shoulders helplessly as far as attempts to halt the process were concerned. "Basically it's incurable; one is entitled to hope (but only to hope) that if affection, sensitivity, and intelligence are found in one's environment, the dying embers of memory may be fanned. But in reality the only thing left is care and constant supervision: Persons suffering from amnesia are not aware of what they are doing. The causes of the illness are unknown, as are the circumstances in which it originated."

And yet Porter tried to identify those causes and circumstances. During the war Violet had been energetic, efficient, and always cheerful in her work as an auxiliary in the military hospital near Guildford. She was popular and highly thought of. Derek worked in one of the military offices in London and was able to live in their old apartment in Chelsea. They saw each other every week to ten days. No, no, at the beginning there was nothing to indicate that the illness had been brought on by her "wartime experiences" (as he had written in his first letter to Agropoli). It was not until a year after the war that the first symptoms appeared, leading him to postpone their return to Italy. These were still harmless symptoms that he took for absentmindedness. If he had looked a little closer, he surely would have seen that she was becoming different: at her easel, in conversation, in domestic life, in love. But above all in her reading. With a bizarre insatiability she consumed literature about war atrocities, with which she had had hardly any contact in her provincial hospital, and which she knew mostly from the air raids on London. She refused to talk about it; her reading became a kind of exclusive, purely private rite. Every evening she closed her book with a face that seemed seared by flames. In bed she was stiff and tense, and would not allow him near her. He gave up his trips to Oxford, where he had been encouraged to resume his archeological studies. He was quite simply afraid to leave her alone in the apartment; one of the indications of the change taking place in her was a fear of leaving the house. Yet all in all, though the change was worrying, it did not presage further disturbances. Shortly before their return to Agropoli, for which he subconsciously held great hopes, her condition took a turn for the worse. In the mornings she would sit for hours in front of a canvas on the easel, touching it with a brush held in trembling hands and smoking one cigarette after another; every so often she would set aside her brushes and palette, twist a lock of hair around her dirty finger and remain motionless in this position for a long time, in a profound somnambulistic torpor. He lacked the courage to shake her out of it, remembering from his childhood the belief that a sleepwalker woken by the touch of a hand will fall down like a heavy stone, and can be seriously hurt. So he sat still at his desk, building his little figures out of plasticine and not taking his eyes off her. At that time too he began to keep something in the manner of a journal, but more about Violet's transformation and his watching over her than about his own experiences and thoughts.

She received with indifference the idea of going back to Agropoli; she, who during the war had frequently dreamed of the path leading to their little house on the Castle hill, about the sea rocking the fishing boats tied up at the shore. But she offered no resistance, and even showed moments of concentration and resourcefulness during the packing of trunks and suitcases. Despite this, Porter was unable to shake off the impression that it was an inert object, and not a living being, that he was taking to Italy.

## VIII

Two DAYS OF BAD weather confined me to my home. As commonly happens in Naples, nature took revenge for a long period of sunshine: It rained ceaselessly, the sky oppressed the city with leaden clouds, and buses and cars moved slowly through streams of water. For a moment the idea came to me of calling the judge; after all, stories can be told over the phone too. The idea came to me and immediately went away again; Ludovico's narration had for me become indelibly associated with our walks along the promenade.

I decided to make use of the pause to digest the story of the Porters, guessing vaguely, from clues dropped here and there by the Judge, where it was heading. I quickly abandoned this intention. Father Zeno unexpectedly and peremptorily broke into my thoughts. What was the meaning of the story the doctor had told me about how every now and then he would vanish for a long time, and would be brought back to Bagnoli by the police—"lost," struck by a sudden attack of amnesia, which shortly before his death, in the hospital corridor, he had called a "hot breath from the desert"? Where did that phrase of his come from? To what extent was it a true expression of his own feelings, and to what degree was it rhetoric overheard or consciously borrowed from teachers of the art of preaching?

I was fascinated by the phrase, but in an instinctive way, as sometimes happens with a line of poetry, whose overpoweringly evocative imagery precedes our understanding of its meaning. This time everything seemed to be muddled up: the memory of Father Zeno's last, fatal heart attack, and a picture presented by my imagination of Father Zeno circling on a pathless plain, a freshly burned field. He was walking ahead, turning back, stopping and shielding his reddened face with his hands; then walking forward again and again turning back like a drunken man, staggering, the only man, a man spurned by the world, a man unaware of his own existence.

## IX

ON THE BASIS OF Porter's statements Judge Ludovico established the critical point in Violet's illness from which began a

steady decline, devoid of the possibility of any check. It was a summer night when Violet woke up suddenly with a sharp cry: "Where
am I?" Porter took her in his arms; she was trembling like a little
bird with a broken wing held in someone's cupped hands. He was
stunned. He kept repeating, automatically, helplessly: "Derek,
Agropoli," and covering her burning face with kisses. She did not
respond to these caresses, though she drew close to him. Then she
leaped out of bed, sat in the corner by the easel and repeated
quietly: "Where am I?" in the imploring tone of a prayer, paying
no attention to his presence there. At daybreak she fell asleep in a
sitting position; he carried her carefully to the bed.

Ludovico came to a stop and leaned against the wall; he was
visibly tired, and perhaps also moved by the story. We stared without speaking at the inlet in the gap between two boulders of the
breakwater, where a flock of seagulls was playing in the sunlight;
they flew so nimbly that their bellies brushed against the surface of
the sea, then they burst upwards into the air like white shells.

"Yes," said the Judge after taking a rest, "yes, it's hard not to see
that as the critical point. Not to know where you are! What torment! But did Violet feel it in some way? I don't think so. She was
already crossing to the other side. Derek Porter reckoned differently, though."

He believed there was still a chance of helping Violet—of seiz-
ing hold of her hand, and forcing her to wake up, as was once done
with sleepwalkers. The Judge saw this belief or hope as proof of the
fact that despite the doctors' diagnoses and deductions, as well as
his own observations of the progression of the illness, Porter was
unwilling or unable to come to terms with the obvious. When it
comes down to it, what is hope? Impotent rebellion against despair.
Whoever says that one can't live without hope, is simply asserting
that one cannot live without constant rebellion.

It's easy enough to say "rebellion" or "resistance." But the daily
facts associated with the constant and ever-quickening process of
deterioration raised a smooth, dull wall between Porter and his
wife that could be neither pulled down nor broken through. When
he looked at her, she had the unmoving eyes of a blind person, and
a gaze that posed the question: Who am I? He undressed and
dressed her, bathed her, brushed her hair, and fed her, pushing

small pieces of food into her mouth—she acquiesced to everything without demur; but if he had not done these things, she would have performed no action of her own free will. Except for one thing: trying to quench her perpetual thirst. She was capable of drinking liters of water and juice, like someone scorched on sun-baked sands. Though, I am sorry to say, this did not induce her to be able to use the bathroom on her own: If he did not intervene in time, she would dirty herself; and she had utterly lost her sense of smell. He tried to remove her from her torpor with recollections, prefacing every episode from the past with a sacral: "Remember?" No, she did not remember, and it was not even certain that she heard him at all, trapped, it appeared, as if beneath a bell glass. Sometimes he would get the notion of sitting her in front of a blank canvas stretched out on the easel and sticking a brush and a palette with paints in her hands. She would sit without moving for a long time, then hurriedly, impetuously, as if furious, she would cover the canvas with lines, blotches, and daubings, like young children make when their parents ask them to draw.

Time went by, and in Agropoli people gradually grew accustomed to the sight of Porter alone as he locked the house (having hidden the matches and disabled the tap on the gas bottle) and left to go to the local shops; or traveled to Vallo to do the shopping.

The fact that she had reached rock bottom, irreversibly plunged in amnesia, he understood when she asked who she was and what she was called. Had these questions been addressed to her, she could not have answered them herself. "They were both stuck in time," murmured Father Ludovico. "She, with the gentleness of a person suffering from paralysis; he, struggling ever more powerlessly, with ever greater resignation, to drag the little house in Agropoli from where it had run aground on dead, timeless shallows."

## X

THERE CAME A DAY that Derek Porter did not expect. He had already in some way become resigned to the fact that his wife's illness was incurable; he had given in, and felt that from the flames of rebellion only smoldering embers remained. He knew that the only thing he could do for Violet now was to take care of her with unceasing tenderness until her death. He believed in this and counted on it, praying in his soul that he would outlive her and not leave her on her own. The thought that he might die first—while she would live on in solitude, not knowing who or where she was—was a source of torment to him.

Yet even in his darkest thoughts, he did not entertain the possibility of what was an utterly unexpected, even unimaginable turn of events. Could he have foreseen that amnesia is contagious? On that terrible day, at the beginning of autumn, a day partially hidden by the soot-stained window between him and the seashore, a day of obstinate depression, he sat on the couch by that window, from time to time glancing at the corner where Violet still lay asleep in bed. He suddenly realized that the material of his own memory was coming to resemble a tattered and moldering piece of cloth that would soon begin to fall apart completely. "He was fully aware," Judge Ludovico was quick to clarify, "that in him the process was of a different character, that it was not a copy of his wife's illness but a consequence of it." They had been so closely bound together since the moment they had met at college, had so separated themselves from their environment, as a couple had so isolated themselves from the world (in a certain way even during the war, not to mention their time in Italy), that Porter's past was reflected in his wife's past and vice versa. Violet's illness rendered the mirror of Derek useless to her. But for him the mirror of Violet had broken, shattering into tiny fragments. He was condemned to lose his memory because he had lost the sole participant and witness of his own past. It sounds strange to say, "he was infected by amnesia." Yet in the inquiry, in Porter's statements, that expression recurred many times. From that autumn day he came ever more frequently to understand that his past was shrinking to the period of Violet's illness. People struck with amnesia lose the awareness that they have lost their memory; their life dries up into a series of trivial material facts which took place a moment ago, and soon themselves dry up in turn. Porter did not lose this awareness; he knew that the exclusive nature of his relationship with Violet condemned him to accompany her in her illness. "Just listen, my good sir"—Judge

Ludovico came to a sudden stop—"listen to the metaphor he used. He said: 'If progressive amnesia can be likened to the excision of successive portions of memory, then Violet's "operation" was performed under anesthetic, while mine took place without it, while I was fully conscious.'"

His relation to Violet underwent a rather clear, though slow, change. He never neglected his duties as guardian and nurse, continuing to look after his wife with all his former diligence; but drop by drop the tenderness went out of all his actions. He noticed the change, and yet, to his own surprise, he felt no pangs of conscience.

Autumn passed and winter began, which in those parts was not so much cold as soaked in damp. A large part of his day was taken up with chopping firewood and heating the house. And then, in southern Italy, when a "good" or "clean" spring comes, nature explodes with unbridled impetuousness and liberality, and there seems to be a rivalry between the green of the plants, the blue of the sky, and the sprightly green-blue reflections on the sea. To break the monotony of his life, Porter would go fishing early in the morning. He would sit on a rock in the small bay, from where he could keep an eye on the house in which Violet was still sleeping.

## XI

JUDGE LUDOVICO: "In his statements he was cooperative (he put up no resistance); he was clear-sighted, truthful, and straightforward. Right up until the crux of the matter, to which, after all, the inquiry was to have led step by step. At that point he stiffened and closed up, if not completely, then almost so. No, he didn't attempt to deny anything or to lie; but his eyes showed his pain as he struggled to tear the broken words or monosyllables from his throat. It took me a great deal of time and effort to reconstruct that last round of questioning into a statement. He signed it without reading it through."

On the night of the 22nd to the 23rd of April he awoke shortly before dawn, with the feeling of anxiety that a nightmare brings on. He did not remember what he had been dreaming about. He sat in the armchair, his heart racing, and stared at Violet. She was sleeping peacefully, her breathing regular. It was probably an illusion, a hallucination of his, that a smile appeared on her lips. It may have been caused by a contraction of her drawn features (she had virtually stopped eating of late). He remembered that her real or imagined smile had stirred something like anger in him, as if it were absurd proof that Violet had deliberately "infected" him. He stood up in a trance, took his pillow from the bed, and put it over the face of the sleeping woman, pressing down with all his strength. Strength was not necessary; Violet did not move a muscle, only her bare arms turned livid. After some time he lifted the pillow. Violet was dead. He went back to the armchair; the crazy thought occurred to him that he could live with her like this for a long time, that he could love the dead Violet. He left the house, first covering her face with the pillow. Still in a trance, he slowly descended the stone steps to the sea; he looked at the pink-colored horizon and noticed that the dawn had now properly broken. Without undressing he walked into the sea. He did not feel the cold; quite the opposite—he was lashed roughly by a hot wind. He went deeper and deeper; the stony sea floor disappeared from under his feet, and water flooded his ears and his eyes. To this day he remembered how his heart had filled with joy at the thought of drowning.

He was rescued by fishermen returning from a nighttime fishing trip. As it later transpired, silently, and not knowing what he meant to do (the extravagance of foreigners!), they had been watching him from behind a rocky outcrop.

## XII

THE TRIAL IN Vallo della Lucania lasted one day. At the beginning Porter confirmed all of his statements, and in a soft voice answered *colpevole*—guilty—when the president of the tribunal asked him how he pleaded. He seemed not to be interested in the course of the proceedings, but sat in the dock with lowered head. He shrugged and remained silent whenever his court-appointed defense attorney leaned towards him to whisper something in his ear. He raised his head and listened with an expression of approbation to the prosecuting attorney's speech. The jury found him guilty, and the president of the tribunal announced his sentence: four years, including the six months he had been in prison during the inquiry. "I deserve life imprisonment; I'll administer it myself," said Porter in a loud voice. That evening Judge Ludovico visited him in his cell. For that conversation—about which he "preferred to remain silent"—he paid in the nighttime with his first heart attack.

Porter served only a year in Ascoli Piceno; the remainder of his sentence was remitted for good behavior, and he was sent back to England. Apparently he hid himself in some little provincial town in Scotland. Was he still alive? Was he serving his "life sentence"? After his return to England he donated his little house in Agropoli to the Archeological Society in London. Professors and students from London would sometimes stay there. The last sojourn of this kind ended tragically: In the night, after the visitors had left to return to England, the house was razed to the ground by a fire probably caused by the carelessness of those just departed. The site, now only flattened black ruins, a patch of black desert, remained the property of the Archeological Society.

For the first time on our walks, having seen Judge Ludovico remove a nitroglycerine tablet from his pocket and slip it quickly under his tongue, I took his arm.

The sun was sweltering; we walked all the way to the end of the jetty, where we could sit beneath the lighthouse on a broad step and calmly breathe the warm air of the bay.


*February 1993*

# THE EYETOOTH
# OF BARABBAS

## I

IN HIS *Storia della città di Roma nel Medio Evo*[1] Gregorovius devotes a separate chapter to the "cult of the relic" in the ninth century. One can immediately sense a trembling of the historian's normally calm, sober, dispassionate pen. What a strange, mad century! What a fever swept over it! For was it not a fever, the high fever of a sudden bout of sickness, that desire to possess anything that went by the name of holy relic? In our age people talk of "gold fever"; in saying this, we imagine the wild faces of the miners, and the crimes committed in the struggle over gold deposits. In the ninth century the historian's imagination evoked similar faces, similar crimes amongst those hunting for relics. To Rome (for Rome was at that time the largest deposit of relics), pious and less pious pilgrims traveled from all over the world to dig with their greedy hands in the earth that concealed the treasures. The most valuable kind of treasure was considered to be the whole remains of some saint; such a treasure could only be afforded by a rich purchaser (whether lay or ecclesiastical). Other searchers had to content themselves with skeletons, skulls, tibias, or fragments of bone. "The pilgrims," writes Gregorovius, "could not leave the holy city without bearing away some consecrated momento. They bought relics from the Catacombs, as visitors of the present day buy jewels, pictures, and marble statues." Lastly, it must be noted parenthetically that the

[1] History of the City of Rome in the Middle Ages.

ninth-century cult of the relic also gave rise to a wave of mass pilgrimages. Crowds took to the roads, above all traveling to Rome, the city of Martyrs and Apostles, with the profound conviction that in addition to sacred relics they would also find there the holy keys enabling them to open the gates of Paradise.

Of the Romans, Gregorovius recounts that thanks to their innate practical sense they were always able to reap a profit from the passions of the rest of the world, continually supplying the rapidly growing trade in holy remains and relics and images of the saints. Naturally, there were cases of fraud—the sale of fakes, wool pulled over the eyes of naive newcomers. Priests overcome by "rising greed and cupidity" distinguished themselves in the role of "guarantors" in this process. Custodians of cemeteries kept guard at night "as if against hyenas lurking in the darkness." When the Popes consented to the removal of the authentic remains of saints from Rome, magnificent processions were organized; along the way invocations were sung to the dead saints, calling on them to confirm their saintliness with miracles, while in the cities of France, Germany, or England that were their destinations, the weary processions were greeted like returning victorious warriors. It is hard to believe: The fever rose so high that criminals were let out of gaols, given certificates of temporary release, and sent to Rome, that *refugium peccatorum* (refuge of sinners), so they could attempt to redeem their sins and as the fortunate finders of relics in the Eternal City earn a reduced sentence.

In 828 a group of Venetian merchants overcame many an obstacle and survived numerous perils to bring back to their home city from Alexandria the remains of the apostle Mark, soon to become the patron saint of Venice. In 840 the remains of another apostle, Bartholomew, arrived in Benevento in truly miraculous fashion: In a marble coffin they had floated on the oceans and seas from India to the Aeolian island of Lipari; in that year, the island was plundered by the Saracens, and the bones of the saint were thrown out of their grave. A hermit of Lipari devoutly gathered them and took them to Benevento, where the local Lombard Prince Sicard "honored the Cathedral with them in splendor and glory, amid unspeakable rejoicings of the inhabitants."

∎

IT IS WORTH remaining a little longer in Benevento, with Gregorovius still as a guide. "The anxiety for saintly relics was scarcely
anywhere more fervent than at the court of the last Lombard rulers
of Italy. As in the fifteen and sixteenth centuries Popes or Princes
were enthusiastic in collecting antiquities and manuscripts, so
Sicard, sending his agents to the islands and along the coasts, collected bones and skulls, entire bodies and relics, which he de-
posited in the cathedral of Benevento, thus entirely transforming
the temple into a museum of sacred fossils. We may imagine the
alacrity with which he was served. As other monarchs extorted
tribute from the conquered, he made use of his wars to extort
corpses. He forced the people of Amalfi to surrender the mummy
of S. Trifomena, as his father Sico, driven by the same fanaticism,
had previously obliged the Neapolitans to surrender the body of
S. Januarius."

What Gregorovius fails to mention, as if embarrassed and
somewhat wearied by this fever of the century, is that Prince Sicard
reached far beyond the borders of Italy in his quest. He was particularly drawn to the hunting grounds of the Holy Land, and so he
created a separate team which operated solely on that route. We
shall not occupy ourselves here with reflections on whether, in his
emissaries' efforts to fulfill the dreams (or whims) of a generous
master, he was deliberately or unknowingly deceived. Besides, who
knows what tests credulity was put to in those times—or in general,
what was credulity and what was carefully concealed disbelief, in
times of such proximity of the miraculous and heavenly with the
everyday and the earthly. The fact of the matter is that the emissaries of the Lombard prince never returned from the Holy Land
to Benevento empty-handed, and Sicard had no cause to complain
of their sluggishness or ineptitude. Quite the opposite: When,
kneeling before him with the humility required before a ruler and
the reverence called for by religion, they laid out before him the
holy relics they had brought, he unstintingly gave gold for the
fruits of their labors, and for the labor itself, performed in a distant
country. The chronicles noted what they brought in the year of 844
alone: a sleeve of the robe of the Holy Mother of God, the helmet

of the Roman soldier who nailed Christ to the cross, a piece of the boulder that closed off the Lord's tomb, a large sliver from the Cross, Pontius Pilate's sandal, and the eyetooth of Barabbas. This eyetooth was the source of the greatest wonder in the Cathedral treasure-house. "Yellowed, but not rotten," writes a medieval chronicler, "it amazed viewers with its sharpness and its size. For Barabbas, who is often relegated to the background in the holy story, was an important figure in the mystery of the Crucifixion." The chronicler's view was shared by Prince Sicard, who placed the eyetooth of Barabbas in a prominent place in his treasure-house, like a dazzling jewel of uncommon worth.

## III

AND I TOO, the author of this narrative, also share the same view. There must be dozens of stories, legends, poetic works, as well as psychological studies and theological treatises about Barabbas. That he should strike the imagination and provoke one's curiosity, surely no reader of the Gospels can doubt. Yet in that fascination there has always been the element mentioned by the medieval chronicler—of something secondary, accidental, undefined. Barabbas captures one's attention briefly; he was a minor character thrust upon the stage, and not one of the leading actors in the holy drama. A contemporary historian of Christianity says of him: "He comes from nowhere and is headed into the unknown. He appears unexpectedly, passes by barely noticed and perishes . . . He enters history for one moment only, so as to be freed in His place. He does not even have a name. Bar Abba in Aramaic means Son of his Father, and who is not Son of his Father? The veil that has hidden Barabbas's past has also concealed his future. There were many wrongdoers in Jerusalem's prisons; the chronicles are silent about them, and the historians say nothing either."

Before I explain why Barabbas is for me a significant figure in the Gospels—an important player, though in the mask of a minor one, as he was for some time in the Middle Ages (at least in Benevento during the rule of Prince Sicard)—I will pause to consider two examples of literary speculation about him.

**IV**

GIOVANNI PAPINI, the author of *Witnesses to Christ's Passion*, made Barabbas a solitary figure—despised and driven away by those about him, spurned by all creation, as if he were a specter, wandering without purpose upon our earth of the living as a fugitive from the land of the dead. He is an intruder, both for the high priests and the Christians. Caiaphas has his servants throw him out of his house. Peter shows him a little compassion and does not refuse him absolution, but, calling him "a wretched criminal condemned to live," tells him never to appear before the eyes of the followers of Christ. In Bethany, on the slopes of the Mount of Olives, Barabbas meets Lazarus, miraculously raised from the dead, who discloses a great secret to him: Life is not always better than death. In despair, and unable to find a place for himself anywhere, he hangs on desperately to a single idea: to kill Pilate, the man responsible for his suffering. Arrested by the guards of the Public Prosecutor of Judea, at the latter's verdict he dies on the cross in exactly the same spot where, forty days earlier, the prophet known as the King of the Jews breathed his last. Truly, the prisoner of the dungeons of Jerusalem "released in His place" did not long outlive the Son of God and Man.

Papini's book was written in 1938, and so it is reasonable to wonder whether the Florentine author, often praised for the originality and vitality of his mind, had not *ante litteram* hit upon the trail of existential alienation. For that is how he portrays Barabbas: banished, and isolated from the world. Being a religious writer, and a fervent one at that, in the character of Barabbas he may have intended to depict the fate of a person affiliated with no faith whatsoever. A solitary, cursed man. The real Barabbas, about whom I will say more below when I return to Benevento in my narrative, seeing himself portrayed this way in *Witnesses to Christ's Passion*, would have smiled, and in that malign, vicious smile, would have revealed his eyetooth.

The leitmotif of Pär Lagerkvist's novel *Barabbas* is the coming to maturity of the wrongdoer freed in Christ's place. This process is a slow one, going on for over thirty years, and taking place in Jerusalem, then on Cyprus, and finally in Rome. Like Papini,

Lagerkvist begins with a Barabbas alienated from the world, rejected, lost, and stupefied at being "condemned to live." What is new in the Swedish writer's story is the way Barabbas thinks almost obsessively about the Crucified One; his fascination grows more intense every day, and with every year it absorbs his whole being more and more. Knowing from the first moment that Christ died "in his place," Barabbas gradually comes to the realization that He also died "for him." Here he is a single step away from embarking upon the road to conversion. "Jesus' disciples spoke of his having died for them. That might be. But he really had died for him, for Barabbas, no one could deny it!" Since he, Barabbas, was supposed to have died on the cross, the Crucified One had taken his suffering upon Himself. And if He sought to suffer for him and for others, if He craved suffering, like a traveler lost in the desert craves water, then what remained for Barabbas and the followers of the Crucified One to do? To honor His suffering with their own suffering, to pass through a world set about with sharp rocks and thorns, to continually battle their pain with something to which Christ's disciples give the name, unfamiliar to Barabbas, of "faith."

Old already, yet still hale, he arrives in Rome as a servant in the household of a Roman patrician. Here he keeps looking for Christians; though it sometimes seems to him that he is able to recognize them immediately by their faces, his quest is fruitless.

On July 19th in the year 64 he is walking down the street when flames begin to erupt from the windows of the houses. Rome is burning at Nero's command. For Barabbas the fire in the imperial capital is a sign that the Crucified One has returned to earth. He throws lighted brands into the houses to aid this second coming. Rome burns for six days and seven nights. Nero accuses the Christians of setting the fire. Thrown into the Mamertine prison, they await execution, which means crucifixion. Amongst them is Barabbas, who has been caught red-handed. "When, on the cross, he felt death approaching, that which he had always been so afraid of, he said out into the darkness, as though he were speaking to it: To thee I deliver up my soul. And then he gave up the ghost." He repeated the words he had heard thirty years before, when from a place of hiding on the top of Golgotha he had stared into the face of the Crucified One.

**V**

AFTER A LONG nighttime conversation with his wise and trusted advisor, the Public Prosecutor of Judea has decided to release the self-styled King of the Jews. Thus, the birth of Christianity does not take place. This is how Roger Caillois finishes his novel *Pontius Pilate*. In essence he is asking openly whether Christ's victory would have been possible without the Passion.

In the books by Papini and Lagerkvist there are to be found similar questions, though they are under the surface and never asked outright: "What if Pilate had rejected the demands of the Israelite high priests and the Jewish crowd, and not released Barabbas in His place? What if Barabbas had died on the cross, and a free Christ had moved on to continue His teaching without His martyrdom? Would Christianity have come about under such circumstances?"

Caillois's overt question is raised as an elegant and rather subtle intellectual puzzle, with a hint of irony and skepticism. The hidden, unspoken questions of Papini and Lagerkvist take us in a different direction: By presenting Barabbas—with certain differences of emphasis—in the grip of an incomprehensible fate, and by plunging him in the sometimes romantic semi-darkness brought on by his banishment from the world (only the English word *outcast* properly describes this state), they both underline the accidental nature of his role in the story of the Passion. It is somewhat as if he were the rock that triggers the avalanche. True, both writers strove to turn him into a *living* boulder, but they were not able to divest him of the qualities that are neatly captured in the phrase "from nowhere and to nowhere." That he was in reality the antagonist of Christ, accompanying Him unnoticed like an Evil Shadow, fully conscious of the work he was doing or seeking to do, was clearly understood in the ninth century. Was anything left of the treasure-house of Prince Sicard, the owner of the relic of Barabbas?

**VI**

IN BENEVENTO I stayed at the Hotel Rocca, near the ruins of the Lombard fort. The city—from 571 to 1033 the capital of the Principality of Lombardy—had retained traces of those almost five centuries of its past; but these traces were unfortunately scant, and largely obliterated or densely covered over by more recent accretions. The only object that could have competed with the Arch of Trajan in Rome—which has remained in excellent condition to this day—had been the Cathedral, built in the seventh century and remodeled in the twelfth; *had been*, that is, until the last war (till 1943 to be exact) when, with the exception of the façade and the campanile, it was destroyed by Allied bombs.

And yet it was for this Cathedral that I came to Benevento, though I knew of course that it had been bombed in August 1943. The Germans had not left the city till October of that year, after the Anglo-American forces had landed at Salerno; and so—who knew?—perhaps during those two months they had worked feverishly to organize and protect the cimelia that had survived, if, that is, they were not tempted to take them for themselves. My letters of inquiry in this matter, sent to the Office of the Conservation of Monuments in Benevento, went unanswered. From old guidebooks it became clear that Prince Sicard's treasure-house had been located in the cellars of the campanile; and thus it was permissible to hold out a faint hope that it had been protected from the explosions and flames of the air raids.

It must seem to the reader to be naivete, bordering on mental obfuscation or even madness, to hope to pluck from eleven centuries of history the treasure-house of Prince Sicard including the eyetooth of Barabbas—for that was mostly what I was interested in. Eleven centuries! A stormy torrent of time whose influence could not have been mitigated even by building several levels beneath the ground (the old guidebooks from the eighteenth century spoke of a hiding place carved out of the rock in the lowest chapel, by the steps leading to the cornerstone of the campanile). Did I really entertain such illusions? Obviously so; a sober gaze is a useless antidote to a sudden onset of maniacal imaginings. But I believe that somewhere within, at the moment of my departure for Benevento, there lurked another, more modest and realistic calculation. I was hoping that in the former capital of the Principality of Lombardy—as in almost every historical city in Italy—the people had an enthusiasm for rummaging around in their own history and

legends in an amateurish or half-scientific way. How many provincial books and pamphlets had I seen and studied, all published at
the author's own cost! How many "cranks" (in the opinion of mutual friends) had I had the opportunity to meet in the provinces,
their lives consumed in probing seemingly trivial and inconsequential details from the history of their own town! Could not the eyetooth of Barabbas in the treasure-house of Prince Sicard be such a
trivial detail of history or legend in Benevento? During my month-
long stay in that city I discovered that I was not mistaken in my
expectations.

## VII

FATHER MAINARDO, the venerable keeper of the Cathedral, heard
me out patiently, not saying a single word and continuing to shuffle
the papers on his desk. When he finally looked me in the eye, in his
gaze there was a mixture of readiness to assist me and a delicate,
barely perceptible derision. Still saying nothing, he simply gestured
for me to stand from my chair and walk with him out into the hallway. From the window of his room on the first floor of the lofty campanile a group of people could be seen staring at the façade of the
Cathedral. I followed him with a feeling of embarrassment, taken
aback, put out of countenance by his silence. I had expected at least a
few words concerning the purpose of my trip to Benevento.

An elevator—which, judging from the date on the factory
name-plate, was a recent acquisition in the campanile—took us to a
chamber immediately beneath the belfry. Through a small opening
in the wall, the city could be viewed as clearly as if it were an architectural model. It looked as if Father Mainardo, in accordance with
the vague letter of introduction from his friends in Naples, intended to treat me as a tourist, and completely ignore my real interests, which I had laid out before him right at the beginning of
my visit. Luckily I suppressed my reaction of irritation. We returned to the elevator, and I saw him press the lowest button,
which was marked *Grotta dell'eremita*.

We rode down to the very bottom of the campanile, passing
Father Mainardo's office on the first floor. There was a gust of cold

cellar air. The "hermit's cave" was hewn out of the rock; it was here that the construction of the campanile had begun in the seventh century. In the rebuilding of the twelfth century it had been converted into a chapel—with an altar in a recess of the rock, and with sacred hangings (frequently replaced) covering the coarse, bare stone walls.

My companion became somewhat more animated, yet without abandoning the role of a *cicerone* accustomed to the tourist routine.

"The hermit was Helos, a Greek from Egypt. Before he asked Prince Sicard for his consent to remove himself from the world and live in seclusion, he was his advisor and priest. It was he, Helos, who first sparked off the Prince's enthusiasm and then supervised the finding and collecting of holy relics. It was also he who established the Cathedral's treasure-house, which was transferred to this cave when, with the acquiescence of his master, he became a hermit and at the same time the custodian, as we would say today, of the Prince's collection. He survived his master by ten years; he died in his cave in 869, after seventeen years of work and prayer in total isolation. Yes, work. He made an inventory of the Cathedral museum pieces that had been entrusted to his care. At one time the museum occupied the entire cave. Today meager remnants are all that is left."

Father Mainardo suddenly took me by the arm and led me behind the altar, to a side alcove in the rock of the recess. He bent down low, and lifted a heavy curtain covered with rich embroidery and incrustations, which concealed an immense ivory casket, the superb work of some Byzantine master. Beneath the lock, it bore a faded and barely legible inscription: *Sicardus Princeps Beneventi Servus Christi*. When the lid was lifted an empty interior appeared: At the bottom of the casket there was merely a little dust and soil. I could not refrain from asking when Prince Sicard's collection had disappeared.

"I don't know exactly. In any case we found the casket empty after the Germans left Benevento. Along with the relics a sheaf of parchments in Helos' handwriting had disappeared."

"The Germans stole the contents of the casket—relics of dubious authenticity—and yet they didn't touch the priceless casket itself?"

Father Mainardo did not reply. Anger flashed in his eyes. We rode the elevator to the first floor in silence, and our parting was cool.

## VIII

FOR ME, A LONG walk has always been an unfailing way of calming down. The beginning of April had left the way wide open for spring: The sun was sweltering, the trees on the streets had turned green, and in the conversations of passers-by there could be heard a note of excitement full of joyful relief. I wandered without purpose around the city, stopping before storefront displays and venturing into narrow blind alleys, where surprised looks followed me through chinks in the shutters. Despite its impressive historical past, Benevento is not one of those cities frequented by tourists with Baedeker in hand, and so *uno straniero* is an object for curiosity with a mixture of distrust.

Circled by a ring of mountains on the horizon and situated on a hill, Benevento drops gently towards a plain upon which two rivers converge. Beyond the city I came upon a path that led across fields, and then through a small grove to a clump of fresh, lush vegetation, a sure sign of water. There I lay down on the grass, in the shade of a sizeable bush. The sky was cloudless, like a silk canopy of a faintly ashen color stretched tight overhead.

It had been perhaps ten years since the dream I will describe in a moment. At that time I was spending the summer in the Alps; my mornings were devoted to writing and reading, while after lunch I would go off on short mountain hikes. What I was reading each day, chapter after chapter, was a book by the American religious scholar Jeffrey Russell: *The Devil: Perceptions of Evil from Antiquity to Primitive Christianity*. That day I had reached the chapter entitled "The Devil in the New Testament." It would seem that the Gospels were familiar to me, and yet I was struck as if only now I learned that Christ called Peter Satan, when Peter attempted to lead Him from the way of the Cross that was ordained for Him. He called Peter the Devil because Peter sought to turn him away from his Passion. He also called Judas the Devil, for steering Him towards His Passion by his betrayal. Yet it is usually Judas who is identified with the Devil; Luke goes so far as to assert that Satan entered into him. Russell remarks: "Judas is such a close counterpart of Jesus that one senses an analogy between their relationship and that of the doublets so often found in mythology. The analogy may even be closer: In the great scheme of salvation the God knew from all time that Jesus would be the savior and Judas the betrayer; and as the betrayal of Judas was necessary for the Passion of Christ, the God might be said to have chosen Judas for his part in the act of salvation as well as Jesus for his . . . The Devil has his genesis in the God himself. He is a counterpart, a doublet of the good Lord. He is the shadow of God."

On that day, after I read this chapter, I had a dream in my remote mountain chalet. I dreamed only of a Voice, resonant, almost imperious: "No, not Judas! Barabbas!" And as I lay with half-closed eyes on the meadow outside the gates of the ancient city of Prince Sicard, I could not avoid the sensation of reliving anew my dream of ten years earlier. This was why I had reacted so emotionally to the medieval chronicler's mention of the relic of Barabbas. I knew what his eyetooth meant. In the theriomorphism of that time (that is, demonic manifestations in the form of animals or their attributes), a large eyetooth was the identifying mark of the Devil, just as today it is the insignia of a Vampire.

## IX

I RETURNED TO MY hotel in the early evening. The porter handed me my key and nodded towards the hotel's small parlor. Father Mainardo was sitting there. He was waiting for me, and agreed to eat dinner with me in the hotel restaurant. At first we exchanged casual remarks about trivial, indifferent things. Finally, towards the end of dinner, I could no longer stand the strain.

"To what do I owe this visit?"

"There was a misunderstanding between us. I know what brought you to Benevento. I imagine that you did not believe what I told you about the remains of Prince Sicard's treasure-house. I can't help that, though I can direct you to persons who, like me, saw the empty casket after the Germans left Benevento. If the Church had wished to get rid of those ridiculous—I repeat, *ridiculous*—relics, those mementoes from the crazy ninth century, it had hundreds of opportunities over the past ages to remove the contents of the casket; but it did not do so, because it attached no importance to curios with value only as museum pieces. The eyetooth of Barabbas! A new perspective on the character of Barabbas! The Lombard princeling listening intently to the elucidations of his priest—later the hermit—who allegedly wrote everything down on a sheaf of parchments! I say 'allegedly' because no one has read those ancient Greek parchments, with the exception, I believe, of a grammar school professor of Greek and Latin at the beginning of this century. He was given permission to do so by the Bishop of Benevento; but the church authorities wouldn't allow him to record the contents of the parchments in a pamphlet, with translations of Helos' selected fragments. I don't know how the matter ended; I arrived in Benevento thirty-five years after Bishop Vizzini's interdiction and the professor's protest. I don't even remember the family name of the professor, only that his first name was Bartolomeo. The Bishop took the position—rightly, in my view—that it is not permissible to disturb the harmony and inner symmetry of the Gospels and their transmission with unauthenticated versions coming from goodness knows where, brought from the Holy Land by Prince Sicard's emissaries over eight hundred years after the Crucifixion of Our Lord. Whenever anyone has expressed interest in Helos' parchments and the so-called 'eyetooth of Barabbas'—and you are not the first to do so—the church authorities have sent the petitioners away empty-handed, including the times before the Germans emptied the casket. I know about this from stories told me by older clergymen. I don't wish to be importunate, but it's difficult to suppress the unhealthy curiosity of an old priest: What was it that so fascinated you about the 'eyetooth of Barabbas' in the treasure-house of Benevento Cathedral?"

"A dream."

"A dream?"

"Ten years or so ago I dreamed of a voice—a powerful voice that seemed to come from beyond, which said that we do not appreciate the role of Barabbas in the holy story. It may just have been my impression, but in that voice I heard a warning: There exists a force which impels one not to appreciate it. This dream was brought back to me when I came across a medieval chronicle, in which the author made special mention of the eyetooth of Barabbas amongst Prince Sicard's treasures."

Father Mainardo smiled and glanced at his watch. It was late; I asked whether he would let me walk him back to his home next to the Cathedral. His attitude toward me seemed to have changed; he had become sympathetic, and at the moment of our parting was even cordial. As I returned to my hotel that night, deliberately prolonging my walk, the feeling would not leave me that what he had said was a deliberate and rather ingenious mixture of truth and falsehood; and that in that combination he was trying to secretly convey something of great importance to me. What was it?

## X

I MUST HAVE BEEN very tired, and slightly tipsy from the wine I had drunk during my dinner with Father Mainardo, not to have immediately figured out what it was that he was attempting to tell me. Deftly, *en passant*, he had quite simply informed me of the existence of a pamphlet based on Helos' parchments, and had even given me the first name of its author—a professor of Greek and Latin in the local grammar school, who lived at the beginning of the century.

I doubt whether there would be any sense in describing the details of my quest for that pamphlet. I think that the rhythm of my story should take on the same impatience that guided my actions.

At the grammar school I was permitted to examine the registry book of the school, from its founding in 1870 to the present day. Around the turn of the century the teacher of Greek and Latin was a Professor Bartolomeo Protocristiani. In the entry devoted to him there was a list of his publications (all brought out by the author), in the area of classical philology. The list included the title *La zanna di Barabba*, with an addition in parentheses: *preparato ma non pubblicato per divieto categorico dell'Eminentissimo Vescovo di Benevento* (*The Eyetooth of Barabbas* . . . prepared but not published due to the categorical interdiction of His Eminency the Bishop of Benevento). He was by nature a misanthrope and a confirmed bachelor. Embittered by the Bishop's prohibition (amongst the faculty he was considered a model of piety), he took early retirement and moved back to his native San Bartolomeo (between Benevento and Lucera), where he died in 1903 in his family home. "In Professor Protocristiani our school has lost an outstanding scholar, a paragon of integrity and a great educator of youth. We salute his memory!"

San Bartolomeo is more a large village than a town. The first boy I asked on the market square led me to the *casa Protocristiani.* On the way he explained to me that no one lived there but a very old woman with four cats. She turned out to be the great-grand-daughter of the Professor's brother, a childless widow; she was a talkative old lady bent with rheumatism, barely able to walk, and yet with an intelligent face and a canny gaze. As God is my witness, I had no alternative than to resort to a subterfuge I thought up on the spot: At the University of Naples, a project had been started to honor the eminent Professor; unfortunately not all of his papers had been issued in print, and so I had been given the task of photo-copying his unpublished manuscripts. No, Malvina Protocristiani would not even hear of lending the Professor's manuscripts so they could be copied in Benevento; the best she could do was to permit me to read them or look them over in her presence, and perhaps take some notes. She was the last of her line; she was well aware of her duties, until the Good Lord should call her to Him. She was to guard her priceless treasures: the books and manuscripts of the Professor, and the four cats. After her death the University of Naples would be able to add the Professor's works to its library col-lection (that would certainly have been what the Deceased would have wanted), while the cats would be looked after by her distant cousins who lived near Lucera, in return for the house, which she had left them in her will.

She led me to her bedroom, where the "Professor's works" oc-cupied the top two shelves of a cabinet with glass doors. The mas-ters of the room were the cats—fat and ponderous, dozing in the armchair and on the window sill. I am not certain that I was suc-cessful in controlling the trembling of my hands as I reached for two notebooks at the end of the lower row of books. The thicker notebook bore on its cover the title *La zanna di Barabba* and a subtitle in Latin: *Sine Diabolo nullus Dominus* (Without the Devil there is no Lord God). The thinner notebook, really just an exercise book, was only half-filled with writing and was entitled *La scomparsa di Barabba*—the Disappearance of Barabbas.

## XI

AS I SAT AT A small table by the glass-doored cabinet and, with pencil and notepad in hand, began to read Professor Protocristiani's thick notebook *The Eyetooth of Barabbas*, there was something rather extraordinary about the atmosphere surrounding me. The old lady lowered the blinds over the windows, sat on the bed, and watched me closely. The four cats spread themselves upon the bed and stared at me nervously with their hackles up, as if at any moment they might run away or leap onto the table. The situation was not conducive to a quiet, meticulous reading; the author's small, though clear, almost calligraphic handwriting often turned before my eyes into muddled, illegible rows of letters. I was on edge and agitated. I was on the verge of saying something inappropriate, causing the old lady to take the notebook away from me and order me out of the house. Fortunately—truly fortunately both for myself and for our knowledge of Barabbas—the old lady was simply testing me. My face obviously conveyed the proper combination of diligence and respect for the manuscript before me, because after an hour had passed she stood and shuffled out of the room, returning for a short while with a kindly smile and a cup of strong coffee—a reward for the "professor from Naples" (as she called me), who had passed the test and proved himself trustworthy. As if at a given signal, the cats on the bed calmed down; their fur ceased to bristle and their eyes drooped sleepily.

The further I read, the more taken I was with the Professor's conscientiousness and restraint as a commentator. He had set himself the task of giving a clear and accurate synopsis of Helos's account; the passages he quoted verbatim he gave in the original ancient Greek and then in his own translation. He refrained from "enriching" or "modernizing" Helos with his own remarks and reflections. In fact, he permitted himself only two things: His was the subtitle *Sine Diabolo nullus Dominus*; and it was he who at the end of the work added a commentary which I will cite word for word, as it deserves, at the relevant point.

Helos' account was based on the reports of Prince Sicard's emissaries, who brought the relics back from Palestine. He questioned seven emissaries in great detail. The text indicates that he spoke with each of them separately, later comparing their stories for verification, and occasionally resorting to confronting the witnesses, as if he were intimately familiar with investigative methods. He himself made sparing use of his own commentary and interpolations, though he did not avoid them when the need arose. Thanks to this, it was not hard for me to extract from the text his own view—which was so skillfully and emphatically given that it could not have been merely the product of the emissaries' reports. It was Helos who stated that "Barabbas, who is relegated to the background in the holy story, was an important figure in the mystery of the Crucifixion"; a statement which in all likelihood was not so much inspired as simply confirmed by the reports.

The reports of the emissaries, in turn, naturally and understandably drew their life-blood from stories heard in the Holy Land, both from the sellers of the relics and from others met by chance at bazaars or taverns, in houses, or at camping grounds. One theme recurred constantly: Barabbas was not a secondary character, a nameless bit player in the holy drama, a wayside stone by chance unleashing an avalanche, a criminal "released in His place" because the dice happened to fall out one way and not another in a Great Game which neither cared about him nor concerned him. Before he was thrown into a Jerusalem prison for murder, he had acquired a "name for himself" (the expression used in Helos' text) as a hater of Christians. It was a blind and passionate hatred, not understandable in an ignorant and godless cutpurse. Whenever he met anyone suspected of being associated with Christ's disciples, he would seem to shake with anger; he would clench his fists, narrow his flashing eyes, and mutter something to himself, while foam appeared on his lips. At a certain point he began to accompany Christ and His followers at a distance. When they stopped to rest, he would hunker down for a while in the wilderness at a distance where he could observe them; and he would either sit calmly with his eyes half-closed, or would splutter incomprehensible curses, making himself hoarse, and wave his arms like one possessed. Only Christ would watch him in thoughtful silence, on one occasion saying sorrowfully: "Bar Abba, Son of his Father. Where I am, there he is. For all time." His disciples looked at Him in astonishment.

One day he vanished. He had been arrested for the rape and murder of a woman known in the Christian community. Beaten unconscious and thrown into the dungeons with a death sentence over his head, in his chains he did not stop cursing the King of the Jews and His adherents. As he cursed he revealed his eyetooth, terrifying the other prisoners who lay beside him. Amongst them he was feared and obeyed.

The high priests and the populace that they stirred up knew exactly why he should be the one to be "released in His place" by the Public Prosecutor of Judea.

## XII

IN THE NATURE of things a synopsis of a synopsis doubly impoverishes the qualities of the original, and sometimes simply loses them completely. I am aware that I have been unable to convey even to a modest extent how much effort and talent the worthy Professor Protocristiani had invested into making Helos' ninth-century account accessible to our age. At times it can be seen clearly—though as if through a light mist—that Prince Sicard's mentor and favorite was not only a shrewd and intelligent investigator, but also a narrator with considerable powers of poetic expression. At other points the evidence of this is direct and tangible. In the ancient Greek original and in his translation, the Professor cites his description of Barabbas obstinately accompanying Christ and His disciples at a distance, crouching in the desert, silently or in an onset of furious ranting. It is an exquisite passage! I am not surprised that it provoked the translator's only commentary in *La zanna di Barabba*: "In the analysis of literary works, the Germans quite frequently make use of the term *Doppelgänger*. This is what was for Helos, and is for me, the Bearer of Evil (*Il Portatore del Male*), never leaving the side of Our Lord, who brought to the world the Light of Good (*La Luce del Bene*)."

The thin, half-filled exercise book entitled *The Disappearance of Barrabas* made a melancholy impression. Either the aging Professor's powers were deserting him, or he already knew that the attitude of the Bishop of Benevento towards his publishing plans was unfavorable (not to say hostile), and he had lost much of his original enthusiasm. In either case, the presentation of Helos' last chapter was hasty, full of deletions and corrections, though it was also freer in the sense that the Professor did not deny himself certain personal interpolations (at times made in a delicately provocative tone).

Readers of Lagerkvist's novel will recall how Barabbas bragged to Sahak that he had been present at "the Master's Resurrection." "No, not so that he had seen him rise from the dead, no one had done that. But he had seen an angel shoot down from the sky with his arm outstretched like the point of a spear and his mantle blazing behind him like a flame of fire. And the point of the spear had rolled away the stone from the tomb, pushing in between the stone and the rock and parting them. And then Barabbas had seen that the tomb was empty."

Let us overlook the writer's poetic license and preserve from the quoted excerpt two details that are of the essence for us: the entrance to the tomb blocked by a stone (or rather a boulder), and the empty tomb seen by Barabbas.

In his final chapter Helos tells of the last years of Barabbas that are known to us. The "one released in His place" assembled a gang of bandits with whom he traveled the country, marking his trail with murder, robbery, and fire. But as he grew more and more impulsive and violent, he also felt more and more weary, and angry at everyone and everything; his anger was like an illness, with paroxysmal attacks. One day, in his huge, shaggy head, covered in wounds, there was born a crazy notion: He had a desire to spend a night with his companions in Christ's empty tomb, as if he wished once again to feel His Presence and perhaps also, crushed by the weight of time, to steal from Him the secret of immortality. They reached the tomb in the evening; with difficulty they rolled the heavy boulder away, and lay down around the rock walls, treating themselves to the wine they had brought, while Barabbas finally managed to quell his companions' fear with his loud laughter. At midnight, all of a sudden it became light; a gash of lightning appeared in the sky and for a long time did not go away, after which there came an extended peal of thunder, as if the earth were rolling to the edge of a precipice. The walls of the tomb cracked, and the massive boulder at the entrance crashed onto those lying there. It fell directly onto Barabbas' face, breaking his nose and knocking all his teeth out. Bleeding profusely, the men finally succeeded in moving the boulder aside. They broke out of the tomb and ran off every which way. Barabbas' companions saw him rushing forward with great bounds unparalleled in a mortal man. He was never seen again.

"But I," Professor Protocristiani concluded his summary and translation, "see him still. I see him every day, wandering the desert, with his eyetooth grown back even sharper than before, in the vain hope that Christ will come to earth to perish at last by his hand, which clenches into a fist at the very thought. For all time, Bar Abba."

*July–August 1990*

# BEATA, SANTA

OVER THE COURSE of the year my relations with the largest newspaper in southern Italy, *Sud*, had broadened, and strengthened to the point that the editors decided to extract me from the narrow constraints of my original "specialization." That specialization, within which the newspaper and its occasional contributor had remained up till then, was the political problems of Eastern Europe and Russia. Now, the editor-in-chief invited me for a coffee in his office, announcing as soon as I crossed the threshold: "You're a writer, and you shouldn't fester away in this narrow pigeonhole— and one that's become even narrower of late. I have a proposition for you, which at least to begin with is partially connected with your homeland and with Eastern Europe."

He placed before me a press release from one of the agencies which was terse in that typically journalistic way, and which, it appeared, the other newspapers had not picked up.

"As you see, the story is set in Macera, which is situated high above Potenza. There's only one bus a day from Potenza to Macera, ten kilometers or so up a steep and rather bumpy road. It returns to Potenza for the night after dark. We'll reserve a room for you in a good hotel near the bus stop. There's no hurry. In my view the matter is delicate and rather sensitive; it resembles material for a story more than a series of reports. If you're interested in the idea, find what information you can in Naples and tell us when we should book the hotel in Potenza."

* * *

"FINDING WHAT INFORMATION I could in Naples" was easier said than done. After my first and only attempt, it turned out that a short trip to Rome was necessary. The dispatch from the agency, which I had read over and over (so that in the end I knew it almost by heart), as usual in the case of such dispatches, contained only a dry account—like the skeleton of a living being that has been picked clean.

Before the outbreak of the civil war in Yugoslavia Marianna K., a young woman from a village near Kielce in Poland, had been invited to Goražde by her sister, who towards the end of the Second World War had married a Bosnian physician she had met when she was sent to do forced labor in Germany. The couple had twin daughters who were considerably older than Marianna. The physician and his wife (she was also a doctor) had perished on the street from the bullets of a Serbian sniper. The three girls—the lady physician's daughters, who were about thirty, and her seventeen-year-old sister—had fallen into the hands of the Serbian army during an "ethnic cleansing" operation. Imprisoned in a women's building, and at the disposition of the Serbian soldiers, for four months they were raped every night—either in their own building or in the soldiers' quarters. The two daughters (one of whom was pregnant) made successful attempts at their own lives immediately after they were released from their "service." Marianna was also pregnant and decided to have the child—both out of her own free will, and convinced by an Italian Catholic monk from a mission in Sarajevo. With the aid of his brothers in Potenza, this cleric arranged for her to come to Italy. The priest in the small town of Macera near Potenza took her in and entrusted her to the care of his mother in the presbytery. The doggedness with which she was preparing for the birth of this child of rape, spending every free moment in the church in prayer, won her the admiration of the inhabitants of Macera (though it was not clear whether this applied to all of them). Her devotees called her *Beata* or even *Santa*.

* * *

THIS APPELLATION WAS not the invention of the God-fearing residents of Macera. It had first appeared in an unsigned piece in the Episcopal Bulletin of Potenza; from there the piece had made its way, in the form of a reprinting, on to the more significant pages of the Archepiscopal Bulletin in Naples. In this manner it took on the flavor of a semi-official designation, or in any case, one with the backing of the Cardinal Archbishop.

In Naples I knew a priest, a "cavalier of the pen," as he called himself—in other words a scribbler who dreamed of publishing his ghastly "religious" poems, yet was incapable of going beyond descriptions of church ceremonies that appeared in the Archepiscopal Bulletin. After lengthy persuasions, he revealed the "editorial secret": Both the note in the Episcopal Bulletin in Potenza and its reappearance in the Archepiscopal Bulletin in Naples were the work of a "high-ranking dignitary" in the Vatican. Reluctantly, and asking me to keep the secret, he gave me his name. I could not even hope to stand before the stern countenance of the cardinal himself, but I learned by chance that his personal secretary, Father V., was a reader of my writings. This simplified matters. In return for the promise of a signed book, he agreed to a meeting in a café near the Santa Anna Gate.

Father V. was a young man who made a favorable impression on me; he was brisk and "all-knowing" ("behind the Bronze Gate a person has to know everything"), with a lively intelligence. He devoted the opening of our meeting to some interesting remarks about my writing. Then I signed the books I had brought for him. Finally I stammered out timidly: "I have a certain request too." To begin with he frowned in a rather ominous manner, but I realized that this was probably part of the official ritual. In the end, when delicate pressure was applied, the wellspring of my interlocutor's knowledge opened up, and he made little attempt to hide his satisfaction at being the informant of "such a well-known and respected personage."

One thing he knew for certain: His superior had sent the recommendation to the Bishop of Potenza and the Archbishop of Naples at the urging of someone higher than himself in the church hierarchy. But he did not know who this was, or at any rate he assured me that he did not, dismissing my guesses with a slightly offended silence.

Before we parted he suddenly felt the need to compensate me for what he believed to be my serious disappointment. There was much to suggest that in the young pregnant Polish woman, who out of maternal love had decided to bring a child of rape into the world, the Vatican saw an example. *"Un preclaro esempio della virtù cristiana*—a shining example of Christian virtue," he added, rising from the table.

As soon as I returned from Rome to Naples, I accepted the offer of the *Sud* editor and gave him the date of my departure for Potenza.

\* \* \*

POTENZA IS AN UNSIGHTLY city. It is a curious thing that in Italy cities of middling size are either very beautiful or very ugly, as if it were the nature of Italian aesthetics to recognize only extremes. In Italian cities beauty possesses a clear historic center and from there has outgrowths to the adjoining neighborhoods and as far as the outskirts. The indeterminate character, or even lack, of a historic center renders the rest of the city commonplace and coats it in grayness. To walk around it is to encounter images that are worth neither observing nor remembering.

A draw in Potenza—or rather in its distant environs—is the figure of the sixteenth-century madrigalist and criminal Carlo Gesualdo, the Prince of Venosa. In the opinion of experts (including Aldous Huxley), he was one of the most outstanding composers of madrigals; in the opinion of criminologists he had few equals in his cruelty. He had a beautiful young wife, whom he had long suspected of unfaithfulness. Having guilefully orchestrated just such a betrayal in a bedroom in his palace in Naples, he ordered his servants not only to kill the lovers but to hack them to pieces. He fled beyond the jurisdiction of Naples to his family estate at Venosa west of Potenza. Books about him, portraits of him, picture albums of Venosa, tawdry pictures depicting the crime, long poems of folk *cantastorie*, and recordings of his madrigals were the principal articles sold to tourists in the city; in all probability he was its only claim to fame.

The hotel was indeed next to the bus stop, but I arrived in Potenza before evening, too late to risk a trip to Macera. I merely called the presbytery. The mother of the priest, and then the priest himself did not hide their satisfaction that I was Polish: "At last she'll be able to speak her own language.'"

Indeed, she knew only a few sentences in Serbo-Croatian, and her two-month stay in Italy had taught her that characteristic pronunciation of Italian by foreigners with no ear for languages—a mixture of distorted sounds and ancillary gestures. Her joy at meeting me was so unrestrained that she seized me by the hand, brushed my cheeks with her lips, and kept repeating, "O Lord, thank you, Lord," as if I were a relative of hers. In one sense I was. We came from the same region; her father was a woodsman in the vicinity of Zagnańsk, halfway between Kielce and Suchedniów.

We sat in a well-shaded arbor next to the presbytery; it was the end of August, and the heat of the *solleone* was not yet over. To begin with, she silently stroked my hand; from time to time she wiped her eyes with a handkerchief and kept whispering, "Lord, thank you, Lord." Father Pietro had told me confidentially when we met that she was in her fifth month (he had also immediately added in an even lower voice: "We call her *Beata*, *Santa*, but the name makes her angry"). Her silence, which lasted perhaps half an hour, gave me an opportunity to take a good look at her.

In the faces of Polish women one may observe—more frequently than with other women—a pleasant and engaging ordinariness. They are neither beautiful nor ugly, but rather, as the expression goes, agreeable. Who knows if the Madonna should not be modeled after just such faces, without the excessive sweetness of the Renaissance, or the gloomy melodrama of Gothic. Gazing at Marianna as she leant against a column in the arbor (she preferred to stand rather than sit on a lawn chair), I thought of Piero della Francesca's *Madonna del Parto* from the chapel in Monterchi: The Madonna was older than Marianna, of course, but had an agreeable peasant's face with regular features and a straightforward expression in her searching eyes. Or perhaps the association was brought to mind by the fact that Marianna's dress opened on her belly just like in the painting by the Italian master, a few unfastened buttons emphasizing her condition in such a way as to suggest that its resolution was close at hand (though I knew that in her case, she was only in her fifth month). But in this description I have omitted the most important thing: In both her face and her figure, she seemed barely more than a grown-up girl. This came across especially in the shape of her mouth, which every so often was twisted fleetingly by a grimace of sadness or a slight trembling of the lips; at these moments her eyes misted over with tears.

\* \* \*

AT OUR FIRST MEETING, after she calmed down and broke her silence, we immersed ourselves completely in an evocation of our native region. Naturally her memory was fresher and more vivid as she had been away only a short time: No more than a year and a half had passed since she left the forester's lodge near Zagnańsk. Before my own eyes, after so many years, there passed images as if obscured by an opaque screen. But in the end my memory, half-dead, revived, and I grew better and better at keeping pace with my ever-so-young interlocutor. We picked berries and mushrooms in the dense woods around Zagnańsk, flushed out hares in the glades and clearings, fished for minnows under the rocks of streams and for larger fish in the rivers, and followed the railroad tracks, so as not to get lost, through the dark old woods of Tumlin. She knew our Black Pond in Berezów, because she used to pass by there with her mother on the way to Michniów and Wzdołowy, where she had relatives who also worked in the forestry administration. She was so excited at these wanderings, so happy! This may explain, and partly justify, my mistake: I asked why she didn't return home to have her child, rather than rely on the hospitality of people who no doubt were kind, yet were strangers, with whom, additionally, it was difficult to communicate. She blushed abruptly, turned her head to the side and placed both hands on her stomach without saying a word. I realized my truly unpardonable indelicacy and quickly resumed our cheerful, nostalgic journey. She looked askance at me in gratitude. How could I not have guessed that her decision had not erased the sense of a shame not of her own making? And shame, as everyone knows, is most painfully felt amongst one's own people.

In the evening I returned to Potenza and without eating supper I lay down on the hotel bed, chewing over in my mind the bitterness caused by my embarrassment. In all probability—small consolation!—I had understood subconsciously that the editor's proposition had been one of those crazy notions that reveal the ambiguities (not to say more) of journalism. But I came to understand this fully only now. It was obvious that I would be able to speak about everything with my young countrywoman, *except* what happened to her in Goražde. In my behavior I had to consign her misfortune to oblivion. For her, I had to be a source of relief, not of increased stress. Nor could I reveal the real reason I had come from Naples; luckily Father Pietro had introduced me as a Pole whom the Neapolitan archbishopric had persuaded to visit a compatriot in this parish near Potenza.

The next morning I intended to clear the whole matter up by telephone with the *Sud* editor. Before I fell asleep I was haunted by the last image I had taken from Macera. A small group of elderly men and women (from Macera? or Potenza?) had come to the arbor by the presbytery, led there by a very young priest whom I did not know. They touched Marianna's stomach with their fingers, then kissed them piously and folded their hands in prayer. The girl fled, literally fled, from the arbor, in her haste forgetting to say goodbye to me. And I instinctively recalled the custom common in the South of touching a casket as it is brought out of the church to the hearse, and then of kissing one's fingers.

\* \* \*

I WAS SURPRISED by the sensitivity of the *Sud* editor; I had taken him for a typical journalist, prepared to hunt for any sensation without the slightest moral scruples—*by hook or by crook*, as the English say. He heard me out without once interrupting, despite the fact that I had prepared a longish explanation. When I finished, there was a lengthy silence on the line. "I understand you perfectly," he said finally; "in your place I would have done just the same. But since we paid in advance for a week at the hotel, I suggest you make use of it for the rest of the time and visit your fellow Pole each day. She needs it." I was touched and conveyed this to him.

It was true that I had sworn to myself I would avoid even the faintest allusion to Marianna's Serbian experiences and would pay no attention to her pregnancy. But beneath this vow lay another truth that could not be suppressed: All my thoughts perpetually circled around these things that were strictly forbidden from being expressed in words. And so I watched her half-childlike face, talked too much even and too frivolously, anything to elicit her smile and a flash of merriment in her eyes; yet at the same time in my thoughts I was far away, *over there.* There was nothing to be done about it, just as nothing could be done about my gaze, which from time to time, momentarily and unconsciously, lingered over her belly. I comforted myself that she did not see my quandary, and that I had managed to impose on her a feeling of growing closeness and fondness, *despite* her past and her condition. I was pleased at every sign that I was gaining her trust, and that she was loosening up and relaxing beneath the burden she carried.

From the newspapers I knew that women released from Serbian "ethnic" captivity had few problems in terminating their pregnancies if they wished to do so, and if the instinct to live was sufficiently strong not to plunge them day after day in thoughts of suicide. What had tipped the scales in Marianna's case? Was it the piety she had acquired at home, inculcated in her by her parents since she was a child? Or was it an irresistible maternal instinct? Irresistible, in spite of the circumstances of the conception, in spite of the trampling underfoot of the Christian principle that a child ought to be the fruit of love, not of hatred? I was not even sure whether she was capable of hatred, with that childlike face of hers, and those eyes transparent in their purity. Or perhaps she had been persuaded to have the child by the Catholic monk from the mission in Sarajevo; perhaps he had seemed to be a spokesman for her father? Perhaps she was too frail and young and had been unable to resist his insistent arguments? In what language had he spoken to her? There were no answers to these silent questions, which multiplied in my mind. One brought with it another and another; there was no end to them. I took her hand in mine and drew her to me like a wronged daughter deprived of speech. I did this all the more boldly because once she confessed, without being asked, that she did not have, and did not want to have, written contact with her parents. This imposed orphanhood evidently helped her to bear her arduous trial.

\* \* \*

My week was coming to an end and urgent business was calling me home. On my last day I took a very early bus to Macera in order to catch the return bus at one o'clock and the train back to Naples at two.

Marianna was still asleep in her little room near the arbor. Father Pietro's mother entertained me, serving me coffee in the arbor itself. Her son had already come back from morning mass and was receiving the faithful in the dining room of the presbytery, which, every morning, was transformed into his "office." Muted voices came from inside; the priest evidently took care not to make too much noise. So did his mother—though in the fashion characteristic of older people, with the anxious expression of one entrusted with some secret. This secret—or rather the nagging concern—of course related to Marianna. It sometimes happened that, like today, she woke up very late, and her morning hours of sleep were strange. Lord, how strange they were, not like sleep so much as a long swoon: She would not move, she was as white as her bedsheet, and she appeared not to be breathing, her hands interlaced over her stomach like a dead woman prepared for her funeral. "The doctor from Potenza put our minds to rest, my son's and mine; but can doctors be trusted? You hear so many stories about the mistakes they make! Take a look yourself; I'll just crack the door open and you'll be able to see through the gap."

In the darkened room with the shutters closed, the sight was indeed disturbing. As I looked I tried to catch the slightest movement of her neck, a twitch of the skin or of a vein; I stared at her wide open mouth, her hands crossed lifelessly over her stomach, and her eyes under their heavy lids. Her state had the appearance of sleep without breathing.

The girl came to the arbor right at noon, as the bell in the church tower was ringing. She sat opposite me on a lawn chair, still not fully woken up. For the first time I observed in her something of a double response. One moment she would be stroking her stomach thoughtfully with the smile of happiness or satisfaction shared by all expectant mothers; then the next, with her right hand she would seem to push the unborn child away from herself, and for a split second her features would sharpen into a grimace of aversion, perhaps even of suffering.

We had little time left to say our goodbyes. She stood up from the chair and with a complete lack of constraint nor any hint of bashfulness, she threw her arms around me; with tears in her eyes, she rested her head on my shoulder. "Remember," I consoled her, "Don Pietro has a telephone in the presbytery. And it only takes four hours to get to Potenza from Naples."

\* \* \*

AFTER TWO BRIEF CONVERSATIONS I realized that she was not fond of the telephone. More—she was afraid of it for some reason. The third time she asked Father Pietro's mother to apologize to me, and to say that she was tired and did not feel up to coming to the phone all the way at the other end of the hallway. I switched to writing letters; she responded quickly and elegantly, in the style of a good student, who furthermore had learned legible penmanship. Every letter of hers asked when I would come again. "I'd like to talk at least a little more in my mother tongue. I don't think I'll ever learn Italian, though Father Pietro Scoppola and his mother, Donna Margarita, are very patient and very good to me."

In the second half of October there was a longer break in my work and I would easily have been able to take advantage of it to visit Marianna and her guardians. I put it off, however, until I was driven from my home in the space of a few hours by a package that arrived from the editor of *Sud*. I received it in the late evening; I set about reading it immediately, and at dawn I was already sitting on the train to Potenza.

It was an oral testimony, given by a forty-year-old Bosnian woman, a childless widow, and transcribed by a member of the international human rights commission. She provided her name and her address in Goražde, but I prefer not to include this information. She had once been a beautiful woman, the members of the committee stated; but the person who had stood before them was old and broken. She had come to them of her own accord, neither asked nor encouraged by anyone; it was clear from her first sentences that she wished to testify at any cost, and to do so as fully as possible, without omitting even the most shameful details. She regarded her deposition as a double punishment: one administered to those who had wronged her, and to herself for her role as helpless victim, incapable of an act of despair or courage. The latter component was even stronger in her testimony; at times it seemed that the author of the account was torturing herself with a peculiar, unrestrained relish, as if this were now all that was left to her in life. Nevertheless—and this was also striking—she retained a cold and sometimes repellent precision in the telling of her tale.

She had been in a group of one hundred and eighty young, and more or less good-looking, women who had been gathered in Goražde by an "ethnic" dragnet organized by the Serbian soldiers. It was sufficient to have Bosnian connections, even distant or entirely accidental ones (it was here that I found out which group this was, since the testimony included mention of a young Polish woman with two half-Bosnian nieces). The formal purpose was "racial improvement"; in reality, of course, it was to create a brothel for the common soldiers. The women were first held in a closed building where the soldiers came at night, chose a partner and relieved their needs in front of all the others. At the beginning, this involved beating any resistant partners till they bled. Later, resistance weakened and was replaced with a dulled passivity. It could be taken that on average each woman was raped multiple times each night by three different soldiers. This subsequently brought a desire for more "intimacy"; the soldiers took their chosen women to their quarters in their own barracks. In the end a telephone was installed in the building and the women were selected and escorted to the caller by one of five guards belonging to the "internal services." After four months the occupants of the building were released and dispersed. At this time, in the estimation of the author of the testimony, a third or more of the women were expecting. She had heard of suicides, but no one knew exactly how many there had been. Many had chosen to have an abortion. She herself had been three months pregnant and had directed her first steps to a gynecologist she knew.

The statement consisted of about seventy typescript pages and had been translated (for the use of the international press) into English, French, German and Italian. From the editor of *Sud* I received the Italian translation with the annotation: "Return to editorial archives." I will of course say nothing of the details which the author of the testimony scattered freely throughout—with such a generous hand, and such a desire to cause herself pain. I have long been of the opinion (a view that is increasingly disregarded, even mocked, in the world, both in newspapers, magazines, and television, and in literature), that there exists a certain impassable boundary concerning what it is permissible for people to say about other people.

The editor of the document, a member of the Commission, who had been given the job of making it read a little more smoothly, evidently had rather pretentious literary leanings, since he had decided to preface the testimony with the curious epigraph: *Para eso habeis nacido*—For this you were brought into the world. This was the title of an etching by Goya from *Los desastros de la guerra*, depicting piles of dead partisans and a witness to the crimes, who, staring at them, cannot prevent himself from vomiting.

* * *

I ARRIVED IN POTENZA in the morning. The stores and cafes were already open; I found a more modest hotel, also near the bus stop. Some psychological block prevented me from leaving immediately for Macera. The weather was autumnal: the usual southern October, gloomy, drizzly, and close. There was no sense in wandering for a short time around the unprepossessing Turkish baths of the city. In the hotel I availed myself of the shower, which was not working properly, and, tired from my trip, settled in the armchair by the window. It looked out onto a small side street; with an odd sense of relief I gazed at the infrequent pedestrians. I was seeking a way to calm my nerves, which had been set on edge by my reading in the train.

Once again I had come to understand the faulty way in which the imagination works. Before reading the report, on the basis of my own life experiences and my need for the greatest possible realism I had had an image of the Serbian "ethnic cleansing." It had fallen far short of reality.

The truth I had read rendered the picture of Marianna quite

implausible. Was it possible that after all she had experienced she was the way she was—or rather the way I had come to know her, a young girl firmly rooted in her childliness, and, it seemed, spiritually unscathed? And would I be able to consign my fuller, new-found knowledge to oblivion as I looked at her and talked with her? It would not be too much of an exaggeration to say that I was now afraid of my meeting with Marianna.

I appeared in the presbytery in the afternoon, to the delight of all three of its inhabitants. In the eyes of the priest and his mother I detected what looked like a hint of concern; in Marianna's eyes the joy was unadulterated. She was just getting ready to go for a checkup at the clinic (Macera boasted fine medical services), and I agreed without hesitation to accompany her in place of Father Pietro. The friendly and well-mannered doctor, a native of Macera, was pleased by the results of the examination. He predicted her term to end in December, and warned that sometimes there may occur a fever beforehand (Marianna nodded as I translated the doctor's caution). Aside from the tablets and fortifying syrups that had been prescribed already, he recommended lying down for at least two hours each day, and taking walks. The opportunity for a walk presented itself right then. She took my arm and hung onto it with the trustfulness of a daughter; that was in all probability how the inhabitants of Macera saw us, like father and daughter, clinging to each other in familial closeness. Marianna continually received greetings and good wishes from passers-by, and that may have been the only thing to cloud her enjoyment of a long stroll filled almost entirely with this young girl's voice, talkative as never before. Her desire to speak was unsurprising, after a period of "conversational fasting." I was happy both for her and for myself, since the thoughts I was mulling over in my mind demanded my silence.

We returned home before dusk; the priest and his mother reminded Marianna of her obligation to lie down for two hours. Without putting up any resistance, she went into her room and closed the door behind her. The three of us sat in the kitchen, drinking wine with water. The shadow of concern I had noticed on their faces straight after I arrived at the presbytery naturally had a cause. In subdued voices, almost in a whisper, they told me that their ward would sometimes (not always) talk during her afternoon nap. Naturally she spoke in her mother tongue, which they did not understand. So it was impossible to be sure whether they were ravings without meaning, merely words that rose to the surface of a shallow sleep. What if she was saying something that she did not dare tell them when she was awake? What if there were something she wanted? On one occasion the priest entered her room quietly and watched her from the threshold. He was struck by how her face had changed—it was devoid of its usual sweetness—and by the fact that in this language, foreign to him, the words sounded so gruff. It may be that they were overreacting and had no need to worry; but they asked me to listen to what she was saying as soon as there was an opportunity. Because now—you hear how quiet she is?—thank heaven, nothing was disturbing her peaceful doze.

Two days later the "opportunity" presented itself. And it did so so suddenly that the priest and his mother jumped up in their seats, giving me a look that was simultaneously questioning and imploring. I tiptoed into her room (for the first time!) without releasing the gently depressed door handle. The blinds were lowered to darken the room; on the bare wall opposite the door, over her bed, there hung a photographic portrait of the Pope. Behind the head of the bed stood a tall crucifix and beneath it a prie-dieu that was also quite tall. The girl on the bed was not just talking, not just expelling words; she was in effect shouting but rather quietly, as if choking, as she strove to hold back a storm of tears. And, judging by her face with its sharply set features, also a storm of rage. She lay on her back, her dress fully unbuttoned; her swollen belly looked as if it were about to burst. I leaned over her, trying to catch the exact words she was uttering. If someone had seen me in this pose, they would undoubtedly have been taken aback by the expression on my face: I am certain that it alternately flushed red, then turned chalky white.

"Oh, it's understandable," I said to the hosts, who were waiting for me outside the door as I closed it gently, "that sometimes memories of her painful experiences in Yugoslavia come back to her." The priest and his mother sighed simultaneously as if on cue. The next morning I was called back to Naples. I was grateful for the summons. I arranged with the hosts that I would come again around December 10th; the doctor had predicted a due date in mid-December. They invited me to stay at the presbytery in a tiny but entirely bearable room next to Marianna's.

\* \* \*

MY FIRST DAYS AT home, once I had dealt with current urgent business, consisted of an attempt to compose myself. In the evenings especially, when I had torn myself away from the routine of daily work, I would either sit at the table with the notes I had brought from Potenza (made on slips of paper in the train), or pace about the room like a caged wild animal in a sudden fit of irritation.

On the slips of paper I had written down the words, phrases, sentences, and exclamations I had managed to make out from Marianna's half-sleeping delirium. I will not cite them here, just as earlier I did not cite the testimony of the Bosnian widow recorded by the members of the international commission. And for the same reason. What was of the essence, however, were not some scraps or other of Evil, repellent, turning one's stomach and instilling terror, the kind of things which journalistic and "literary" seekers of "naked, undisguised reality" use to titillate, and poison the minds of, the so-called "general public." What was essential was always, and still is, Evil itself.

I do not recall which famous writer should be credited with the assertion that literature is a constant meditation on death. I would add: and on the power of Evil. In both cases literature strives to comprehend the incomprehensible, to perceive the imperceptible, to shed at least a little light on the "heart of darkness." But it usually acts as though there were a clear line of demarcation separating Life from Death, and Good from Evil. Whereas for me what is important, though hard to fathom, is and always has been the border region, Conrad's "shadowline," which represents motionlessness, a lifeless survival amid elements lying in wait. There is no death, or none accessible through direct experience, beyond the boundaries of life. There is no Evil, creeping up deceitfully from afar, beyond the boundaries of Good. The law of osmosis applies here.

But does it really apply; can we feel it? On the surface it does; what is more, it seems banal to us. But it is one thing to know about it, and quite another to see it. Just as I saw Marianna's pure, childlike little face beneath her vulgar words and hardened, twisted countenance.

\* \* \*

WE RENEWED OUR correspondence. Despite the fact that I wrote short and sometimes banal replies on postcards of Naples (many years before I had discovered this way of dealing with my lack of epistolary talent), she wrote longer and longer letters with ever greater gusto. She had decided to tell me everything about herself, from her earliest childhood memories to her graduation from the co-educational high school in Skarżysko. There was no doubt that she was telling me all this—and including details that I found excessive and even amusing—in order to provide some relief from her loneliness. She knew that I was a writer, and this may have given her additional encouragement, since her efforts to write *well* were all too evident. Shortly before she was due and before my departure for Macera, she mentioned in passing, delicately, I am tempted to say, blushingly, about her "boyfriend" in high school. But she had lived in too strict a household, under the watchful and jealous eyes of her parents and the local priest, for that budding emotion to have come to anything. Besides, after graduating earlier than expected, with straight A's in her graduation exam, as a reward she was sent to stay with her older sister in Bosnia.

I reflected on the reasons of my attachment to Marianna. I believe that the main one was simply the fact that I was fascinated by her misfortune. (A very close friend once said to me: "Isn't it the case by any chance that you fall in love with any human suffering?") Before I even met her, I had been indignant at the Church's appeal to women in her condition—to find within themselves the Christian courage to give birth to those children of violence and hatred and to suppress the temptation to procure an abortion, thus postponing until the future their natural, Christian longing for a child of love. An aura of "saintliness" surrounded Marianna—which in my view had been orchestrated by Church circles; yet she aroused my admiration because she was impervious to this aura, treating it with indifference and a touch of irritation. Why then had she decided to give birth to a child of violence? How had she overcome within herself the anger of a woman shamed, deprived of her dignity, beaten and abused, and remained attuned to the signals of the life that was beginning inside her—growing, maturing, and with every movement undermining her own life? It was this that had me spellbound, and drew me to her with an irresistible force. No, for me she was not "Beata, Santa," she was a creation of instinctive generosity and goodness astonishing in one of her age. And there was one more thing that in the interests of complete truth I must not conceal: From the moment when I heard her half-sleeping ravings and saw her altered face, I liked her even more for the tangle of conflicting human emotions in her. I did not want her to be a "pure saint" from a lithograph; I wanted her to be a "real saint"—in other words, one who is profoundly tainted.

* * *

I KEPT MY WORD, and on December 10th I knocked on the door of the presbytery. I was put in the poky little room next to Marianna's. The lack of space was of little consequence, since from the very first moment it became clear that I only had to sleep there (and even then I had to be prepared to jump up from my camp bed whenever my neighbor called). During the day my two hosts—and, without saying anything, Marianna herself—expected me to be constantly present by her bed. To begin with, I was not certain that this was in fact what Marianna herself wanted, so diplomatic was she, and seemingly so allergic to any inordinate concern for her. Later on I discovered that it was her idea; she had not dared to approach me directly, instead charging Father Pietro and his mother with making the request and asking them to keep the secret. She had suddenly become afraid, now the birth was imminent. It was an arduous pregnancy, if one can say such a thing; she walked about the room with difficulty, and returned to her bed with relief, as if it were a haven. She had visibly aged, and had acquired narrow wrinkles and furrows; though at times she would briefly regain her former freshness, and the pretty, childlike shape of her mouth. She did not resist when I stroked her hand and sometimes enfolded it in my own hands; on the contrary, she smiled gratefully. I also sometimes happened to stroke her face and kiss her lightly on the cheek, which brought a tear to her eye. She yearned for tenderness the way a weary traveler longs for water in the desert. We talked the whole time about our native region; I would never have suspected that so much could be said about it. But we never said a single word about her stay in Bosnia, even about the happy times before the outbreak of war. I would have sworn that during her attacks of fever or her after-dinner naps, she lost touch with herself to such an extent that the "other" Marianna did not leave the slightest mark on her. She emerged from the dark and evil welter like a new-born baby, having utterly cast off the integument of the metamorphosis I had experienced with such feelings of agitation as I watched and listened.

The young physician from Macera called by every two or three days, expecting the birth to come any moment now. In the clinic he had arranged a special room for her. He had also arranged for a good gynecologist from Potenza to be present, since it was out of the question to take her on the bumpy road all the way to the Potenza hospital.

Father Pietro's exalted talkativeness, his fondness for "religious" allusions—for example, to the calendar, as Christmas was approaching—and his gestures (he was constantly placing his hands together piously and raising his eyes to heaven)—all this brought more and more visits every day from "pilgrims" of both Macera and Potenza. Whether I liked it or not, I found myself playing the role of a somewhat tough bodyguard to Marianna. No one aside from me and the priest's mother had the right to cross the threshold of her room.

\* \* \*

THE BIRTH PAINS BEGAN in the late afternoon of December 19th. She was immediately taken, shouting, and under a pile of blankets, to the clinic. From the presbytery I could hear her hiccup-like cries at the clinic, and that was my only contact with her. No outsiders were allowed in the clinic; this order had been given by the young local doctor, apparently on the instructions of the gynecologist from Potenza, who had told them he would be there in half an hour. I say "apparently" because there was continually someone running up to the presbytery from the clinic. We heard that the doctor from Potenza had arrived with the Bishop of Potenza, who was greeted by Father Pietro. I sat in the kitchen with the priest's mother; we gazed at each other in silence, alarmed at the intensifying cries. They finally ceased around nine o'clock. A quarter of an hour later Father Pietro rushed into the kitchen. "*Taglio cesareo*, Caesarian section," he muttered in a terrified voice. And he ran off to the church.

The continuation of the story is a summary of chaotic pieces of information gathered from the street. A boy was born, exceptionally big, and the mother fell into a profound swoon. Later on, at midnight, she did not react as they tried to put the child to her breast. The priest was allowed a five-minute visit to the clinic. He refused to say anything about this visit, but merely kept crossing himself and praying in a whisper.

Marianna died at dawn the next day, December 20th. At midday the church doors were opened. Fortunately it was not possible to get too close to the deceased, since she was surrounded by a dense palisade of tall, thin candles; this alleviated the concern that people from the crowd would rush forward in order to kiss the casket. Marianna's face was serene and placid; it made one think of a first communion more than a funeral. A small crucifix had been put in her intertwined fingers. Between her breasts had been placed an oval medallion with an image of the Madonna. The child was taken by some nuns from Potenza.

A funeral mass was said on December 22nd by the Bishop of Potenza, assisted by Father Pietro. He too spoke at her grave, which was piled high with flowers and wreaths. I was not paying particular attention to him; I was irritated by the dominant theme of *un preclaro esempio della virtù cristiana*. It was cold; the wind blew, the hard clods of earth fell quickly on the lid of the casket, and the crowd hurriedly dispersed like a flock of frozen sheep. I threw in my handful of soil, embraced Father Pietro and his mother, and, chilled through, dragged myself back to the presbytery for my bag. A stranger from Potenza took me in his car to the train station.

In mid-April of the following year I had a visit in Naples from the young doctor of Macera. I inadvertently gave an inward smile as I listened to his story. He was the great-great-grandson of

Flaubert's pharmacist Homais, an anti-clerical "progressive," though in this case an intelligent and witty one. He could not understand Marianna's death; everything had been done as it should. His learned colleague from Potenza had also been tormented at the thought of what he would say to the Bishop of Potenza (you understand, sir?). The child? A strong and healthy boy; the Ursuline sisters of Avellino had taken him in. And Don Pietro? Still in search of miracles *ad maiorem Dei gloriam*, he was telling people that right after the funeral he heard sounds coming from the grave, as if she had not died entirely. A month ago there had been an exhumation in the presence of a *monsignore* from the Vatican and a doctor from Rome, which our Don Pietro regarded as the next step required in the process of beatification. But you know, for the last week he had been morose and had stopped talking; someone from above must have put a stopper on his eloquence. The doctor from Macera was "eloquent" too; I breathed a sigh of relief when I had accompanied him back to the metro station.

\* \* \*

MY INTUITION TOLD me that I should go and see Father V., the secretary of the influential cardinal from the Roman curia. This second meeting was made possible by a fortunate coincidence: Toward the end of July a new book of mine appeared in Italian, and at the same time a Catholic publishing house in the north brought out a small book by Father V. about St. Francis. I bought it and read it (it was very fine), then wrote a letter to Father V. complimenting him on the book, and with the letter, sent along a copy of my own book inscribed with a warm dedication.

A week later I received a reply. Father V. was in seventh heaven, and did not even try to conceal his delight. He suggested a meeting. I invited him to lunch in a pleasant little restaurant near the Vatican on August 7th. He accepted the invitation and the date.

I knew all along that the success of my enterprise depended above all on whether I could for a moment become an actor. To begin with, then, I concentrated on his little book, and would not listen to the complimentary remarks he made about my book in return. It came the more easily to me because at the beginning of the year I had made a careful study of a massive work, by a female Church historian from the University of Pisa, on the question of "the stigmata of St. Francis," a book that impressed me with its erudition and its skillful exposition. It went without saying that Father V. also knew the book, and so our conversation, liberally washed down with wine, became an erudite tournament, interspersed with my own laudatory references to his book.

Over coffee and brandy I decided to show my hand a little. I mentioned casually, *en passant*, our previous conversation. He fixed his eyes on me. I held his stare, knowing that he was testing me, and that he was hesitating. In this duel of gazes, this meeting of looks, which lasted unbearably long, I held out to the end. He drank another glass of brandy and grew lost in thought, nervously wiping his forehead with a napkin.

I have to give him his due. In a split second he turned from a lively and elegant interlocutor into a profoundly and sincerely shaken man, without a shadow of dissemblance. "It's a tragedy, a fearful tragedy," he repeated. It was obvious that he was truly perturbed; there were suddenly bags under his eyes, and despite the ventilation, large beads of perspiration appeared on his forehead.

I cannot exactly re-create his story (which was interrupted from time to time with a dry sob and the expression, "I'm casting this into your soul as into a deep well"), and so out of necessity I present a recapitulation, a woefully plain summary of the "fearful tragedy."

Father Pietro's euphoric news about sounds coming from the grave the day after the funeral, passed on in an entirely different tone by the episcopal curia in Potenza, alarmed the relevant department of the Vatican (that which deals with beatification and canonization processes). A prelate from Rome set off for Macera, accompanied by a doctor working for the Apostolic Capital. An exhumation was ordered; no one was allowed to be present except for two gravediggers from Rome, both sworn to silence. When the lid of the casket was removed the dead woman was found to be turned on her side, her face distorted in a grimace of terror, her eyes wide open and frozen in this way forever, her fingers spread; she had let go of the crucifix, and the medallion with the Madonna had slipped down between the body on its side and the wall of the casket. Her

bristling blond hair seemed longer, as did her fingernails. Marianna
K. had been buried alive, plunged into a deep, cataleptic sleep that
cannot be recognized without pricking the body, a method used
since the Middle Ages till the beginning of our century. What is it
caused by? Father V. had read the report by the Vatican doctor, but
the technical medical terminology had rendered it hermetic. Such
a case, the fault of no one and unique rather than merely rare (Father V. used the Italian expression *più unico che raro*), naturally dis-
qualified the beatification process. A martyr's death must be an actual death. What he meant was: a different *kind* of death.

The August heat beat down as if from a blast furnace; crossing
the bridge over the Tiber, I remembered the good times (after the
war), before the river had become polluted and infested with rats.
In those days one could go down to one of the jetties and bathe
in the slowly moving water. On the other side of the river I
was miraculously able to catch a cab going to Termini. I did not return to Naples. At the last minute I squeezed onto a train marked
*Roma-Potenza.*

I spent the night in a hotel, breathing with difficulty, and concerned the whole time about my heart. At six in the morning I took
the first bus to Macera. The little town was still asleep; the streets
were deserted, and I was able to make my way to the cemetery un-
observed. Marianna's grave was still covered with flowers (partly
withered now); judging by appearances, it seemed that a fresh
wreath had recently been added, with a banner on which two quo-
tations by John Paul II were written in golden letters: "Mother-
hood is often an act of heroism" and "Mothers are the heroes of
our times." On the gravestone of brand new marble there was only
Marianna's given name and family name and the dates of her birth
and death; beneath this was the inscription *Madre di Jan*, and lower
still, in large letters a parsimonious valediction: REQUIESCAT
IN PACE.

The cemetery in Macera has another gate on the far side,
which leads down to a path that zigzags its way to a working-class
suburb of Potenza. Once, on one of our walks, I stood there with
Marianna, but we were afraid of the steep descent to the path.
From above we could see a woman climbing up to Macera with a
cardboard box on her head; it was evidently heavy, since she

stopped to rest every few steps. I thought of the brilliant scene with the great Anna Magnani in Rossellini's unfinished film *Stromboli*. A prostitute is returning to her native village in the mountains with a suitcase tied with string, after she has been away for many years in the big city. She walks slowly along, stopping from time to time; her face is damp with the effort, and her black Sunday dress is covered with patches of perspiration. The scene is unparalleled in all of world cinema; it is a modern-day Golgotha. I said this to Marianna; she blushed and whispered: "Don't blaspheme." And then, after a few minutes of silence, when we had already left the main gate of the cemetery, she added in the same whisper and blushing even more intensely: "What you said is beautiful and true."

I jumped down from the little crag onto the path, intending to return to Potenza on foot. Beyond the hill, on the horizon was the sun, red as if at sunset; despite the heat of August the greenery had its morning freshness. The turned-down boughs of the trees, the ashen grayness of the rocks, skeins of night fog dispersing from the meadows, creeks glistening by the path—Lord, how wonderful is the work of Your creation! And yet descending the hill, I only looked down, like a man who has blinded himself. There are moments in life when the rich, extravagant Beauty of the World mocks us cruelly and wounds us till we bleed.

*August 1994*

# THE HEIGHT OF SUMMER

## A ROMAN STORY

### From My Journal

I READ IN MY *Journal Written at Night* from August 15, 1977:
"The name of *Ferragosto* (the height of summer, August 15) is a
shortened form of *Feriae Augusti*, which were established by imperial decree in 18 B.C.; thus, this pagan holiday in August (which in
the later Christian calendar became the Feast of the Assumption) is
two thousand years old.

"Whoever on Ferragosto gazes upon a motionless Rome from
one of its belvederes, whoever in the ancient part of the city ven-
tures down alleyways empty of passers-by and with blank windows
in all the houses, ought to know that in the shadowy, sticky, stifling
swelter of the rooms behind the shutters, in the heads of the few
people still remaining in the city, thoughts of suicide are often
hatching. This is confirmed by the statistics, which speak with a
dramatic flourish of a sudden, uncontrollable 'paroxysm of self-
destruction' each August amongst those unwilling or unable to flee
the city."

### Report of the Public Prosecutor's Office

LAST YEAR, IN 1995, the "paroxysm of self-destruction" yielded a
particularly abundant harvest. On the night of the 15th to the 16th
of August, nine people took their lives. The report of the Rome
public prosecutor's office, prepared by Special Sergeant Tarantino
and signed by Captain Flavio Carbonari, included a complete list

and a somewhat superficial description of the victims *di codesta notte maledetta* (of this accursed night). The sergeant explained the reason for this expression, which was scarcely appropriate in the bureaucratic language of police reports. The temperature had passed a hundred and five, and during the day there had been numerous cases of "heart failure" in the hospitals and several fatal heart attacks in the city.

The list began with the death by suicide of an elderly couple. The *villino*—a small house with a yard—was on the outskirts of the Prati neighborhood (at Via degli Scipioni 67). He, Ettore Palombini, a retired grammar-school physics teacher, was 74. His wife, Elvira, a housewife, was 72. They had committed suicide in their tightly sealed kitchen by turning on the gas. The prosecutor's office had been called in the morning by an anonymous passer-by alerted by the smell leaking out. They broke the windows with a metal rod they found in the yard. The time of death was approximately three in the morning (the sergeant and two police officers had been accompanied by the doctor on duty from the prosecutor's office). Between the couple on the floor lay a dead parrot. It had probably died earlier, because it had been taken out of its cage. The sergeant had described what had happened as a "tragedy of loneliness" and even added that it may have been the death of the parrot that drove the childless couple to this "desperate measure." The captain inscribed a small question mark in the margin with a regular pencil.

Second on the list was Monsignor Maurizio Zubini, a high-ranking official in one of the departments of the Vatican's Civil Service, who lived in a large apartment building opposite St. Peter's (Via Porta Cavalleggeri 113). He was 40. In the early morning a messenger from his department had come running with an important document for him to sign. He had been alarmed by the lack of response to the doorbell. The prosecutor's office was contacted by a telephone call from the Vatican department. The Monsignor had been found dead (and naked) in his bath, with a plastic bag over his head tied at the neck. When he lost consciousness, but probably before he died, he had slipped down in the bathtub, which was filled with water, but the inflated bag had kept his head above the surface, his eyes wide open and a terrible grimace on his livid face. His building was completely deserted, but in the neighboring one the team from the prosecutor's office was able to find the caretaker and his wife in an apartment in the wall of the closed gateway. Yes, they knew the Monsignor well; for a week or so, in the evenings he had been coming home from his office upset and irritable, barely in control of himself (despite the fact that up till that point his relations with his immediate neighbors and the other residents of his building had been cordial). He lived with a young theology student named Marco, who was his nephew. The caretaker's wife winked knowingly and laughed. Her husband too gave a vulgar chortle. A week and a half to two weeks ago, Marco had left. He had been seen one morning getting into a cab with a large suitcase. It was then that the Monsignor's behavior had changed. His next-door neighbor from his building, a wealthy store-owner, the night before he had left for the coast, had apparently heard through the wall a constant pacing and frequent sobbing. The dead man had left no letter. The sergeant ventured the suspicion of a homosexual relationship. And by this sentence too the captain wrote a small question mark in pencil.

In the Trastevere district, at Via Anicia 15, near the Basilica of Santa Cecilia, there is a two-story house behind a low wall with a roof terrace. The terrace is clearly visible from the street, which made it possible for a police officer on his morning rounds to see a naked body hanging from a beam protruding from an alcove on the roof, which served for washing laundry. The police officer tried to make his way to the roof, but the main door of the house was locked; so he jumped over the wall into the small, untended, weed-infested yard, and there, at the back, he spotted a second flight of steps on the outside of the house leading to the roof. He climbed these steps to reach the terrace. The naked body hanging on the rope fastened to the beam belonged to a young man who was already dead. In the corner of the terrace, by the alcove, lay the naked body of a young woman who had been strangled: There were visible marks of strangulation on her neck and her tongue protruded from her mouth. The police officer passed through the terrace's unlocked door, and on the landing saw another open door into the apartment. He went in and from there called the prosecutor's office. After this, he ran downstairs, where he noticed a strong smell of gas. The concierge's house was in the yard, built onto the

inner side of the wall. He managed to wake the concierge, who was
sound asleep. When they broke the windows of the downstairs
apartment a cat staggered out; it was unclear how it had survived,
other than by a miracle. In the kitchen lay the already dead bodies
of two elderly people.

Our team (the sergeant continued in his report) arrived at Via
Anicia at seven in the morning. With the aid of the concierge the
following was established: The elderly couple on the ground floor
was retired and lived an isolated life; they rarely had any dealings
with the other inhabitants of the building, but were occupied exclusively with their cat. Vincenzo Bernardini, a retired official in
the internal revenue office, was 69; his wife, Amelia Bernardini,
who for five years had been seriously ill with a nervous disorder,
was 71. And here too the sergeant noted: "tragedy of loneliness."
And here too the captain added next to this phrase a small, barely
perceptible question mark in the margin.

The couple on the terrace were American: Bryan Wright, 30,
and Nancy Thurston, 28. The doctor determined that between the
strangling of the woman and her friend's death by suicide, about six
hours had passed. Marks in the dust next to the woman proved—or
at least indicated—that before he hanged himself, the man had sat
by her dead body for a long time. On the inner thighs of both,
patches of dried semen could clearly be observed. The doctor had
no doubt that everything had happened after repeated sexual inter-
course. On the table in the dead couple's apartment the sergeant
found some kind of certificate or authorization in Italian, on the
stationery of the Office of the Conservation of Monuments. Bryan
and Nancy, art historians from a university in California, had been
living in Rome for six months; they were authorized to conduct research on Cavallini's fresco *The Last Judgment* in the Basilica of
Santa Cecilia. In the sergeant's report the words "tragedy of love"
could be seen to have been rubbed out with an eraser. This investigator from the prosecutor's office evidently had a compelling urge
to reveal his own sensibilities within the bureaucratic prose of the
report. Which, as was equally evident, did not meet with the approval of his stiff, matter-of-fact superior.

The eighth and ninth suicides of that "accursed night" of August's Ferragosto took place within the borders of the Rome's Jew-

ish ghetto. At six in the morning (reported Sergeant Tarantino) the telephone rang in the duty room of the prosecutor's office. It was hard to understand the woman caller because she was crying so terribly, in sobs that at times turned into shouts. Yet they managed to extract an address from all the sobbing. Via della Vecchia Sinagoga, at the intersection with Via del Portico Ottavia, number 13, sixth floor. The group went there at once. It was an old, crumbling building with four stores on the first floor; there was no elevator, only a cracked staircase pocked with holes. On the sixth floor the door was already open in expectation of the police. By the bed upon which the suicides lay, sat a middle-aged woman who wept continuously. She was Rachele Viterbo, a widow and mother of two grown children. She was the sister of the man who had killed himself—Vittorio Ferrarese, 75, a mechanic. He lay entwined on the bed with Miriam Matera, 65, a cleaner at the synagogue. They had taken an overdose of sleeping pills; the bottles that were included with the report had been lying on the floor along with an empty bottle of wine. From the chaotic story, continually interrupted by outbursts of tears, it appeared that the witness, Rachele Viterbo, had been waiting for some friends to pick her up in their car to take her to Ostia for the day; and as she came down from her apartment in the attic, she had knocked loudly at the apartment on the floor below, where her brother lived with Miriam. She had been worried by the silence inside. She pushed the door with all her strength and the feeble lock gave way. A considerable effort was needed on the part of the doctor and the two police officers to disentangle the two suicides, who were locked tightly together in a human knot. In the end this "stunt" [sic!] succeeded. According to the doctor, death had occurred soon after midnight. The dead couple were placed beside each other on the bed. Their faces were chalk-white and calm; they looked younger than they were. Nothing conclusive came from questioning the dead man's sister. She cried and shouted and pulled her hair out; what she said in broken sentences was incoherent. The interview had to be postponed till another time. For the moment we know nothing. At the end, the captain sealed the report with a large question mark in the middle of the page, which became lightly smudged because of the poor quality of the pencil; it looked like a bird with a curved bill. Beneath it, at the bottom of the page, the captain printed the following: "This annual phenomenon, which is growing ever more grave, should be analyzed by a commission of specialists in psychology. Perhaps with the participation of a priest. To be carried out soon."

## Analysis of the Commission of Psychologists

CAPTAIN CARBONARI GOT what he wanted; not on the scale that he had intended, it was true, but nevertheless his ambition was honored. The proposal from the public prosecutor's office, backed by the relevant department of the Ministry of Internal Affairs, led to the creation of a three-person commission, comprising Maria Teresa Verace and Giancarlo Portella, psychologists from the University of Rome, and Father Antonio Bertoni, the religious advisor at a drug rehabilitation center near Ladispoli. From their side, the prosecutor's office appointed three junior officers whose job it was to gather materials and evidence for the commission's use. The commission was to meet once a month in the lounge at the prosecutor's office, for a period of no longer than six months. It agreed to keep Captain Carbonari informed of its analyses. The commission was given two additional months to produce its final report. The members of the commission were of course given a monthly stipend, from the budget of the Ministry of Internal Affairs.

The inclusion of a priest from a drug center was striking. It indicated, first and formost, a link to the old tradition of treating suicide as an illness ("an illness marked by a longing for death or a fascination with death"); consequently, that the commission had set itself the goal of discovering why the highest incidence of this illness—becoming greater with every year—fell on the day of the height of summer. It was curious and surprising that it was precisely Father Bertoni—the drug priest, as he was jocularly known—who at the inaugural meeting of the commission cautiously warned against such an approach. He was supported, also cautiously, by Professor Maria Teresa Verace. The analysis began with the suicide of the Palombinis in their villino in the Prati district. A description of the tragedy, as detailed as possible, was prepared by Professor Giancarlo Portella on the basis of materials provided by the three junior officers from the prosecutor's office.

The materials, mostly papers from the prosecutor's office and the accounts of neighbors, presented the suicides in the Prati district as a couple who had lived for several decades in "almost" complete isolation in the small villa they had inherited from the husband's family. Ettore, the husband, had left each morning for the nearby grammar school, where he had no friends amongst the faculty; he returned home for a late lunch, then from six to eight gave private physics lessons in a laboratory that had been set up in the turret on the roof of the villino. His wife Elvira was only seen during her brief morning shopping trips, when she visited the stores on the Cola di Rienzo. After that she did not leave the house. They never went out into the center of Rome or to the neighborhood cinemas. They had been unable to have children, a fact that the neighbors knew from an indiscreet doctor. Yet despite this they had seemed satisfied with life. Their satisfaction turned into something more when, around the age of fifty, they decided to adopt a little three-year-old girl from Elvira's home region of Lucania. The word "almost" used above refers to the change in their lives after the appearance of their adopted daughter in their home. It was a small change but a change nevertheless. They would sometimes go out for a walk when Rosetta was tiny; when she was old enough to be enrolled in school, her adoptive father, the grammar school teacher, dropped his private lessons and devoted himself entirely to Rosetta's education. Her adoptive mother took care of her upbringing, teaching her to play the piano among other things; this was something she had excelled at as a young woman of marriageable age. The retirement of the grammar school teacher coincided with Rosetta's getting married. She was eighteen, and had fallen in love with a much older man who reciprocated her feelings; immediately after the wedding he took her away to Argentina, where he had been promised a well-paying job. At the time of her adoptive parents' suicide Rosetta was the mother of three children. And that very summer she had been planning a visit to Rome so that the "grandchildren" should get to know their "grandparents." It might have seemed that the anticipated arrival of the guests from Argentina was a good thing in the lives of the lonely inhabitants of the villino in Prati, with their parrot. But these were appearances only; sickness was lurking the whole time in the shadows.

Father Bertoni was the first to speak. "Where was there here," he asked with a delicate hint of irony, "any indication of suicide as illness, especially that of a longing for death? In the moment of happiness of two lonely old people—non-believers who did not practice any religion, incidentally, and so were all the more lonely, yet who had taken radical steps to conquer their loneliness?" Professor Verace nodded. Professor Portella objected: Who knows if it was not the case that they were all the more keenly and painfully aware of their own loneliness before death, as they waited for a family that was not their own but borrowed from elsewhere—especially at the very time when their own "child" had died in its cage? The Professor failed to convince his colleague and the priest; Professor Verace even reproached him for the "artificiality" of his "extremely far-fetched interpretation." The influence of Ferragosto on the "tragedy of loneliness" (the phrase from the report of the prosecutor's office was adopted after all!) was set aside for later discussion; but it was accepted as a possibility that suicide is not exclusively an illness, and that it is not necessarily associated with despair (as Kierkegaard had argued).

It became clear at once that the suicide of Monsignor Zubini did not allow for any speculations or hypotheses, in view of the absence of any reliable "objective" evidence or testimony. Furthermore, Father Bertoni excluded himself from the discussion from the start, which the two psychologists respectfully accepted. As a cleric he did not wish to encroach upon the intimate affairs of another cleric. It was even proposed that he could return to the center outside Ladispoli, but he declined the suggestion, and sat the whole time at the round table with lowered head. He appeared to be dozing, but on several occasions the others were able to see that he was listening attentively.

The Vatican office in which Monsignor Zubini had worked categorically refused to comment. Even more—there was no attempt to conceal their sense of outrage at the sight of the junior officers. Out of necessity, then, the commission had to rely on the interviews with the caretaker and his wife. They confirmed their first statements, yet despite the natural talkativeness so typical of their occupation, they refused to go into details. The young Marco had been from Como; the police there were instructed to question his family. But it transpired that after leaving Rome he did not go to his family in Como. All trace of him had vanished; he had probably fled abroad after emptying the coffers of his clergyman lover.

On the other hand, under the lamp on the Monsignor's night stand a card was found, containing just one sentence: "I ask the Almighty for forgiveness." And amongst the books on the top shelf of the bookcase they discovered a small clothbound notebook. It was the Monsignor's personal journal; it was so personal that when passages from it were read aloud, Father Bertoni put his hands over his ears. Fortunately for him, the two professors restricted their reading to a few extracts. These were enough for them to pronounce that the cause of suicide had been the breakdown of a man consumed by an unrestrained passion. As before, in the case of the Monsignor they set aside till later the question of why he took his life on the day of the height of summer, even though his young friend had left him at the beginning of August.

The case of the American couple in Trastevere on Via Anicia required information from the United States. The investigators from the prosecutor's office, let in at the beginning of the session, presented with obvious satisfaction a "complete dossier." After this they were asked to leave, since it was a principle of the commission that meetings should involve only the three members, without additional participants.

Though the dossier looked slim and scant, it was indeed complete. An extensive letter from the American embassy in Rome provided the information from the States, which was organized and clearly set out. Bryan Wright, aged 30, and Nancy Thurston, 28, came from Kansas City and were the children of very wealthy parents. They were brought up together and attended the same grade school; they were regarded as "engaged" from a very early age (he 16, she 14), with the approval of their parents, who lived near each other. He waited for her to graduate from high school and they attended Berkeley together, studying art history and taking Italian classes. The label of "fiancés" that had been given them in Kansas City stuck at Berkeley. They were inseparable. They did everything together: classes, homework, vacations at their parents'; the only exception was that they stayed in separate rooms in the dormitories, though that ended when they rented an apartment off campus. They were good students, and the art history department at the university arranged a one-year stay for them in Italy. After they graduated and before they left for Italy, they had a sumptuous wedding in Kansas City. But both kept their maiden names. The first stage in their Italian studies was a stay in Rome, where they were to conduct research on Pietro Cavallini's *The Last Judgment* in the Basilica of Santa Cecilia. After six months they were to have moved to Siena.

The letter from the American embassy was accompanied by a note from the three junior officers made after their visit to an American clinic in Rome, which had recently been set up in a wing of the Gemelli hospital. Of this visit the investigators from the prosecutor's office were particularly proud; they had gone there one day on a hunch, for no particular reason. It turned out that Bryan and Nancy came to the clinic every month. Nancy was concerned that she was not getting pregnant and was undergoing special gynecological treatment. Bryan, who had had tuberculosis as a child and had subsequently been completely cured, had grown used to having himself "inspected" by a doctor he knew. His last visit was on July 12. Bryan had asked for a checkup. His blood had been taken, and on July 13 he himself had brought to the clinic the results of the analysis, which had been performed at a laboratory on the nearby Piazza Trastevere. He left the clinic in a state of agitation. The investigators' note left no doubts: At the clinic they had been told that Bryan was in the beginning stages of AIDS. In all likelihood he was bisexual.

Father Bertoni—as the "drug priest" probably considering himself a specialist on the related topic of AIDS—attempted to reconstruct the sequence of events on Via Anicia. He made use of the term "amok" to describe the mental state of the young American. It was a state (he explained) which clouds all the powers of the mind and often leads to the emergence of aggression. Professor Verace, with the consent of her university colleague, permitted herself to "present a scenario," which of course was "hypothetical." On August 15th, Bryan and Nancy were lying naked in their room, having taken a shower one after the other or together. As dusk fell they dragged their mattresses outside onto the terrace. Around ten o'clock, in a fury Bryan took Nancy repeatedly; she was frightened and acquiescent. At about midnight once again, as if driven crazy by the sweltering Ferragosto night, he possessed her again; this time she put up some resistance. His hands tightened around her neck. Then, like someone befuddled by fumes, he sat for six hours beside her body. When he came to at daybreak, he hanged himself.

At this meeting Ferragosto was associated with an attack of rage. Father Bertoni asked for the word "amok" to be included.

Just as the previous "American" case had combined a murder and a suicide, so the "tragedy of loneliness" on the ground floor of the house on Via Anicia turned out to involve the same combination, only with the roles reversed. This was revealed by the autopsies ordered by a suspicious Captain Carbonari. Vincenzo Bernardini had first been rendered unconscious by his wife, and then dragged into the kitchen, where the gas tap had already been turned on. Amelia lay down next to him, first placing the cat between the inner and outer windows (they had installed double windows for the wintertime). This explained how the cat had miraculously survived.

The commission had a limited field in which to conduct its analysis. This was a woman who was ill with a nervous complaint; and so one could only speculate as to whether it was the intolerably hot night that had set off the impulse to commit murder. The couple—parents of an only son who worked in the small industrial town of Biella in Piedmont, where he lived with family—had, according to the inquiries made by the investigators of the prosecutor's office (and confirmed by the son), enjoyed a happy marriage up until the onset and steady progression of the wife's sickness. In her moments of calm and lucidity, she was afraid that she would be sent to a psychiatric institution. If the suicide of the Bernardinis was indeed a "tragedy of loneliness," it was only in the sense that the wife did not want to die herself, and did not want to leave her husband alone in the world, evidently not trusting the protective instincts of their son.

In any case, in its analysis the committee could not get beyond one point: to what degree Ferragosto had played a role in exacerbating the nervous complaint to its utmost limits. None of the members of the commission doubted the direct link between these two factors.

The investigations, interviews, and informal conversations conducted in the Rome ghetto yielded a report that had something of a novella about it.

The members of the committee unanimously entitled this novella "Romeo and Juliet of the Days of Contempt." The rather extravagant marriage of Shakespeare and Malraux was the idea of the whole commission, and the faces of all three shone with what is known as creative pride.

In the idea there was indeed something exceptionally fitting and telling for our lamentable age. In 1942, Vittorio Ferrarese was 27 and Miriam Matera 17. Their love, boundless and all-consuming, was the pride of the ghetto. Even when they parted for a brief time (Vittorio used to leave the ghetto despite the strict official regulations), their being apart seemed an eternity; and when he came back they would greet each other as if after a long separation. Both families were opposed to this wilful engagement. Vittorio was the only child of a wealthy merchant, while Miriam was the daughter of a widowed railway porter, who did not imagine that the girl would ever move out. Vittorio managed to graduate from technical college before the race laws were introduced, and in the eyes of the ghetto's inhabitants he was considered a "wise man" (it was true that he was a bookworm); Miriam was illiterate, and from the age of fifteen had been a cleaner at the synagogue. They loved each other as if it had been meant to be from the day they were born (despite their significant age difference). They were lovers, disregarding the rules and traditional customs of their elders.

Vittorio had been a communist activist from the age of twenty-three; as the situation grew more intense, the underground party prepared for his escape. Towards the end of 1942 he was smuggled through to Genoa and onto a Soviet ship. He was arrested in Kharkov for "counterrevolutionary activity" and exiled to Vorkuta. He was freed in 1954 after the "Malenkov Amnesty." But it was not until 1960 that he was "rehabilitated" and could return to Rome.

Miriam fell victim to a German roundup in the Rome ghetto on October 16th, 1943. Those fit for work were transported to Auschwitz. She avoided the gas chamber, and returned to Rome in 1945. She only found her way back to the ghetto because she was with a group of survivors who took care of her. It was not clear whether she had lost the ability to speak, but in any case, in the beginning, for three years she did not say a single word. Yet she obviously remembered her former life, since immediately upon her return she resumed her work as cleaner at the synagogue. She was fed like a beggar with whatever came to hand; and she moved into the tiny apartment of her father, the porter, who had been killed. The state of the emaciated and speechless girl led the ghetto doctor to send her for tests at the hospital in Aventina, where he did occasional work. His worst fears were confirmed: In the camp Miriam had been included amongst the "guinea pigs" and her womanhood had been permanently damaged. She did begin to speak, but it was as if she did not remember her fiancé. And yet she threw herself at his feet weeping when he returned from Russia in 1960—a shadow of his former self, a haggard and sickly man, old before his time. They moved into his apartment together. After his father's death he continued his business, though on a smaller scale; his father's inheritance he shared with his sister. Miriam could have stopped working in the synagogue, but she was deaf to all of her companion's persuasions. They were once again seen about the ghetto, arm in arm and always silent. They held each other as tightly as when they were found dead after their suicide.

The authors of the police report added at the end, with apologies, a few clumsy but sincere words of emotion. Professor Maria Teresa wiped her damp eyes with her handkerchief. Professor Portella's voice also broke as he read the report.

Father Bertoni began his attempt at analysis with the rather surprising contention that in his view there was a lack of substantial material to analyze. "It really was a moving novella," he continued, "whose psychological roots lie in regions unfamiliar to us. Which of us can reconstruct or even imagine the fate of a communist from the Rome ghetto, persecuted in the country that he considers his ideal homeland? Who will dare to expose the drama of a young girl, of her sudden transformation from young love to crippled adulthood?" This led the commission quickly to adopt the principle that silence was the only option in the face of the impermeability of the material and the defective nature of language.

"But we do not have the right," said Professor Maria Teresa quietly, almost timidly, "to forget the main problem in our analyses. Starting from 1960, this Romeo and Juliet of the Roman ghetto could have chosen any night, over many years, to cut the thread of their sufferings, which I would call a barren love—the desperate embrace of a life cast out and made hollow. Why did this fall into the abyss, into eternal sleep—caused only by a stone nudged by God or by fate—take place on that accursed night of August 15th to 16th?"

The commission's final meeting came to a close with the decision that this case too—though without an adequate analytic framework—would be included in the work on the conclusions.

### *Conclusions of the Commission of Psychologists*

OF THE CONCLUSIONS of the commission of psychologists it can be said that unfortunately they were conclusions in name only. The good will of the commission's members was evident: They wished to give something to the prosecutor's office and the Ministry of Internal Affairs in return for the taxpayers' money that had been spent on them. Alas, these efforts bordered on the comical, as in the case of the expert opinion they had sought from doctors, on the subject of changes in the organism under the influence of the "rising curve of hot weather." After all, they were supposed to describe the *psychological* transformations of the human personality when it is subjected to the invisible pressure of the height of summer, Ferragosto, and not the long-familiar individual cases of attacks of insanity in those who are *physically* vulnerable to rising body temperature. (In the ancient Roman chronicles one occasionally finds mention of naked madmen running out of their houses on the night of Ferragosto and rushing towards the Tiber, not so much to cool down in the waters of the river, shallow in the summertime, but rather to fall victim to the bites of the riverside rats—bites which brought them immediately to their senses.) The psychological elements in the conclusions were sparse and flimsy: the emptiness of a deserted city and a deserted apartment building; the impulse to reflect on one's past life and to take stock, which rarely occurs in normal circumstances during the rest of the year; an indeterminate fear brought on by a sudden weakening (especially in older people); the effect of the "distant echo" of one's own voice, which can be dangerous if it becomes necessary to call for help. All these psychological causes were valid, but only partially so. What was still missing was a common denominator in these nine so disparate acts of desperation, beyond the simple fact of suicide. And also missing was an answer to the main question put before the commission by those who had created it: Why did this outburst take place on the night of the height of summer? Against the background of the shallow and rather insipid conclusions presented, Father Bertoni's appeal sounded unexpectedly strong: "Note in the conclusions that no one, with the exception of the unfortunate Monsignor from the Vatican and possibly Miriam in the ghetto, felt a living connection with God; I don't draw any far-reaching inferences from this, but I think that among all your conclusions mine is richer, and more deeply grounded in the reality of human life."

From the beginning, those who convened the commission made no secret of the fact that the results of its work should suggest to the prosecutor's office, the Ministry of Internal Affairs, and the legal advisors of the City Council at least an outline for preventive measures; that, in other words, thanks to the commission's inquiries, it would transpire that the sinister phenomenon accompanying Ferragosto could be overcome or at least diminished. As far as this was concerned the members of the commission confessed to being utterly helpless. "The thought of suicide," Professor Verace added from herself, "is like a flower, requiring a long time from bulb to bloom." Father Bertoni elaborated on her comment: "The poisoned flower of a soul abandoned by God grows slowly; none but God can uproot it."

*From my Journal*

*Entry of July 16th, 1972.*

"MANY YEARS AGO I happened to be staying in a squalid little hotel in Rome near the Termini station on the climactic day of August 15th, which the Italians celebrate as Ferragosto. The city was deserted, the heat indescribable. I lay naked on the wretched wet mattress; once in a while I would clamber off it to put my head under the faucet and to stare down into the dark well of the courtyard. The only occasional sound was that of the wheezing elevator, as a passing soldier brought a girl from Termini for an hour. Even the lovemaking in the neighboring room took place quietly and sluggishly, without shouts or the creaking of springs. Today I am unable to recreate the lazy, disconnected course of my thoughts, but I remember that they drifted back and forth across the space of past years, and that there was in them a slowly growing rage (which according to Kierkegaard is the principal face of despair). Around six in the evening I felt something that is hard to describe, a hole in time, the sucking pump of the abyss. I stood at the window. I was wrenched from a trance by the pain in my hands, which were convulsively gripping the handles of the shutters. A moment later there was a brief buzz of activity on the streets and the city revived for a while; in the neighboring building someone sang a popular song in a tuneless voice but at the top of their lungs. On the radio the midnight news announced that *alle sei della sera circa*—at around six in the evening—four people had taken their lives in various neighborhoods of Rome."

### The Mute Universe

I REMEMBER WHAT happened next, though I did not record it in my journal. After the midnight radio news, with a last effort of will I turned off the bedside lamp and fell into a sleep that was as deep as a swoon. I awoke at two. The entire floor of the room was black with cockroaches. Apparently, this happens frequently in the old apartment buildings of Rome: The high temperatures drive the cockroaches from the heat inside the walls, and they squeeze into the room through cracks between the bottom of the wall and the baseboard. They restrict themselves to the floor, where they form a dark carpet that quivers in places. At dawn they crawl back where they came from and the room once again seems relatively clean.

I managed to dress myself standing on the bed and with the aid of water from a carafe I cleared myself a path to the door. I ran downstairs and woke the sleeping porter, who reluctantly unlocked the door onto the street. There was nothing left for me but to wander aimlessly around Rome till sunrise.

Now, after two in the morning, the city was absolutely empty. I made my way to the Tiber, hoping that at least some feeble damp breeze from the river would allow me to catch my breath. And I set off walking straight ahead along the river, resting from time to time on the low wall. In the end, tired, I decided to go down to the water and descended some steps near a locked-up jetty. Someone had left a leaky boat by its entrance. I was able to lie down in it reasonably comfortably.

I lay there, staring now at the starry sky, now at the boulevard on the far side of the river. It was completely deserted; not a single nighttime passer-by was to be seen on it. Deserted and mute, for no sound came from anywhere, other than the slow plash of water in the dried-up channel of the river and the scrabbling of rats in the trash on the bank.

This mute Rome put me in mind of Pascal's "mute universe" in his *Pensées*. I always believed—and on that night of Ferragosto in Rome I did so more than ever—that Pascal was the only philosopher who was able to bring us closer to our own degradation, and to the truth of the "hidden God."

Two of his thoughts I used to repeat constantly in my mind. "We are separated from hell or heaven only by life, the frailest thing in the world." And: "Knowledge of God without knowledge of our own abjection gives rise to pride; knowledge of our own abjection without knowledge of God gives rise to despair. Knowledge of Christ is in between, since in it we find both God and our own abjection."

But most important is the "hidden God," and more frequently and obsessively even the "absent God." Behind his "hiddenness" or "absence" there unfolds the "mute universe," indifferent to our existence, sentencing us to perpetual homelessness. Or perhaps not "behind" but "before" it, since everything is a veil concealing God? In either case, in this "mute universe" we are lost, left only with our own power (or our own powerlessness), cast down upon a "deserted and terrible island."

Re-creating in my memory the fragments of Pascal's thoughts, I continually came up against the question: What if the feelings that penetrate human hearts undergo such a powerful compression that they extinguish all lights, and drive those hearts into a dark, impenetrable jungle? One does not have to be a philosopher in order

to think and feel this way, at the lowest level of existence. And it occurred to me then that that was exactly what was happening to certain people on the night of the height of summer, when the "mute-
ness of the universe" strikes and the veil concealing God is at its
most opaque, prompting a terrifying fear that He may not be there
at all. Why on that particular night and not on any other? That I
cannot explain, nor, I believe, can anyone else. But I still felt the
pain, weaker but still persistent, in my hands, with which I had
fought off the sucking maw of the chasm outside the window. How
many people that night had similarly resisted the temptation to depart, or the sudden terror of nothingness?

I fell asleep once more as the night drew to a close and was
brightened by the coming day. I woke when a kick rocked the boat
I was in. It had come from a man passing by with a fishing rod and
a bucket. He looked round at me, laughed aloud and shouted: *È
finito il Ferragosto!* And indeed the sunrise had rapidly taken Rome
in its embrace. I went up the steps from the riverbank to the boulevard and, refreshed and chuckling quietly to myself, I walked off in
the direction of the Piazza del Popolo. More and more people were
emerging from open doorways. Several cars had even driven onto
the square. I climbed the winding road to Pincio, which was still
deserted, though the water cart was already spraying the avenues.
Pincio, the garden where my love had been born! I leaned with my
whole body against the balustrade, which always permitted me,
whenever I was in Pincio, to take in all of Rome in a single admiring glance: the Piazza di Spagna, Condotti, the Tiber, St. Peter's.
The sunlight splashed like the water from the water cart. The
streets, the boulevard, and the squares darkened with occasional
pedestrians who brought life to the motionlessness of the dead city.
I do not pretend to have uncovered the secret of Ferragosto. A secret it will remain forever (out of reach of the authorities who
dream of preventing the "paroxysm of self-destruction"). For me
the height of summer was, is, and will remain while the earth still
exists, a time of collision between our life and our death.

*April–May 1996*

# ASHES

## THE FALL OF THE HOUSE OF LORIS

*The storm was still abroad in all its wrath . . . The radiance was that of the full, setting, and blood-red moon . . .*
—Edgar Allen Poe: *The Fall of the House of Usher*

I

HERE IS MY JOURNAL entry from June-July 1977:

"The Aeolian Islands, off the coast of Sicily, or in the poetic language of tourism, the Seven Pearls: Stromboli, Panarea, Salina, Lipari, Vulcano, Filicudi, and Alicudi. Two days a week a boat leaves Naples in the early evening. Night falls soon after Capri is rounded. For a moment the red tail of the sunset still drags along the furrow of the sea, then it is swallowed up by a pure and absolute blackness.

"The first pearl to be fished out of the darkness is Stromboli, just before dawn. As the ship is dropping anchor, the end of the night looks like a slow unwrapping of the day from beneath black bandages. Strip after strip, layer after layer, the dense gloom reluctantly disperses; a tongue of fire emerges from the crater and immediately disappears again in a quick flash, the ferrymen's barges loom, and the light goes out from the lighthouse on the rocky pinnacle off the island. Now Stromboli can be clearly seen. From the black sand on the beach, to the white patches of houses and the greenery with its extraordinarily rich variety of hues that in places turn purple and yellow, to the bare black cone of the volcano. The first pearl rather recalls a boulder retrieved from the ocean floor, or a record of something hollowed out, turned on a lathe, hewn and hammered, shaded with colors.

"The second pearl is Panarea, my destination. Considerably smaller, three kilometers long and two wide, with two hundred and fifty permanent inhabitants, a classic Sicilian landscape: brown screes of cinders, gray-green expanses of rock and *piante grasse*, a rich cactus plant adorned with a gaudy, feverish rash of flowers. The one record from the past is the prehistoric village on Calaiunco, a rocky promontory in the shape of an anchor. The circular remains of stone shacks on the rim of a high cliff, the earth burned to ashes, while down below the emerald sea corrugated like trembling tin foil; behind my back bare pink rocks and thistles with carnelian-red flowers. The tourist guidebooks recommend another curiosity, which also has a hidden flavor of the prehistoric. The *alba lunare*, or moonrise, is known in other places too. But it is perhaps only here that a wan day emerges with such marvelous primordiality from the pallid disk in the sky.

"Out of season the life of the island revolves around three points: harbor—church—cemetery. In the cemetery I found a gravestone with an inscription that embraces the whole cycle. A fisherman of Panarea 'always had oar and net in hand, worshiped God, loved life and the sea, and died at the age of one hundred and ten.' In the tiny harbor, people wait for boats; in front of the church they wait for it to open. The procession on the day of the patron saint of the island, St. Peter, is a march by a handful of castaways.

"For many years the meager soil of the island has not been cultivated, if one excludes a few vegetable gardens. The former vineyards and small fields have long grown wild and become covered with weeds, there being no one to take care of them. The more enterprising inhabitants have fled either to the mainland or abroad. The feckless remain, saving up the money earned during the season for the inactive remainder of the year. Everything is brought from Sicily or from the mainland; only bread is baked on the island. But even those who have remained mostly leave after the season for temporary work in Sicily. In fall and winter the island is deserted. In the part where I am staying, between the cemetery and the prehistoric village, there are barely two families patiently awaiting the spring. *La vita si ferma, tira solo il vento.* Life comes to a stop, and only the wind blows. The Aeolian wind."

\* \* \*

AT THAT TIME I was staying with my Florentine friend Loris Berardi in his house called the Villa Toscana, set on a low hill; its various windows had views of the entire island and around it the sea. During the day that sea was fixed at the horizons to the scorched gray sky, and in the evening and night till dawn was coated with the reddish glow of the moon. For the moment Loris had come to his villa alone from Florence; his Russian wife Marina had taken their child to visit her relatives in the States and would spend only August on Panarea. Loris was not fond of solitude, hence the invitation extended to me. I was delighted to receive it, since I had long dreamed of a vacation on one of the Aeolian islands.

I met Loris in 1975. He came to Naples with a letter of introduction from a mutual friend, Roberto, a first-rate essayist. I was struck by one sentence in the letter: "Remember that the bearer truly loves literature, and that is something more than rare these days; and that he decided to visit you in Naples for precisely that reason, promising himself a long conversation." Loris and Roberto had become friends in New York, where as anti-fascist émigrés they had spent seven years from 1938 till the end of the war. Loris was exactly the same age as me; in May 1969 we had both turned fifty. Roberto was older than both of us.

My guest knew little of Naples, so I showed him Santa Chiara and the art museum in Capodimonte, and then I took him to Cumae. There, in the deserted Cave of the Sibyl, he began to tell me more extensively about himself. He was the youngest son of a wealthy Florentine family. When his father died, he and his two brothers inherited a tidy fortune: a café in the center of the city, a huge workshop producing men's and women's clothing, and a house outside the city. The necessity of joining his brothers to handle the inheritance took him away from the university, where he had just begun to study in the literature department. He had had no particular political views other than that he hated violence, and in general the Forza glorified in the thirties. This aligned him with the anti-fascists—though in a superficial way, without any organizational ties. And it led him eventually to leave Italy a year before the outbreak of war. He was in no way forced into emigration: He was neither politically engaged, nor affected by the "race laws" that Mussolini had at that time (rather reluctantly) introduced. "To tell the truth," he explained, lowering his gaze, "what made up my mind for me was a feeling of disgust. One day I was walking down the Via Po in Rome, where the Ministry of Culture, the notorious Minculpop, was situated. The poet V. C., whom I knew well from Florence (he was often at our home), and whom I admired as a poet, was just leaving the building. With trembling hands he opened an envelope, took out a check and breathed an audible sigh of relief. I stopped in front of him deliberately, not saying a thing; I couldn't even bring myself to stammer out a few words of greeting. When he saw me he waved the check in the air and said with a feeble smile: 'Yes, yes, Loris, always remember what they force us to do.' I remembered, I remembered well. Two months later, in September 1938, in Genoa I boarded a ship bound for America."

This story also reflected his attitude to literature. He was nineteen years old; since the age of sixteen literature had been like a Church to him. Brought up in an atmosphere of religious indifference, he felt the need (as he put it) of "another dimension." He treated his favorite writers a little like high priests. Those were not the best times for people of his "denomination." The outstanding poet V. C. was part of a long line, and one that was growing ever longer. As I describe Loris today, in 1994, I cannot help but feel moved (and saddened) at the thought that he belonged to the vanishing tribe of readers. In other words, the vanishing tribe of seekers of the "other dimension." Literature has ceased to be an experience. Books in bookstores are merely goods which sell better or worse, and about which the booksellers know nothing, where before, they were seasoned advisors with whom keen purchasers could enter into discussion.

It soon transpired that we both liked more or less the same authors and the same books. There was something bizarre and at the same time emblematic in the scene of our conversation. It sometimes happened that in the afternoon hours no one visited the Cave of the Sibyl, as if the tourists instinctively feared the "magic" time, when the gloom inside the Prophetess' lair clashed with the sun at its zenith outside. We sat side by side on a stone bench at the end of a subterranean hallway where according to legend the sound of the Sibylline oracle—from the famous *antro*, a grotto hewn out of the rock—could be heard the loudest. Whenever I went there— and when I first moved to Naples I found myself there often—I was overcome with disquiet, possibly even fear, and on the back of my neck I felt the cold touch of something unknown, as (apparently) happens at night in a cemetery to lonely hobos or visitors. This time, as I chatted with Loris I did not feel anything of this kind, but it did seem as if someone was tying our fortunes together with a se- cret knot. And instinctively we both gradually lowered the tone of our conversation, lending it the character of an almost conspirato- rial whisper. "People like us," he laughed, "will be banished to the catacombs." "People like us?" I replied in an echo. But of course I knew what he meant. The world was ever more plainly saturated with routine and habit, such that it was sometimes doubtful whether traditional friendship or traditional love could survive.

That evening he left for Florence, with a brief stop in Rome to have dinner with Roberto. I knew that we had entered upon the path toward friendship: shorter or longer, straight or winding, but headed for the goal we both desired. Oh, if I could have known how painful that goal would be!

\* \* \*

MY TWO WEEKS ON Panarea in 1977—the last week of June and the first week of July—consisted in the mornings of bathing in the wonderfully clean sea; in the afternoons of siestas and unsuccessful attempts at reading, and from dusk (when the heat abated) till mid- night of explorations of the little island. It was a tiny flake of the world, and its charm lay in its miniatureness. If the postvolcanic sea bed ever managed to produce a *maremoto*—a marine earthquake with waves as high as New York skyscrapers—Panarea would dis- appear for ever into the abyss. Along with Loris' villa, though its turret might hold out for a moment longer above the swirling, seething mass of water.

Thanks to the volume of Edgar Allen Poe's short stories I spotted on Loris' bedside table, the appearance of the Villa Toscana immediately made me think of the Ushers' house in the title story. True, it had nothing of the gloominess of that mansion, being rather a dinosaur of late nineteenth century architecture; yet, as in Poe's story, its ugly, pretentious walls, columns and crenellations conveyed a strange presage of ruin. The father of the Berardi line, a Tuscan nouveau riche, after he bought his extensive but encumbered property from a bankrupt aristocrat (who became its manager), had built this mammoth construction for some unknown reason on distant Panarea, where for a long time the few locals treated the place almost like a temple. In guidebooks of the period it was mentioned alongside the prehistoric village of Calaiunco.

Loris let me stay in the turret, which was surrounded by a terrace; from its back edge there was a three-story-high chasm between the house and a vertical rock face. It was true that in the afternoon hours the turret turned into a red-hot bread oven; but later, the opening of all four windows produced a sufficient breeze, and at night even a pleasant chill. The hosts, Loris and Marina, slept on the ground floor in a large room lined with bookshelves and decorated with paintings and reproductions. Next door was the room of their twelve-year-old daughter Irina.

It did not take long to walk round the island. But our explorations led up and down, on wild diagonals, sometimes through dense scrub, with stops by deep holes in the ground; we made visits to cottages in the distant corners of the island, and spent hours observing the fishermen with their nets and poles (I myself dug a still serviceable fishing pole from the lumber room under the stairs in the villa, and returned to the passion of my boyhood). Our explorations, then, recalled the free breaths people take when they have been poisoned by life in the city. Time dragged in rhythm with our carefully placed steps, and in fact virtually ceased to exist, being measured exclusively by the changes of light, of the sky, and of the colors in nature. The sense of separation from the world was a constant source of delight, which could be expressed only by silence. We were silent then, aside from infrequent utterances, as if a dislike of conversation were part of the natural order of things. We would sometimes call at a modest café at the harbor to drink a coffee and hear the Panarean gossip (which was so uninteresting as to be charming evidence of the little island's blessed sleepiness). We ate dinners in a "restaurant" near the beach: a rickety table and always the same meal, *pescepada* and a bottle of white wine. We liked to go by the cemetery: Never in my life have I seen a cemetery so permeated with an atmosphere of serenity and eternal rest.

In the evening little lights would go on in the cottages along the coast that had mostly been built by summer visitors from the mainland. As we passed them we could see kerosene lamps or candlesticks on the tables, as in the Villa Toscana (the generators were used to operate the refrigerators). It was the summer visitors, most of whom were wealthy, who fought against the electrification of Panarea, raising bitterness and even anger in the hearts of its permanent inhabitants. The former came here in the summer in search of the "primitiveness" that the locals found so burdensome.

We spent the evenings, usually till midnight, amongst the rocks and piled stones of Calaiunco, the prehistoric village, the remains of which had been preserved more in the minds of archeologists than in reality. From there the sea, slightly pink beneath the immense lantern of the moon and smoothed to the point of deadness, became something that one reads about in fairy tales and myths.

I watched the *alba lunare* or moonrise from the boat that was to take me back to Naples. Loris waited on the jetty till the anchor was weighed. He had three more lonely weeks till his wife and daughter arrived. "Christmas in Florence!" he shouted. "Christmas in Florence!" I called back like an echo. I returned home in a state of euphoria, of delightful stupefaction.

**II**

In mid-December of that year (1977), in accordance with my promise, I set off for Florence. On the way I stopped off in Rome and naturally turned my first steps towards the apartment of Roberto and his wife. Our friendship went back a long way, almost to the day I had settled in Italy. It was what could be called an intellectual friendship—that is, if "intellectualism" and all its aspects were not so debased, and underpinned with progressive inanity (the adjective can refer equally well to progressive paralysis as to "progressivism"). I sometimes asked myself how Roberto had been able to maintain such purity and integrity of thought, heart, and soul (the last being these days so persistently thrust into obsolescence), all linked inseparably with an intelligence of the highest quality. The answer would probably have been his reflex—more even, his immediate impulse in every case, following the lead of Simone Weil, to abandon the camp of the victors for the side of the defeated. It was a reflex nourished by a distrust of grand systems, doctrines, and ideologies; and by a need for a "cosmic *pietas*" in the face of the metaphysical impermeability of the world. He used to call our times the "age of bad faith," a nihilistic reaction to all moral norms and precepts. If "good faith" can be considered the exact opposite of "bad faith," then his attitude constituted an openness to anything grounded in clear and honest reasoning and an unremitting quest for the truth along with the greatest emotional sincerity.

He and I regarded each other as close friends—indeed, our friendship contained an element of brotherhood even—but I did not consider him my master. He was, however, a master for Loris, who, with his hankering to be a disciple, was good material for pupilhood. I had already had various masters in the distant and more recent past. But I was pleased by the awareness that my new friend was a student of Roberto's, since, as he did not belong to the guild of writers, he had the valuable quality of disinterestedness and objectivity. And—why should I hide it?—subconsciously, as I now realize, I counted on sharing him with Roberto; for in me too, the passage of years had stirred modest aspirations to mentorship.

At the dinner table, and afterwards in armchairs over coffee, Roberto and his American wife Ruth told me how they had met Loris and how they had quickly become friends with him. In New York the Italian anti-fascist émigrés—(the Italians who had emigrated for economic reasons, who were mostly Americanized, were "pro-government")—the émigrés, then, used to gather in the evenings in the club of the American radicals in Queens. One evening Loris appeared there. To begin with people treated him with suspicion, especially because he said nothing, and seemed to listen all too attentively to the discussions (in New York there was no lack of police agents sent from Rome); but the second time he came he joined in the conversation. He spoke clearly, sensibly, and with commitment; he analyzed the mood of his peers in Florence, warned against the creation of a "professional anti-fascism," and stressed the importance of natural resistance in thought and deed. He regarded his coming to the States as an act of weakness; he could have successfully stayed and worked in Florence, but he could not stand the growing fascist boorishness, the epidemic of vulgarity and deliberate coarseness. Their eyes fixed on *Il Duce*—who was crass both by nature and for show—and on his sidekicks, the Italians prided themselves on what was claimed to be "the straightforwardness of the common people," even in the houses of the wealthy middle classes and the salons of the aristocracy. A certain instinctive inner elegance, combined with an abhorrence of clamorous, programmatic aggression, was conserved, at least partially, amongst truly simple people from the lower levels of society. Refined people concealed their refinement, educated people were embarrassed by their education, while the clergy seemed to forget their calling. The fascists' "serried ranks" and "oceanic mass meetings" that filled the squares to bursting, and the ever more widespread "life in uniform," were accompanied by a stampede to break out of the traditional rules of community life.

Loris was immediately popular; everyone took a liking to him. At that time he was still receiving money from home, but the payments ceased soon after at the bidding of the Italian authorities. He found his ideal job, though a poorly paid one, working in an international bookstore. There he met the charming Marina, child of a Russian family which had managed to escape abroad after the revolution and come to the States via Germany and France. Only her brother, who was in the American armed forces, and her sister, a nurse in a Chicago hospital, were still alive. Like Loris, Marina had broken off her studies at the university, in the medical school, out of a lack of money. She learned how to make patterned fabrics, painted plates, and artificial jewelry, and this provided a decent source of income. She was lame from birth, which had kept her from military service after America entered the war. She was and still is truly charming, said Roberto's wife. It was and still is agreeable, she added, to look at that loving couple, Loris and Marina. Their daughter had been born late on, when they had already returned to Florence, and they were both approaching fifty.

\* \* \*

MARINA, LORIS' WIFE, was charming indeed. And it was indeed agreeable to observe this couple, still in love with each other and still affectionate after almost forty years of marriage. Marina's limp was hardly noticeable, apart from the fact that walking clearly tired her and that she had to sit for a short time at frequent intervals. She had a lovely face, still fresh despite her age, and huge, sorrowful eyes that were simultaneously sweet, like those of the Madonna in Tuscan paintings. The problem was their twelve-year-old daughter Irina; but more of that later.

The Berardi family home, a substantial farmhouse with some land, an orchard, and a small vineyard, was located outside the city in Monte Oriolo, near Pian dei Giullari, where the great Florentine historian Guicciardini had once had his residence. It was truly hard to believe that one had to drive for only ten minutes to leave the perpetual crowds of Florence and pass into this classic Tuscan landscape, with its rolling hills and roads lined with cypress trees; it was pervaded with tranquillity, and in winter was still and transparent as a drawing on glass.

Loris' brothers had moved to the city, and so he had become master of the entire family house outside Florence (his brothers had also turned the Villa Toscana on Panarea over to him). Both of them were content. Loris would proudly show his extensive and ever-growing library. In the season Marina would busy herself in the orchard and the vineyard, and (with the help of the local farmers) even tried to cultivate the land. Along with that, in an upstairs room she set up a workshop for her handiwork. It seemed—and such was my first impression when I arrived on Christmas Eve— that there was not a cloud on the family's horizon.

There was one, however—dark, small, yet laden with lightning and thunder. Irina, Loris and Marina's young daughter, had been born with a hearing problem. She was not deaf and dumb; the percentage of hearing she still had was sufficient for her to hear things that were said to her slowly and in the light, whether daylight or artificial, for she helped herself by lip-reading; and also she could speak herself, though her voice was guttural, seeming to rise from the bottom of a well. But her disability—and this was the thunder and lightning—kept her in a constant state of irritation and aggression; and it also kept her parents in a condition of watchfulness—defensive and powerless, filled with fear and feelings of guilt—despite the fact that they had done no wrong and loved their only child only too much. I knew nothing of this before my arrival in Florence; neither Loris on Panarea, nor Roberto and Ruth in Rome had seen fit to warn me of the girl's handicap. She herself was so pretty, and so harmoniously combined two kinds of beauty, the Russian and the Tuscan, that for a long time, as we sat down to Christmas Eve supper, I could not take my eyes off her. I was all the more surprised, then, by her infrequent, short, somewhat angry utterances. At bottom she preferred to remain silent, which indicated that she was profoundly and painfully conscious of her infirmity.

Loris' connections made it possible to send her to a convent school, where she was given a seat in the front row and received a great deal of special consideration and attention, without any objection from her schoolmates. She was popular; but this was to little avail. The atmosphere in the Florentine house was oppressive and perpetually tense; it was only in the late evening, when Irina went up to her room next to her mother's workshop, that the three of us could talk downstairs with a sense of relief.

I knew Florence reasonably well, but I did not fancy wandering around the city on my own, especially at Christmastime. Loris was busy despite the holiday, and I was reluctant to ask Marina to accompany me, bearing in mind her lameness. I decided to suggest to their daughter that she join me on my daily walks. Her parents were amazed and delighted when she accepted without a moment's hesitation. They did not, or would not, notice that she wanted above all to get away from her parents. Besides, what did it matter what the real reason was! In my mind (and perhaps in my heart) I had already conceived the intention of winning the friendship of this brusque, rude, permanently bristling young girl. I hoped that she would gradually thaw out; and it became a point of honor for me to break through the shell in which she was enclosed.

Loris dropped us in the city by car in the morning, and in the evening he would pick us up at an appointed place, different each day. Lunch was to be taken in a restaurant.

It was a mild Florentine winter, not sunny, but lit by dazzling white light. Walking around a city like Florence is an uninterrupted series of moments of joy; towards evening one's capacity for reception is reduced to a minimum, and there is nothing for it but to collapse into an armchair in some café and close one's tired eyes for a while. Every place so frequently seen before—church, museum, palace, stretch of street—seems for a moment to be viewed for the first time. And each time the heart beats anew, just as when a beloved face reappears after many years, a little altered, it might appear, a little older, yet deep down still bearing its old expression, which once inspired love and may do so again. In the end, such walks are like wading through treasures strewn by a generous hand. Frequent diversions to the Arno provide a chance to catch one's breath and to rest one's eyes. The river, which is so forbidding in times of floods or even when it is merely in spate, has about it a lustrous softness that is like the soothing undulations of the Tuscan hills.

An additional pleasure in those wanderings about the city was something that is usually off-putting: the crowds of tourists. It was a source of delight to me to elbow my way across squares and down streets, to rise on tiptoe at the back of the throng the better to enjoy an altar or fresco in a church, a painting in a museum, or the incrustation on an ancient gateway of some palace. And to lift Irina up so she could see it all with me. Who knows if it was not the breaking of the ice that gave me the greatest satisfaction on my walks with her? Because she quickly grew close to me, became friends with me even, seeking me out in the crowd with an outstretched hand, asking to be picked up to see the precious objects. At times she laughed (while her parents had complained that she did not and would not laugh); it was a hollow and loud laugh, to be sure, accompanied by sounds reminiscent of the scraping of a knife on glass, but for me, her companion and guardian on those Florentine peregrinations, friend of her father and soon to become a friend of her mother, it was a laugh I had longed to hear. Her parents barely believed my evening reports from our walks. For— strange to relate—everything stopped the moment we crossed the threshold of the house in Monte Oriolo. Irina assumed her "domestic" character, so disagreeable, if not painful, for her parents.

What is more, she also changed her attitude to me, as if the tokens of friendship offered during the day in the city no longer held good. I pretended not to notice this, but in my evening-time conversations with her parents it was hard for me to deny that it was for them she reserved all her "prickliness," as they called it. The end of my stay in Florence was drawing near. On the morning of the last day I took Irina to Santa Maria del Carmine. We sat for a long, long time before Masaccio's fresco *Saint Peter Healing the Sick with his Shadow*. When I rose to leave, she held me back with her hand. And it was only then that I noticed tears in her eyes. No, she was not crying. Her expression was hard and angry, out of keeping with her dreamy, tear-filled eyes. Loris, whose workshop was close to the church, came for us as we had arranged, shortly after the bells of the Florentine churches had chimed twelve. That day we returned home for lunch. Her eyes dried; she moved away from me on the rear seat of the car. Our friendship of the previous two weeks all at once seemed nothing but a phantasm. As soon as we arrived back home she refused to join us for lunch; she ran upstairs to her room and locked herself in, and we did not even say goodbye to each other before I left for the train station. Loris gave me a parting gift. He seemed embarrassed, and asked me not to open it till I was in the train. And in the train I was delighted to find a beautiful edition of *The Fall of the House of Usher*, by Edgar Allen Poe, in the original, along with Loris's translation (that was probably what he was embarrassed about) and published by him, with illustrations by an artist of the nineteen-twenties who was unfamiliar to me, but who was strikingly similar to Kubin, the author of *Die Andere Seite* (I give the German title since I am not aware whether this book— *The Other Side* in English—has been translated).

**III**

READING LORIS' TRANSLATION (which was exemplary!) simply refreshed in my memory *The Fall* (or *Ruin*) *of the House of Usher* (the Italian title had the word *Rovina*, ruin, instead of *Caduta*, fall). I had read the story many times during the years of my fascination with

Edgar Allen Poe, my "Poemania" as my friends jokingly called it. And I regarded it as one of the best of the great American writer's tales. Yet I have to confess that my admiration was instinctive, and not based upon any analysis of the work; in a word, it was something like the evaluation of a wine-taster who praises the taste of a wine after a couple of sips, knowing little or nothing about the secrets of its origin and manufacture. It was for this reason that the slim volume I had been given offered me a double surprise: Loris' translation and his short, three-page afterword.

I never suspected such subtlety and insight in that "unlettered" booklover (as he described himself). His very brief essay gave a concise summary of Poe's writing and went beyond, into realms of literature of which the American poet and short story writer was one of the fathers. First, the combination, more: the union, of precise description (of setting, characters, events) with an awareness of the abstract significance of the work. "In this story, which I have translated in my amateur way," wrote Loris, "in the foreground there can be seen an admittedly rather monstrous, yet distinct concreteness of persons and landscapes. But they are not the goal in themselves; they conceal an essence or spirituality, which is not susceptible to ordinary realistic description. As the hero and his twin sister, and the Usher mansion reflected in the tarn, brush up against the human condition and the mysterious decrees of fate, they cease at once to belong to tangible reality, but instead are transformed into phantoms of themselves."

Loris went further, uncovering a distant relationship between Poe and Kafka. Was the House of Usher not a Castle, and did Roderick and Lady Madeline not live like K. in the shadow of a sentence? Loris set great store by what Kafka says in *The Trial*: "You have probably read somewhere that the sentence condemning a person often falls from an accidental word spoken by an accidental individual at an accidental time." Poe was indeed obsessed with "sentences," but he refused to regard them as accidental. On the other hand, God is absent from the story. Then what? The sentence grows inside a person from year to year like a fatal hereditary disease—a disease of the whole of humankind. Until the moment when everything falls apart: The House of Usher crumbles, and Lady Madeline in her death throes drags with her her brother, who has been struck by an attack of fear. They both die together; the narrator of the story runs away in terror, but does he succeed in escaping his fate? Does he manage to flee the gusty wind, the ominous full moon, the ruins of the house being swallowed up by the surrounding marshes? According to Loris, Poe was a poet of the ineluctable fall of human works and the spiritual cancer that lies dormant in a person's soul and then quickly grows to maturity. I believe he overgeneralized from the work he translated. The writer's works include both similar and different stories.

And overgeneralizing from *The Fall of the House of Usher*, as if it were a summation of Poe's writings, in a few sentences, and in a manner that was clear to me though it was hard to pin down, he brought to the story his own personal character. I could not have said where this impression came from. Perhaps I recalled the association I had made with the Villa Toscana on Panarea, seeing the volume of Poe's stories on Loris' bedside table? Or perhaps there now loomed more vividly the specter of my Florentine evenings with Marina and Loris, and the strange feeling that they were more like brother and sister who loved each other boundlessly, than a married couple? In their love and their mutual tenderness there was something particular, that is unknown in relations between husband and wife. I put it down to the fact that they were as alike as twins, even physically.

## IV

OVER THE NEXT THREE years we lost touch almost completely. I did not know what the reason for this was. I knew only that a short, chance meeting in Rome revealed a Loris I had never seen before, reserved, stand-offish, unwilling to enter into conversation in the old spirit of our friendship. He was in a hurry; he answered my questions evasively and, taller than me, he stared before him over my head. We had met in a café on the Piazza del Popolo. He quickly said goodbye and hurried out. I was convinced that his haste was a pretense. No one answered the phone in either of their houses—in Florence during the year, or over the summer on Panarea. It was as if both had turned deaf and dumb. Once I called

Loris' office in Florence. He answered and immediately excused himself for lack of time. Roberto and Ruth had identical experiences. Something bad had happened in Loris and Marina's life. We racked our brains over what it might be.

We learned the truth when it was already too late for any friendly advice, assistance, or intervention. And we heard it not from Loris or Marina but from Loris' brothers.

It was they who proposed a meeting in Rome at Roberto and Ruth's, asking me to be present too. With Loris's consent. We met in May 1980.

Loris' brothers, self-possessed and matter-of-fact, exaggeratedly ceremonious, and a little embarrassed by the visit, were "people of business" outside their brother's sphere of interests; nevertheless they were very fond of him and in some sense proud that he in fact had "such" interests and "such" friends. Their story (for that was how they began it) was concise and direct, and did not require additional questions to be posed along the way. It was only once they finished that room for a possible "council" opened up.

Irina's condition had worsened in the spring of 1978 to such a point that, on the advice of the Italian doctors (principally that of an eminent specialist from Padua) they had decided to take her to see a famous professor in Berne, Switzerland. That is, her hearing problem had not grown worse, but the girl had become absolutely *intrattibile*, both at home and in school. This Italian word emphasized by Loris' brothers meant quite simply that with every day the threads still connecting Irina to her environment were snapping. She had closed up, *si chiudeva in sè*, at a rapid pace; there was a danger that she would stop talking completely, though physiologically, the percentage of hearing she still possessed had not changed. A great deal indicated that she wanted—she herself wanted, out of desperation—to cut herself off from the world; it was an exceedingly rare case, practically speaking, unique, since as a rule those partially deaf and dumb make stubborn, even convulsive, efforts to hang on to the world. Her hopeless and helpless parents had the impression (as Loris once put it to his brothers) of watching their only daughter drown in a whirlpool and of being unable to stretch out a hand to her. It was then that they took the advice of the Paduan specialist: Maybe the famous Swiss professor would be able to suggest some remedy. They decided to take the matter into their own hands, without any words of advice or caution from family or friends; they cut themselves off from the world like their daughter.

The Bernese professor, the leading authority on illnesses of hearing, with his assistants submitted Irina to two days of tests and analyses. She bore it all obediently, agreeing even to certain rather painful procedures; the whole time there was a glimmer of hope in her eyes, and from time to time she gave an engaging, trustful smile. The professor's final verdict, which he presented in conversation with the parents and in the presence of the girl (she had compelled them to agree to her being there despite the protests of the professor), was as follows: Hearing defects as severe as hers had a few years ago been the subject of attempts to replace the dead nerves with microscopic electronic plates. The whole problem had been from the very beginning, and still remained, how to create surgical instruments that were accurate, and invisible to the naked eye. So far it had not been possible to make reliable instruments of this kind, but there were doctors in Paris and in Stockholm who were prepared to operate now, with a high percentage of risk: Where the operation was not successful the patient could lose what hearing they still had, in other words they could go completely deaf. He, the Bernese professor, would not take such a risk, but would wait till the microscopic surgical tools could guarantee one hundred percent that the plate could be inserted properly into the dead nerve. He had conducted the tests and analyses on Irina's ears, counting on the possibility of palliative measures if it had been a question of her having a relatively mild hearing disability. Alas, the results were not favorable. There remained a choice, then: Either to wait—no one knew how long—along with Professor F. for a totally safe operation in Berne; or to take a risk in Paris or Stockholm. The professor wrote the relevant addresses in Loris' notebook.

The operation in Stockholm was not successful. Irina came out of it entirely deaf. Though she did not wholly lose the abilities she had possessed beforehand: By following the speaker's lips she could understand roughly what was being said, and she could also still speak herself, though her voice was even more guttural and hollow.

But she sank consciously into utter isolation. She refused to continue attending the convent school. She lived (according to Loris's
brothers) with eyes that looked but did not see, and with no connection at all to her family. Her parents lived in constant fear that
she would "do something bad to herself." They had decided to take
Irina to the house on Panarea at the beginning of July. Remembering how during my brief stay in Florence I had been able to strike
up some kind of communication, however modest, with the girl,
Loris had asked if I would spend some time on Panarea during the
summer.

The "council" after Loris' brothers' story, then, was brief.
There was nothing to discuss. After a few trifling explanations,
there came a cheerless silence. I broke it by promising that I would
arrange my summer vacation so I could spend August at the Villa
Toscana.

## V

THAT AUGUST WAS TOUGH work for me. To begin with Irina
would go down to the beach with me in the morning; we would
rent a small boat and sail out onto the open sea. In the heat it was
necessary to keep jumping into the water in order to avoid sunstroke. Whenever the girl, who was an excellent swimmer, moved
far away from the boat, I would follow her like a lifeguard. There
were moments when she teased me and tried to get away; but most
of the time I had no problems with her. But there was no way to
overcome her psychological resistance, and I had to bid farewell to
our former closeness in Florence. She had "closed up" to me too.
Her parents stayed home in the mornings. They went down to the
sea in the late afternoon, while Irina and I were sleeping after our
long bathe, I in the turret, she in her room or on the terrace.

At the time she was fifteen; nature had compensated for her
physical disability. She was already a young lady, very comely and
with the figure of a grown woman. And she was aware of her
beauty and her physical maturity. She brightened up fleetingly
(though without smiling) when the boys on the beach turned to
look at her.

Our evenings together were especially onerous. Since we did not eat lunch, the dinner table was the only opportunity for all four of us to meet together. We did not know, Loris and Marina and I, how to behave. A conversation amongst the three of us, without paying any attention to Irina, drove her to her room immediately after dinner. Attempts to arouse her interest and participation by a slow explanation of everything that was being said around the table (done in particular by Marina) not only failed to produce results, but caused her to stiffen up: She sat with stooped head, bristling, on the edge of her chair, as if just about to leave. Truth be told (though none of us would have said it aloud), we could not help breathing a sigh of relief when we saw her stand from the table after the meal was over. And it was only then that we felt the artificiality of our conversations in her presence; we would either choose a long-awaited, blessed silence, or listen to records till late at night.

The height of August, the traditional *solleone*, dried up the island with a wave of windless air from Africa. It was impossible to walk in bare feet across the scorching sand on the beach; stones cracked in the low walls surrounding the houses, the ashen sky turned a darker gray, while the trees and bushes, even the *piante grasse* or cactuses, lost their green color, withered, and became covered with the hot dust that hung in the air. Bathing shrunk to a sliver of time after moonrise; the seawater turned into a hot, sticky soup. We were too scared to use the boat. We spent almost the whole day in the house; only after dusk had fallen did we dare to venture onto the terrace.

The nights not only provided relief; with their beauty and their faint breezes, and their skies so rich they seemed to be encrusted with jewels, they also brought equilibrium back to the world. From my turret I observed a group of young people bathing at Calaiunco. From that time on, after midnight, when the rest of the house was supposedly asleep, Irina would slip out by the back door and would half-walk, half-run to Calaiunco. This repeated night after night; she would return before dawn with an expression of enchantment on her face. She did not know that I was watching her from the turret. No, I could not be in any doubt about what was going on at Calaiunco amid the rocks of the promontory, on the narrow beach. But I was so happy, as I furtively followed her with my gaze the next day, and I turned a blind eye to her fifteen years and kept the secret from her parents; and when, one night before dawn, she spotted me upstairs as she was passing on tiptoe through the gate, we became accomplices. Our familiarity from Florence was revived. Loris and Marina were convinced that it was only a question of their daughter's renewed affection for their friend. And they were happy too. I was concerned about one thing only: whether she and her partner (for I was quite sure she had a "regular" boyfriend at Calaiunco) were taking precautions. I consoled myself by thinking that this partner was older than her and knew what he was doing. On the other hand, unfortunately, I was equally certain that it was a question of a short holiday romance. And sure enough, toward the end of August she came back home soon after she had left, her hands covering her eyes, which were probably filled with tears.

Luckily, a few days later we all boarded the boat for Naples. And we said our farewells at Naples harbor, by the taxicab that was to take them to the train for Florence. Loris and Marina hugged me and kissed me in turn, naturally as an expression of gratitude. And Irina? She threw her arms around me and pressed her wet face to mine.

## VI

AFTER MY SUMMER vacation in 1980 I had no time for any business other than my own. Certain family affairs had to be put in order; and I was suffering from intermittent pains about which my doctor friend could say nothing clearly, recommending hospital tests that were out of the question for me at that time. I say at that time because after a long unfruitful period I had at last begun to write again; the new text, as I worked on it, seemed more and more important and absorbed me utterly. I am one of those writers with a very slow pen; furthermore, my own nature and my quiet discipline led me to fill breaks intended to provide a breath of relief, and to allow me to rest my mind, with the writing project that was lying on my desk and slowly moving forward. At such times it happens that though I seem to be conversing with those close to me, in reality I am absent; I even dream, not the Freudian "remains of the day," but of fragments of my growing manuscript.

Yes, as always in such circumstances, I was absent or only half-present; I dealt with domestic issues unthinkingly, gave short answers to the questions of my wife and children, read letters inattentively (and failed to reply to them), and reduced phone calls to the absolute minimum necessary, which was undoubtedly off-putting for those on the other end of the line. The egotism of the so-called "creative process" is uncompromising, if not simply cruel; it would surprise many a reader to know the price that is paid in practice for the expression of pure feelings.

That egotism pushed the Berardi family to the side. I persuaded myself that on Panarea in the summer I had "done my bit," that the time had inevitably come for me to disengage myself from "other people's dramas." And so I quickly brought Loris' telephone calls to a close, forgetting what he had said after I hung up. I treated Marina's calls in the same fashion. Matters were made worse because Roberto and Ruth had left for a year to the States, where Roberto had been asked to lecture at some university. In other words, there was silence from Rome, which had played such an significant role in our triangular friendship. Today I am deeply ashamed of my behavior. And rather disgusted at the evasions, the hiding-places, and the traps created by my wanton ego.

I was jolted from this state in May 1981—my sobering up, incidentally, being aided by the words "The End" that I had written in the manuscript—by an unexpected visit from Loris' brother, who had come to Naples for a few days on business. He was staying in a large hotel on the promenade and invited me to dinner there.

After we had exchanged the usual pleasantries, I realized from the very beginning that nothing had gotten through to me from the hints dropped by Loris and Marina over the telephone; hints, because (and I understand this perfectly) they were unwilling to talk openly, and by phone at that, about matters which were of the greatest importance to them, and at the same time which perturbed them. With a winsome embarrassment, Nicola, Loris's brother, gave me gently to understand that my Florentine friends had preferred to think of me as having suddenly turned deaf and stupefied, rather than entrust their "painful secrets" to the telephone. Those "painful secrets," were that after their return from vacation, Irina had "gone sexually wild" (Loris's brother's expression). Of course, her parents had been unaware of the inauguration of that "wildness" on Panarea in August. In any case, the pretty, ebullient girl approaching sixteen threw herself wholeheartedly into a series of romances with boys. They did not even know whether it was only with her peers, since grown men often drove her home late at night or in the morning. She carried herself defiantly, as if she considered her behavior in some childish way to be a form of revenge upon her parents for the fact that she had been born with a hearing defect. And they were afraid, quite simply afraid to intervene; for they ran the risk, or so they thought at least, of losing her for good.

After dinner that May evening, we walked along the promenade towards Mergellina. It was already warm; we stopped frequently to lean against the wall overlooking the boulders by the shore, and it did not require a great deal of intuition to know that Nicola had not finished his story. And sure enough, in a café near the speedboat harbor, twisting in his seat, he added the epilogue.

This prematurely awakened sexual appetite (he said almost in a whisper) was not so bad. When it came down to it, it could be regarded as nature's compensation for her disability. Loris and Marina consoled themselves that it had gotten her out of her perpetual unhappiness, though this consolation was underpinned by an obvious delusion: Through her dalliances, Irina was giving vent to her desperation and her rage, above all her rage. Soon, a few months ago, she had found herself amongst a circle of drug addicts. At that point it was no longer possible for them to deceive themselves. She was constantly wheedling money from her parents; she sometimes spent long periods away from home, and she had become aggressive. Then, on the day of her sixteenth birthday, March 23rd, 1981, she secretly packed a traveling bag and disappeared from home. She left a brief note on her bedside table: "Don't come looking for me. *Addio.*" Loris did go looking, however, and in the end, by a miracle he found the only clue at a travel agent's. Her name appeared on the list of a group of people who had bought airline tickets for a flight from Milan to Delhi. It was too late to regret the fact that at the beginning of the year Loris had yielded to her demands and, in accordance with the regulations, had signed her application for a passport; and that he never dared to refuse when she asked for money. What was he to do now? He wanted to travel to India, which was like looking for a needle in a haystack. At least he should not go alone. There was a silence. Nicola finally plucked up his courage: "Is it true that you were in India years ago?"

I knew what he was driving at as he looked timidly into my eyes. Without a moment's hesitation I agreed to accompany him back to Florence the following day.

He had a car; at my request we drove to Rome, where I had asked to be able to stop for a couple of hours. We did not take the freeway but the old highway, the *Domiziana*. For some time I had been growing weary of the emptiness of the freeway; the old highway, which passed through towns on the way, took longer, but a road that led among people and houses seemed to go more quickly than a journey on the ribbon of the freeway (though the opposite was true). For those who meditate on the nature of time, this is a small contribution to the phenomenon of its relativity.

Before leaving Naples I called a friend of mine in Rome and invited him to dinner in the neighborhood of the Piazza di Spagna. My friend, known familiarly as Giovannino, was a journalist with the largest newspaper in the capital. He specialized in narcotics, and in journalistic circles had been nicknamed the *narcologo* or *narcogiornalista*. He was indeed an expert in this area; he was often invited to international science and law enforcement conferences. Irrefutable proof of his expertise were several attempts on his life in dark Roman side streets, which, though unsuccessful, served as warnings; there had even been a (fortunately not very large) bomb placed in his apartment by someone pretending to read the electric meter.

We ate dinner quickly, leaving the serious conversation till the coffee. Nicola listened without saying anything. In fact, by and large, I did too, only asking my friend for minor clarifications from time to time and jotting them down in my notebook. Naturally, I asked him about India. For the last three years the region of Benares or Banaras (or to be precise, Varanasi) had become a favorite destination for Italian drug addicts. The reason for this was unknown. It was true that narcotics were easily obtainable there, and that they were cheaper than in Europe; but for this a high price was paid in homelessness, the difficult conditions of daily life, and the somewhat hostile attitude of the local population. And so when it came down to it, the draw for the Italian drug addicts, whose numbers were growing from month to month, was a mystery. They gathered under the open sky in fields from which the Indian peasants would continually chase them off at dawn, and also on a long stretch of sand on the shore of the Ganges. Except, Giovannino explained with a melancholy smile, when they were drawn to a large nearby area where the dead from the local villages were cremated daily. The dead from amongst the Italian drug addicts could also be cremated there; it was a universal rite, in which nationality and religious affiliation had no meaning. All one needed was kindling and wood.

Giovannino did not know why I was interested in these things, though like a good journalist he tried to sniff it out. Nicola called Florence from the restaurant. We arrived in Monte Oriolo late, around midnight; Loris and Marina were waiting impatiently for us.

## VII

AFTER HIS BROTHER'S phone call from Rome, Loris had already managed to buy two round-trip tickets from Milan to Calcutta via Cairo. From Calcutta to Benares the journey had to made by train, since flights were fully booked for the next few weeks. Marina, who had been dissuaded with great difficulty from traveling to India herself, accompanied us to Milan in her brother-in-law's car. The plane departed in the evening. At the airport Marina threw her arms round her husband and wept aloud like a hurt child. Loris was pale; I took him by the arm. He did not resist but, on the contrary, clung to me, and continued to do so in the plane, even as he slept. Brave, strong Loris could not control his own inner sense of relief. The night-time connection in Cairo refreshed him somewhat. At the train station in Calcutta we had time to eat lunch before squeezing ourselves into the train for Benares, which was packed right up to its luggage racks, and on the roofs of its cars. Probably because we were foreigners, the two of us were allowed to occupy one seat by the window.

I was in India for four days in 1952, on my way home from Burma to London. Less than twenty-four hours of that time was spent in Calcutta. I quote here from my journal entitled *Voyage to Burma* concerning my main experience there: "Not far from the temple of the goddess Kali, behind a low wall there is an open crematorium. In air trembling from the heat, the vertical trails of smoke look like shuddering pillars and rise skyward from pits of varying sizes, where the relatives of the deceased surround their remains with bundles of wood and dry twigs. Some of the pits contain no more that a handful of white ashes, but in many of them, from amongst the smouldering branches there protrude arms and legs that have escaped the flames. People enter and leave the crematorium as indifferently as if they were taking part in some anodyne folk ceremony. The smell of burned bodies and of burning wood fills the air, smoke stings the eyes, heat throbs from the flames of the fires, and the sweltering sky beats down, reducing the earth to a yellow-brown shell. We flee through the entrance gate and go down a few dozen meters to the Ganges, where only a thin stream flows down the middle of the dried-up river bed, and white cows lie motionless in the damp ooze by the banks."

We passed parched yellow fields dotted with streams and puddles that were sucked dry by the sun and drunk greedily by the spongy earth. On the paths could be seen small groups of half-naked, barefoot men with turbans wound round their heads, carrying long sticks, some stepping behind a mule or an emaciated horse. On the horizon, like a mirage, stretches of green appeared and disappeared. The train moved slowly, puffing laboriously, and in the vicinity of small stations swarms of ragamuffins would run after it and beg in shrill voices.

We dozed in our corner; each time we woke up our eyes met the same picture. The rumble of the wheels on the tracks and the chugging of the locomotive were the only proofs we were moving—the view from the window suggested rather motionlessness. And that motionlessness, as I recalled from my previous visit, seemed to reign everywhere; it appeared to represent a paralysis of the entire country. Of course, this was only outside the big cities. The latter, espe-

cially Calcutta, and Delhi too, were the frenetic, delirious opposite
of motionlessness.

In the moments when I woke from dozing, I furtively studied
Loris' face. It bore an expression of fear mixed with confusion; the
unchanging landscape, perpetually multiplying itself, must have
deprived this new arrival of the hope of finding anything or anyone
in this country, lost in its admittedly shallow, yet stubborn sleep.

We finally arrived in Benares at night. Using a combination of
words in English and gestures, a rickshaw driver brought us to a
hotel and promised to take us the next day to the destination of our
journey. He knew what we were looking for—he repeated *Italian,
Italian*, and then *droga, droga*, the Italian word for narcotics.

I doubt whether I will be able to give an accurate description of
our destination, just as I doubt we will ever establish the real reason
for the Italian drug addicts' invasion of a scrap of field and beach
thousands of miles from their home country. I already mentioned
that the cheapness and relative availability of narcotics was not to
be disregarded, but this explained little. Also not to be ignored was
the argument (put forward by my friend the Roman journalist) that
especially among young people who have only recently become involved with drugs, there is talk of the need to create a kind of com-
mune, beyond the reach of even the surreptitious glances of their
countryfolk; but this too provides only a limited explanation. It
must then be accepted that it is a matter of some irrational drive,
the source and essence of which those concerned do not themselves understand.

The rickshaw driver took us down a narrow road to the edge of
a cultivated field and declared firmly that he would not go any further. It was obvious what he was afraid of: Farmers were looking
angrily in our direction, armed with something in the nature of
grappling irons, as well as their agricultural implements. Beyond
the field there extended a long, broad stretch of sand washed lazily
by the waters of the Ganges.

On this sandbank there were dozens, if not hundreds, of young
people, boys and girls. They looked like sleepwalkers or drunks,
staggering as they walked, now squatting, now standing; some lay
without moving, probably asleep. At the end of the farm track
there was an outpost of the Indian police under an awning set up to

keep out the sun. One of the three policemen spoke good English. He very politely gave us the most important information. The laws and ordinances of India did not permit any intervention. Drugs were not forbidden, and anyone with a valid passport and a visa could come here. Nor, in a country where one of the largest cities, Calcutta, held the record for the greatest number of people sleeping on the streets (with about a million homeless) was anyone prevented from living on the riverbanks. The only way to stem the tide of young Italian drug addicts was to introduce visa restrictions; this had been done, but only recently. At the present time, over two hundred people lived and took drugs on the beach by the Ganges. Three policemen were on duty here day and night to protect the newcomers from the attacks of farmers; they in turn were protecting their cultivated fields that at the beginning (in other words two years ago) had been trampled upon and destroyed in the night as the best place to sleep.

For some time now there had been an increase in the number of drug addicts killed by overdoses. In the nearby crematorium they had been given eight pits in the first row, which ran parallel to the beach. They themselves had to find wood and kindling, but this was not difficult. What was harder, however, was to make the Italian drug addicts comply with the requirement of registering those who had died and been cremated. They were not cremated like the local Indians, wrapped in a white shroud, but fully dressed, with all their belongings, including their documents. In the course of two years the police had managed by a miracle to record twenty-three deaths, though it was known that (especially in recent months) an incomparably larger number had died. Here was a copy of the list sent to the Italian consulate in Delhi.

Luis was white as a sheet as he studied the list; he was barely able to hold the paper in his hands. After this, we went between the small fields down to the river, accompanied by the courteous policeman. It rapidly became apparent that there was no sense in questioning those sitting or lying there. Our inquiries about Irina were answered with far-away, hazy, vacant stares. But we were looking for a living Irina, and so we turned onto their backs all the girls who were sleeping (or rather in a torpor or trance). Eventually, at the edge of the beach we noticed a boy sitting somewhat to the side and gazing

at the water. He was only partially under the influence, on the borderline between stupefaction and what remained of his lucidity. Yes,
he had become friends with a girl called Irina, who was deaf and
dumb, though she spoke and understood a little. "Actually, I loved
her," he added, lost in thought. "She died the day before yesterday;
she injected too big of a dose." She had been cremated the previous
night in the third pit on the left. No, he would not go there now, not
for any price. He would probably return to his native Bologna.

At this point I should change the tone of the story. I cannot do
so; I want to finish this chapter as soon as possible. The policeman
led us to the crematorium. The third pit on the left was filled to the
brim with ash, and so Irina was not the only one in it. Nevertheless
Loris knelt down and poured a few handfuls of ashes into a plastic
bag the policeman handed him. Before leaving Benares he bought a
metal urn engraved with the inscription *Ashes for the Almighty*. His
eyes were dry and he had almost stopped speaking entirely. His
brother Nicola informed me later in a short letter that the urn had
been placed in the cellar of the Villa Toscana on Panarea.

## VIII

IT IS HARD TO BELIEVE it, yet what I will say now is the truth.
In the course of the following four years, until September 1985, I
saw Loris and his wife only once—at Roberto's funeral in Rome on
November 18, 1983. After his first heart attack in the spring of that
year, Roberto had regained his health to the extent that he could
take up writing again; on fine days he would go for walks with Ruth
or with his friends (including me), around Rome, which was at
once so lovable and so unlovable. At that time nothing portended a
sudden end. But a sudden, and unexpected, end is characteristic of
heart disease. He had just recorded a discussion for the radio; in a
cheerful mood he entered the elevator on the fourth floor and was
beginning a light-hearted dialogue with one of the participants in
the discussion, when all at once—the moment the elevator began
to descend—he gave a quiet cry as if he were choking, and slipped
heavily to the floor. Death came immediately; one might have said
his heart broke, or was pierced by a dagger.

We took our leave of him at the Verano cemetery. Ruth leaned on the arm of Roberto's brother; his sister walked behind the coffin between Loris and Marina. My customary embrace with the latter couple at the graveside was amongst many others, and was striking for its silent conventionality. Outside the cemetery gate Loris summoned a taxi and he and his wife went to the station to catch the next train to Florence; they were "alas unable" to take Ruth and Roberto's brother and sister back to Ruth's apartment. It was I who did so. As we drank coffee we talked more about our absent friends from Florence, than about Roberto. Ruth whispered: "Everyone regards their own pain as the most important and the deepest— even when it's abated in comparison with the fresh pain of others."

The pain of Irina's parents after her death had not abated despite the two years that had passed. I saw something of this in the short and infrequent letters that Loris' brother sent me. In the most recent one, he said that they had shut themselves up in Monte Oriolo, seeing no one; on weekdays Loris went to his office overlooking the Arno, answered the telephone curtly and reluctantly whenever he took calls himself if his secretary was away, and returned home on the stroke of five. Marina did not show herself at all; she neglected everything by which she had previously lived— the garden, her handiwork—and spent whole days listening to music recordings, or sitting motionless in her daughter's room, staring at the photographs of her on the walls (pictures from her childhood to her flight from Florence). They had stopped spending their vacations on Panarea. "I believe that in Naples," Nicola concluded his letter, "there are frequent cases of withdrawal from the world, with apartments becoming transformed into sepulchers or cemetery chapels after the loss of loved ones. But in Florence?"

To withdraw from the world after the death of loved ones, to turn one's apartment into a sepulcher of the living was to me—on the basis of my Neapolitan observations—a way of maintaining contact with the dead. In it there dwells a subcutaneous fear that a return to the world will become a betrayal of shades, a betrayal of people who are still alive thanks to us alone, and who are condemned to a slow second death as we immerse ourselves in life after they die. I have never seen such an apartment in Naples, but I am well aware that the Neapolitans' intimacy with death is an imperishable characteristic of some if not all of the inhabitants of this city. It is expressed both in the buoyant atmosphere of visits to the cemetery, and in the peculiar way in which graves are treated, sometimes going so far as the famous case of the widower who installed a telescope on the roof of his apartment building trained right on the grave of his wife in the local cemetery, and spent many hours staring through it. Yes, that is Naples, very material in its dealings with the dead; in this respect Nicola was right. But there is also a broader phenomenon that extends beyond the ancient Greek south—and thus beyond the territory of the Kingdom of Naples and the Two Sicilies—encompassing the whole of Europe, if not the entire West. It is a phenomenon that was described and codified—at the height of the Enlightenment!— in a book by a German monk named Herlicher: *On the Summoning of the Dead*, a sort of handbook intended to facilitate the communion of the living with the souls of their deceased loved ones. Even in Florence . . .

In the summer of 1984 chance would have it that I had to travel for a week to Stromboli, where part of my family was taking a vacation. From there, in my friends' motor boat, I landed at the harbor on Panarea. The excursion was to take no more than half a day, from lunch taken in the restaurant by the harbor, until dusk.

The owner of the restaurant—"plenipotentiary" of the Berardis on Panarea and my close acquaintance in the past—gave me the key to the Villa Toscana. He did not omit to point out reproachfully that for some time now Loris had stopped sending money for the upkeep of the villa; nor had he responded to written requests. If I happened to meet with him in Rome or Florence, could I warn him that in the Panarean climate this meant condemning the villa to slow disintegration?

I saw for myself the accuracy of his warning when I crossed the threshold of the villa. It had not been aired out, and as a result its walls were covered with mold, the ceilings were drooping, in the corners cobwebs contained masses of dried insects, and the books on the shelves were damp. The steps that led upstairs creaked ominously, while the doors to the turret and to the cellar (where the urn with Irina's ashes stood) had rusted and fallen off their hinges, blocking the way. On the floor the tiles were loose and in places dislodged. It was a woeful and a moving sight; I remember that I whispered quietly to myself: "The fall of the house of Loris." I had scarcely uttered these words when an invisible hand propelled me towards the bedside table next to Loris' bed. Here lay, just as before—though damper than the books on the shelves, almost wet and with the corners of the pages eaten by ants—the copy of the Selected Stories of Edgar Allen Poe, *The Fall of the House of Usher*.

At the harbor on Panarea, in the summer there was a small telegraph office in operation. Before I returned to Stromboli I sent a cable to Loris. It went unanswered. It was not until the middle of August of the following year that a long letter from Loris arrived in Naples. It began the final, terrible chapter in our relations.

The letter was long, chaotic, and agitated. Even its form conveyed Loris' nervous tension. Its content, its essential content, had to be extricated from the convoluted, frequently broken-off sentences, which were written as if they had been accompanied the whole time by a dry weeping. He began with an apology, which thank God was brief and stayed within the bounds of dignity. "Understand me, the plight of our daughter drove me to mental illness. I had two friends, you and Roberto. You I beg for forgiveness. As for Roberto, I still have a faint hope that he died with an awareness that I was mortally hit and wounded. Now I turn to you not just asking for forgiveness, but also asking for help. A month ago Marina was diagnosed with breast cancer; she was operated on immediately, but it was too late. The doctors say she can expect to live to the end of the year at the latest. But she doesn't want to die in Florence; she wants to close her eyes forever on Panarea. Since nothing will dissuade her of this, I finally agreed (true madness, for various reasons which I do not have to explain to you); and we leave at the end of this month. I can't manage on my own; come in September if you can get away from your work and your family. I know I'm asking a great deal of you. I have nowhere else to turn."

That was the only lucid part of the letter. The rest, complex and confused, could be called a muddle. I read it several times over, with a heavy heart, testimony to my friend's troubled mind.

## IX

I ARRIVED ON September 10th; I could not get away any sooner. The house on Panarea had been cleaned up only superficially, since the presence of someone seriously ill precluded more extensive repairs. The front and back doors and all the windows had been opened, so the still-hot September sun had quickly dried the mold on the walls, but had not entirely succeeded in dispelling the mustiness that hung in the air. The maid that Loris had hired swept the spiders' webs from the corners of the ceiling, washed the pitted floors and the creaking stairway, and carried out onto the lower terrace the moldiest of the books, tools from Marina's workshop, and kitchen implements. It had not been possible to open the rusted, collapsed door to the turret; the same was the case with the door to the cellar. Later on Loris broke them down with an ax and took them out to the shed, so that the cellar became a part of the first floor, separated by a few steps. The house took on a more tolerable appearance, though it retained signs of its former neglect; one had the impression of rot that had temporarily been suppressed but was lurking still in the walls. Since access to the turret was blocked, I slept in Irina's room, with her orphaned, sick mother next door; and of course Loris too, who now slept on a separate bed set slightly aside from Marina's.

Every two days a doctor came from Stromboli in the morning and brought whatever medicines were needed. He would return before lunch (which we ate by Marina's bed). She could no longer stand; Loris washed her and sometimes took her solicitously to the bathroom, and sometimes helped her in bed. I admired how obliging and dexterous he was as a nurse, but then what was there to admire, as he did it all with an expression of contentment on his face?

Loris and I divided up the day. He received the doctor. In the mornings he was at Marina's beck and call, and also helped the girl in the kitchen. I went out in the morning and came back for lunch. After lunch, I thrust Loris out of the house and was on duty at Marina's side till dusk. When evening came, we both accompanied her, often till midnight; though usually Loris and his wife sent me off to my own room around ten o'clock.

September was hot, but agreeably so; it was a mellow heat with occasional breezes from the sea. I wandered about the island half-dressed, from time to time jumping into the sea to cool off, or dozing in the shade of the trees by the cemetery wall. Knowledgeable inhabitants were predicting a rainy, unpleasant fall; some were already preparing to leave for Sicily earlier than usual.

Strolling about the island was like a journey around one's own room. The place was too small for the walk to possess its own natural "course"; within a quarter of an hour I would cover the distance between the harbor and Calaiunco. I knew every rock, every bush, every dip in the path. I also knew all the inhabitants, who frequently stopped me for a short chat. *Come sta la moglie di Loris? Speriamo.* "How's Loris' wife? Let's not lose hope." In the afternoons they were not able to talk to Loris, since he mostly slept in a gully between the rocks on the beach.

This was our life as the summer drew to a close. At that time Marina was not feeling so bad; severe attacks of pain came relatively rarely, and passed after shots of morphine. Worse was the insomnia. It was her sleepless nights, which were also his, that Loris would recover from in his afternoons on the beach.

I wondered why she had so wanted to leave Florence for Panarea, knowing full well—after all, she had studied medicine at one time—that she was going there to die. I did not speak of this with Loris; in general, from the beginning, we were joined in a pact of silence regarding Marina (and Irina). It was ridiculous to suggest that she wished to pass away close to the urn containing her daughter's ashes; for the urn could easily have been brought to the house outside Florence. She was drawn to the island by something very personal and mysterious, something (such was my vague but most abiding conjecture) that arose from the history of their love and their life together; and also—though this is hard to explain clearly—from the feeling that the island itself gave one: a sense of the boundary between life and death, unstable, and rendered indistinct by the sea all around. One does not die once and for all, forever, at the moment of death staring at a shard of space, entering another dimension with a light step. Thanks to the separation of the island from the rest of the world, the cosmic *pietas* had a sister: a cosmic death-without-death. But at the time, as I thought about these things I immediately accused myself of literary-philosophical exaggeration. It was to turn out to be closer to the truth than I had imagined.

After lunch, when my watch began, Marina would doze off for a short time; that superficial, shallow sleep would be interrupted by quiet moans as she continually shifted position in bed. From the beginning she asked me to hold her hand in my own hands. As she moved and groaned she often tugged her hand out of mine, while I had the impression of catching or letting go of the hand of a drowning woman. Loris once saw Marina's hand in mine; he turned pale and quickly left the room.

At four she would rouse herself, drink a coffee that had been prepared beforehand and was now cold, take her prescribed tablets, and dab her face with eau de Cologne; then every day she would request "her record." It was Schubert's string quintet, written allegedly a few hours before the composer's death. Even though I was no expert, merely a music lover, I drank in the quintet with a lump in my throat and an ache in my heart; and with a strange admixture of liberation. For me it was a brilliant work, about mortal agony ending with a triumph over death. "There is no death," as Tolstoy's novella about Ivan Ilyich concludes, a moment before the decease of the hero, in the gleam of a distant light. It sometimes happened that, tired of listening to the "favorite record" (she had not wanted to bring any others from Florence), she made me read poetry aloud—me, a person deprived of the gift of diction. She loved Russian poems, though from home she had only a poor knowledge of the language of her parents. But it was as if the sound alone took her back to her old, forgotten roots.

In the evening Loris and I outdid each other in eloquence in order to capture and retain her attention as long as possible, well aware of the fruitlessness of our efforts.

Immediately after the war, in London, I was present as someone close to me was dying of breast cancer (which had spread, just like Marina's cancer). One day she was visited in the hospital by a former friend who was passing through London, and at a moment of pain written on her face, he placed his open hand gently and tenderly on the place where the breast had been removed, in a gesture of affection, of love, for her sick body. The grimace of agony on her face, faded away and was replaced by a soft smile. I

knew that the man who had done this and achieved such an unan-
ticipated effect had once been the lover of the dying woman; and
so I could not expect that Marina would react in a similar way to
my hand, placed to ease the pain on the thick bandages in the
place where her breast had been, as if in a lover's trance. And yet
she too looked into my eyes with a smile of gratitude. Loris
turned his head away.

* * *

IT WAS OBVIOUS THAT there had been a change in her relationship with Loris. Whether it had come after the death of their
daughter I did not know. I saw only his growing suffering, and her
growing indifference. It may have been that that was why he had
not wanted to be alone with her and had implored me to come to
their house on Panarea.

From the middle of October the predictions of the locals began
to come true. The rain poured down with infrequent breaks in the
afternoons, and the sea rose stormily, washing over the beaches and
some of the jetties at the harbor. The doctor from Stromboli was
unable to visit every other day; he took advantage of moments of
calm, kept his visits to a minimum and, during them, did not conceal
his haste and urgency, almost panic. To tell the truth, he was not really needed. We had considerable reserves of medicines and needles,
and his medical examinations were a meaningless formality. Marina
entered the stage before death; her pain grew more intense and
would not let up, and it was marked no longer by the soft moans of
before, but shouts that had to be suppressed by force. We were helpless; Loris wandered about the room only half-conscious. Marina
asked for her bed to be turned to face the sea. She stared intently at
it; I was convinced that the sight brought her hope of finding a relief
for her attacks of pain. And she succeeded. A strange miracle occurred that confirmed my earlier intuitions (which I had reproached
myself for being exaggerated). With her gaze Marina seemed to
reach beyond the horizon of the sea, to sail there, far away from us,
and then to return to us. She was throwing down a challenge to
death as it approached; she was *taming* it. And we truly did not know
if she had died on the morning of November 3rd, with her eyes open

and still living, fixed with some superhuman, lifeless force upon the billowing waves of the sea. It was only that force, the immobility of her gaze, her final gaze, that convinced us she had passed away. Loris closed her eyelids, knelt by her bed, laid his head on her breast and burst into tears in what seemed like a weeping of all weepings, all the weepings he had hitherto suppressed. Her arm was hanging from the bed; I took her wrist in my hands, not so much doing once again what she had asked me before, as driven by a need to check whether she really was dead. Yes, yes, she really was; her pulse had stopped. But for me, beneath her eyelids, there were still the remains of unextinguished life. "You will come back," escaped my lips (or to be precise, the lips of this reader of the monk Herlicher's book *On Summoning the Dead*). I said these words aloud; and they brought Loris out of his lamentations as if he had been struck on the back while he knelt. He rose and looked at me in his old way, like a friend—but with a glimmer of something between surprise, faith, hope, and trust. It was at that moment there was born our silent covenant, which for him turned first into a profound animosity towards me, then later into apathy and depression.

## X

THE ONLY CARPENTER on the island built a primitive coffin and fastened its lid with hooks. From the Panarean fishermen Loris rented a motor boat with a crew that was to take him and the coffin to Messina. There he intended to get on a regular passenger ship to Palermo. This turned out to be unnecessary: Messina too possessed its own small crematorium. Three days later he reappeared at home with an urn bearing the inscription *Eterno Riposo*, Eternal Rest. We went down to the cellar together and placed Marina's urn next to Irina's. He allowed me to hug him, but I sensed resistance; he did not return the embrace and would not let me kiss him. In all likelihood he had noticed the signs of my visit to the cellar during his absence. He hesitated a moment, then of his own accord came up to me and rested his head on my shoulder, just as he had at the beginning of our journey to India. After a brief reflection, he had evidently decided to continue believing in our covenant.

During the three days he was away, the house on Panarea became the site, or rather the birthplace, of strange things which I cannot pass over in my story if I wish to continue it without concerns about so-called credibility. I know perfectly well that the writer's pen hesitates to describe phenomena that are too elusive, afraid precisely of their elusiveness, that is, their existence beyond language. Yet one should not ignore something that from time to time fleetingly reveals its existence.

After Loris' departure the atmosphere was so electrified, so full of invisibility struggling to become visible, that the house, in which I had remained on my own (we had dismissed the maid), forced me into stillness; yet it was not a voluntary stillness, but that of a man tied by unseen bonds. I could not leave the house; I was able only to move with some effort, between the four walls of Marina and Loris' room. In the evening, as if knocked over by someone, I collapsed onto Marina's bed, and fell into the very depths of sleep, from which there was no returning. I saw Marina on the other side of the window through which, towards the end, she had stared at the sea. She was saying something to me, but I heard nothing other than the name of Loris repeated over and over. In the end she vanished; I saw the sea, and Irina lying in the shallow water by the shore, her face buried in the sand. I woke at midnight. And, again as if impelled by someone, I went down the stairs to the cellar. I sat on a chair by Irina's urn, and was surprised to see that the inscription *Ashes* had disappeared from it. And I fell asleep in a sitting position. I was swallowed up by a dark dreamless sleep. In the morning I left the cellar and staggered to the telephone. It was dead. Everything was dead. Someone's touch brushed against the back of my neck, like in the magic moments at Cumae. I did not hear the sound of the sea, nor did I hear human voices. I had the sensation that time was standing still. I must have tripped and fallen onto the rug by Marina's bed, because that was where Loris woke me when he returned.

The words "You will come back," uttered at Marina's shade immediately after her death were confirmed by the apparitions in my dreams; Loris' vigilance was stretched to its limits when, as soon as we had greeted each other, I told him about the three lonely days I had spent in the house after he left for Messina. From that point on

he accompanied me everywhere like a faithful dog, and his eyes followed mine wherever I turned my gaze. I suppose it was in this way
that he understood our wordless covenant: He believed that with
me, thanks to me, he would enter the circle of visions that only I
was able to summon. But my apparitions did not recur, neither in
dreams, nor all the more so in my waking hours. I merely heard from
time to time someone's footfall (which he did not hear); and twice, in
the doorway to the next room I saw a white human figure made of
mist or smoke (which he did not see). Did Loris feel as if he had been
robbed, as if I had stolen all that was dearest to him? It was entirely
likely; in any event, our silent agreement was dissolved, giving way
to antipathy, if not something like a grudge. If I had not been afraid
to leave him alone in the house on Panarea, I would have gotten on
the first boat back to Naples. Before long he fell into a depression
and spent entire days sitting in the cellar beside his two urns. In the
evenings I literally had to carry him out of there, blue with cold, and
set him on the couch next to the lighted fireplace. He seemed not to
recognize me, staring at me with a blank gaze.

I telephoned Florence. Nicola came without delay. We closed
up the house, and despite the bad weather we took Loris (who
presented no resistance whatsoever), and crossed to Messina,
where we boarded an express train for Milan. I got out in Naples.
Nicola and his life partner planned to move into the house in
Monte Oriolo while Loris remained in such a "pitiful" condition.
We promised each other we would stay in constant contact.

## XI

LORIS NEVER EMERGED from that "pitiful" state. Viviana,
Nicola's companion, looked after him as if he were a child. One of
Florence's most eminent doctors had shrugged his shoulders helplessly: "It's a rather rare illness, which could be called a rejection of
life. It's incurable, though it does not necessarily end in suicide."

One night at the beginning of spring Nicola and Viviana heard
a very loud cry from Loris' room (which had been Irina's). The
door was locked from the inside. It took them a long time to break
the lock. Loris had died kneeling on Irina's childhood stool by the

window; his head lay sideways on the windowsill, and his left hand was pressed against the pane with his fingers splayed, the right clutching crookedly at his heart. In the drawer of the night stand, there had been for some time a brief letter from him. He asked to be cremated, and for his remains to be placed in a third urn in the cellar of the house on Panarea. The urn, made in Florence, bore a verse from the Bible in Italian: "For ashes thou art, and unto ashes thou shalt return." Nicola took it to Panarea alone, not even asking me to accompany him.

I did go with him, however, in December, when, alerted by the "plenipotentiary" of the Berardi family on Panarea, he drove by car to Messina and there rented a motor boat that was capable of reaching the island in the brewing storm. The alarm raised by the "plenipotentiary" was justified. Lightning had struck the turret on the terrace and had cut away part of the wall of the upper floor, such that the stability of the entire house was threatened.

We stayed with the "plenipotentiary," who was happy to rent out rooms both in and out of season. From our chilly room Loris' house could clearly be seen. We arrived in the evening and decided to delay our inspection of the "scene of the crime" till the next day. Fate spared us the need to do so.

The storm grew continually stronger; the waves of the sea, which had not been particularly dangerous during our crossing, were stirred up eventually into a small *maremoto* or seaquake, and struck with a sudden roar against the house. Water poured in through the broken doors, then flowed out again, only to renew its onslaught. Where did the flame come from in the lower window by the door? Wherever it was from, it quickly engulfed the whole first floor of the house, and was extinguished gradually as the incoming waves washed over it. The house was breaking apart, and overhead in the sky, as in *The Fall of the House of Usher*, from amongst the clouds there briefly appeared the "blood-red moon."

*January–February 1995*

# NOTEBOOK OF WILLIAM
# MOULDING, PENSIONER

*Explanatory comment from the acquirer of the notebook*

ALL OF THIS WAS a simple matter of chance. In June of last year, 1991, I took myself off to London for a month, at the request of my dear, aging friend L. My great attachment to her proved insufficient for me to swallow such a large (or rather such a lengthy) portion of London. My relationship with that city is characterized, to put it mildly, by a severe allergy. A literal, physical allergy. After two weeks there I began to suffer rather frequent headaches and dizzy spells during the day, while in the night I would have such intense attacks of breathlessness in my little upstairs room that I would drag myself out of bed and stand by the open window, sometimes for half an hour at a stretch, sometimes even for a whole hour. To look at sleeping Putney (for that was the neighborhood in which I was staying) in a dense gloom with a purple hue, utterly still, as if it were no longer alive, as if it had been turned into a huge cemetery—no, this was more than I could bear. To the attacks of breathlessness was added an indefinable fear; I had the feeling that I was in a boat made from a nutshell, rocking gently on the waves of a grayish-yellow ocean untouched by even the slightest breeze.

Two weeks of my stay were behind me, and two more were still ahead. I tried to shorten them with visits to museums and art galleries, and with walks in the parks of London (once I even made an expedition to Hampstead Heath, where I had lived for a few years after the war); twice I passed the afternoon in the empty Everyman Cinema situated near L.'s house. When I was running out of ideas, and was struggling to conceal my condition from L., whom I loved so dearly, I received a phone call from an acquaintance of mine from the time of the war and its immediate aftermath. We arranged to meet for coffee in "Polish London." A beggar in the post war, my acquaintance had turned into a relatively wealthy man; his wealth he owed to "a life in the little world of auctions." This was how he himself put it; and he meant just that he knew all the auction houses in the city, going around from one to another each day, and from time to time was able to buy something valuable for a song and later sell it at a profit. "An expert eye, an expert eye," he repeated with a proud smile. "No," he hastened to explain, "I'm not talking about the famous auctions on Bond Street, where old masters or priceless furniture or family jewels fetch giddy prices; people like me don't even dare to show their face in those kinds of places. I mean the little auction 'huts'" (he used that word) "in various districts of London" ("this city has inexhaustible resources!" he added), "where belongings are sold after the deaths of regular folk, who were sometimes unaware of the value of what they had. Come with me tomorrow to Willesden Green; a professional auctioneer from the 'hut' there has told me they're expecting a minor sensation."

I knew Willesden Green; it was there, near the Underground station, that there lived a Polish doctor with whom I was "registered." When I visited him in the evenings for an examination or to collect a prescription, I would walk along as if I were having to feel my way, so dark were the streets in the pale, yellowish glow of the street lamps. In the day, presumably, the dreariness gave way to the usual London tedium and the monotony of little houses devoid of greenery and deserted, as if the plague had passed through.

The auction hall was indeed a hut; it must at one time have served as a store for building tools, a stockroom, or a temporary firehouse. There were twenty individuals at most assembled for the auction; they wore old-fashioned clothing, and their faces were so sorrowful they looked as if they were taking part in a funeral service. In a strange and incomprehensible way, against the background of the odds and ends stacked against the walls, they created something of a Dickensian atmosphere. Also Dickensian, lifted directly from etchings by the famous illustrator of Dickens' novels, was the auctioneer—a short, restless man who kept skipping about,

leaping onto the podium, and tapping his gavel on the table for
no apparent reason. Soon, however, a reason presented itself. A
wooden trunk was placed on the table. My acquaintance was all
ears.

The auctioneer talked rapidly, continually spitting on his
threadbare waistcoat; he spoke with a slight cockney accent, but
was more or less understandable. A year ago, in July 1990, at the
age of eighty-five, had passed away Dick Mulbery, *Mr. Chief Hangman of England*, the principal executioner of the country, who had
been sent into retirement in 1956. As a pensioner he had moved to
Putney under a new name, Bill Moulding; before he retired, he had
lived with his unmarried sister in Willesden Green. After his tragic
death, his sister sold the little house in Putney and brought all his
remaining possessions to Willesden Green. In this trunk—he
knocked on the wooden lid with the gavel—were three valuable
objects to be put up for auction today. Before he began to name
and display them, he drew something of a sketch of the executioner
in words "that made your blood run cold." The first object was a
black hangman's cap with eyeholes, "used from the first to the last
execution." The starting price was £100; it rose to £250, and my
friend bought it at this price. The second object was a thick pair of
stiff and, as it were, callused leather gloves, in which the executioner had "opened the trap door and brought death to the condemned man." The starting price was again £100; this time, after
heated bidding with a woman in a plush mantle and a black veil, my
acquaintance had to pay £470. He leaned towards me and whispered: "I can get two thousand pounds at least for both of those
things." Before taking the third object out of the trunk and showing it to us, in a voice aimed to elicit shudders of fear the auctioneer reminded us that "Mr. Chief Hangman of England—for those
present in this hall the famous Dick Mulbery—in his ten years of
work hanged 433 men and 17 women. *Can you imagine that?*[1] And
he wrote all this down in the *Notebook of William Moulding, Pensioner*, as the inscription on the green cover reads." After the starting price was called there was a silence, then three people brought

[1]Phrases and passages in italics are in English in the original. (translator's note)

it up to £140, and silence fell again. I turned to my friend: "I'd like to have that notebook." He called £150; no one made any further bids, and all three objects were returned to the trunk. He was well known there so the formality of writing a check took only a moment. "The notebook is my gift to you. After all, we were in the army together. You can repay me in whatever way you see fit." I took Moulding/Mulbery's notebook back to L.'s, and did not say a word about my acquisition. I spent the rest of my stay reading the notebook at night, while my remaining days in the city, of which I was (to put it gently) not very fond, passed more quickly from that moment on—in long conversations with L., and without my usual complaints about London.

Before I left I sought out the house in which Moulding/Mulbery had spent his retirement years. (The address appeared on the cover of the notebook.) It was a handsome detached house with a large garden; it was on a street which contained few buildings and which led to Putney Cemetery. His former home now housed the Bible Society. And at the cemetery, with the help of a keeper won over by a tip, I was able to find his grave and meditate over it for a while. It was marked by a large, new cross with an oval-shaped enamel plate: *William (Bill) Moulding, an Honest Godly Man, R. I. P. in Loving Sorrowful Memory, His Sister Mabel Mulbery.*

## Notebook of William Moulding, Pensioner

1.     NATURALLY, IT WAS A piece of false advertising for the auctioneer to claim that Mr. Chief Hangman of England "had written it all down in his notebook"—the "all" referring to the executions of over four hundred men and almost twenty women. His notebook was not in the slightest a journal of his operations, or a register of executions, but a loose, unstructured set of jottings begun in 1956, after he retired. In this respect the title *Notebook of a Pensioner* accurately reflected reality. Furthermore, it was not clear why it had been started, or to what purpose. In many places Mulbery/Moulding had stuck in clippings from the newspapers, not unduly trusting his own literary skills—and rightly so. He was a terrible writer. He had only finished elementary school, and as exe-

cutioner he had picked up a pen for only two reasons: to sign the certificate of execution and to pick up his wages. It is probable that as a young man, after he settled in London, he wrote letters to his girlfriend in Cardiff, but no return letters were found amongst his few papers, so this is open to doubt. In practical terms he was barely literate.

Furthermore, his handwriting was clumsy and awkward, probably reflecting a sluggish mind. I had great difficulty deciphering his sentences and organizing them into some kind of order, not to mention his lengthy notes, which were a chaotic muddle of thoughts full of gaps, half-expressed ideas, or words quite simply dashed off on the run. For this reason I will only rarely quote actual passages from the notebook; and I will do so solely in cases where he managed by some miracle to stammer out something like a rational utterance.

How did it come about that he bought at W. H. Smith's that two-hundred-page exercise book in its stiff green binding and under the printed inscription *Notebook* added *of William Moulding, Pensioner*? A large role must have been played by his inactivity as a retiree, especially a lonely one who had little idea what to do with his long days. Yet I believe that the real stimulus came from elsewhere. In an October, 1956, copy of the *London Illustrated News*—of which he was a loyal reader till it ceased publication—he found a photograph of himself, a high-quality reproduction on thick, glossy paper, with a short accompanying note saying that the *Chief Hangman of England, Mr. Richard (Dick) Mulbery*, had recently taken "a well-deserved retirement, after ten years of exemplary work in the service of his country and society." Underneath this, the very conservative magazine had placed in a decorative frame an editorial encomium to the executioner: "Joseph de Maistre wrote that the executioner hangs and cuts on the strength of a special decree of the Heavens, and that without him principles would give way to chaos, thrones would come crashing down and society would fall into confusion." Mulbery certainly did not know who Joseph de Maistre was, but, I suspect, he wished to keep as a souvenir this page from the "News" that bore his likeness with the weekly's congratulatory text. It cannot be ruled out that it was for this purpose he decided to purchase the notebook at W. H. Smith's.

* * *

2.   MR. HANGMAN (from now on this is how I will refer to him, to avoid having to choose between his real and assumed names) may have had plans to write a short autobiography, because the first lengthy entry was an account of his life up to the point when he assumed a "responsible position" (his own words) in London. Or—and this seems more probable—he had been called on many times by his superiors to write an official curriculum vitae, and he had fixed it firmly in his inflexible head.

In any case, from the account it could be learned that he had been born on May 1st, 1905, in Cardiff, as the only son of a miner named Jonathan. His sister Mabel was much younger than he. His mother was called Margaret; her maiden name was Peabody. His father worked with his unmarried brother John in a coal mine. John lived with them in an attic room. Every day at supper their father would read aloud a passage from the Bible, and at that time everyone had to be present at the table, even tiny Mabel. The boy was eighteen years old and was soon to go down the mine for the first time when his father and uncle, in response to an application they had submitted, were given jobs as guards at the London prison of Wormwood Scrubs. He remained in Cardiff with his mother and sister and worked at the pit. When his mother died of consumption, he was thirty. A girl by the name of Rose Willis was his fiancée. After his mother died, his father brought his sister and him to London. Right at that time his father and uncle had become executioners, carrying out their duty by turns. His father was proud to be enacting the verdicts of divine justice. He gradually prepared his son to take over from him; in the meantime the latter was also employed at the prison. The engagement with Rose was broken off, and the future Mr. Hangman ceased to think about beginning his own family. His father and uncle died in the air raids on London shortly before the end of the war. Their successor conducted his first execution in 1946. "I worked for ten years. In this occupation that is a lot; my father and uncle died after seven years of honorable service."

Beneath his autobiography Mr. Hangman stuck in a cutting from the *Evening Standard* entitled *Shame*. The author of the text, a city reporter for the London afternoon paper, had gone to Willesden Green intending to conduct an interview with the recently retired executioner. Miss Mabel Mulbery, the hangman's sister, had informed the reporter with tears in her eyes (*no wonder!*) that her brother had moved, no one knew where, and had changed his name. Why? While he had been the executioner, everyone in the neighborhood had treated him with fearful respect. Once he retired, every day he encountered insults in the pub, and people turned their heads when they saw him on the street. When he noticed people moving away from him in the pew, he ceased attending services at the Methodist chapel. Where was he living now? Had he left London? Miss Mabel stared for a long time into the reporter's eyes, then replied: "I don't know, he didn't give his address or his new name even to me. *Oh, what a shame!*" Did he not sometimes visit his sister? He had come once, late at night. She had sat in front of him crying; and he had stroked her face with his large hands. Under the clipping stuck into the notebook he had written: *I am dead to my sister. I am dead to everybody on earth, but not to Heaven's ruler.* He used this expression rather than the word *God*, having perhaps learned by heart de Maistre's dictum concerning the "special decree of the Heavens." (In later parts of the notebook he would refer to de Maistre as *That very wise French gentleman*.)

3.        I GAZED FOR A long time at the photograph cut out of the *London Illustrated News*. The date in the corner showed he was in his fiftieth year of life, though he truly did not look like a man on the threshold of retirement. But his years of "special" service counted double, perhaps even triple—they were "special" in consideration of the emotional stress. His uncle John, after working for five years, had spent three months in an institution for the treatment of nervous disorders. At the beginning of the twenties there had been a well-known case of an executioner who had tried to take his own life.

His face in the photographic portrait seemed to belie that "specialness." It was expressionless, rough-hewn, with a low forehead, a hard gaze beneath thick brows, and a jutting lower jaw (a sign of decisiveness, or of cruelty?); it put one in mind of the face of a traveler or explorer, with its combination of strength and courage. A woman would have exclaimed: "Goodness, how handsome he is!" The notebook was silent on the subject of his romantic life, though one bizarre sentence appeared to suggest that Rose Willis had broken off their engagement out of fear; it was not inconceivable that this was because she had discovered what course his life's journey had taken. Another sentence—set apart from the rest of the text, and isolated on a separate page—was interrupted in the middle of a word and might have indicated something about the erotic preferences he developed in his retirement: "I liked the boys from the choir" (probably in church), "and from the sports field, *but they panicked* (!) *when I tried to approach them.*" And then immediately afterwards: "*They misunderstood my intentions.*" It was quite possible that these intentions were entirely innocent, the result of the indistinct desires of an old bachelor attracted by youth.

His unchanging, frequently repeated claim to fame was that the official annotation on all four hundred and fifty reports of the completed sentences declared that the execution had gone off *without a hitch*. A great many things contributed to this evaluation on the part of his superiors. In one of the longest and, relatively, most correctly phrased entries in the notebook, Mr. Hangman had been unable to deny himself the satisfaction of a detailed explanation of exactly what these things were. He even titled this passage *High Efficiency*.

The *meticulous preparations*, he wrote, which guarantee that an operation will go *without a hitch*, should begin the day before the execution. In the early morning Mr. Hangman and his assistant discreetly take measurements of the height and weight of the condemned person, to determine the distance of the drop (after a long period in prison, the original information in the files is usually out of date). "Discreetly" means that the condemned man himself should not be aware of it, and so in most cases this involves surreptitiously sliding open the screen on the peephole in the cell door. In the evening on that same day, there is a rehearsal using a stuffed sack that weighs the same as the prisoner, in order to ascertain that the chosen length of the noose will neither choke him too slowly nor tear his head off.

The following day, two or three hours before the execution, Mr. Hangman enters the cell. He has to be very polite, but without feigning an excessive cordiality. This is a psychological *turning point* which is difficult to carry off and unfortunately not always *successful*. If the condemned man shakes your proffered hand, you can reasonably suppose that there is a fifty percent chance everything will go smoothly, *according to plan*. If he refuses, you can expect unpleasant surprises. In general, however, he does shake hands, with an exaggerated eagerness, as if he subconsciously expects relief or aid from the kindly executioner. *What a strange animal* [sic] *a man is!*—This is the only philosophical exclamation in the *Notebook of a Pensioner*. In those cases where the condemned man takes the hand offered him, he might be inclined to play a game of dominoes and smoke a cigarette—a very desirable thing.

It is important that shortly before the appointed time, the condemned man should be sitting with his back to the door through which the executioner enters in the company of the officials and a clergyman; for there occur (albeit rarely) incidents of resistance, and in such instances, instead of a calm departure from the cell, the condemned man is dragged bound and struggling to the place where the execution is to take place. Among the condemned men who put up resistance there are occasionally raving madmen who mark their final journey with blasphemies, curses, and spitting. When the condemned man sits with his back to the door of the cell, the procedure takes on the speed of lightning and works like a well-oiled machine: The door is opened briskly, and the prisoner's hands are tied behind his back; then comes the *almost solemn* procession to the scaffold. The appropriate place on the trap door has been marked ahead of time in chalk. The condemned man's legs are bound, and over his head is placed a white hood and the noose with its moveable copper ring. Mr. Hangman dons his black hood and pulls on his gloves. *Everything is fit and ready*, this description concludes, not without a note of boastfulness in its tone.

4.        THE NEXT CUTTING was glued in without mention of the name of the newspaper it came from, only the date 1963: It was a long and unsigned article entitled *The Hanging of Edith Thompson Forty Years Ago*. The compiler of the *Notebook of a Pensioner* must have been familiar with this case, which had been notorious in his profession (if one can use such a term), but only from hearsay; he probably heard about it from the stories of his father and uncle,

who could not have played a direct part in it themselves, since it appeared in the judicial annals in 1923.

Edith Thompson was a plain, sickly woman approaching thirty. She had a meek and obedient husband, a worker on the nightshift who treated his wife with proper respect and whose only dream was to have a child. No, the doctor informed them, they could not have a child. The husband, till then a teetotaler, turned to drink and became violent and aggressive, though he continued to behave well towards his wife. In the next house there lived an unmarried policeman who began by flirting over the garden fence then soon became Edith's lover. (At the trial she swore that she had at least wanted to have someone else's child for her husband, whom the doctor had found to be sterile.) One night the husband had returned home two hours after he left for work; suddenly feeling ill, he had passed out at the factory, and was bleeding. He found the lovers in his marriage bed. Despite his weakened state, he threw himself on the policeman with an iron crowbar. He was stabbed by his rival thirteen times with a kitchen knife. At the trial the policeman testified that Edith had badgered him, repeatedly calling on him to murder her husband (she sobbed quietly as she listened to his testimony); he also said that he was acting in self-defense. He was given six years in prison, while Edith received the death penalty "for inciting her lover to murder her husband" (this was the wording of the sentence).

During the execution, the condemned woman's innards literally dropped out—*her insides*, wrote the author of the article, *fell out before she vanished through the trap.* All those who were present at the scene paid the price afterwards of nervous illness. Executioner Ellis attempted suicide a few weeks afterwards. Some time later Morton, the governor of the prison, was described as follows by an official inspector: "I have never in my life seen a person whose external appearance was so altered by mental suffering." The prison chaplain Murray described the scene of the execution in these words: "When we had gathered, it seemed utterly beyond belief that we were there in order to . . . Dear Lord, the impulse to rush forward and save her by force was for me almost impossible to suppress." The assistant governor of the prison, Miss Cronin, a woman who was tough by nature and who did not easily yield to her emotions, said of the hanged person: "I think that if she had been spared, she could have become a very good woman." The conclusion drawn by the article's author was brief. From the example of Edith Thompson, forty years after her hanging, it was clear how wise, necessary, and humane (this was the writer's emphasis) was the abolition of capital punishment. The retired Mr. Hangman did not agree with this. In rather twisting and incoherent words, evidently written in a state of irritation, he emphasized (*"I would like to stress"*) two points. First, the article suggested, without stating it openly, that Edith Thompson may have been innocent. "I want to say once and for all that there are no cases in which a person who is condemned to hang by a decree of the Heavens (*as that very wise French gentleman says*), and finds themselves in the hands of the excutioner, is innocent; since they have been condemned, they are guilty, *absolutely guilty.* Secondly, an old regulation of the Execution Service requires categorically that before a woman is executed she must be made to wear tight and waterproof underwear, to avoid the kind of inconvenience described above." Either Executioner Ellis forgot about this (which would be surprising) and thus acted in a highly *unprofessional* manner; this may later on have driven him to make an attempt on his own life. Or, in 1923 "the waterproof material with which they made the special underwear for women condemned to be hanged had not yet acquired the high quality it possessed during my own period of service."

5.     IN THE YEARS AFTER the war, I often visited my friends in Putney. Whenever I traveled by tube from Hampstead, I had to wait for a bus at the bus stop opposite the station. On the other side of the street was the Bible Society, in a small, decidedly ramshackle house that, in the distant future, was no doubt destined to be bought and demolished by some building firm or by the local housing authority. In the afternoon and early evening hours, I would observe those going in. For the most part single people, they would arrive at their spiritual harbor with an effort, taking slow, tired steps and opening the door as if with relief. Once, standing at my bus stop in the bitter cold and the fog, I decided to warm up for a while in the Bible Society. Yes, the majority of its denizens were

elderly; they sat in silence on benches around the tables, some dozing with their head drooping on their breast. The young people's job was to read the Bible aloud, to comment on it, and to answer infrequent questions. Around the walls there stood glass-doored cabinets with copies of the Bible in various languages open for display. The dominant mood was of austerity, isolation, shelter during the storm. The Bible was a light in the darkness, an anchor, a guarantee of the One Path—to a much greater degree than the church liturgy.

As I gazed at these aging folk, I thought of a poem by Cavafy, to whose poetry (in English) I was addicted in those days, one entitled *Old Men*. "In ruined bodies dwell the souls of old men . . . How they have been worn down by the life they have led. And how they are afraid to lose it, how they love it." Another poem by Cavafy, *Walls*, came to mind when (unaccosted by anyone as I entered) I took in the whole of the Bible sanctuary, or rather refuge. "They have built walls around me, thick and high . . . Imperceptibly they have closed me off from the outside world." These old folk had closed themselves off from the world in a dilapidated house in Putney, barricaded in on every side by the Bible, intent on its verses, believing that it is possible to flee the world and take cover beneath the protective wings of the Almighty (and Just) Lawgiver and Judge.

It was right here that Mr. Hangman came almost every day in his retirement. It was close to his house. For a few hours he could breathe freely, reminiscing about his childhood, and recalling the Bible evenings around the family table in Cardiff; he could, more importantly, be confirmed in his conviction that he had once fulfilled his obligations in accordance with the spirit of the Old Testament. The New Testament he regarded, following his father's teachings, as espousing *a religion of weaklings*.

Every so often he recorded his visits to the Bible Society in his notebook, always in words which showed (clumsily it was true, but clearly) that they were a source of respite and relief for him.

Until 1970. Yet before I attempt to reconstruct from the *Notebook of a Pensioner* just what happened in 1970, I will broach a topic which has hitherto been passed over, that of subtle distinctions in the work carried out by Mr. Hangman. Though he tried to conceal them, there is no doubt in my mind that such distinctions existed. He inaugurated his ten years of service with the hanging of Baronet Hawkings, an English aristocrat who during the war had broadcast Nazi propaganda from a Berlin radio station. The harvest in the aftermath of the war was plentiful. On one occasion, in the course of less than twenty-four hours he hanged twenty-seven war criminals. And he recalled the one event and the other euphorically; the phrase *without a hitch* here carried a particular undertone. I believe this was because the death of his father and uncle from German bombs had been a severe blow to him. He could not fail to experience the taste of vengeance.

Yet despite his remarks—indifferent, "professional" and devoid of any compassion—about the hanging of Edith Thompson, he was not good at dealing with the execution of women (though he carried out these executions irreproachably). The reason for this he was unable or unwilling to reveal in his notebook. But the instinctive reluctance, the grimace of nervousness on his face, could not be concealed the few times he mentioned the hangings of women. Just as he could not hide the sigh of relief he must have uttered when, a year before he retired, he hanged Dorris Norton, about whom there were mutterings amongst lawyers that she would be the last woman in England to receive the death sentence. She had poisoned her lover's wife. The evidence was weak and ambiguous, but she herself confessed to the crime with a strange and ardent passion at the very beginning of the trial. That was enough for the jurors and the judge. In the press the campaign to end capital punishment was gaining strength every day; the sentence was announced and carried out as it were in a hurry, with a presentiment that from now on no woman would mount the scaffold.

In 1970 then, in the wintertime—and that winter had been called the harshest in London for half a century—a new person appeared at the Bible Society. She belonged to the circle of lecturers, readers, and interpreters. Her age was hard to pin down; she was between forty and fifty years old. He noticed immediately the resemblance she bore, and also the fact that during the lesson she never took her eyes off him. Dorris Norton was the only one of the four hundred and fifty he had hanged whose face he remembered well, perhaps because according to the rumors she was to be the last woman on the gallows. And the newcomer looked like an older copy of her. As he left in the evening and, as usual, wrote his name in the attendance book, he glanced at the column of names. Ruth Norton. She could only be Dorris' sister—one who made a person think of twins. That day he returned home uneasy and on edge—*I was terribly agitated.* Why had she been staring at him so insistently? Did she know his identity? At the Bible Society he went by the name of William Moulding, but he had expected that at some point someone would recognize him. The truly odd thing, *what was really strange,* was that from the first moment he had taken a great liking to her; he had wanted at last to have a female friend. Not a friend in *that* sense—he had just turned sixty-five, and took care of *those* matters very rarely, at a brothel in Fulham—but simply someone close with whom he could go to the pictures or for a walk, whom he could invite for afternoon tea and for long conversations. He realized two things at once. The first was the fact that he had hardly ever had a conversation with anyone for longer than a quarter of an hour. His talkativeness he had lost in Cardiff.

Ruth Norton came to the Bible Society for only a month. She announced her departure before she left, at the end of the lesson, adding that she was being transferred to Birmingham. She said her goodbyes to everyone. Him she pushed into a corner, and said to him briefly in private: "Your name is not William Moulding. You're Mulbery, the former executioner. You hanged my sister Dorris. I want you to know that I know. The rest belongs to your conscience. I loved Dorris."

The next day he did not go back to the Bible Society. Nor ever again. The memory of Ruth on the lecturer's podium was for him *unbearable.*

6.     THE SECOND THING that he had suddenly realized was even more burdensome, and brought about a long period of *desperate confusion.* (This state was something entirely new to him, and induced a feeling of panic and, at times, a pounding of the heart so violent that he attempted to overcome it by lying motionless on his bed and staring at the ceiling.) For me the phrase itself was something entirely new and startling, coming from his pen.

For he had come to realize that with the exception of Dorris

Norton, he did not remember a single face of the four hundred and fifty people he had dispatched to the next world. All of them had merged into a dark mass, a great black boulder—it had to be black—that crushed him to the ground; this, despite the fact that with his hands he was trying to push it aside or at least hold it back. This effort seemed to him, perhaps rightly, the cause of the sensations he was experiencing with his heart.

This was not such a problem in the daytime, when he could wrestle with his feelings. But at night! His sleep was nothing but *a nightmare*: Now he seemed to make out some human features imprinted on the black boulder, features which did not sound a single chord in his memory, and were completely voiceless; now there was nothing but pure blackness, fluid yet slow-moving, like a stream of ooze riding up into his mouth, nose, and eyes. He would wake up with a cry, thanking God that he lived alone and that no one could hear.

He wrote in his notebook in printed letters: "I cannot stand this hell any longer." *In extremis* he had an idea that on the face of it seemed sensible. He wrote a letter to an official he knew in the Home Office, in which he asked to be provided with the files (including photographs) of the people he had hanged in the ten years from 1946 to 1956; he explained his request by saying that he was planning to write his memoirs in order to supplement his meager pension. This idea had allegedly been suggested to him by a professional ghost writer. He received a cold, two-line reply: Employees of his rank of service (underlined) were prohibited from publishing memoirs (Special Activities Act of 1903). Naturally, this ban did not extend to journalists, and so soon (as if at the wave of a magic wand) he saw the entire window of a bookstore taken up with copies of *The People Dick Mulbery Hanged*, by Johnson and Muir. In the middle of the display a copy had been placed open at an illustration showing six prison shots of people whose names were given and whose cases were described in the caption at the bottom of the page as *probable judicial errors*. His own photograph from the *London Illustrated News* appeared on the title page. At that time he blessed his decision to move from Willesden Green and once again forbade his sister to give anyone at all his address in Putney. Luckily his house in Putney, by the cemetery, was set apart and often seemed to go unnoticed.

He read Johnson and Muir's book twice, with considerable difficulty, stumbling over unfamiliar words and legal terms on the way. To begin with he angrily rejected the notion of *judicial error*, even with the qualification *probable*. Later, he came to question his confidence in his own judgment, especially while he stared for hours at the photographs of those who had been hanged. The authors of the book had managed (just how, was their professional secret) to gather forty-eight pictures—eight illustrated pages with six prison photos on each. From the perspective of our times it was striking (and inspired some confidence) that they had elected not to acquire, by guile or money, family photographs of the condemned from their surviving relatives.

These pictures riveted his attention with a growing power. The text—stories of the crimes of the people he had hanged and of their trials—aroused his growing indifference. He kept returning to the eight pages sewn into the book. Of the forty-eight faces—including five women—he did not remember a single one. Something mysterious was going on within him which he could not comprehend, let alone put into words. *What has happened to me, what is happening to me?* This question rose many times from the tangled, garbled writings in this part of the notebook, with a kind of dramatic, helpless emphasis. To regain his mental equilibrium he retreated instinctively to the principle that *they were all guilty, all of them*. It was to no avail. Even their guilt—once again beyond dispute—drove him towards them, and at the same time away from the world. Once, he had wiped them from the face of the earth with that simple *without a hitch*; now he was following close behind them, though not feeling within himself any sense of guilt, whatever that word meant in the mouths of people such as Ruth. Compassion? This participant in the meetings and lessons of the Bible Society did not understand the notion. Dark clouds sailed through his reeling mind.

But in one respect the faces saved from oblivion brought him a certain relief. His dreams were different. The dark, heavy stone vanished, and the stream of black ooze ceased flowing; their place was taken by the faces from the photographs. He woke now not with a cry, but with a cough, which, with one unaccustomed to shedding even a single tear, stood for a dry sob. The place of his *desperate confusion* was now occupied by the *community of human misfortune*. This gave him a momentary feeling of calm. Occasionally he thought fleetingly about taking his own life; very fleetingly, for no more than the twinkling of an eye—he had been brought up to have contempt for suicides. Death could only be granted by the Supreme Judge, either by Himself, or through the avenging arm of another. Instead, he created a substitute for departure: In Putney cemetery he bought a plot for a grave, enclosed it with a low fence, and went there whenever the weather permitted; "standing as if over my own buried remains," he experienced moments of a curious satisfaction, if not happiness. Finally, in mid-July 1990, as he was returning home from the cemetery along the usually deserted street, he was accompanied at a distance on the other side of the street by a small group of boys singing and playing guitars; they were tall, laughing, colorfully dressed, with shaved heads . . . *I was almost happy*, were the last words of the notebook.

7.     THE REST HAS TO be reconstructed. I know roughly what happened on the night of July 18th, 1990, but only very roughly. The circumstances are extremely vague and swathed in mist. My London acquaintance—who had bought *The Notebook of William Moulding* for me and whom I repaid upon my return to Italy with a handsome watercolor by a rather well-known Neapolitan painter—my acquaintance, then, expressed his willingness to prepare and to send me "exhaustive press documentation." It was indeed exhaustive, comprising almost a hundred press clippings from July 10th to 25th, which covered the whole period of the public's interest in the so-called "affair of executioner Mulbery."

It was exceedingly difficult to establish the exact course of events; and so the journalists had not refrained from patching the large gaps (which seemed as if they would never be filled in) with guesswork and imaginings.

The real identity of the murdered man came as a surprise. His sister, when she learned the condition in which the body had been found, refused to be driven from Willesden Green to Putney for the purposes of a formal identification, justifying her decision on the basis of a heart complaint, a condition confirmed by her doctor; nevertheless, she signed an official statement saying that from 1960 her brother, Chief Hangman Mulbery, had resided in Putney under the assumed name of William Moulding, and that though she had known his address, she had revealed it to no one, at his own "strict and categorical request." The police were satisfied, albeit reluctantly, with an identification at a distance.

In all the articles it was taken as a certainty that for a few days (probably from July 15th) a "group of young predators" from Roehampton or Wimbledon had been following the solitary old man (he was 85!) in Putney, shadowing him from the cemetery entrance to the gate outside his house. Everything indicated that, taking advantage of his cheerful disposition in those days (according to the testimony of the cemetery keeper), and that he was probably not suspicious whatsoever, they invited themselves into his house for a drink around six in the evening on July 18th. From the autopsy the doctors estimated that the torture had begun at around eight and lasted till midnight, when he died. What this torture consisted of (his mouth had been gagged immediately) could only be surmised from the police's refusal to allow the details to be published in the papers. One policeman had muttered as he stared intently at the ground: *Absolutely indescribable*. At a press conference the officer heading the investigation said: "It is beyond belief that such a thing could be thought up by human beings." The attackers were finally arrested on December 4th, 1990; had it not been for the abolition of the death penalty, all five would have ended up on the gallows. They had not touched the house in Putney; they stole neither money (there were three hundred pounds in the table drawer) nor valuable objects, but only wrote slogans on the white walls in their victim's blood. These slogans, in accordance with a police directive, also went unreported in the papers. The obscenities they contained, marked by a disinterested, impulsive hatred, were apparently something monstrous, and in any case were not fit to be quoted in the press. The most fundamental point was that not one of these slogans contained any allusion to the position the dead man had held for ten years before his retirement. The torturers and murderers had no idea that they had spent four hours ill-treating a former executioner. Their choice had been random; they could equally well have tormented another person to death *for fun*—on the next street, or in a different, distant neighborhood of London.

It took a considerable effort, and a great deal of nerves, to gather the remains of Dick Mulbery/William Moulding into a casket. His sister did come to his funeral, however, with the permission of her doctor. The "pieces" of the deceased (for this is unfortunately how they must be described) were incinerated at the cemetery crematorium. Along with the dead man's sister, a Methodist preacher, an official from the Home Office, and a police officer took their leave of the urn with the ashes. Dick Mulbery's testament was found in his cupboard: He left everything to his sister, on condition that his house would be sold at low cost to the branch of the Bible Society opposite the East Putney Underground station.

### Farewell to London

DESPITE MY ATTACHMENT to L., within me there was growing a vow never to visit London again. An indirect though important role in this was played by my cardiologist, who advised me against making any longer journeys. In this case "longer" meant to foreign places, out of reach of his supervision.

But it happened to me—especially after I finished reading the *Notebook of a Pensioner*—that in my imagination I would tramp about London for hours on end, amongst other things hoping that I would come to understand where my "London allergy" came from. There was no doubt that to a large extent it arose from my personal experiences from spending five years after the war in that city. It is a truism that one loves, or at least likes, places where one has had pleasant experiences, whereas places of painful experiences are repaid with antipathy. But in my case even that rule operated only to a certain degree, since I remember London repelled me as soon as I moved there, when nothing at all had yet happened to me, and my life in London was still a blank, unwritten page. Well then? If I had understood why William Moulding's notebook had so intensified my aversion towards London, I might have gotten to the "heart of darkness." But I did not understand, and merely yielded from time to time to the need to roam the streets of London in my mind. "That city will go with me," said Cavafy of

Alexandria. I could say something similar about the handful of large and small cities in my own life. But not about London. That city, ponderous and morbidly overgrown, would never go with me. And perhaps it was here that there resided the "heart of darkness"—about which I knew only that I was incapable of reaching it in any way.

What was curious was that my imaginary wanderings steered clear of places I knew well from my five-year sojourn after the war. I wished to avoid a gaze imposed by hurt. The route I took was "the Moulding route": Holloway Prison, in which he had hanged women; the house in Willesden Green in which up to a certain moment he had lived with his sister; the house near the cemetery in Putney in which he had been tortured and killed. In the end, in my imagination I also dropped by the Bible Society that now occupied the place. An elderly lady (who knew if it was not Ruth Norton, sent once again to London?) was reading and commenting on the Book of Ecclesiastes. With relish, in a dramatic voice, she emphasized the constant motif of Koheleth the preacher: "vanity and chasing the wind." Twice, with tears in her eyes, she read this passage:

> *I praised the dead*
> *which are already dead*
> *more than the living which are yet alive.*
> *Yea, better is he than both they,*
> *which hath not yet been,*
> *who hath not seen the evil work*
> *that is done under the sun.*

As I left and turned toward the cemetery, for some unknown reason I repeated aloud, in an altered form, Melville's exclamation:

OH MULBERY
OH HUMANITY.

*July–August 1992*

# THE SILVER COFFER

*Christmas 1991*

THE HISTORY OF THE Silver Coffer, on the first anniversary of its death.

Jim Vodnick had been my friend since September 1945, the year in which Rome was liberated. In those days, in Rome, we all drank like fish—the Americans out of joy, the Poles mostly from sorrow and a sense of disillusion. So how did it come about that every now and then I would drink with Jim, a lieutenant in the American tank corps, despite the fact that we were drawn to the bottle for completely different reasons? How could I stand his often rowdy mirth in the small taverna near the Piazza di Spagna that was frequented mainly by American troops? Quite simply I was fond of this ever so young lad, amazingly well read for his age, sensitive, witty, bursting with energy, yet sometimes plunging into a depression so deep that I, of all people, had to extract him from those depths (though fortunately this occurred rather rarely). I first met him in the lounge of the office for those working on Polish and French army magazines. He appeared there one morning "out of curiosity," searching for some contact with Poles. He knew about his distant Polish heritage, but that was all; he did not speak a word of Polish and had virtually no conception of Poland, since his parents had brought him up in deliberate isolation from anything to do with the country where his grandparents had been born. He had begun his military career, at the rank of second lieutenant, in the Normandy landings; his regiment had been transferred to the Italian front at the beginning of 1945.

After I moved to England in 1947 I lost touch with him. I received no reply to the letter I sent to his address in Rome (he had a fine apartment near the Milvio bridge, overlooking the Tiber; he had been given it when he had been seconded from his regular assignment to the military authority of the Eternal City). This could have meant that he had returned to his home regiment in northern Italy, or that he had been included in the partial demobilization, and had finally entered some university in the States; or perhaps he had simply decided not to continue our wartime friendship. The latter seemed most likely to me; I myself—were it not for the Silver Coffer—would soon have forgotten about my Roman libations with Jim.

\* \* \*

AT THAT TIME I had seen the Silver Coffer just once, during my only visit to Jim's apartment on the Tiber. It was very beautiful and very old. It was clear that in the past it had been regularly cleaned, but despite this the silver was streaked with curling matt-black discolorings—proof of its age. Perhaps fifty centimeters in height, yet not tall enough for it to be called a chest, its four sides were covered in shallow bas-reliefs in exquisite metalwork: the Road to Golgotha, the Crucifixion, the Entombment, and the Resurrection. The convex lid was engraved with the face of Christ, a little like the magnificent, dramatic visage in Piero della Francesca's *Resurrection*. The bottom bore in smooth silver the coat of arms of those who were probably the first owners: a quiver full of arrows and a pennon with the letter D. The lid was attached by silver-plated, or perhaps solid silver, bands in two corners. It was massy, and looked very heavy, yet the Coffer was surprisingly lighter than it appeared; without particular effort it could be lifted—empty of course—in two hands. What had been kept in it, what had it been for? It could not have been a jewel box, since aside from a hasp it lacked a strong lock. It was too precious to have contained domestic odds and ends; and it seemed too narrow for ledgers. What then? The only thing I could come up with, also under a question mark, was that it had held important family documents.

I was more than fascinated by it; I was bewitched. During that one visit to Jim's apartment, I could not take my eyes off it; I studied it from close by, then went up to express my admiration with the touch of my hand. Besides the wonderful handiwork, there was something extraordinary about it, as if it were a fragment of an unknown story. Jim watched me with a smile; it seemed that only now, thanks to me, was he beginning to discover what he had.

I did not even have to ask him to tell me how he came into possession of the Silver Coffer. He told the tale freely, with relish, with satisfaction, even a hint of pride—though it was a matter, perhaps not of theft, but let us say, of the "spoils of war." In Normandy his tank regiment had been pushing the Germans back in a slow retreat, and had encountered stiff resistance at a monastery situated five kilometers outside of some small town. The monastery greeted the American column with heavy fire. The fight went on all afternoon; at dusk the American tanks were preparing for a final onslaught, when there came an explosion: Before they retreated, the Germans had mined a part of the building on the side nearest the road. One wing of the monastery survived. The place was empty, since, as it later transpired, the Benedictine monks had been expelled previously. It was decided to halt the march here for the whole night. In the nighttime Jim walked amongst the sleeping soldiers, shone his flashlight across the shattered walls of a long hallway, and kicked open one cell after another, until in the last one, near the window above the monastery cloister, which dangled over some rubble, he noticed something poking out of a pile of debris in the corner and glittering in the beam of the flashlight. It was the Silver Coffer. He gently dug it out and without a moment's hesitation decided it was his "booty." Wrapped in canvas and tied with a string, from that time it became part of his wartime baggage.

Was he, like me, enchanted from the first moment? No, not really. He had wanted a "souvenir." It never even occurred to him that the monks would eventually return to the monastery and would gather what was left of their belongings. Sensitive, intelligent Jim had rapidly been corrupted by the "rules of war."

And so I forgot about Jim, as, incidentally, I had forgotten many of my other comrades in arms, with whom my friendship had not lasted into postwar times. I did not even try to find out what had subsequently happened to him. But I will be honest: I did not forget his "spoils of war." The Silver Coffer lived on in my thoughts, and sometimes appeared fleetingly in my dreams. And as time went on it gradually assumed complete autonomy, and eventually became entirely independent of its fortunate owner. It existed on its own, as if it were a living thing, imbued with its unknown past, closed in on itself and jealously guarding its secret: an object that had never been touched by human hands other than those of its creators. It is easy to see that after one encounter in Rome, the Silver Coffer had become an obsession for me, as sometimes happens with a woman seen once in a crowd or a landscape glimpsed from the window of a train.

\* \* \*

In November 1955 I settled in Naples. One Sunday a few months later, in the spring of the following year, I set off to visit the Bay of Amalfitano. I was lured by Ravello, which I had seen very briefly immediately after the war. I drove up the hill, parked my car on the cathedral square and walked to the delightful Villa Ruffolo, which, in a single breath, guidebooks of the time described as having hosted Wagner and Victor Emmanuel during the process of his abdication. Ravello had always been regarded as a town popular with rich English and Americans, and so it was not surprising to constantly hear the sound of the English language in cafés and restaurants and on walks. All at once, behind me I heard a voice I recognized, interspersed with familiar bursts of laughter. Yes, it was Jim Vodnick. I turned around and could barely recognize him. He had put on weight—I ought to say he had become bloated; he had aged greatly (he was only thirty-two!), and he had the red, puffy face of a drunk. We threw our arms around each other, and my eyes clouded over with tears, brought on, I suspect, more because of the Silver Coffer than from meeting my wartime friend. It was twelve noon and Jim was already well in his cups; but he managed to tell me in a half-coherent way that after I left Italy he had married an Italian woman in Rome, made a lot of money ("never mind how"), and moved with his wife to Ravello, to a villa near Cimbrone which he had bought "for a song" and which had a magnificent view over the bay. I was thinking of one thing only: Would he invite me to his home or not; would I be able to see the Silver Coffer? (I did not doubt that it was still in his hands.) He in-

vited me to dinner, which was sumptuous and generously washed
down with alcohol; I met his wife, Clementina, who was ever so
pretty, and ever so empty-headed. We reminisced a little about
Rome after the war, and I waited in a state of constant tension as to
whether I would see it . . . After dinner we passed to the next
room for coffee and brandy, and there, in the corner by the window
overlooking the bay, stood the Silver Coffer on a small round table.
Jim had evidently forgotten about my fascination with his "wartime
plunder," since he sat in an armchair with his back to it and went
on with his drunken ramblings, paying no attention to my furtive
glances towards the corner of the room. Poor Jim! During those
ten years of "making money" and all the rest, including his move to
Ravello, he had not merely become physically coarser. His entire
refinement and intelligence had also disappeared. He no longer
had any interest in books, and at times he was vulgar, though a dis-
cerning eye could not help perceiving a certain desperation beneath the veneer of boorishness. It is with regret that I use that
word, but unfortunately it is appropriate. At the same time one had
the impression that in some way, provocatively, he took pride in
this boorishness, vaunting it ostentatiously.

From that time, for many years we would see each other twice a
year, at Christmas and Easter. And always in Ravello, where I
would be invited to a "Lucullan feast" (as Jim liked to call it). For
reasons unknown to me, perhaps connected with his "business interests" (which, he added with a smile, were "rather dirty"), he
never came to Naples; even his frequent journeys by air he began
and ended in Rome. Our wartime friendship did not revive; at a
stretch, one might call our relationship one of "familiarity," but
things settled down pleasantly enough at this level of mutual con-
geniality. It was hard for me to tolerate his wife, with her eternal
babbling, and flirting (rather than hurting him, this amused him).
How long did it all go on? Let us count: From the spring of 1956,
to the late fall of 1990. I believe I need not add that every visit of
mine to the Villa Clementina was above all a visit to the Silver Coffer. Once, on Easter Saturday 1975, the Pasquetta left me, alcoholi-
cally speaking, in such a state that in the evening the drive back to
Naples was out of the question. I slept on a fold-out armchair in
the room of the Silver Coffer. I remembered that night for a long,

long time. I awoke at dawn with an aching head. Through the window a vivid blood-red sun was emerging from the sea on the horizon. The stillness of the bay—leaden gray or matt silver at daybreak, with not so much as a ripple—seemed like a carpet spread out for the Coffer in the corner of the room by the door onto the terrace. I pushed the door open and stepped out with the Silver Coffer in my arms. I felt a trembling, as if I were embracing a living creature, and hugged it to my breast. I was without doubt well on the way to losing my senses. Then I put the Coffer back in its usual place and did not sleep till morning, watching the rising sun caress it with its golden rays. Is it possible I had a presentiment then that the Silver Coffer *was*, in its own way, a living being?

In November 1990 Jim died of apoplexy; I learned about it in a letter from Clementina. Her letter also contained the information that in his will, he had left everything to his wife, with the exception of the Silver Coffer, which (in his words) "ought to belong to my friend, who fell in love with it the minute he saw it." Good, kind Jim! His former refinement had penetrated his thickened skin after all.

I drove to Ravello the next morning. I drank a coffee with Clementina, and had to listen to her long story about her husband's last moments (*"poveretto*, he had an easy death"). The whole time I was on tenterhooks; nevertheless, I listened politely as the widow prattled on, and even—something that required no mean effort—supplemented the abundant bouquet of her recollections with a few modest little buds of my own. At last, thanks be to the Almighty, I was on my way, with the Silver Coffer in a cardboard box on the seat next to me, along what may well be the most beautiful road in the world, around the Bay of Amalfitano, towards my home in Sorrento. How happy I was!

\* \* \*

SOON AFTER MY RETURN home from Ravello, at Christmastime—with a feeling of satisfaction I was already becoming accustomed to the Silver Coffer on its special wooden pedestal in the alcove in my room, and I both greeted the day and prepared for sleep by tenderly caressing its sides and lid—I noticed with dismay that it was blackening. Further, I suspected it was doing so irreversibly, since the narrow matt-black marks were growing wider every day. From the moment I had come into possession of the Coffer, I had cleaned it every few days with silver cleaner. And now this had ceased to work. Why?

Friends recommended a museum conservator from the silver department of the former Royal Palace, a man said to be of great knowledge and expertise in the matter, and also of great personal charm. In light of this strong endorsement, I managed to invite him to our home for coffee on Boxing Day. He examined the Silver Coffer closely, declared it to be the work of a "true artist" of the sixteenth century, and ascribed its sudden blackening not, as I suspected, to the constant humidity in Naples (which is not so intense in Ravello), but to "natural processes of aging." It was his opinion that silver objects have a "life expectancy," like humans. There comes a time when no one is capable of preventing the yellowing of the complexion, the appearance of spots on the skin and the growing number of wrinkles. So it is with silver. The longer the blackening of the silver is fended off by cleaning, the more sudden and rapid is the subsequent process of decay, the metal's own form of decrepitude. "And this Coffer, which I confess is exceptionally beautiful, looks to be around five centuries old. I'm surprised by how light it is. In all probability the sides are hollow inside, and the plates with the bas-reliefs have been inserted with a little space between them and the interior walls. It's possible to check, even though the naked eye can't detect any signs of assembly. A superb artist and a consummate craftsman."

That evening, using a magnifying glass, I conducted a minute examination of the sides and the top and bottom edges of the Coffer. I found nothing. The craftsman was such a master that he had disarmed even the armed eye. The next morning, in light that was brighter than that of a lamp, I renewed my examination. I surprised myself by my own stubbornness, underpinned by a certainty, the absolute certainty of my inner clairvoyance in this search, by means of which—I do not know why, though perhaps I was led by some intuition—I promised myself that I would discover something more than the secret of the Coffer's construction. At last, in the early afternoon, while the sunlight was still strong, I spotted under the bands attaching the lid, two narrow lines that looked as if someone had stuck a hair on the edge. I pressed one of them with the blade of a small knife. The line widened. Pushing down with greater force, I depressed a small slat that was set into the rim of the Coffer, completely invisible. It was exactly the same with the opposite rim. My museum conservator had been right: Beneath the slats, between the two interior walls and the plates with the bas-reliefs, there was empty space, filled with something that looked like paper. They were small sheets of a delicate parchment of uni-form size, which at first glance seemed well preserved, but which, once they came into contact with the air, would probably be diffi-cult to hold in the fingers without the risk of crumbling. With the help of a pair of tweezers I succeeded in extracting them from both sides and laying them on the table. In all there were twenty-four sheets covered on both sides with rather small handwriting, in Ital-ian and in places in Latin. I trembled at the sight of the first and last words. "I, Cesare Baron Demagno . . ."; and the signature "Abas Petras," beneath which was the date of 1560.

\* \* \*

FOR RESEARCHERS OF sixteenth-century chronicles the story of the Demagno family is one of the most interesting and intriguing. It can be said without exaggeration that there are as many versions of it as there are authors. But the theme common to all of them, re-stricted to the bare facts (if facts are ever bare), is as follows.

Baron Federico Demagno, the owner of two castles in Apulia—one between the towns of Altamura and Gravina, the other between Mottola and Palagiano, near Taranto—having declared himself on the side of the French against the Spanish, in 1528 was forced to flee the Kingdom of Naples for France. In his summer castle of Panicale (the second one mentioned), at the Baron's order part of the family remained behind with some servants: his twenty-five-year-old daughter Teresa and his son Cesare, three years her senior, who was in charge of the surrounding estate. The older castle, the family's an-cestral home on the Gravina River, Baron Federico left in the care of his wife Caterina and their other two sons, Moro and Lorenzo. It was called Turrita. It was actually within these walls that most of the lives of the Demagno family had been spent (usually only the three summer months were passed in Panicale Castle). The flight of Baron Federico occurred during the move, at the beginning of June, and so out of fear of Spanish reprisals it was decided to separate the family in two, keeping watch in both castles.

Teresa Demagno was a poet. She dreamed of leaving the tedium and isolation of her imprisonment at home, and in her poems sought forgetfulness and consolation. Also a poet was Don Miguel Molinos, a Spanish captain from the fortress at Taranto, and the owner (through his Italian wife) of the property of Pastorizia, halfway between Taranto and Panicale. The tutor from Panicale traveled every Sunday to Pastorizia, where he taught Molinos how to write in Italian. Don Miguel, who had never seen Teresa, sent some of his Spanish poems to her through the tutor, receiving in exchange Teresa's Italian poetry. It was an innocent correspondence between two poets which could have led to deeper feelings, had it escaped the watchful eye of the Spaniard's Italian wife. Cesare, Teresa's brother, a hot-headed fellow always ready for a quarrel, did not know about it. One Sunday at dusk, watching from the window of the castle he noticed the tutor handing Teresa a roll of papers. He ran quickly down to the castle courtyard. Explanations, pleas, and entreaties were to no avail. Straight away he stabbed the tutor to death. On Monday, at dawn Teresa was found dead in her bed, with signs of strangulation. Cesare had vanished. It soon transpired that he had galloped on his horse to Pastorizia, where he had lain in wait, and shot and killed Captain Molinos. The triple murder forced him to flee the Kingdom of Naples. He evaded his pursuers and succeeded in reaching France. There, according to all extant chronicles, he entered the Benedictine order ("penitent and asking God for forgiveness"). He was transferred from monastery to monastery in order to "obliterate the traces of his earthly wanderings." None of the chronicles gives the name of the monastery where he ended his monastic peregrinations. It is only known, from somewhat uncertain sources, that, "devoted to the Lord in body and soul, and by the grace of God having a heart changed through unceasing prayer," he became abbot of that monastery and "passed away in God after reaching the age of seventy-eight." Few in the order knew his real name. He died as Abbot Peter. Of the

Demagno family he was survived only by his brother Moro, seven years his junior.

When many years ago, succumbing to my weakness for ancient chronicles, I came across several versions of this sixteenth-century *storia di passione*, I promised myself that I would visit the places where it had been played out (the chroniclers used the word *passione* to mean the passions of the noble families). Chance would have it that right at that time I was asked to give a lecture in Bari. The invitation to Bari turned into a short journey around Apulia.

From Bari I drove first to Altamura, and from there I took the road along the Gravina River (or rather creek) to the castle of Turrita. It was uninhabited; even the lower chambers were unoccupied (which in southern Italy happens quite rarely—in most instances the homeless live off the wretched remains of noble splendor); the four turrets were crumbling and half missing, and only the ruins of the walls were still standing. Inside, where fragments of the walls of the lower floor could be seen, wild plants had taken root and were spreading rapidly. I did not dare climb the stairs leading upward; they were overgrown, and the grass between the stones indicated that they were loosened. On that cloudy October day the heavy gray sky seemed a reflection of the ruins. Turrita, situated in an empty field, was repellent and caused a slight shiver of fear. I moved quickly on, along the road signed Mottola-Palagiano.

The castle of Panicale was entirely different, though it too had been built in an isolated spot. It was much better preserved in its handsome, rounded construction, with a single turret and a terrace on the roof, and a row of half-bricked up windows around the whole rotunda. In its massiveness it resembled a fortified stronghold; and it could have led one to ask why no one had thought of restoring it as a historical site or as a place to live. Had they been afraid of the shadow of what had happened here in the sixteenth century? From the entry way and the courtyard there was a broad view of the valley, which turned behind the spur of a hill extending forward, and melted into the dark wall of the woods. Behind those woods there probably began the descent towards the sea at Tàranto.

When I turned round I noticed a slim column of smoke rising from a large concavity in the wall next to the gate (which had likely once been a place to leave horses before entering the courtyard of the castle). An old hobo was sitting by a small campfire and warming his hands as he heated water in a kettle. He was on his way from Taranto. The previous night he had slept in the barn at Pastorizia, with the permission of the owner of the property. The estate, he explained to me, lay between the curve of the valley and the woods. From where we were its buildings could not be seen.

I imagined the scene: Tall Cesare unfolds the roll of papers, after which he shouts and shouts; with a single thrust he brings the poor tutor to the ground, stabbing him in the heart with a dagger. Little Teresa, cowering in the concavity of the wall, shields her eyes with her hands . . . On the upper floor of the castle I went into the hallway and stood at a window; it had once been the window of a room (as could be seen from the half-rounded, irregular shape of the wall). Perhaps it was right here that it happened? What happened? I leaned against the rough wall and closed my eyes for a moment. As if in a hallucination I heard words whispered without a hint of anger or hatred, followed by the moan and rasp of a woman's voice. Then all went quiet. I opened my eyes; the castle was plunged in dead stillness, while from below there came the barely audible sounds of the hobo's song, occasionally interrupted by something between a cough and an old man's wheezing.

\* \* \*

AS CAN BE SEEN, I was well prepared for my reading of the manuscript found in the Silver Coffer. From one of the chronicles I knew even more: that the Silver Coffer was the favorite object of Teresa Demagno, who made it her secret hiding place; she entrusted to it her own poems and later also the poems of Don Miguel. Cesare Demagno, as he fled the castle of Panicale after committing two murders and raced to Pastorizia to carry out a third, was not so swept up in his attack of rage as to forget to take as a memento a little piece of his Italian past, which was probably over for good. He snatched up the Silver Coffer.

What, for the love of God, led me to postpone my reading of Abbot Peter's manuscript that evening; what evil spirit whispered to me to leave it till the following morning? Was I afraid that the glaring light of the electric lamp would damage the delicate sheets of parchment, which were over four hundred years old? Was I too excited by my discovery, and so (bearing in mind my heart problem) preferred to cool off a little overnight? God alone knows, if He happened to be reading my thoughts and feelings. It was enough (and as I write about this a year later, I feel the old pain returning) . . . it was enough that I covered the manuscript, which was spread out on the table, with a silk cloth; and when I took it off the next morning . . . What pen can describe what I saw? During the night, as a result of extended exposure to the air, the manuscript had quite literally disintegrated into tiny pieces—as if someone had systematically, sheet by sheet, torn it up into scraps. I sat at the table, thunderstruck. An impulse of rage at myself almost drove me to take those wretched, crumbling remnants of the precious manuscript, some of which had turned to dust, and throw them in the trash. Luckily, after a few moments of inner struggle, the voice of discretion prevailed. Equipped with miniature tweezers, I determined to preserve—or rather to attempt to preserve—at least the small flakes of the old abbot's story, which the daylight had shattered and broken; the story had managed to survive such a huge length of time in the dark, hermetically sealed hiding place of the Silver Coffer, only to fall apart in the clumsy hands of its late, accidental discoverer.

At the bottom of the first sheet a fragment had been saved with a fairly long though incomplete sentence: "T. was not only my sister, and I was not only her brother, we were . . ." This could be regarded as a key to the abbot's whole story, miraculously saved. And as a sensational confession, refuting the drift of all the chronicles of the time, irrespective of the various versions of events that they contained. For in all the versions the three murders committed by the young Baron Demagno served as an example of the lofty —certain later commentators on the chronicles added: blind, impassioned, morbid, insane—sense of family honor in those times: Without any proof, on the basis of an innocent exchange of letters, the brother's hand had not wavered as he punished "the sullying of the name" of his sister (who also met with death). The chroniclers themselves, though they mostly maintained objectivity in their writings, were not always able to control the traces of outrage that could be read between the lines.

I did not find another sentence like this (or one as long as it) in the powdered remains on my table. At most there were two or three words here and there, which allowed one to speculate, and stimulated the imagination, forming the separated spans of a ruined bridge across an abyss of silence. I spent the whole day over the remains of the abbot's story. In my efforts there was something of the solving of a brain-teaser. Eventually I created a certain picture for myself, full of gaps and question marks, which I shall present in rough here, though asking historians of the period to bear in mind that in this picture it is difficult (for me too) to separate the reporting—the reconstruction of scraps of the document—from the imagination of its finder, who was attempting to extract something from it before its ultimate disintegration.

Teresa and Cesare Demagno had become lovers in the castle of Panicale when their father's order had separated them from the rest of their family. But their sinful love had blossomed earlier, at the castle of Turrita, hidden naturally from those around them (there was a frequent juxtaposition of the words Turrita and *segreto*, and of Panicale and *passione*). Teresa must have soon come to her senses, for later there appeared in fairly close proximity to one another, the words *distacco, dolore, furore* (separation, pain, anger). In the next set of words that had survived there most often occurred *sospetto* and *sangue* (suspicion, blood). It was probably at this time that there began—not sufficiently noticed by Cesare—the exchange of poems between Teresa and the Spanish captain, through the mediation of the tutor who traveled regularly every week to Pastorizia. The last words of the abbot's story (before his signature) were shocking evidence of incurable madness or demoniacal possession. Let us remember that Cesare was writing those words as a sixty-year-old abbot of a Benedictine monastery, more than thirty years after he had strangled his sister to death. These words he wrote in Latin: *Teresa tota mea* (Teresa, all mine).

The version of the murderer-Baron of Apulia as "repentant sinner" in a Benedictine cowl turned out to have been merely a legend. Amongst the remains of the manuscript I did not find a single word or even half-word of a Christian penitent. It was the chroniclers who had regarded it as expedient, perhaps even edifying, to end their stories with the image of the abbot "devoted to the

Lord in body and soul, and having a heart changed through unceasing prayer." I am prepared to believe that he went through the motions of penitence, that he lay prostrate at the base of the altar, that he prayed for hours (for otherwise he could not have won the confidence of his superiors in the order), but would a true penitent end his tale with that terrible *Teresa tota mea*, emphasizing after all those years his "exclusive right" to his strangled sister? Would he not have asked God for forgiveness, instead of reaching out his hands defiled by crime to the wretched shade of Teresa, as if even that were his exclusive property? His hard heart did not flinch till his last breath. He lived eighteen more years. If he had known the blessing of regret, and of pure brotherly love, it would have been sufficient to burn the document concealed in the Silver Coffer.

Why, for whom, did he leave that document? Of the whole Demagno line only the childless Moro was still alive; he died seven years after Cesare. His elder brother Lorenzo had perished in a duel soon after Cesare's flight to France. The Baron had passed away in Paris, and a year later, in the castle at Turrita, his wife joined him in death. So then? There exists only one possibility. The abbot of the Benedictine monastery intended to mock the aura of saintliness almost that hung over the "penitent sinner." He counted on someone coming upon his story, the record from beyond the grave of a crime and an inextinguishable, sinful love; and also to hear from beyond the grave, a burst of satanic laughter in an austere monastic cell.

I gathered from the table the handful of pieces of parchment and poured them into the Silver Coffer. Now it was an urn filled with ashes.

\* \* \*

*December 31, 1991*

CHRISTMAS MARKED THE first anniversary of the death of the Silver Coffer. On the last day of the year I gave it a burial. Since in my journal I celebrated the anniversary of its death, in these same pages I must not omit to commemorate the anniversary of its burial.

In my journal . . . It may seem strange that I decided to include the tale of the Silver Coffer, which has the appearance of material for a short story, alongside such different matters—to introduce it into the dimension of the real that is characteristic, in one form or another, of any journal (which contains after all, or should by its nature, writing that is the opposite of invention). But to begin with, whether or not anyone believes it, the story of the Silver Coffer is not invented. Secondly, for a long time now I have taken every opportunity to speak out against the opposition of strangeness and naturalness (or verisimilitude). Whoever closely observes reality, whoever trains themselves to notice the apparent "strangeness" of many of its manifestations, knows that we allow ourselves to be limited and bound in our way of looking at "natural or plausible" events, seeking in them exclusively that which appeals to our sense of realistic level-headedness. There is no division into "strange" and "natural" things. There is—if one absolutely insists—a division into "common" and "uncommon" things, things that are "ordinary" and those that are "difficult to grasp." Is not the "naturalness" of the (allegedly fantastic) stories of Edgar Allen Poe proof of this? Does it not give pause for thought that Dostoyevsky was an avid reader of the "strange" tales of Hoffmann?

And so I turned the Silver Coffer into an urn for the ashes of the abbot's story. And I set about writing a short report in Italian which would, if only in an imperfect way, record my discovery for the Neapolitan historical review. I expected that the editor of the quarterly, a historian of sixteenth-century southern Italian history, who had written a commentary on one of the chronicles of the triple murder in this family of Apulian aristocrats, would be grateful and pleased to publish my text.

The next morning I simply froze when I saw the Silver Coffer in the alcove in my room. I did not believe my own eyes; a sudden rush of fear caused me to back towards the door, as if I were subconsciously seeking a way out. That the Silver Coffer was doomed to eventually become covered with a matt-black coating, I knew from the museum conservator. But it was *completely* black, and of a terrifying black never encountered in nature, intense, *ominous* (this is the only adjective that can convey my impression). I got a grip on myself and approached the alcove, though without touching the Coffer. The bas-relief of the Crucifixion on the side towards me had flattened and turned into something like a shapeless pustule. I overcame my feelings and turned the Coffer on its pedestal. All four sides had been afflicted with the same leprous malady. Each side seemed to resemble a human face; and each face had a different expression, if "expression" is the right word for an indescribably nightmarish grimace. The countenance of Christ that had graced the lid had disappeared completely. I lifted the Coffer off the wooden pedestal. The bottom, with the coat of arms of the Demagno family, was unmarred and immaculately silver.

On December twenty-eighth I made a decision, paying no heed to the sudden worsening of my already poor state of health. Yet what I meant to do required a few days' preparation. A driver I knew, who was familiar with the place I had selected, was not free till nine in the evening on New Year's Eve—he made the proviso that the trip should not take more than an hour, because with the mounting paroxysm of the New Year, by ten o'clock the streets of the city were already strewn with sharp fragments of iron and glass, and sometimes also unexploded rockets. The trip did not take longer than that. We drove to a sea cliff not far outside the city, an almost vertical drop, that in the last century and the beginning of the present one had often been chosen by suicides. I bore the once Silver, now black, Coffer, wrapped in a cloth; it was heavy in a way it had never been before. Once, that night in Ravello, I had held it in my arms like a beloved living being; now it was dead and resting on my lap, and I thrust it instinctively away from myself.

It was dark in that deserted spot; I climbed up a muddy path to the top of the cliff. Below, the deep sea was roaring and striking regularly and fiercely against the rocks. The noise of the sea drowned out the fall of the Coffer; I saw nothing, and heard only a brief and faint splash.

We drove out of the darkness onto a lighted street, and then on to the broad avenue that led via hairpin bends to the center of the city. The red sky was already crisscrossed with a net of fireworks; the rumble and snap of firecrackers intensified in the air. Two hours remained till the new year of 1992. What a bright, colorful and noisy setting it was for the funeral of the most valued of the many treasures that from all accounts had once belonged to the house of Demagno!

# UGOLONE DA TODI

## OBITUARY OF A PHILOSOPHER

1.     MY OBITUARY STORY will be brief. Brief, and dry as a bone: devoid of dramatic tensions, psychological probings, or lyrical embellishments. I will give each of its mini-chapters a number so that it will be a chapter, but it will also bring to the reader's mind the sections of an official document. My title makes it clear that this is a document of decease (though it will contain a great deal of biographical and bibliographical information about life and about transformation). A document of the decease from our world of the philosopher Ugo Ugolino from the city of Todi, also known as Ugolone da Todi, in obvious allusion to the thirteenth-century author of the *Laudi*, Jacopone da Todi.

At four thirty in the morning of the sixth of May of this year, I was present at his death. What is more, it was I who, taking the place of his wife Orsolina, numb with grief in the corner of the bedroom, closed the philosopher's wide-open eyes, took his hands where they hung from the bed, and crossed them upon his breast. Having performed this last earthly service for the dead man, I pushed the shutters back from the windows and pensively greeted the daybreak over the roofs of the Umbrian town.

2.     I WITNESSED Ugolone da Todi's death at close hand, but I had been an observer—sometimes close by and at other times from a distance, at times more sympathetic than others—of a considerable portion of his life and his philosophical work.

I met him for the first time in the penultimate year of the war, in Sorrento, where, after escaping from an armed unit that the Germans had formed in Rome, he was teaching Italian to Allied soldiers in convalescence. In a sense, then, I can say I was a student of his, although he didn't teach me the subject for which his writings were soon to make him famous. Before he was drafted into the army, he had managed to complete his doctorate in Bologna with a dissertation on Hegel. (And he was so knowledgeable about Hegel that after he defended, he was given the nickname *Dottor Begriffo*.) We were brought closer together, and even linked intimately from the beginning, by Orsolina. She came from a poor Sorrento family, and had studied philosophy in Naples. She was his friend out of love for philosophy, and mine out of love for the well-supplied Allied canteens in an Italy that was starving at the time. We constituted a relatively happy threesome in those less than happy times.

I was excluded from their frequent philosophical disputes, patiently awaiting my own appearance on the scene in our three-sided arrangement. I lacked an interest in philosophical matters, and even more so a solid background in philosophy. Above knowledge of philosophical systems I value knowledge about the lives of philosophers. Ugo—many years would have to pass before he acquired the flattering name of Ugolone da Todi—Ugo then, I sensed, had a most interesting and colorful life ahead of him.

3.   WHEN I MET HIM, he was already the author of a thick volume entitled *Prolegomena to Hegel's Philosophy*, an expanded version of his doctoral thesis that was published during the war. (I might add in parentheses that the sound of the word "prolegomena" sent him into a state of strange exaltation; prolegomena were to be encountered in many of the titles of his subsequent books.) He considered himself a proponent of *idealismo gentiliano*. Gentile, incidentally, supervised his doctoral debut in Italian philosophy. For some time in Sorrento, this allegiance manifested itself in the ostentatious sporting of a small black pointed beard, a token of loyalty to fascism. He shaved it off one day after a long discussion with Orsolina, declaring openly that he was embracing *idealismo crociano*. In the journal *Filosofare* founded in Naples, he published an essay titled *Perché non possiamo non dirci crociani*, which of course was a clever reference to Croce's own essay *Perché non possiamo non dirci cristiani*—"Why We Cannot Not Call Our-

selves Christians." His philosophical conversion was received as a noteworthy "advance payment," though no more than that, on the threshold of the post-fascist period of purges. It was only later that he took his next step (after Gentile's murder by partisans in Florence) with *Prolegomena to a "Philosophy" of Fascism*—an apparently lethal critique of the Sicilian philosopher—and won greater trust and, in 1947, an associate professorship at Perugia. At that time he married Orsolina and settled in Todi, in the house his parents had left him when they died. This was the house in which he himself was destined to die on May 6th, 1983—at the height of his (in the eyes of some) admittedly controversial fame—or in the depths of philosophical and real decadence (according to others).

But I am getting ahead of myself, when I ought to be capturing in a few words the image of the still-young philosopher as I remember him from Sorrento. His eyes, black as pitch, were so mobile that they made your head spin as you stared into them during a conversation. His avalanche-like eloquence was filled with erudite references, sudden changes of direction, sentences piled on top of one another like skyscrapers, thoughts spun from a never-ending skein. This last characteristic meant that Orsolina frequently had to help him extricate himself from entanglements of his own making, exhausting herself to within a hair's breadth of collapse. My job was to send the philosopher out on a walk and then to revive Orsolina efficaciously.

4.      AFTER THE WAR THE two of them took up residence in Rome. Times were still hard, and so I still saw Orsolina frequently. The philosopher was chained to his desk day and night, writing the Prolegomena that, it would soon transpire, were to be the turning-point in his university career.

In 1947, as mentioned, he was given the opportunity to teach in Perugia, and so also to marry Orsolina and to return to his native Todi. I moved to London, where from time to time I received letters from Orsolina. They arrived at increasingly longer intervals and were increasingly more laconic and reserved, not because of the physical separation so much as the growing spiritual distance between us. It was not at once that Ugo (accompanied, and aided, by his wife) scaled the greatest heights of human thought. First he disposed of idealism in his book *Critica dello Spirito non puro*, which was immediately perceived to show "great promise," and won the author a full professorship. After this, from the ruins of the "impure Spirit" he brought out his three-volume *Prolegomena to Marx's Philosophy*, which was universally acknowledged as a "scientific monument." Orsolina informed me that they were both invited to join, and then were received into, the Communist party. For a short time Ugo was mayor of Todi. And it was at that time he acquired the appellation of the *filosofo di Todi*, or more tenderly, and with a hint of historical reverence, *Ugolone da Todi*. He was offered a seat in the senate. He refused it contemptuously, but he did agree to write a concise article *In Praise of Stalin's Linguistic Theory* for the party's philosophical journal. It was 1953.

5. AT THE BEGINNING of that year two universities, in Moscow and Warsaw, awarded honorary doctorates to Professor Ugo Ugolino. I learned about this in Munich, where I now lived and worked—from the press and from postcards that Orsolina sent from both capitals. He returned in a blaze of glory to Perugia, where he was promptly elected rector of the university. This I read about only in the newspapers, since there had begun a two-year period of silence from Orsolina.

When we renewed our acquaintance, after I moved to Naples, Orsolina did her best to explain the reasons for her silence; unfortunately, her explanation was exceedingly vague and evasive. The Great Ugolone (as she now called him, with a glint of devotion in her eyes) had allegedly experienced a major crisis. On the one hand there had awoken within him a will to act, and even a "lust for power" that had been dormant since his youth and the time of his early years as a philosopher: He regretted having rejected the office of senator, and had ambitions to assume the chair of the President of the Academy. On the other hand, he was so enmeshed in his latest work, *Nietzche's Holy Philosophical War Against Christianity*, that even Orsolina, experienced as she was in the arts of rescue, couldn't disentangle him. Couldn't or wouldn't? O wife of the philosopher, wife of the potentate of human thought, who will pay you the homage you deserve; who will bow low before your quiet, devoted efforts as you accompanied greatness?! The still-tangled mess of writings was consumed by the flames. In the nick of time. The spirit of the age required other flights and conquests of thought.

It took him barely six months to write the massive volume *Open Marxism*, which appeared towards the end of 1955 and, according to experts, revolutionized the revolutionary thought of the philosopher of Trier. The philosopher of Todi had achieved a triumph. During the hurried writing of his book, he had grown a beard as long as the work he had created, and as long as the beard of his revolutionizing predecessor. He shaved it off in order to greet his election in November, 1956, amid storms of applause, as President of the Academy. Western universities presented him with honorary doctorates and invitations to give lectures; western Academies competed for his consent to be numbered amongst their foreign members.

6.      THE WORTHY ORSOLINA saw to it that the greatness of her Great Ugolone was not jeopardized. What was to be done? How was he to be protected from the ambuscades of fame? In her husband's name she gratefully confirmed receipt of his honors, and politely postponed the lecture invitations until an undetermined future date. Her husband needed a long rest, and above all a radical change that would be conducive to enriching and deepening his philosophical meditations. It was decided that they would travel to the Far East for six months, including a three-month stay in India on the way.

Their journey lengthened to a whole year. After they flew back to Italy I spent an evening with Orsolina in Rome. She had managed to leave the sick philosopher in Todi under the requisite care, so she could make a quick trip to the capital to conduct several urgent pieces of business. She didn't conceal the fact that he was ill, though she strove to downplay the matter. During our meeting she seemed absent, anxious about something, despite the fact that she was continually putting a good face on it. She found it difficult to conceal her haste. She spoke of "superficial nervous symptoms" and of a "temporary depression." However, her husband had returned from his travels with a suitcase full of notes, and she trusted in the therapeutic powers of work.

The work took him four years; its fruit was the two-volume

*Prolegomena to Buddhist Philosophy.* Four years, during which Orsolina was once again silent; in response to my letter, she asked
me to "have respect for philosophical seclusion." The new *Prolegomena*, which for me was virtually unreadable, made little impact
in the academic world. The most guarded reviews spoke of the
philosopher's "well-deserved exotic vacation," and the harsher ones
of "a rather worrying interlude, which one hopes will not last excessively long." Ugolone resigned as President of the Academy; he
took another year's leave of absence from his university in Perugia;
and from the pile of old offers to lecture abroad, dug out an invitation to Berkeley—or rather, Orsolina dug it out for him.

7.     YET THE TRIP NEVER came about. The nervous symptoms returned, this time, evidently, more seriously, since the news
reached the media. There also subsequently appeared in the papers
a reassuring interview with Orsolina: Her husband was already
fully recovered, but for the moment he preferred not to leave Todi;
his admirers around the whole world would soon find out why; oh
Lord, nothing could be kept secret from the press, so yes, Ugolone
had begun a new book.

The word "soon" unfortunately was spoken rashly, to say the
least. Years went by and the philosopher of Todi was almost forgotten; while the book continued to be *in statu nascendi*—a "work in
progress." It did not appear till 1972. In terms of size it was relatively modest (in comparison with the weighty tomes that Ugolone
was fond of producing): three hundred pages in all, plus fifty pages
of footnotes in small print. It was titled *Critica della regione non
pura*. It instantly became a sensation, with a hint of scandal even.
And—today I can admit this openly—it was the only one of
Ugolone's books that I was able to get through, reading rather attentively and in places feeling curiously moved.

I was, in all probability, moved by the less than philosophical
passion with which Ugolone attacked "impure reason"—enmired
in materialism and empiricism, and leading us into the wilderness
of anthropocentric pride. There existed for him another reason,
unfeignedly pure, that arced like a rainbow between us and God.
"Religion in the Bounds of Pure Reason": It was not without cause
that the title of his final chapter was borrowed from Kant; just as

the title of the book as a whole referred to Kant (although at many points in the text the philosopher of Todi underscored his own originality and the independence of his thought from that of the philosopher of Königsberg).

*Si è venduto corpo e anima alla Chiesa*—"He's sold himself body and soul to the Church": This was the verdict, dominating over weak dissent, of Ugolone's former admirers and students, who only now realized that the *Prolegomena to Buddhist Philosophy* was far from an "exotic vacation" or an exploratory "interlude," but rather an organic stage in the development of the philosopher's thought. The definitive seal was stamped in hot wax by the *Osservatore Romano*, which published a two-page polemical article about the book entitled *Una mente elevatissima* (*A Most Sublime Mind*), illustrated with a photograph of Ugolone and Orsolina in the garden of his family house, a picture of Todi cathedral, and a drawing of the tomb of Jacopone in the Church of San Fortunato in Todi.

8.      1975 BROUGHT A GREATER, a much greater sensation. How it had been made possible is hard for me, as an uninitiated person, to say; suffice it to report that with the personal consent of the Holy Father—possibly on the basis of some kind of dispensation releasing the philosopher of Todi from his married state (his marriage with Orsolina had in fact only been a civil one)—he entered the Franciscan monastery in nearby Assisi. Orsolina became, practically speaking, the widow of *Fra* or *Frate* Ugolone, who was still alive, yet living in voluntary seclusion *intra muros*.

In the first year of her "widowhood" I saw her very frequently, as she spent long periods in Sorrento with her unmarried sister, who owned a souvenir stand on the Piazza Torquato Tasso. She had become uncommunicative, testy—and extremely pious, as if by attending early masses and participating in the local Rosary brotherhood, she was trying to stay at the side of her husband after his miraculous transformation into a friar. I finally understood that seeing me was disagreeable to her, because of her memories of the past; when this became clear to me, I removed myself discreetly into the shadows, emerging from them at Orsolina's urgent summons two days before Ugolone's death.

But up until that point, following his fate meant simply follow-

ing his work. The monastery had regarded it as an honor to take in
such a famous and contrite sinner, and so every effort was made to
allow him to continue his work. Whatever Fra Ugolone could not
find in the monastery library was brought, with the Prior's intervention, from other libraries. Initially, he dropped his philosophical studies and meditations in favor of historical research. He wrote
a book about the monk and hermit Pietro, or Pier, of Morrone
near Sulmone, who had been elected Pope in the thirteenth century. Evil tongues sought in it an encoded expression of the author's own unbridled ambitions. His few defenders recalled that
Celestine V had stepped down from the Papal throne with his *gran
rifiuto* (great refusal) after a six-month reign, finishing in the dungeons on the order of his successor, Boniface VIII. In any case
some distant echoes of this discussion must have reached the ears
of Fra Ugolone, because he fell silent for a long time. All of a sudden, in 1980, two books by him appeared simultaneously: one
about St. Francis of Assisi, and the other about Jacopone da Todi.
They were regarded as "spiritual exercises bordering on pure mys-
ticism." A year later Fra Ugolone came down with a serious illness
which the doctors could not fathom, and which was resistant to
treatment or drugs. Thanks once again to the personal intervention of the Holy Father, he was released from his monastic vows
and returned to Orsolina.

9.      THE ILLNESS WAS indeed mysterious. The only doctor
bold enough to suggest a diagnosis (with a question mark) spoke of
something halfway between catatonia and catalepsy. One way or
another, the medical profession was helpless as its practitioners
leaned over Ugolone's bed of pain: His limbs would turn stiff,
sometimes violently, sometimes less so; he had difficulty swallowing food, even in liquid form, due to contractions of the throat;
there occurred a dulling of all his senses close to atrophy; he sank
into silence; and certain of his reactions indicated that his memory
had been significantly impaired.

And yet (as Orsolina told me) immediately after he was brought
home from Assisi there had been a pronounced, though unfortunately short-lived, improvement in his condition. Above all he had
recovered his speech. He had spoken constantly—with difficulty it

was true—of one thing: His intention of writing a philosophical autobiography, combined with a philosophical treatise. For the last work of his life he came up with the title of *Il Paragone*. Where did this title come from? He had been struck by two of Jacopone's *Laudi*, both of which began identically. The first was written after the election of Celestine V and began thus: *Che farai, Pier dal Morrone? Sei venuto al paragone.* The second was composed after the author of the *Laudi* had been imprisoned in a monastery cell on the orders of Boniface VIII and began so: *Che farai, Fra Jacopone? Sei venuto al paragone.* On the title page of his magnum opus Ugolone intended to place the inscription: *Che farai, Gran Ugolone? Sei venuto al paragone.* "What will you do, Great Ugolone? You have come before the . . ." The word *paragone* meant for him not just "baptism of fire" but also Judgment: upon himself, the world, God. He dreamed of a new definitive philosophical system: "transcendental paragonism."

How short-lived and illusory was that improvement! The sickness took him once again in its inscrutable possession, adding new symptoms to those already mentioned. He was afraid of the darkness. He suffered from insomnia. From time to time he would utter isolated words in a throaty voice and repeat them over and again, as if the sound of the words had become detached from their meaning. He so loathed being alone that Orsolina had to hold his stiffened hand day and night, while every time she went away from him, he responded with an inarticulate weeping and moaning. Brave, good, faithful Orsolina! Her tribulations dragged on for almost two years. When, summoned by a cable, I appeared in Todi on the evening of May 4th, she told me all about those two years, crying profusely, yet relieved—and not letting go of the hand of her husband, who gave no indication that he heard or understood anything whatsoever of her story.

The end came before dawn on May the sixth. I pulled Orsolina away from the dying man and sat her in an armchair in the corner of the bedroom. Ugolone was wheezing softly. I moved my face close to his. He gasped out a barely audible word, and gave up his insatiable spirit. Insatiable? I realized what that word had been, later, as I stared musingly over the rooftops of the Umbrian town: *Basta!*

After the funeral I drove Orsolina to her sister's in Sorrento. She died there, in somewhat obscure circumstances, on May 14th. Her death emboldened me to write this obituary of the philosopher of Todi.

10. POSTSCRIPT TO THE *Philosopher's Obituary.* Over his grave, my thoughts turn to the deaths of other philosophers. I am tempted by a comparison with Nietzsche's, but in Ugolone the flashes of madness were too scant and too transitory (concealed perhaps by Orsolina). At a pinch, though, I could imagine him as the author of a new *Antichrist,* although it was only *in nuce* that there existed the project of *Il Paragone,* a book in which he was preparing amongst other things to pass judgment on God; while (as I mentioned) the unfinished work on "Nietzsche's Holy War Against Christianity" had been destroyed by fire. I was utterly unable, on the other hand, to imagine the philosopher of Todi, even in his Franciscan habit, embracing and kissing a donkey on the streets of Assisi.

Comparisons with the death of Kant seem to me more vivid, if slighter. The Polish writer Bolesław Miciński says in his *Portrait of Kant:* "He was alarmed by the trees growing outside his window, and, tormented by nightmares, he wrote a note: Avoid bad dreams. Avoid bad dreams—this is like saying to a poplar tree: Wither, or to a cloud: Clear up. One would have to be completely devoid of psychological feeling not to perceive in this memorandum to oneself a lust for the power that would regulate the revolutions of the heavenly spheres and determine the flight of swallows."

Miciński's remarks concern the period preceding the final days of the philosopher of Königsberg; I am struck by that "lust for power," which I also had sensed in the philosopher of Todi.

Kant's dying was described by Thomas De Quincey in *The Last Days of Immanuel Kant,* based on the accounts of eyewitnesses— principally the friend most devoted to the philosopher, who had the Polish name of Wasiański.

In the last days of his life Kant lost his sense of time, taking fifteen minutes for a period of several hours. He was afraid of the darkness; and he, who previously had been prevented from falling asleep by the faintest sounds, and the narrowest cracks in the shutters after they were closed for the night, now had a lighted lamp in his bedroom, and had an upright clock brought in so the constant ticking would accompany him in his sleeplessness. He was unable to write his own signature: As De Quincey, after Wasiański, explains, this was not because of worsening eyesight, but from a profound disturbance of his memory, which caused him to forget which letters made up his name; then, when the letters were repeated to him, he was unable to recall their shape.

"He sat with sightless eyes, lost in himself, and manifesting no sense of our presence, so that we had the feeling of some mighty phantom from some forgotten century being seated amongst us."

Lastly, he had problems with swallowing. On the day of his death Wasiański placed a spoon against his tightly compressed lips. Kant pushed it away and whispered: "It is enough!" Wasiański recounts: "It is enough! *Sufficit!* Mighty and symbolic words!" De Quincey adds in a note: "The cup of life, the cup of suffering, is drained. For those who watch, as did the Greek and the Roman, the deep meanings that oftentimes hide themselves (without design and without consciousness on the part of the utterer) in trivial phrases, this final utterance would have seemed intensely symbolic."

SUFFICIT!
BASTA!


*May 20, 1983*

# THE EXORCIST'S BRIEF
# CONFESSION

*"Inner experiences, even the simplest ones, are either
so holy that nature itself jealously mounts guard for
them, or they are so abject that they are not worth
revealing to others." Holy or abject, they possess their
own form on the borderline between speech and silence;
it is a kind of disordered, fitful confession whispered in
one's thoughts.*

—Lev Shestov

I AM OLD, VERY OLD; in January of the coming year, 1989, I shall
(God willing) turn eighty-four. My memory sometimes fails me
and my thoughts are often confused; my vision and hearing are
growing worse; and reading tires me so quickly that I am wont to
fall asleep over a book or a newspaper. The older I become, the less
mobile I am and the more attached to my dark and damp little den
on the ground floor of a building by the Piazza San Domenico. For
the last year, a woman who lives on the second floor has been paid
to bring me a single hot meal a day, at one in the afternoon; she
prefers not to call me to her table as she used to. Coffee in the
morning and tea in the evening I make myself; I need nothing
more, and besides, I could afford nothing more on my modest in-
valid's pension.

I leave home rarely and reluctantly, like a fugitive from his hiding place. When I do happen to go out on a fine day, I move along
the street at a snail's pace, brushing against the walls of houses,
with the walking stick that a lame man needs to keep his balance

and to drive away pesky children. I, who spent almost my whole life in Naples since I was a young boy, who knows its every stone, am afraid of it in my old age; I shake with fear in the throng on the street, and feel my weak heart thumping in panic. Because I do not see or hear well? No, no, the truth should be told. I am afraid that some bad person will recognize me and shout: *Un prete spretato!* A defrocked priest! Because it is enough that someone good greets me with a friendly: *Caro Padre Vito!* (Dear Father Vito!) out of respect for my former position as clergyman (though former only in a certain sense, since the sacrament of priesthood is irreversible) for me to calm down somewhat. But for a short time, for a short time only. So have I perhaps grown averse to people? Perhaps I have observed them and listened to them enough in my life, and now I love my den precisely because it ensures my solitude? Yes, yes, nothing except my den with the little shrine in the corner by the window, nothing except God and his old and faithful, though spurned, servant. Is it right to turn away like this from the world and from people? Whoever like me has been an exorcist for five years, has a right to his solitude, even though many may well regard it as an escape. The merciful Lord looks into my heart. And he sees, I believe that he sees.

I have come to write this confession for the following reason: May is almost over; from the window of my den the only tree I can see is covered with leaves and blossom, yet it was not until today that I resolved to take my first spring walk. The course of my infrequent morning trips is always the same: from the Piazza San Domenico to the Piazza Gesù, and before my return home a rest at the majolica cloister of Santa Chiara. I sat there on a vacant bench in the shade (the sun is harmful to me), and I may have nodded off; because the moment I opened my eyes, at the other end of the bench I saw . . . Great heavens! Doctor Pontormo, the federal prosecutor in Turin at the time of the tragedy in Brumiera, my accuser in that terrible trial! I knew him at once; while he, after so many years—almost forty—either did not recognize me hunched and dozing there, or had not even noticed me, for he was facing away from me and engrossed in conversation with his companion. I caught some scraps of their discussion: They were speaking of the "satanic Turin" that had recently been described in the papers;

about the "city in the hands of the Devil," with its spate of murders, and growing number of "narco-satanic rites." Doctor Pontormo's companion mentioned the recent increase in the number of diocesan exorcists in Turin. Doctor Pontormo gave a sarcastic laugh, but I did not catch his reply; I only heard my name mentioned in it.

I stood up from the bench in a state of agitation, almost trembling; I barely managed to hobble home. I threw myself on my bed and lay there without moving till lunchtime. Is it not time now, on the threshold of death, to emerge from silence? I never made confession concerning the end of my career as an exorcist, skirting round it in the confessional. May that which God, the one God, read in my heart then and continues to read, be finally recorded on paper.

* * *

FOR MANY YEARS I have been in the habit of reading a few pages of St. Augustine aloud to myself in the evening. In this way I have read the *Confessions* I do not know how many times; so many that, were it not for my weakening memory, I might well be able to recite it whole or in parts without looking at the page. Now that I am to begin my own confession, I invoke two passages to which I am particularly attached: "Man is himself a great deep. Thou dost number his very hairs, O Lord, and they do not fall to the ground without thee, and yet the hairs of his head are more readily numbered than are his affections and the movements of his heart." And: "How did it come to be that I had no inducement to evil but evil itself. It was foul, and I loved it. I loved my own undoing. I loved my error—not that for which I erred but the error itself."

I invoke these passages to aid me, though they only partially apply to me—I myself could not say to what degree. St. Augustine received a miraculous gift from God: that of touching in people even those wounds which they do not possess, yet they feel with their entire being that they could possess them. A person is a great deep, however unable to see that deep within. People can love Evil, their undoing and their ruin, even though they regard as hatred that sinful love which the abyss conceals.

It is not easy for me to speak of my childhood and adolescence, yet how on earth can I say nothing at all if I am setting about a confession? I grew up in the midst of Evil and fear. My father was a peasant, the owner of a modest cottage and two hectares of land in the Apulian village of Collemanno. A drunk and a brute, he beat my mother, my sister, three years my junior, and me, for the slightest reason. We lived in perpetual fear. St. Augustine says: "Either Evil is that of which we are afraid, or Evil is the fact that we are afraid." The Evil in our house was twofold; but it had one face, inebriated and enraged, I do not hesitate to say diabolic: the face of my father. I was approaching the age of fifteen when before our eyes, my mother's and mine, he raped his twelve-year-old daughter. We watched without moving, paralyzed by fear—I with my eyes wide open, my mother sobbing quietly and covering her face with her hands. From that moment on he did the same frequently, ignoring the girl's cries, laments, and pleas; they did nothing but fan the rage of a possessed man. One day I threw myself upon him with an iron poker. He wrenched it from my hand with a laugh (the same laugh he gave every time he forced himself on my sister); then he laid about me with the poker, furious, roaring, blindly lashing out. One of the neighbors ran to the police station. My father was locked up; I was taken to the hospital with several broken ribs and a fractured left leg. I spent six months in the hospital. My mother never once visited me there. I found out later that my father had hanged himself in his prison cell, and that my mother had quickly sold our farm and left with my sister for distant relatives in Argentina. Before her departure she had left part of the money from the sale with the priest in Collemanno, who used this dowry to send me to the Jesuit college in Naples, as far as possible from my native village. The good Don Vincenzo died soon after. My mother and sister had erased me from their lives; they never contacted me, as if they wished to kill the past and forever drive away the shadow of the Evil that bound us together. I was left alone in the world, an orphan and a cripple, lame in his left leg.

I am too old and weak, my head is too confused, and my hand trembles too much as I write, to draw my confession out unnecessarily or to litter it with details. It must be short. I have to make it in time.

I graduated from the college and entered a seminary; in 1935 I was ordained as a priest and assigned to a parish in upper Naples. At the same time I taught Latin and Greek in the college where I had once been a student.

It seemed to begin with, in the college and the first years of the seminary, that I was becoming spiritually healed, that the time filled with study and prayer was assuaging the pain in my heart, which was open to receive God trustingly. Yet in the last year of the seminary there came a change so sudden that I found myself at a crossroads, thinking in panic about my impending priesthood. My memories stirred in me. From nothingness almost, my father's face came back to me and haunted me day and night; in the nighttime especially, I awoke terrified from dreams of him, feeling stifled and with an impulse to flee. That face, so terribly caustic and insolent in its expression, combining cruelty and mockery, distorted with a grimace of victorious Evil, gradually became for me the countenance of the Devil. I lived as its prey, seeing my own powerlessness, which prayer no longer helped. At times, in my torment I believed myself to be infected by my father's possession. Fortunately God took mercy on my benighted soul. I was suddenly overcome by a calm that was oddly sweet and mild, rather like the relief afforded by the rapid fall of a fever after sickness, when a blessed coolness flows rapidly into the exhausted, burning body. How joyfully, with what bright and pure faith I greeted the day of my ordination!

But from that crisis on the threshold of my priesthood something remained: I was drawn to the study of exorcisms. I avidly read both the church's pronouncements and its handbooks for exorcists, and lay books on the history of exorcisms in Italy and other European countries. Was I preparing for future service in the struggle against the Prince of Darkness; or subconsciously performing private exorcisms on myself?

Word of my studies and readings evidently reached higher up, because soon after the war I was sent to Turin, where one of the three diocesan exorcists had died, and a second had asked to be relieved of his duties and had entered a monastery. At that time I was forty years old. We were all emerging from the war, which some had called a time of mass possession.

\* \* \*

IMMEDIATELY UPON MY arrival in Turin I met the one remaining exorcist there. He was unfriendly and distrustful towards me; I suspect that in this newcomer from the South he sensed someone with a propensity for pagan "magic" disguised as the work of the church. I also paid a visit to the remote monastery outside the city that had received the exorcist who had retired.

He had a mild, slender face, with two sorrowful eyes, thick, snow-white hair, and a bitter smile playing about the corners of the mouth. Father Ulderico himself had asked to be removed from his position as exorcist, despite the fact that he was not yet either old or infirm. Why? Was there a shortage of people possessed by the Devil? Quite the opposite: Their number had increased to such an extent that he was no longer able to keep up with his responsibilities. Exorcisms are of two kinds, "ordinary" and "formal." The ordinary ones are not such a problem; all that is needed is holy water and a prayer written by Leo XIII invoking the Archangel Michael. The formal ones are long, laborious, and often tense and dramatic; they require patience and perseverance. Amongst the possessed there are many sufferers from epilepsy, and nervous illness such as hysteria; but by labeling them this way one cannot drive the Devil out of them. Amid the satanic harvest of unrest he had been concerned by the growing number of children, innocent children, who had been recently included . . . No, God forbid, his faith had not wavered within him, but something new had appeared that he had never sensed before. At one time—it was not to be denied—he had been afraid of suddenly seeing the terrible face of his opponent, as he felt his hot breath during exorcisms. Yet the fear was always accompanied by renewed courage, the fine courage of his calling. Now, though, an icy chill reached to the marrow of his bones. He had definitely lost the zealous gift of the exorcist—of this he was certain. This was why he preferred to hide himself away in a monastic cell.

I was dispirited by my meeting with Father Ulderico. I was tormented by the thought that my own experiences might sully the work I was to be doing in Turin; I doubted myself—armed, it was true, with priestly learning, yet marked somehow with the stamp of the Devil. I paused for a moment at the gate to my apartment by the church of San Gregorio, and, ignoring the torrential rain, I stared for a long time into a large puddle in which gusts of wind, passing mist, and the reflections of street lights now delineated, now erased a sinister face which (I believed) I had forgotten. But it did not force its way into my dreams either that night or the following ones. A hair's breadth from new doubts and irresolution, I concluded that this was a good sign. Heaven was watching over me; I prayed that it would not abandon me, but would continue to extend its protection over me.

It sometimes happens in Naples that the city is beset by a June hotter than the height of summer. I find it difficult to bear such a sudden transition. I gasp instead of breathing, my head is heavy, the old pain in my left leg makes itself felt, and weakness keeps me in bed during the day. Perhaps I should set aside my confession for a while . . .

\* \* \*

IN OPPOSITION TO Father Ulderico, I was guided by the principle that nervous or mental disorders are not forms of possession. In the face even of illnesses such as epilepsy—that were once classic for exorcists (and still occur today)—we are helpless, and should confess our helplessness, refusing to perform exorcisms despite pleas and entreaties. I, following the lead of St. Augustine, sought Evil in those enchanted by it, since according to me true possession is precisely true love of Evil. But how is that love to be properly recognized and then to be overcome? I own freely that with the passage of time, the exorcisms I performed gradually acquired the quality of a soulless routine, and I lost faith in their effectiveness. Whether they were ordinary or formal, they did not reach to the source of that accursed and poisoned love where it lies hidden deep in the human heart. And so, as I dutifully took the beaten path of the exorcist, I sought other, more personal ways; for example, I visited the possessed in their homes, which could not have met with the approval of my superiors. In the fifth year of my stay in Turin I counted on the possibility of being quickly sent back to Naples.

* * *

I REMEMBER THAT September morning in 1950. The woman who came to see me immediately struck me by her resemblance to my mother. She was short, stooped, frail, worn down, and timid; her face was lined with premature wrinkles, and her hair was thinning. Though probably my age, she looked elderly. She further resembled my mother in her movements: She frequently hid her face in her hands, her eyes were constantly cast down, and she kept shifting to the edge of her seat as if she were forever on the verge of standing and leaving. In her handsome, tear-filled eyes there was panic, though this word does not fully convey their expression of someone pursued and encircled on all sides. Every time she had to look at me, she crossed herself furtively with a small gesture over her breast. That was what my mother used to do whenever she could not avoid looking at my father.

She had come to see me about her daughter Rita. When she began to tell me about her, I turned numb as her disordered sentences reached my consciousness, and a lump grew in my constricted throat; at several times, to her consternation, I rose to my feet. Not only did she remind me of my mother, but her home in the Piedmont village of Brumiera, at the entry to the Susa valley, was almost a replica of our cottage in the Apulian village of Collemanno. "God is putting me to the test," I said to myself. "He wants everything to come back that, with his aid, I have tried to bury forever."

In Brumiera they owned a small grocery store. Her husband had been drafted into the army in 1942 and had not returned from the war; his name appeared on the list of those missing in action. When he went to war, Rita had been fourteen. Seven months later she had given birth to a child, a malformed boy with a huge head who was congenitally deaf and dumb, and capable only of a vegetative, supine life. "He was her son and her brother," she whispered, and bent towards the ground with her entire body as if she wished it would swallow her up. From this point in her story she no longer used her daughter's name, calling her instead either *la indiavolata*, or *la indemoniata*, or *la posseduta dal Male*. "I'm living in hell, I'm living in hell," she kept repeating. The girl had already tried twice to set their house on fire. She would say nothing to her mother for days on end, and was afraid to appear before other people; at times her speech was replaced by such heart-rending cries that the neighbors would come running. And a laugh not of this world, a laugh that her mother had never before heard. Who knew if her lengthy periods of apathy were not even worse: At such times one could do anything with her, since she was not there, alongside her mother and child, but in a sleep from which no one could have woken her. "What's to be done, what's to be done?" I had to jump up when she threw herself at my feet and began kissing my hands. The parish priest in Brumiera had sent her to me with a letter of recommendation: *Reverendo Padre, fate l'esorcismo a questa nostra povera Rita, salvate la sua anima cristiana*—"Reverend father, perform an exorcism on this poor Rita of ours and save her Christian soul."

The next day they both appeared. Rita did indeed allow her mother to lead her by the hand like a passive somnambulist. She was taller than her mother, well-proportioned, carelessly dressed but good-looking, with a shock of tousled black hair; in her behavior she was docile and utterly absent. She did not say a single word to me, and did not even shake my hand when she met me. She merely fixed me momentarily with an evil, angry glance, after which she sank back into her apathetic indifference. She was probably unaware of who she had allowed herself to be taken to and why; at least that was the impression she gave. As I looked at the two women, I realized that thoughts of my mother and my sister had come over me too much for me to be capable of performing exorcisms, even of the half-hearted and routinized kind I had grown used to of late. I had gooseflesh, and my hands trembled.

But I got the better of myself. I said litanies over Rita as she knelt, interspersing them with curses addressed to the Evil One; I was thoroughly unsure whether I was following the prescribed order. The only thing I was certain of was my attention, fixed intently upon the blessed host I held in my raised hands. We were approaching the end of the ceremony when she tipped back her head and knocked the host from my grip with a powerful swipe of her hand; her angry, evil look met my gaze, and she tore herself from her apathy with a laugh. That laugh, dear God, that laugh . . . It was like the laugh of my father, coming to me from the depths of a well.

In October the priest in Brumiera informed me that Rita's young son had died. The somewhat unclear circumstances of the child's death led the judicial authorities in Susa to commit Rita, at her mother's request, to an institution in Vercelli for patients with nervous disorders.

\* \* \*

THE INSTITUTION WAS run by nuns, and so I was able without much difficulty to obtain permission to enter its grounds. What really led me to pay my first visit, and several subsequent ones that November, cannot after so many years be the subject of overly detailed inquiries. This much I know for sure: that I was acting under the influence of an irresistible impulse, and that my need to check on the possessed woman between the performance of successive exorcisms was not the most important thing. I did not even believe that in Rita's case there would be any further exorcisms; nor did I want there to be. Amongst all of the many cases in my practice as an exorcist, hers was unique. With Rita, I felt at a loss. Her loathsome, sacrilegious gesture had confirmed her possession, more: According to the handbooks, it constituted crowning proof of it; but at the same time it showed her to me in a new light. Up till now, in possession I had seen a diabolic incitement to a love of Evil; now I beheld (or so it seemed to me) a woman possessed in whom there was as much hate for Evil as love of it; who in turn convulsively embraced Evil and desperately rejected it. "Man is himself a great deep, O Lord!"

Sister Emilia, who was responsible for looking after Rita in accordance with the doctor's instructions, told me about her first days in the institution. She had incessant attacks of fury; she would throw herself upon other people, spit out words (this was Sister Emilia's expression) that were either obscenities or were incomprehensible to anyone there; she would rip to shreds the dresses she wore and scratch her own body till it bled. Injections of sedatives were of little avail, and so at times they had to strap her to her bed. After days of frenzy (continued Sister Emilia), unexpectedly, as if they had been cut off or whisked away by some hand, there followed days of apathy. She would become a child of over twenty, melancholy, unrelenting in her speechlessness, deaf to the world about her; she was obedient and utterly dependent on those who were taking care of her. She was capable of lying motionless in her bed for hours, or of standing, also without moving, beneath a tree in the park or by the wall of the institute.

My visits fell during a period of apathy. That November was mild, rainless and windless, and a cold sun shone. With the nuns' permission I would take Rita for walks in the park. Did she recognize me as her exorcist? I was not sure of this, for her torpor, her removal from reality, truly had the character of a trance. She was not aware of the people around her and had no sense of place or time. And what about me? I must admit it openly: I waited longingly for every new meeting with her. It was a little as if I had subconsciously come to believe that those walks, during which she listened to me in silence, were the real exorcisms, more effective than the ceremonial ones. Sometimes—very rarely it must be said—she would look sideways at me and give a good-hearted, sweet smile. At such times my heart was warmed with joy; perhaps I was close to victory over my opponent, who was formidable yet whose grip on her was weakening.

Toward the end of November, immediately upon my arrival in Vercelli I learned from the doctor at the institution that at Rita's request he had decided to send her home soon and had already asked her mother to come for her. "To a large extent this is thanks to you, Father," he added.

Our last walk took us to a small pond at the far end of the park. We sat by its bank on the trunk of a felled tree. Rita stared for a long time at the dark surface of the water, notched with the curled-up leaves of water lilies, and suddenly . . . Suddenly there spoke a person who had been *freed*, who had regained her speech, and along with it scraps of distant memories. She recalled childhood outings with her father to the hillside in the Susa valley, to a stream where she would play, immersing her hands and feet. "They were silver, so pure and silver. *Oh, Padre mio*." I did not know whether this exclamation was addressed to me, or whether she was summoning her father from her memory. I should have been warned by a special intonation of her voice in that cry; but in my elation, I did not assign it any particular significance. What induced me, as our conversation continued, to mention in passing the name of her little son? She grew intent, frowned, and looked challengingly into

my eyes: *È morto, poveretto. Sia ringraziato il Signore del Cielo* . . .
*o dell'Inferno*. Ominous words, interrupted in the middle by a quiet
giggle: For the death of her poor little son, she thanked the Lord of
Heaven . . . or of Hell. Just how ominous these words were, I
was soon to learn.

\* \* \*

AND THUS I HAVE come to the tragic crux of my confession. I
have turned this incident over a thousand times in my mind and
have observed it from every side, only to come to the conclusion
every time that in it, something has been passed over, removed to
the shadows, out of fear of the *whole* truth. I know the whole truth;
aside from me, only God knows it; He also knows that I know, and
that I am avoiding it or circling round it, with closed eyes and mute
lips. Yet if death, already creeping in on tiptoe, thrusts a pen into
my hand and compels me to make a dying confession, could I now
wriggle out of its strict injunction, or ignore a signal sent to me by
God? But if I am at last to unclose my eyes and open my mouth, all
I have turned over and examined a thousand times in my thoughts
becomes futile prevarication. The only important thing is that
which I have passed over and thrust into the shadows a thousand
times. The fewer words, the more truth there will be.

On December 20th I paid an unannounced visit to Brumiera.
Christmas was approaching so the idea seemed natural and pious.
Behind it was concealed the beating of my heart as, chilled by my
journey and dusted with snow, I crossed the threshold of the little
country store. Rita's mother greeted me. She scurried out from behind the counter, moved her customers aside, bowed low before
me and called me "our benefactor." This was enough for me to
breathe a sigh of relief. I was led through the small, narrow door
behind the counter into the apartment; Rita's room was at the end
of the hallway. Rita too smiled when she saw me, with that good,
sweet smile, while my heart began to pound once again. We were
left alone as her mother returned to the store.

Rita was busy decorating her room for Christmas; cutouts of
colored paper and silver foil were laid out on her large iron bed. On
the table she had put a glass of wine for me. We spoke freely, con-

tinually changing subjects. "She's freed," I thanked God in my heart, "freed." I was so moved by her story about how at the age of ten she had been taken by her father to Sordevolo to the passion play (modeled on Oberammergau's) that, remembering my priestly calling, I delivered a lesson on Christ's Passion, pacing around the table in my excitement. She listened with bowed head, leaning against the bed frame. All of a sudden she raised her head, ran up to me, threw her hands around my neck and pressed her whole body against mine. Yes, let these words be uttered: I had never felt so happy in my life. I stroked her hair, I may even have brushed my lips against her tear-soaked face. But then I was jolted—how inadequate that word is!—from my blessed feeling by her laugh: It was *that* laugh, arising from the depths, terrible, the laugh of my father. I was stunned. I thrust her away from me with all my strength. What happened next I do not remember, as God is my witness. I came to on my knees amid the shouts of men and the lamentations of women; some people were lifting me up with an iron grip, and someone was shaking me and showering abuse upon me. Rita lay bloodied upon the bed, as two women revived her, dabbing her forehead with cloths soaked in a pail of water, while her mother kissed her feet as they dangled from the bed. Apparently, when I pushed her away with all my might, she fell on the bed and knocked her head against the iron rail. Apparently, I also beat her as she lay there. This I will never believe. But God was witness to what happened: He also knows as well as I do the truth I have been running away from for forty years, the truth that for forty years I have been afraid of, that is too onerous and too terrible to be borne even by a deathbed confession. As I was led to the carabinieri's car with an escort on both sides, my heart was still filled to the brim with the same feeling of happiness that had come over me when I held Rita in my arms. The merciful Lord sees into my sinful heart, which had come to love what? That towards which it fell, or the fall itself?

\* \* \*

THE TRIAL TOOK place in February 1951. I declined to make a statement in the pre-trial inquiry, and I said nothing during the trial itself. I tried above all not to listen, though it was not easy. I could not help but hear Rita's statement, written down and then read aloud in court, since she was still being kept in the hospital. She spoke of my "struggling with myself," may God forgive her. Doctor Pontormo, who was known for his anticlerical views and his antipathy towards the Church, finished his prosecutory speech (to the approval of the public) with the sentence: "First the Devil possessed her, then the Exorcist endeavored to." May God forgive him too. I was given a one-year suspended sentence.

After I returned to Naples from Turin, I supported myself from private lessons, teaching high school students Latin and Greek in preparation for their examinations. My Jesuits avoided me, but they did not stand in my way, and sometimes even helped me discreetly to earn money by arranging lessons. When I was seventy I succeeded in obtaining a pension—just in time, for I had lost my former capacity for work.

In 1955 I had read in the paper that Rita had disappeared. She left the house late one night despite her mother's protests and was never seen again. The police searched the area around Brumiera for several days, to no avail. The newspaper used the expression "into thin air," and in the process it dragged up the "story of the possessed" and that of my trial. I waited in vain for more news in the press; the affair soon quieted down. But, may this be said too, for a long while I hoped secretly that one day I would see Rita in the Neapolitan crowd.

How hot and stifling it is, Lord how stifling, and this is only the beginning of August. This morning, in the summer deadness of our building, I was troubled by loneliness and summoned my courage to go out for a walk. I had to return immediately from the Piazza San Domenico. The sky, which looked so beautiful and clear, seemed to crush me to the ground. And the pressure in my chest is constantly growing stronger from waking up in the middle of the night. How stifling it is, there's no air, no air. Great Lord, Holy and Immortal, Our Father, who art . . .

* * *

AT ONE IN THE afternoon the neighbor from upstairs knocked as usual at her lodger's door with a dinner tray. There was no reply.

This had happened before on several occasions, so she pushed down on the door handle and peered through the crack into the "den." He did not respond to her call; the top half of his body lay on the papers that littered the table. This had also often happened before, that at lunchtime she found him asleep at the table among the newspapers and books. She set the tray aside and went up to him. She nudged him gently, then touched his forehead and stroked his cheek. *Caro Padre Vito. Era buono, tanto buono. Un Angelo*—"Dear Father Vito. He was good, so good. An Angel." The Angel was already cold.

*February 1989*

# DON ILDEBRANDO

## I

THE SURGEON WITH the rather strange name of Fausto Angelini (in English this would be "Angelic Faust") is close to eighty and it is several years since he practiced his profession. Yet his renown is so great that whenever a particularly risky operation is to be performed, the famous Fausto is summoned by the patient's family, for a huge fee, merely to be present, offering verbal advice to the younger surgeons. I do not know how this plays out, and I wonder how his colleagues tolerate it; but the fact remains that the presence of the "angelic" doctor is treated like an absolute guarantee from the bank, or the silent participation of a brilliant civil lawyer in a complex courtroom trial. Is it possible that someone's presence alone could play such a significant role? That sidelong glances toward the Magus could provide sufficient aid or encouragement? Evidently so; I only regretted that I could not even dream of Fausto granting me the briefest glimpse of the operating room from the outside.

He had stopped performing surgery at the age of seventy-five. He himself had noticed that his long fingers had suddenly lost their former dexterity. He clearly had hopes that they would regain their old powers, since in the evenings he would stubbornly exercise them, entertaining himself by cutting out fantastical shapes from the newspaper. He was capable of spending hours in this way, sitting at the vast table in his mansion on the border between upper and lower Naples.

He came from Abruzzi, from the mountain town of Montenero, the pride of which was a rather well-preserved Romanesque cathedral on a narrow square near a precipice. The cathedral was rightly famous as a historical monument, but it alone was not capable of breathing any life into the place. Desolation stared from the few flimsy apartment buildings. Fausto Angelini and his slightly younger sister Veronica were the only children of a healer whose memory was honored as if he had been the lord and father of the town, more important than the steward of the cathedral. Both had died long ago. The doctor came back to his hometown once a year for one month in the summer. He was greeted and sent off with great pomp, while his wizened sister summoned up the will to live for another year; and every day at dawn, during her brother's visit, she would kneel smiling at the altar of the cathedral.

**II**

I CAME TO KNOW him as one of his patients, in the last months in which he was still performing surgery. He examined me thoroughly and quickly, explained that any delay at my age would make an operation on the prostate more difficult, and rejected with an expression of disgust the "modern" method of "freezing" the swollen gland. "We have to open up your belly and cut," he said tersely; "it's not a minor procedure, as many people believe, but an operation that'll keep you in the clinic for two weeks, then at home for a month." He put me on the list at his private (and expensive) clinic. He was likeable and inspired trust. The operation lasted longer than he had anticipated—three hours. When I came out of the anesthetic, though still groggy, I dozed and woke in turn while he talked without a pause and without pulling any punches, speaking with relish, as he sat at the head of my bed.

His fondness for talking and telling stories had struck me at once during our first meeting in his office overlooking the sea. It was easy to surmise the cause. He lived alone, an elderly childless bachelor; he was interested in things that would interest me, as a writer, more than they would his colleagues. We had one other thing in common, beside the fact that he was partial to my work (it turned out that he had read my books). He, a man of the South, suffered from a curious and very rare allergy: He could not drink wine, either red or white. He could, on the other hand, drink

whiskey *like* wine, in large quantities, without a trace of the rash
that the allergy brought on and without ill effects. So we began
to drink whiskey just as soon as the scars had healed from my
operation.

I did indeed spend two weeks in the clinic. I would see Don
Fausto (everyone mostly called him that, not *dottor Angelini* or
*dottor Fausto*, but old-fashioned *Don*, a relic of feudal mores and a
token of social respect) during his morning rounds. He would place
his hand on my forehead, draw back the blanket to check my dressing and say *tutto va bene*, squeezing my hand surreptitiously. I had
the right to regard this, and did regard it, as a sign of our growing
friendship. He was undoubtedly well-disposed towards me from (I
am tempted to say) first glance. He entrusted me to his favorite
nurse, a nun who looked upon him as a saint. The day before I was
discharged he brought me a packet of books tied tightly together.
"Here's some reading for your month of convalescence at home.
We'll have something to talk about when you visit me in the
Palazzetto Panoramico" (this was how people in the city had come
to refer to his mansion high on the Corso Vittorio Emanuele, near
the old Hotel Inglese).

It may sound odd, but during those two weeks in the clinic I
felt completely happy. Happiness in sickness! But that was how it
was, perhaps because of some subconscious association I had with
my short stay in the prison-camp hospital on the White Sea. The
window of my room looked out over the bay. During the day I
would sometimes doze off; but, when the nurse woke me with a
dose of pills or at mealtimes, I would stare at the bay, at the ferries
to the islands, at the private yachts and the fishing boats, with what
must have been the same feelings that the young Albert Camus described in his journal: He was filled with love for the Mediter-
ranean coast and enchanted by it, as if it were the only true source
of life and of its rules.

In the night, on the other hand, I barely slept, afraid even for a
short time to miss what the view had to offer: The sea cut every so
often by long blades of light, the promenade lined with the orchids
of street lamps, and the boom of the waves beating against the
rocks of the breakwater, so regular that it seemed like the ticking of
the sea's clock. The sky was pure dark blue; every so often it ex-

ploded with fireworks from some unknown place, or lay heavily over the bay like a thick multicolored carpet.

How curious it is! I do not possess that which the Russians call the *slyozny dar*[1]; I sometimes think that I wept out all I had to weep, quickly and abundantly, on the threshold of adulthood. But I was choked with tears then just as I had been in my hospital bed in the far North. Yet all those years ago my weeping had been both happy and bitter; now, gazing at the bay, I shed rare, transitory tears of unalloyed happiness.

**III**

MY MONTH-LONG convalescence at home was enlivened by the books from Don Fausto's package. He himself came to see me at irregular intervals every few days; he needed only five minutes to check (with satisfaction) the condition of the wound left by the operation. Every now and then he would bring his nurse (the nun), who would change the dressing. During his lightning visits I sensed that we were continually growing closer, if not yet becoming friends; every time he glanced with a smile at my table, where I had laid out the books from his package and my notebooks.

The thread linking this set of books together was the *iettatura*, which the different authors treated in various ways. The *iettatura*— that is, the evil charm or the evil eye, *malocchio*—stemmed from an ancient belief that the Romans called *fascinum*, and the Greeks *alexiana*. I was not surprised. During our very first meeting, after my examination in his office near the harbor, Don Fausto had referred to the *iettatura* as "the principal interest of my life," adding with a laugh that "medicine, surgery, is nothing but the source of my income."

That the *iettatura* had put down deep roots in Naples, which no one had attempted to dig up, was obvious to even the most casual newcomer after two or three months in the city. In fact, with the native Neapolitans it is glaringly evident: At the sound of the word *iettatura* or *iettatore* a chill runs down their spine. They are quite

[1] A gift for tears. (translator's note)

capable of recognizing the action of the evil eye (or the evil touch, or the evil word); they know at least by hearsay the bearers of the magic, and they try to live in such a way as to pass the danger by until they are in their grave. Woe betide those merely suspected of possessing the characteristics of an *iettatore*; often the burden of suspicion alone crushes them to the ground, and poisons their entire existence. But even more, woe betide those about whom it is known for certain that their eye, their touch, one word of theirs, is capable of striking like an unexpectedly drawn dagger—they live the lives of people touched by the plague, avoided by all, condemned to move along a narrow demarcated corridor traced out by the sinister chalk of isolation.

The *iettatore* causes misfortune; his very presence is a threat. With his evil eye he spreads fires, brings about fatal attacks in the sick, causes storms and shipwrecks, kills unborn children in the bellies of expectant mothers, deprives young women of the gift of fertility, induces complications on the operating table, and brings about accidents on straight roads; with one murderous look he tears down chandeliers in ballrooms, concert halls and opera houses, and with a single glance upward makes old apartment buildings come crashing to the ground.

There is a rich literature of history, customs, and anecdotes concerning the *fascinum*; in the annals of this and other ages can be found fully fledged romances, short stories, and screenplays about selected cases neatly told, with notorious characters; thus, Don Fausto's package was little more than a sliver of rock broken from a large cliff: Dumas' book about Naples, *Corricolo* (with the extraordinary story of Prince Ventignano), Mayer's historical study of folk life in Naples during the Romantic era, Nicola Valletta's classic little eighteenth-century work, *La cicalata sul fascino volgarmente detto iettatura* (or *Discourse on the Charm Known Commonly as the Iettatura*), and Croce's volume, with the chapter concerning Valletta's classic book. Over the centuries the evil eye has encountered many forms of self-defense against its spell, both amongst the common people, and those of high birth. In Naples, when you see a person in conversation with someone on the street secretly thrusting two fingers in the shape of little horns from his hand, you can be sure that he is protecting himself from the alleged evil eye of his interlocutor. Generally speaking, the horn is a basic form of protection from the *iettatura*—in a country cottage, a genuine bison horn, in the cities red horns in the form of fobs on watch-straps or bracelets; occasionally too horseshoes can be found in women's handbags. Such methods cannot have been employed for centuries without proof of a certain effectiveness. The matter can be put differently: The *iettatura* has taken root, and so have protective shields against an assailant lurking at every step; it is as if there were an enchanted circle, enchanted and forever closed. As for me, what convinces me that the action of the *malocchio* is real are the age-old varieties of weapons which are used against it and which have never convincingly been challenged.

The *Cicalata* opens with the author's invocation: "I am filled with an intimate delight at the thought that in our times it is not only the plebeians who flee at the sight of those endowed with the evil eye, but that believers in the *iettatura* include judges in their magnificent robes, knights of the highest rank, expert jurists from the legal profession, masters of the medical sciences, accomplished mathematicians and thinkers, and numerous sages and luminaries of culture. Praise be to our age, in which the torch of learning and the arts burns high and bright; in this way too it is no worse than the happy age of Augustus, when ill omens played the same role that the *iettatura* does today."

Yet Valletta would not be the proud standard-bearer of the Enlightenment if he did not temper his hymn of praise to the *iettatura* with certain "scientific reservations." Since there are no accidents, and everything possesses cause and effect, so the *iettatura* is admittedly a "natural" fact; but at the same time it is also a "psychological" one. Since in the universe every seemingly accidental thing is connected with a causal law of physics, the *iettatura* too is based on some cause. What is the cause? That we do not know; we can only say, or rather guess, that in this case the cause is mysterious. The author of the *Discourse* with his Enlightenment mind would not allow himself to go any further. He raised his baton in the air and froze in this position, leaving his contemporaries and his descendants in exactly the same place where they had been before. A mystery: That was what the *iettatura* had been since time immemorial; that was why the *malocchio* was capable of unleashing misfortune.

And Evil. How could the stalwart Valletta enjoy such authority if his thought did not go beyond "I know that I do not know"? Probably because everyone else thought in like fashion.

With the exception, that is, of Doctor Fausto Angelini, the great surgeon Don Fausto, who was convinced (as I was soon to discover) that the mystery could be fathomed. During my visits later to the Palazzetto Panoramico, I wondered briefly whether he himself might not be a secret *iettatore*. If that had been the case, however, if anyone had had the slightest doubt on that score, people would not have offered large sums of money to try and ensure his mere presence in the operating room after he himself stopped performing operations (and he had just announced his retirement at that time).

## IV

AFTER A FEW TIMES the ritual of our (monthly) evenings in the Palazzetto Panoramico might have seemed tedious. I would arrive around ten; we had both already eaten dinner—I at home, he in his favorite restaurant. In the main room, which was indeed panoramic, with a window looking out onto Capri, on the table there were piles of newspapers, a large bottle of whiskey with two glasses and a bowl of olives. The room was of rather gloomy appearance, and indifferently furnished. On the main wall there hung side by side two excellent copies of Piero della Francesca's *Madonna del Parto* and Rembrandt's *Bathsheba*; in the corner, amid the folds of the window drapes there always flickered a flame beneath a dim picture which, from a sense of discretion, I never looked at closely.

Don Fausto immediately turned to work, in other words to his cutouts; the deftness and speed with which he plied the scissors made one think that this may well be how great pianists exercise their fingers before concerts, or in times of temporary numbness. This was not accompanied by silence—on the contrary, as the glasses of whiskey went down, the host's speech flowed forth. He rarely let me get a word in, and when he did he seemed to set little stock by what I had to say. His eloquence had something declamatory about it. I quickly grew accustomed to it. My whole body was suffused with a pleasant warmth—from the whiskey, plus the evenings at the end of hot days; I listened and gazed at the bay. But I tried not to miss a word of his monologues, which were fascinating, as is always the case when the person speaking is engrossed in the topics at hand and reveals his conclusions at the end of his lengthy reflections. Actually, it would be better to use the singular: Don Fausto always addressed the same topic, and his lengthy reflections always led to the same conclusion.

He was familiar with a huge number of cases of the *iettatura*, and of people known for the evil eye—mostly from history, but also from his own experience—and he told their stories colorfully and often dramatically. He sometimes reminded one of a painter who puts every painting he exhibits in a different frame.

The fundamental theme was unchanging. How can one speak of a "typically Neapolitan or southern superstition," if there are people completely lacking that often fatal ability (and who generally become its victims), while amongst them there live people (of all stations into the bargain) whose evil eye, evil touch, or evil word can be a mortal weapon, and who are at the very least capable of plunging their prey into misery? What does it mean, where does it come from, what is the reason for this distinction? Why is someone born armed with the instrument of Evil (for Don Fausto considered it an innate quality), while the object of their assault may be someone utterly pure and innocent? People, for instance, are born with various kinds of heart, yet a cardiologist can establish without too much trouble the nature and cause of a so-called *malformazione cardiaca*, and may even help to correct the inborn fault with treatment. None of this comes into play in the case of the *iettatura*: A born *iettatore* is an unchanging specimen. Is it enough to say that we are dealing with a question of character, that one person is quite simply born good and another evil? I do not think so. There are cases of those who possess the evil eye but wish to get rid of it, yet they are unable to do so by any means. Usually, though, a person who is evil from the cradle never dreams of suddenly becoming good; he is how he is. So by what means is an individual known as a *iettatore* produced?

In posing this question, Don Fausto occasionally glanced fleetingly at that small picture in the alcove in the folds of the curtain.

Once I arrived early; the maid showed me into our room without a word, and curiosity, plain curiosity, got the better of me. In an old engraving, yellowed and curling under thick glass and almost falling apart, I saw a face that for a short moment made me shudder: a face with a piercing gaze, a pointed beard, in a very tall hat a little like a fool's conical cap. Underneath there was a barely legible inscription: *Conte Francisco Ildes Brandes, 1401–1461.*

## V

IT WAS ALREADY CLEAR that the finger exercises were yielding poor results and so Don Fausto prepared to enter a state of semi-retirement. He promised himself that his last operation would be performed on his sister to remove a swelling from her left shoulder blade (probably malignant, though her brother stubbornly referred to it as benign), which was the cause of her sleepless nights. Veronica, who had grown eccentric and was filled with imaginary fears, lived in Montenero, which she had never left since the day she was born. She refused to travel to Naples alone with a driver; so Don Fausto asked me to go in his car to Montenero and to bring his ailing sister back to the clinic in Naples. I had a few days free and I was also attracted by the idea of a trip to Abruzzi, which I hardly knew at all.

We set off one May morning on the highway to Avezzano with the intention of stopping in charming Sulmona. The terrain was densely interspersed with rivers and broad creeks and was hilly, forcing one to be constantly alert on the sharp curves. The journey to Sulmona took longer than the driver had anticipated. The city of Ovid, an "urban salon," tempted me as it always does to take a chaotic walk (on which I lost track of time); and so it was not until late afternoon that the driver reminded me we still had quite a way to go to Montenero.

From Sulmona the road led to Chieti, where we needed to find a rarely used and poorly maintained side road to Pescara; then, before reaching D'Annunzio's town, we were to climb several kilometers to the top of a hill where the map and a barely visible sign pointed to Montenero. Moving very slowly and driving over numerous potholes, we were able as it were to lead our gaze gradually amongst the walls of Don Fausto's hometown. Immediately beyond the town the empty sky indicated a open space; this was probably the famous precipice, on the rim of which the Romanesque cathedral had been built centuries ago. To the left, and set aside from the town, in a barren, rocky area, there stood a large castle, virtually a copy of the famous castle of Otranto described in the novel by Horace Walpole. I had been unaware of the existence of this castle; my friend from Montenero had never mentioned it in his stories.

Dusk was beginning to fall as our large automobile squeezed into the narrow street leading to Montenero's market square. Veronica, who had probably been alerted by some observer on the road leading from Chieti, was already standing in front of the little apartment building belonging to her family. I use the word "little" because almost everything in Montenero had to be called little, with the exception of the cathedral on the precipice and the castle on the hill outside the town: everything from our hostess, with her prunelike head set on a tiny figure in a mantilla, to the market square ringed by only a handful of buildings, and the wine bar near the cathedral, where the only outside table was occupied by four elderly men playing cards. The town gave the impression of being deserted; beyond the square there was no network of narrow streets, while only one wretched little store adjoined the cathedral courtyard. Later, when our hostess had shown us to the guest room, I decided to take advantage of the late-afternoon light and take a closer look at the cathedral and the castle. No, the cathedral had not been built at the edge of the precipice; it was partially suspended over the void as a result of the constant—and centuries-long!—erosion of the rock on which its foundations lay. For a long time now it had had no steward, as no priest had been willing to occupy the vacated position; so the ragged sexton, who was still fairly sprightly and was probably the youngest person in the town, had the job of opening and closing the door and of sweeping the three naves. The "Castle of Otranto" also seemed to have been undermined by the crumbling of the rocks. In the dense gloaming of the evening it looked quite extraordinary, enwrapped in mystery, just as a peasant of Abruzzi or Apulia is enveloped in his great dark cape.

Anyone who has read *The Tartar Steppe* (its author, Dino Buzzati, is in my opinion one of the most important writers of Italy), whoever has preserved in memory the appearance of the officers in the deserted frontier garrison (and of the space around it, which could not be said to have ended anywhere or led anywhere, to any other inhabited place), must immediately have sensed a similarity of atmosphere. To the naked eye it appeared that there were no families in Montenero; everyone looked like an older person who had long been alone and was slowly drawing closer to the grave. Amongst them could be included Veronica, Don Fausto's sister. Taciturn, mistrustful, as if constantly frightened by something, she made dinner for us and sat down at the table with us herself; she spoke reluctantly, preferring to listen, with an avid expression on her face. As I talked about my friendship with her brother, I mentioned in passing what we mostly talked about (or to be more precise, what he talked about) during my visits to the palazzetto in Naples. She turned pale at the word *iettatura*. After which, complaining of the "infirmities of age," she tottered rapidly off and disappeared behind the door of her room.


## VI


AS PROMISED, WE took Don Fausto's sister directly to his clinic; on the way she fell completely silent, dozing, or pretending to, in the corner of the back seat. The doctor ran out into the street from his office at the sound of three toots of the horn. The meeting of brother and sister I found amusing and moving. It was amusing to see the brother—a giant of a man, well-proportioned and energetic—next to his tiny, frail sister, as he lifted her up from the sidewalk to give her a kiss. What was moving was their dialogue: *Vera, Veruccia, sorellina mia*. The "little sister" repeated with a quiet sob the words "little brother": *Fratellino mio*. Eventually Don Fausto thanked me warmly for what I had done, took Veronica, who was in the great metropolis for the first time in her life, and virtually carried her into the clinic in his strong arms.

My friend fell silent for a while; I did not dare to get in touch with him. I contented myself with calling his nurse (the nun), with whom I had become friends. But Suor Maddalena was niggardly with her information. Don Fausto's sister was being prepared for the operation; it was not known how long this would take. Once she added softly: "There's a danger from her age and her general state of exhaustion; she has a weak heart too." One day *il professore* (as he was called in the clinic) must have guessed who Suor Maddalena was talking with over the telephone; he took the receiver from her hands and said in a changed voice in which there was a certain note of impatience: "We'll have to break off our meetings for quite some time; I'll be the one to call after the operation."

It was not he, however, but his secretary who called with "sad news." Veronica had died that day at dawn. Without asking for permission, I drove immediately to the clinic. Suor Maddalena led me to the dead woman's room. Veronica was covered from head to foot with a white cloth and was utterly drowning on her deathbed, quite lost, amidst armfuls of flowers. Tall, thick funerary candles were burning on either side of the headboard. "Oh, *dottore* (this meant me), *caro amico*, Don Fausto was so strange during the operation, his eyes were so strange." Her whisper broke off, and on her face I saw the frightened look of a person who has said *too much*.

Don Fausto took his sister's remains in a metal casket to Chieti, where the Angelinis had a family plot. I did not see him before his departure. He remained in Montenero for the three summer months, and returned to Naples towards the end of August. From Sister Maddalena's enigmatic whisper I understood only that the great surgeon had failed in an operation that had meant so much to him; that he had been "strange" during the operation—in other words, he had performed below his customary level of mastery. But this circumstance was not revealed either by the young doctors who had been assisting him, or by the nurses. Keeping the secret was a silent homage paid to the Master. Besides, the Master immediately announced that he was parting ways with the operating table, and the faithful silence of all the witnesses of the inconceivable failure sufficed for Don Fausto to continue to be summoned by the families of patients (for a considerable fee), to be present as an "advisor" at particularly difficult operations. Despite, I would imagine, the objections and protests of surgeons of the younger generation.

He invited me to his Neapolitan palazzetto at the beginning of September. He was changed, profoundly changed. He suppressed his irritation with difficulty, avoided my gaze, did not take up his favorite topic, and when the word *iettatura* fell by chance from my lips, he looked at me reproachfully and did not respond. His behavior led me only too clearly to understand that he hoped I would keep my visit to a minimum. I did so with the vague feeling that something between us had snapped, and that it had not been my fault. I put it down to his recent experiences. He politely made it clear to me that we would have to stop meeting. As a parting present he gave me a book recently published in America, entitled *Count Francisco Ildes Brandes—From the History of the Spanish Inquisition*. I glanced at the cover. It bore a reproduction of the engraving that hung amongst the folds of the drapes in his room, above the eternal flame in the little red lamp.

## VII

THE BOOK DESCRIBED the story of the so-called *Marranos* or *conversos*, that is, the Spanish Jews who converted to Christianity. The author took as his point of departure the year 1391, in which there began the massacres of "infidels," "pagans," or "heathens," as they were variously called. There then began a wave of conversions, which some Christians, who had been "pure from the cradle," regarded as a form of pretense to avoid persecution, while others accepted it sympathetically as a step taken in good faith. Beginning in 1440, in Toledo and other cities of Castile, ever more frequent conflicts broke out, even physical clashes, between the *conversos* (accused of secret loyalty to Judaism) and "pure" Christians. The historian estimated the number of honest *conversos* towards the end of the fifteenth century at one hundred thousand individuals, and the number of those stubbornly clinging to the Jewish faith (who disregarded the persecutions), at eighty thousand. The third generation of *conversos* had already appeared; they were generally considered to be unblemished Christians, and were allowed to assume high functions in political and court circles in Castile and Aragon. There were fewer and fewer people suspicious of the conversions;

but they did not cease to act with growing implacability. Although an influential cardinal in Rome and the general of a great order in Castile emphasized outright the authenticity of the *conversos'* transformation to Christians, the opposing camp would not lay down its arms. Despite the assurances of many rabbis (especially in North Africa) that the *conversos* were Christians and not clandestine Jews, despite the complete confidence in the *Marranos* shown by the dignitaries of the court of Ferdinand and Isabel, the Inquisition was on its way. The cause of the Inquisition, discussed extensively in the book, is of less concern; in my reading what was important was the fact that one of the chief accusations brought by the tribunals of the Inquisition was against the "secret Judaization" of the *conversos* for several generations, and their "superficial and false Christianization."

Francisco Ildes Brandes, the main subject of the book, belonged to the third generation of the *Marranos*. He was a zealous, ardently practicing Christian; from his father he inherited the title of Count that had been bestowed by the king, and at the age of thirty-five—the father of a sizeable family (he had a wife and five children)—he was appointed to an almost ministerial office in his native Toledo. He enjoyed universal respect, in some cases even veneration, for his profound honesty and sense of justice. But the enemies of the *conversos* were not wasting time. The Inquisition had been born and was growing stronger every day. The accusations made primarily concerned heresies, heretics, and blasphemies; yet they included ever more frequently and boldly suspicions of "secret Judaization." In 1459 Don (as the Count was universally known) Francisco Ildes Brandes was summoned by the Tribunal of the Inquisition in Toledo, and appeared before it. The allegations seemed inconsequential, but the judges of the Tribunal were capable of turning inconsequential things into serious charges. Tortured in the dungeons and during the sessions of the trial, held up to ridicule by being made to wear the traditional tall, pointed conical cap of the fool, he refuted the accusations with courage and clear-headedness. At the turn of 1460 and 1461 his situation was suddenly worsened by the fact that in some unknown way, through loyal friends and those who believed in his innocence, he had been able to arrange for his wife and children to flee Toledo for Venice. The Tribunal found this to be indirect evidence of guilt, and intensified the trial (which is to say, they simply ordered more frequent and more ingenious tortures); this only made the accused more obdurate, since he had become bolder as soon as his family was safe. In April 1461, at the culminating point of the crossfire of interrogation, accompanied by the administration of physical suffering, Don Francisco all at once drew himself up on his hard stool; he knocked the fool's cap off his head with a bloodied hand, and locked his gaze on the president of the Tribunal, whose name was Hernandez. An incomprehensible thing happened. His piercing stare ("devilish," as people later said) immobilized the members of the Tribunal, and killed Hernandez like a dagger between the eyes. In the confusion Don Francisco broke free from the manacles that usually fettered his hands during the trial, and burst out of the hall of the Inquisition into the street. He was last seen running down to the Tagus, which was swollen from the spring rains. After that he disappeared without a trace. The police deputies sent out by the Tribunal of the Inquisition did not find him amongst his family, who had taken refuge in Venice. He never turned up again, "either alive or dead," as the author of the book put it. The year 1461, without a specific day and month, was taken as the date of his death.

## VIII

FOR THE NEXT HALF a century there was constant talk of the murderer armed with the lethal evil eye. Because those present at the scene did indeed remember Don Francisco's terrible, merciless, steely, dagger-like gaze; and they were convinced that if that gaze had turned on them it would have had the same power over their lives, the power of killing. In 1485 the case was revived by the assassination in Aragon of the inquisitor Pedro Arbués. The author of the book put forward the hypothesis that it was conspirators from the ranks of the Inquisition itself who had raised their hand against the inquisitor of Aragon, in order to strengthen the Holy Office in that part of Spain. Whether or not this was the case, Don

Francisco Ildes Brandes came back to life in the memories and imaginations of the Spanish.

I read the book with flushed cheeks, abandoning my usual habit of looking a book over, "feeling it out," both before and during my reading. This was why it was only when I reached the last page, and before I closed the book, that I discovered inside the back cover a letter stuck under the cellophane dustjacket. It was written by Don Fausto.

He added, from what sources I do not know, to the story presented in the book by the American researcher. Actually, Don Francisco Ildes Brandes had reached Venice in disguise, under the name of Don Ferdinando Ildebrando. He had evidently been able to spend a few hours in Toledo before his escape, since he arrived in Venice with a large purse stuffed with gold. He circumspectly located his family in a handsome apartment overlooking a canal that adjoined the oldest ghetto in Europe; he had obviously drawn the appropriate conclusions from his experiences in Spain. By bribing the Venetian officials he was able to change the whole family's name to Angelini; then he took his eldest son on a journey. Where to? To Abruzzi, where in the environs of Chieti he bought a sizeable piece of land, married his son to a beautiful young Italian woman, and helped him to turn the property into a source of considerable income, which was to serve both the newly established family, and also the family which had remained behind in Venice (with the perspective of an imminent move to the property near Chieti). After this he vanished once again, this time without a trace and for good. Before this came about, Don Francisco (or rather Don Ferdinando), had not only worn a disguise so as to cover his former traces, but had become astoundingly altered physically. His face, once cheerful and benign, was now evil and cruel; before he finally disappeared, he frightened people in Chieti and Pescara as an *uccello di malaugurio*, a bird of ill-omen. They steered clear of him, and were afraid when he was present even briefly in either town.

"This is the true beginning of my lineage in Italy," Don Fausto concluded his letter; "this is why I am sending you this book, which was published last year and was a complete surprise to me, concerning my Spanish roots."

## IX

THE LATE FALL (that is, the end of September and the beginning of October) was so beautiful, so warm and sunny that aimless strolls about the city, even for hours at a stretch, provided a pleasure rare at my age. Since a couple from Luxembourg who were friends of mine were staying at the Hotel Inglese high up on the Corso Vittorio Emanuele, I used to call in to see them in the afternoons, and we would spend long hours sitting in armchairs by the balcony, which opened wide onto the bay. From there (though my friends did not know it) I was able to observe Don Fausto's palazzetto. It was only very infrequently that I happened to see him returning home in the early evening. Now slightly stooped, with bent head and heavy step, he would sometimes stand for a long time at the door before his maid Carmela came running down from upstairs. It seemed that in his absentmindedness, he more and more frequently left his keys at home. In the room that I knew from my visits, he never opened the windows or raised the blinds. He sat there in the dark, so the palazzetto appeared to be without life.

Carmela sometimes met me on the boulevard; she would ask me why I did not come by as before, and would add, gazing at me intently: *Il professore è triste di recente*, the Professor has been sad of late.

Don Fausto invited me to his home once again at the beginning of November, on the threshold of the rainy season. I came at the appointed time; under my arm I bore the American volume by Walter Morden, which I intended to give back. Carmela showed me into the main room, where the fire was lit in the fireplace; she asked me to wait for the Professor, who "would be back any moment now," but she said this in an embarrassed way, avoiding my eyes.

I moved my armchair closer to the engraving of Don Ildebrando. For some unknown reason, I was convinced that Don Fausto was in the house. Also for an unknown reason, my head suddenly began to ache, which had never happened to me before, as I have never been prone to migraines. And at the same time I was overcome by an acute impulse to flee, which I could not act on because my legs had all at once gone numb; they hung from the chair like two lumps of wood. By pushing my hands against the floor, I managed to turn my chair around from the engraving to face the door. I would have sworn that in the picture frame a small hole had been bored, through which someone was watching me. Someone . . . I was the target of an eye aimed directly at me. The eye took me in its possession, seeming to envelop me and smother me, till I was overcome by darkness.

When in the end I came to (after how long I did not know; it turned out later that it had been two hours), Don Fausto was standing over me with a look of deep concern on his face. "You fainted. Unfortunately I was late for our meeting. Let me examine you." Instinctively I did not want this, but I did not put up any resistance. "You're obviously overworked. You should ease up a little."

This was nonsense. At the time I was leading a relaxed life and was doing little work.

## X

THERE ARE DIFFERENT kinds of rainy season in Naples: Some are relatively mild, with rains that are transient and interspersed with brief moments of brightness, and with a tolerable moisture suspended in air which is not so cold, oppressive, and dense as compared to the times when violent rainstorms encase the city in darkness, intensifying the crash of high sea-waves against the boulders on the shore and permeating the air with a keen chill (toward the end of the last century Russian travelers from Siberia complained in their memoirs of the "unbearable cold" in the then unheated apartments of Naples).

Halfway through November there began a rainy season so disagreeable that people left their homes as little as they could, while anyone who did not have their own car found it almost impossible to get around the city.

A short time after my last visit to Don Fausto and the examination he had submitted me to, I fell ill. It was not clear what the problem was. My usual doctor (and neighbor) could find no specific symptoms; he shook his head in puzzlement, and did not refrain from muttering something in a diplomatic and friendly way about an "imagined sickness." This did not alter the fact that I felt as if my whole body had been filled with some poisonous solution. I was weak and constantly sleepy, while sleep brought me no relief, but quite the opposite—I would drag myself out of bed limp and befuddled. In addition, I had frequent bouts of migraines, something I had never known before.

On my own, without any advice from family or doctors, I decided to go away somewhere, to get a change of air—*cambiare l'aria* is an Italian expression that belongs to the repertoire of home cures. The question arose as to where. In mid-December I received in the mail a card with greetings for Christmas and the New Year that had been sent to us for the last seven years or so by the Benedictine nuns in the Umbrian town of Bevagna (which was famous for the sermon that St. Francis delivered to the birds). Yes, Bevagna, of course Bevagna, I repeated to myself.

My wife and I had gone there for the first time about eight years ago, at the suggestion of friends; it was at the time when the spring is already turning into summer. In the small Umbrian town the Benedictine nuns ran (as they still do today) a hotel with a restaurant in the convent, treating the business as a source of income—along the lines of nunneries and monasteries that make a living from the production of honey or liqueurs, for instance, or from embroidery. Nevertheless, it was not possible to rent a room without the recommendation of one of their previous guests; in this manner, there was created a chain of friends, an extension of relations with the nuns, who lived in a special, strictly closed wing.

Bevagna, modest, and attractive in its modesty, is situated near Foligno, an historic medieval and Renaissance city and an important Umbrian railroad hub. From there it is no more than a quarter of an hour by train to Assisi.

We always had pleasant memories of our short stay with the Benedictine nuns. During the day we would ramble around this most beautiful region of all Italy, with frequent trips to Assisi; in the evening, there was an almost family-like atmosphere at the communal dinners; and at night, absolute silence in the convent right through till dawn, when in one's half-sleep, the nuns could be heard tiptoeing without a word to the large chapel, from which there then came a whispered chorus of prayer. At that time we were most interested in Assisi. And now, I was interested too in my urgent need of a "change of air." Perhaps it would have been wiser to travel directly to Assisi and to stay in a hotel there? Probably so, but Assisi was overflowing before Christmas. There remained, then, Bevagna as a "base of operations."

On the day I arrived at the hotel in the convent, the moment I had talked with the nuns that I knew and unpacked my suitcase in the room I had been assigned, I felt better. And in a way that had something of the miraculous about it, like the touch of a magic wand. I had the clear sensation of having crossed some enchanted line, like an exhausted diver emerging onto the surface of the water. I stared with tears in my eyes and with a touch of euphoria at the roofs of the buildings on the other side of the street, observed the movements of the women hanging laundry out to dry on clotheslines, and listened intently to their conversations and their laughter as if it were all happening to me for the first time in my life. As if I had been born anew. These feelings remained with me on the small market square, in the empty nave of the church, and on the low wall round the fountain. Some of the passers-by stared at me curiously; I evidently wore a singular expression on my face. I returned to the convent and threw myself on the bed. I slept profoundly from early in the evening, or rather late in the afternoon, till the slow wintry dawn. I got up in the morning rested and full of vigor. I could not avoid saying silently to myself: I have escaped, I have escaped. Why escaped, and in fear of whom?

Ready for an excursion, I first went to Spoleto. The cathedral below, after one descended all the steps, always enraptured me with its façade. On my way back to the train station I paused beneath the hill with the prison that had once been a medieval fortress. At the rim of the valley, the Umbrian landscape was spread out fanlike at my feet. The winter that year was mild, sunny, by turns warm and chilly. How quickly and effectively that landscape healed!

In Assisi preparations for Christmas were already underway. Even on back streets that were normally deserted, the inhabitants rushed by, knocking into one other in their sudden haste; while holiday-time tourists relaxed in the sun on the squares in front of the churches of St. Claire and St. Francis. It goes without saying that I reacquainted myself with Giotto's cycle in the upper Basilica of St. Francis; and in the dark chill of the lower Basilica, I gazed for a long time at the night star in the portrait by Cimabue. But I was also in a hurry to get to the *Eremo di Porziuncola*, the cell of the Saint and his companions. It was incredible how time had excluded this corner from its operation, how Porziuncola was still living through the past and in the past. I always thought that a living past is balsam for human wounds. I thought so this time too, as I sat on the bench and leaned back against the exposed, twisted and hardened roots of the large bushes amongst which the Franciscan hermits, the "beloved brothers" of the Saint, had strolled for many centuries.

## XI

EVERY MORNING I traveled to Assisi, where I ate lunch; before dusk I took a regular train back to Foligno, and from there a bus to Bevagna. I would be the first in the dining room for dinner, surrounded by the three nuns who waited on the guests. One of them was particularly well-disposed towards me, and one evening, when her two colleagues had gone back to the kitchen, she sat down at my table. "It's not in our best interest," she whispered, "but why should you waste time traveling? The hotels in Assisi are full, it's true, but you could rent a room from a family in a private house." And she thrust a card with an address into my hand.

In Assisi I had no problem finding the address. The single-family house was situated above the city, a little to the side, a few paces from the path leading to the hermitage at Porziuncola, which in my eyes constituted an advantage. It belonged to a pious widow who lived alone and rented out two rooms. The windows of both looked out onto the Basilica of St. Francis. One room was free. The other, as I learned immediately from the owner, had been occupied for a month now by an Irish priest with the strange last name of Ecclesius ("I call him Padre Stefano"), who had lived for years now in Rome at the Irish college there. "He speaks Italian like you or me. You won't get in each other's way. Padre Stefano rushes off to the archives every morning. He comes back in the

evening for dinner." The word "rushes" signified someone young
and physically fit.

And indeed, were it not for the stiff collar of a clergyman in
civilian clothing, he could have passed for a professional sportsman, he was so supple in his movements, and in constant motion.
He covered the ground between our little house and the narrow
street below in leaps and bounds, and there it was obvious that he
would have been happy to switch from a rapid walk to a jog. By the
second dinner we shared in the company of the lone widow, we had
taken a liking to one other. "The Irishman and the Pole," he said
with an infectious laugh as he raised his glass of wine in a toast. I
began to eat my lunches in a trattoria he pointed out, in other
words with him; we would sometimes return home together, and
after supper, when the landlady, who "went to sleep with the chick-
ens," had disappeared, we would sit together till late in the dining
room.

He was thirty years old; he had been ordained in Rome at the
age of twenty-five. He had been sent to study with the greatest exorcist in that city, who had just turned seventy and was preparing to
take a well-deserved retirement. In the Irish priest was combined
an admirable physical fitness with a profound spirituality. And it
was clear that his teacher Armani was a beloved master to him. It
could be sensed right away that he believed in his concepts heart
and mind, without reservation, as he repeated those he had heard
in the great exorcist's apartment in Trastevere or which he had read
in his huge work, *Scienza nuova sul Diavolo*. He had come to Assisi
after a short stay in Perugia, with a clear task: to search in the
church archives for materials concerning the Devil, from the time
of the beginnings of the Franciscan order and its first flourishing. I
could only listen to him, and I did so with immense interest. His
teacher and master was in the course of writing a supplement to the
*Scienza nuova sul Diavolo*, based upon his experiences in recent
years. Had knowledge of the Devil changed or become enriched?
The Devil's strategy had altered. Before, his main goal had been to
prevent people from believing in him. Now, in our times, when he
was only seen by the pious and by country priests (and not all of
them at that), he had emerged onto the illuminated front of the
stage.

"It's enough to look around day after day, to read the newspapers and watch films and television. Everywhere there is Evil, growing, rapacious, unfettered; and underpinned with delectation. *Delectatio morbosa*, a feeling once condemned by the Church. Evil has always been rife, but it has never been so permeated with the element of the *gratuit*, often occuring for no reason. Evil for Evil's sake. What has become morbid is not the delectation of Evil, but our longing after Good. In present-day Italy there are around six hundred satanic sects. Once, at the request of my teacher, I put on a black cape to my ankles, a pointed hat, and a mask with eyeholes, and sneaked into a black mass in the mountains of Castelli Romani. From Michelet's *La sorcière* we know the satanic rites of former times. Above all they were just that, rites; even though they were orgiastic and involved obeisances to Evil, they did not identify with it entirely, and at least some modicum of humanity remained. What I saw in Castelli was a wild and unrestrained rush to the work of intensifying Evil. And it was love of Evil. Beyond that there was nothing."

For a considerable time we were silent, seeking relief in the sight of the Basilica lit up by night.

"The crowds thronging the offices of exorcists are no coincidence. The more powerful the demon, the stronger the need to wrench oneself from its talons. The Church provides assistance in this only unwillingly and without conviction. The majority of bishops don't believe in Satan. They seem not to have noticed the explosion of illnesses, nervous breakdowns, and mental depression, whose source is an evil charm. Two categories of demonic Evil lie in wait to entrap people: *infestazione diabolica*, the persecution of a person by outside forces against which medicine is powerless; and *possessione diabolica* (which is extremely rare), the possession or capture of a person by a demon from within; in this case only an exorcist may be of help, though he won't always succeed. In both cases the evil charm operates in various ways—for instance, through the *malocchio*, the devil's eye, that can do harm in human guise. St. Paul tells how he was often tormented by the Satanic Angel. That, by the way, was how a demon used to be referred to. Most important to remember is one thing: A demon is not an impersonal being, evil in the abstract, but a concrete being who (as St. Peter puts it) like 'a roaring lion, walketh about, seeking whom he may devour.' In the New Catechism it is clearly written: 'Evil is not an abstraction, but indicates an entity: Satan, the Evil One, the Angel who is at war with God.'"

My return to Naples was drawing near. The last Sunday in January was improbably sunny and warm. Padre Stefano suggested a farewell walk to Porziuncola. We sat on a stone bench carved out of the rock to the right of the chapel.

At that time, in my free moments I was reading *The Life of St. Francis* by Chiara Frugoni, a scholar from Pisa who had received an award at the same time as me in Viareggio.

"In 1226," I began, "the Saint was sent to Siena, though his brothers were well aware of the meaning of the constant bleeding, and that the heated bars that were being applied to the affected places on his body were not curing him but merely increasing his physical suffering. Yet he did not die in Siena; his last wish was granted: 'Take me to Porziuncola.' They did so. He lay dying in his cell; he asked that his suffering be eased at night by the singing of *The Canticle of Brother Sun*. This too they did, miraculously extending his fading life. Just before he died he summoned Brother Angelo and Brother Leone, and instructed them to sing the *Canticle* again, but this time with a newly composed verse: 'Praise be, my Lord, to our sister bodily Death, from whom no living person can escape.' They did this weeping, and a few minutes later they lowered the eyelids of the deceased and repeatedly made the sign of the cross over him."

"In that eternal and impossible escape from our sister Death," said Padre Stefano, "is contained everything that needs to be known about humankind. If St. Francis were alive, would he call Evil our brother?"

"It's possible," I replied. "The brother and the sister would be linked by the fact that a person cannot escape from either of them."

## XII

THE RHYTHM OF the narrative should reflect the rhythm of the events that I am recounting.

I had barely crossed the threshold of my home in the evening (complimented by my wife on my successful convalescence in Umbria, visible to the naked eye), when, waking in the middle of the night, long before dawn, at four o'clock (the very worst hour for insomniacs), I found myself in what maritime experts call "the dead zone." All the winds suddenly die, like wet sheets laid down on the smooth surface of the sea; the sky darkens, sails droop, and an ominous silence falls. The sailors are overcome by an irrational fear that they have sailed into an area of motionlessness, of mortal stillness, from which there is no return. If this goes on "endlessly," and sometimes it really does seem as if no end is in sight, among the sailors there occur cases of madness, or at least attacks of hysteria.

The rhythm of the present chapter, then, will reflect this dead interlude which preys on seafarers. My behavior aroused no suspicions; I did what I needed to do, I began writing again, I was (as people said) "in fine fettle." But the dead seascape had opened and extended throughout my entire being; I had become nothing more than its frame. Something—something unclear—had happened in my life, which had been immediately cut short, yet not suppressed. I went on walks as before, yet these were (if I might express it in this way) desolate walks; I was insensitive to my surroundings and to the people passing by. No, I was not lost in thought and hence distracted, but rather hollowed out, waiting for the reappearance of something that had been interrupted. On one occasion, without thinking I climbed to the upper boulevard and in front of the Palazzetto Panoramico I ran into Carmela and Sister Maddalena talking on the street. Don Fausto, or *il professore*, had for some time now been traveling; *si riposa poveretto*, the poor man was taking a vacation, put in the maid, and we don't know when he'll be back. Carmela was in no hurry for him to return; she received her salary regularly from the bank, and had little to do at the palazzetto. In Sister Maddalena's eyes, on the other hand, there lurked the sorrow of abandonment.

Up till this point I have not described Sister Maddalena. She was probably around fifty and had a ruddy country beauty; were it not for her nun's habit, she would not have lacked for suitors in Naples. But if she had not become a nun and not come to Naples from Sardinia, she would have been a good wife and the mother of many children in her own village. During my stay in the clinic I perceived—it was not difficult to do so—that Don Fausto was her secret love. She gazed after him in mute adoration. Naturally, the clinic would not have been an Italian institution if it were not sometimes whispered there, even in conversations with the patients, that years before she had been Don Fausto's lover.

And so my life went on emptily; I lived with bowed head, raising my eyes only to check whether the wind had not risen, and whether the sails were not fluttering in response.

An attack of appendicitis brought me to Don Fausto's clinic once again. After a quick, successful operation I found myself in the same room with a view of the bay. Every evening Sister Maddalena visited me before midnight. She would sit on my bed and always with the same, entirely innocent gesture she would fold my hand in hers. We spoke of trivial things, remembering the Great Surgeon. Then, on my last night in the clinic Sister Maddalena, blushing slightly, her eyes fixed on the bay, said: "Is it possible to kill someone with a look? Oh, how strangely he looked as he was operating on his sister!" It was the second time she had allowed such a troubled, anxious sigh to escape.

At home I received a postcard from Don Fausto in Toledo showing the workshop of El Greco on the Tagus, which had once housed a synagogue. It had taken a very long time to reach me, from Christmas to the end of February. It contained holiday greetings and the news that we would see each other in Naples at the beginning of April.

From my travels in Spain long ago I recalled Toledo with special delight, and in particular the very scene that Don Fausto had sent me, El Greco's workshop in the former synagogue.

## XIII

WE DID NOT SEE each other in Naples at the beginning of April. I learned from him later ("in confidence") that he had remained longer than he had intended in Toledo, having bought a wing of the old building in which (according to historians of the city) his ancestors had supposedly lived before the tragedy of the Inquisition. He spoke in the anxious voice of a man releasing some secret for a bribe.

He appeared in Naples in the first half of August, changed almost beyond recognition, with a long beard and a wild expression in his feverish eyes. He was weakened and unsteady on his legs; his speech was indistinct and stuttering, though his mind was still relatively lucid. With Carmela's help he moved his bed to the room in which previously he had received guests (if our former evenings can be described in this way); he also instructed her to ask me and Sister Maddalena to come quickly. We came the morning after his return; for he had fallen asleep fully dressed after they had moved the bed and had passed the night in a deep sleep interspersed with constant ravings (as we were told by a frightened and tearful Carmela). Sister Maddalena measured his temperature; it was a hundred and three. He recognized us and gasped out a greeting with a reluctant look. His colleague from the clinic, summoned by Sister Maddalena, could find no obvious symptoms of illness; he ascribed the fever to extreme exhaustion. It seemed that Carmela's solicitude was all he needed; yet he protested with an abrupt gesture when we began to depart. And so we stayed, taking turns on duty. The night fell to me, since Sister Maddalena had a period of night shifts at the clinic. I brought a few books and my notebook from home. I imagine that after her night of work in the clinic, Sister Maddalena kept watch by day as she dozed in an armchair by his bed.

Was that watch-keeping, day and night, really necessary? He did not want to be alone, that much was evident to us. But he slept almost continuously; he woke rarely and at such times would gaze around with unseeing eyes, and then fall asleep once again. In his sleep he did indeed rave, but the tattered shreds of words were incomprehensible. He thrashed about in his bed, and sometimes a short cry came from his throat; he was constantly pulling off his pajamas in the August heat. Carmela fed him on fruit juice.

In the course of a week, I managed to catch only three words from his rantings: *malefico*, *iettatore*, and *sorellina*.

During the daytime, the month of August cleared people from the streets and from the city; it was a time of escape from sweltering Naples. People came out somewhat more towards evening.

Not in such numbers, however, that I was not surprised one day to see a crowd hurrying down the alleyways toward the city park and the sea. At the time I happened to be going to the Palazzetto Panoramico for the night; on the way I had picked up a newspaper that someone had dropped or discarded. A huge headline on the front page announced that at noon there had been an earthquake, and that the observatory on Vesuvius was expecting a second quake (the first had fortunately not been particularly dangerous) at midnight or before dawn. I took the paper into the room. Don Fausto was not asleep. He was lying on his bed with his eyes wide open. Without a word he stretched out his hands, and without a word I passed him the newspaper. He glanced at the front page, and I had the impression that he had a lump in his throat and was about to cry. He turned over onto his stomach; something sounded loudly in his chest. Soon he fell asleep.

After exactly a week he got out of bed with no one's assistance, went into the bathroom, where he shaved and took a shower, and returned to the room dressed impeccably. Without looking at me, he said in his normal, sonorous voice: "In September, I'm going to Montenero for the whole of the fall. I'd like to take you and Sister Maddalena there; she'll be put on indefinite leave. I don't yet feel strong enough to stand eye to eye with solitude."

## XIV

AT TIMES A SENTENCE heard from someone will not go away. The more insistently it circles and buzzes around, the more grating it becomes. "To stand eye to eye with solitude": It was probably not the first time I had encountered such an expression, yet it struck me coming from Don Fausto's mouth. It stayed with me for the entire duration of the drive to Montenero, so naggingly that at times I did not hear the fragments of conversation in the car (a rather poor conversation, incidentally, which Sister Maddalena was trying to keep up, drawing monosyllabic grunts from the doctor).

Secrets of the spoken and written word! Neither its sound in speech nor its form in writing is changed, yet, suddenly or gradually, it acquires an aura that is the exact equivalent of nuances in paintings—their colors and figurative composition—when we look at them from different points of vantage. The semantic richness of identical words is miraculous, as miraculous as the variety found in identical forms of expression in art. We communicate in shades; sometimes like blind people reading shapes with sensitive fingers, or the deaf and dumb, who hear more graphically than we do thanks to the reading of others' lips.

In Montenero the residents of the market square seemed to have shrunk even more since the time of my last visit; now it would have been enough to put tall top hats on their heads and short sticks in their hands for them to look like fugitives from the world of Bruno Schulz. The same went for the apartment buildings on the square and the little family houses as we drove into the town. The only things that were unchanged—though they dominated even more than before—were the cathedral overlooking the precipice and the castle on the rocky plateau.

Sister Maddalena took up residence in Don Fausto's empty family apartment, while he and I—so as not to bother her or put her in an embarrassing situation—stayed in the castle. I had a room downstairs, by the gateway, furnished in rudimentary fashion; the doctor was in his regular quarters upstairs, underneath the tower, which was joined to his large sitting room by a staircase. Sister Maddalena cooked meals for us in the apartment on the square, and it was there that the three of us would meet.

At dawn, before breakfast, Sister Maddalena would visit the cathedral. Not for a mass, since there was no one to perform it, but to pray at the altar. She was the only person in the building, until it was closed at twelve noon; none of the inhabitants of Montenero went there. In the afternoon and evening the cathedral was not even opened. It was treated as a historic monument, not as a house of prayer. The townspeople did not cling to God, though at the same time they did not ostentatiously advertize their religious indifference. They simply lived as if their little town were dead, or were slowly preparing itself for the sleep of death. They bent double in prostration before their Gulliver, for that was how the tall and well-proportioned Don Fausto looked next to them. Their forebears had probably once treated his father in a similar manner. It was only the late Veronica whom they had acknowledged as "one of their own," since she was a miniature figure just like them. Every day of my stay in Montenero confirmed in me the conviction that the doctor had brought us to a town that was dead. And that in it he felt himself to be an all-powerful lord.

I was glad to visit the always empty cathedral. The remains of its Romanesque character had somehow been preserved, despite the fact that it was crumbling before one's eyes, ignored completely (for some unknown reason) by the conservation departments in Chieti and Pescara, not to mention the larger cities. I never ceased to be charmed by its Romanesque severity, in particular the massive columns propping up our earthly world, with the Gothic rising toward the firmament. It pained me to see holes in the columns and shards of stone that appeared more frequently every day on the equally pitted flagstones. The unused altar was visibly slipping into the earth; it was bare and transfixed by the murky operation of time, like the figure of Christ on a crucifix. Walking around the cathedral, one could believe that it foretold the death of religion. And that weak-minded sexton, almost devoid of speech, sitting in rags on the steps of the altar after he had swept the naves! He was able to correctly pronounce only two words, which others had doubtless taught him: *Montenero muore*, Montenero is dying.

The doctor's purpose in returning to his hometown had been to overcome his condition—I do not know what to call it. He himself on several occasions used the word "depression," but in my view it was a question of something much more serious. Protracted rains (for a whole week!) at the beginning of September kept us in completely, restricting the doctor and me to reading, and Sister Maddalena to prayer and attempts (without much success) to strike up acquaintances with her neighbors on the square. Don Fausto barely conversed with me at all; he livened up a little only during our meals together. This was how we were supposed to help him "stand eye to eye with solitude"? Luckily, after the initial week of rain a fine fall set in, warm and with startlingly clear skies. We began going on long walks; we visited Chieti and Pescara, and even went off on day trips to Sulmona and Aquila. The whole affair got underway, and Don Fausto became a rather eloquent guide.

But the end of September was approaching—a time that I instinctively draw away from, both in my recollections and especially in my description. Can I hold my pen firmly in my fingers, and will I be able to disarm the reader's disbelief and mistrust?

## XV

It seemed that the castle had been built by Don Fausto's grandfather in the middle of the last century. And for some time he lived there all year round with his family, in the summer usually hosting representatives of other branches of his extended family. Don Fausto and his sister had inherited the castle in their youth. Don Fausto, at that time a freshly minted surgeon already living in Naples, first rented, then bought outright an apartment in Montenero for his sister. He intended to visit her as often as he could, but he preferred to stay on his own in the castle, rather than with her in Montenero. The castle was situated no more than a kilometer or so from the town.

The castle was an architectural extravagance, the work of a Spanish engineer who had been brought in for the job. It combined a farcical anticipation of art nouveau in the interior with the character of a fortress on the outside. In all probability the original owner himself instructed the architect to incorporate the quality of a labyrinth, which deprived new visitors of their most elementary sense of direction to such an extent that there had been cases of guests lost late at night among the narrow passages, the secret corridors, and the many small terraces, and forced, if the season allowed it, to improvise a rudimentary bunk in some recess in the wall or under a broad overhang on one of the terraces. This extravagance was not the product of the architect's unbalanced mind (or that of the first owner), but gave the impression of being deliberate, which may have lent the building its only artistic, and even mysterious, element. One seemed truly justified in suspecting that the creators of the edifice had been fans of Ann Radcliffe's gothic novels, especially *The Castles of Athlin and Dunbayne* and *The Mysteries of Udolpho*. In any case I felt vindicated, and even a little proud, that having seen the castle from close by—but not from the inside—during my first visit to Montenero, I had called it "The Castle of Otranto." Walpole was a contemporary of Mrs. Radcliffe's and his own gothic novel of that name had led a renowned Italian scholar of English literature to compare it with Henry James' story *The Turn of the Screw*, and to dub the eighteenth-century author "the Christopher Columbus of metaphysical fear." Walpole was one of Piranesi's first admirers. That made sense too. When I noticed inside the walls of the castle a completely unnecessary drawbridge linking the two sides of a courtyard over a specially dug moat (which had once probably been filled with water, but was now dry), I recalled what Aldous Huxley had written about Piranesi's *Prisons*: "They give expression to an exquisite purpose-lessness; the stairs lead nowhere, the ceilings support nothing." Perhaps the castle in Montenero was intended by its creators to be related to a prison?

"I waked one morning," wrote Walpole in a letter in 1783, "from a dream of which all I could recover was, that I had thought myself in an ancient castle (a very natural dream for a head like mine filled with Gothic story) and that on the uppermost bannister of a great staircase I saw a gigantic hand in armour. In the evening I sat down and began to write, without knowing in the least what I intended to say or relate." That was how *The Castle of Otranto* was conceived.

One night I woke from a deep, dreamless sleep and, as if directed by an invisible hand, I turned my gaze towards the balustrade of low wooden steps that was visible in the elongated skylight in the ceiling of my room. The steps led up to Don Fausto's sitting room or, in the opposite direction, descended, passing by my room, to the castle gate. In the opening I saw what looked like a cloud of smoke, and my first thought was that a fire had broken out on the upper floor. I was just about to leap out of bed and alert my fellow-occupant when the cloud of smoke began to assume a human-looking form. Especially clear was a large head with no face in a tall, pointed hat in the shape of a cone. Only that could be discerned, and something in the manner of a hand sliding down the balustrade. The apparition moved towards the second flight of stairs that led down to the gate, and disappeared. I lay there benumbed and frozen. I listened intently. For a long time no sound came from Don Fausto's sitting room. Suddenly, however, a barely audible noise was heard, something between crying and dry sobs.

In the crack beneath the door a sliver of light came on, and heavy footsteps sounded on the floor, now louder, now quieter, evidence that the doctor was pacing about the room. Finally the light went out, and the castle was once again plunged in silence, while I fell into a sleep that had in it something of a swoon. In the morning I lacked the strength to get out of bed and go to Sister Maddalena's for breakfast. My breathing was shallow and labored; my head had started to ache. Before noon I managed to visit the still-open cathedral, without calling in at the apartment on the square. I did not want to see anyone. I sat in a pew near the altar, holding my heavy, aching head in my hands and feeling the need for at least a wordless prayer. The sexton paid me no heed as he finished sweeping the side nave. But his torn and threadbare apron reminded me by association that the apparition in the night had been wearing some kind of cape all in tatters.

That day I did not see my companions; I took advantage of the weather and went for a walk down the hill, remembering that at the crossroads about four or five kilometers away there was a country inn. Shabby, smoke-filled, and noisy, it was exactly what I needed at that time. Amid the clamor I ate the only dish on offer, a thick meat and vegetable soup, drank it down with some wretched wine, and with a sense of relief I felt my head clear. Now I could hear those who were talking, or rather yelling, with each other. I was struck by one thing: Without knowing who I was, they sometimes mentioned Don Fausto and Montenero as if they were speaking of a wizard and his domain. In the evening a vegetable delivery man took me back to Montenero in his wagon. I went directly to my room in the castle.

There was no one in the castle; Don Fausto and Sister Maddalena were probably eating dinner and getting ready for a game of cards or draughts, perhaps wondering what had become of me. I climbed the stairs in soft, quiet slippers, without turning on the lights, and cautiously opened the door to Don Fausto's room. Despite the autumn chill the window was wide open. On the table lay scissors and piles of newspapers. On the bedside table was the American book *Count Francisco Ildes Brandes*, with the picture of the eponymous hero on the cover. The little door that led to the narrow stairs up to the tower was open. I could not resist the temptation. The tower, which from a distance gave the impression of being the principal firing point in the fortress, consisted of a single broad room with two windows firmly sealed shut. On the wall between the windows a sizeable, competently painted fresco was quite simply an enlarged version of the Inquisition portrait of Don Ildebrando; yet not (as in the miniature copies on the book cover and the picture in the alcove amongst the curtains in the Neapolitan palazzetto) a portrait to the waist, with the subject seeming to be sitting. Don Ildebrando—his figure stretching from floor to ceiling, and colored by the creator of the fresco—stood in all his grandeur, staring ahead with those terrible eyes of his. And I stood before him, my heart pounding and my feet rooted to the ground. How much time went by? As I tottered down the narrow steps to the doctor's room, then down the regular stairs to my bedroom, I could hear Don Fausto's footsteps on the sheet of rock by which one descended to the castle gate. In the darkness, I just had time to slip into bed fully clothed. Don Fausto looked into my room; he hesitated for a moment whether to wake me, then in the end went up to his own room. He tried to avoid the creaky treads in the wooden stairs.

A few days passed, during which the mood of our little trio improved somewhat. Night after night, till late, I stared from my bed at the balustrade visible through the skylight in the ceiling. I did not for a moment doubt the reality of my first vision, yet believed with a sense of relief that it had been an isolated incident. On the night of Saturday to Sunday we liked to sleep longer, and so I lay engrossed in my reading (for the umpteenth time) of Bulgakov's *The Master and Margarita*. The Russian writer's half-comic narrative tone was intended to arm me against the fears that crawled beneath my skin. Before I turned out the bedside lamp I glanced at my watch: It was three o'clock.

Right at that moment, at three o'clock in the morning, a heart-rending cry burst from Don Fausto's room, or rather from the tower. Not the quiet weeping or dry sobs that I had already heard once coming from his room. It was a cry, together with some words repeated loudly. Maybe he was having a heart attack, maybe he was calling for help? I jumped out of bed and ran barefoot upstairs straight to the tower.

He was kneeling before the fresco, beating his head against the floor like a Muslim in prayer and repeating over and over the same words in Spanish: *Librame del mal*, deliver me from Evil. Each time his head struck the floor he lifted it once again to the image of his distant ancestor on the wall. What I will say next will lead many of my readers to laugh and shrug their shoulders. Yet I will say it anyway, because the present age has been excessive in inculcating in us the cult of "common sense." We observe inexplicable phenomena out of the corner of our eye and pretend that we have not seen them; we read in bolder authors about ghosts or the dead, and regard them as phantasms, products of a sick imagination—anything so as not to jeopardize our "common sense" or to be propelled into the ambit of another dimension, beyond the threshold of "verifiable, tangible reality." We pass through life with one eye all too sharp, yet the other blind, as if covered with a film. Is it enough just to see? No, it is not enough.

Don Ildebrando came out of the portrait on the wall, stepped over the man kneeling and beating his head against the floor, and having done so, without turning round, with his foot extended backwards he kicked him so hard that Don Fausto ended spread-eagled on the floor, frozen into motionlessness. I fled. From my room, I saw a figure moving in a slow and dignified manner down the balustrade, after which I lost consciousness and slipped to the ground.

I came to in the late morning; the full light of day had extricated itself from the darkness, and, with difficulty overcoming my lack of strength, I gripped the handrail with both hands, and climbed upstairs. The doctor's room was empty. Empty too was the tower with the fresco on the wall between the windows.

### The Storm

THE ENTIRE SEARCH came to nothing. It was conducted both by the Italian police and by Interpol. Don Fausto had disappeared without a trace. The Italian police combed the places that he used to visit in Italy. Interpol looked in Toledo. We two—Sister Maddalena and I—hunted around Naples like two bloodhounds on the trail. Warrants were issued, and on the walls there appeared posters with the missing man's photograph and a significant reward for finding him, or at least for a useful lead. Naturally there was a flood of letters and tips from hoaxers. The possibility of suicide was not ruled out, and so two small lakes located near Montenero were dredged.

For some time a popular explanation involved the only monastery in Italy at which complete anonymity was maintained for new initiates, something that extended to the huge cemetery, where the graves were marked only by the name adopted in the order. Yet someone cut this thread, recalling the fact that Don Fausto was a sworn atheist.

Half a year after his disappearance, in accordance with the legal regulations an official death certificate was prepared. This enabled a renowned Neapolitan lawyer to reveal Don Fausto's will, which had been dictated in secret before his last trip to Montenero. He had left the Palazzetto Panoramico in Naples and the wing of the house in Toledo—along with the apartment and castle in Montenero—to the clinic, which had long ago become a cooperative.

Over a year later, toward the end of the fall, the papers and the television news reported heavy rains in Abruzzi. It was a baffling business. From a friend of mine in Abruzzi I knew that after a relatively mild autumn the region usually had a severe winter; roads were covered with deep snow, and villages were completely cut off and had to be sent supplies by air. This time—as apparently had last happened fifty years before—the opposite happened: Fall lashed the entire area with torrential rain and endless storms, while winter did not settle in for good till January, without snowdrifts or blocked roads, and with a warm sun at midday.

The storms inundated the entire region with rivers of water, but they particularly beleaguered Montenero and its surroundings—Montenero, forgotten by God and by people.

Chance would have it—though does chance exist, or is it not merely the composition of events that is neither seen nor comprehended by us?—"chance," then, would have it that at that time I was finishing (once again!) *The Master and Margarita*. As the television was issuing its frequent "special reports" on the "natural disaster" in many parts of Abruzzi, I was reading the last chapters of Bulgakov's novel: "The thunderstorm that Woland (the Prince of

Darkness) had mentioned was already gathering on the horizon. A black cloud had risen in the west and cut off half the sun. Then it covered it completely. The blackness, which came from the west, enveloped the huge city. Bridges and palaces disappeared. Everything vanished in the darkness as if it had never existed. A single streak of fire ran across the whole sky. Then a clap of thunder shook the city. It was repeated, and the storm began. Woland ceased to be visible in its darkness."

Two bolts of lightning descended on Montenero. The first hit the castle, causing a fire that burned out the interior—especially the wooden stairs, the habitable rooms, and the drawbridge, such that the building came to resemble a skeleton. The other struck the cathedral on the unsightly clock tower that had been built onto the Romanesque roof at the end of the last century. The lightning had been sufficiently damaging as to leave a triangular gap in the side wall of the cathedral.

Scarcely had the storms abated, or rather moved away, rumbling ominously, toward the northeast, when a flood descended from the mountains on the horizon. It washed away in its path anything that was too frail, including Montenero. Some of the Lilliputian inhabitants perished in the layers of mud that came in with the water; others made it to the crossroads in the valley, where the mudslide left only a shallow coating.

"Everything vanished in the darkness as if it had never existed."

*January–February 1996*

# SUOR STREGA

IT IS NOT EASY to re-create the life story of persons who not
only remain silent on the subject of their past, but seem consciously and insistently to cover its traces. She herself let it be
known that once, before she entered the convent, she had been
called Cecilia Ongaro; also that she had been born in a village in
Apulia, the exact name of which she preferred—why?—not to
mention. From her too came the information that, having assumed
the habit of the Order of the Discalced Carmelites, located between Siena and Volterra, after a very long and stormy novitiate, at
her own request she received the monastic name of Suor Caterina,
presumably in honor of St. Catherine of Siena. There was no
reason—up to that point at least—to travel to the Apulian village
or the convent hill in Tuscany to enliven her meager biography
with more details.

Up to that point . . . Then, one day Suor Strega ran away
from the order, at the age of about thirty, and began living in
Naples near the Fontanelle Cemetery. The anthropologist Dagoberto, with whom I had recently become friends, was writing his
dissertation at that time on "purgatorial souls" (whose principal
abode is the Fontanelle Cemetery). There he met the former nun,
who still unlawfully wore the habit and went by her monastic
name. Discretion prevents the author from entering into the personal aspects of their relationship at too great a length. Suffice it to
say that my anthropologist friend, instead of continuing his learned
treatise on the Cult of Purgatory, and the cemeterial remains of the
so-called *anime in pena* in old Naples, without Sister Caterina's
knowledge, took a trip to Apulia and Tuscany. He returned not especially enlightened and at the same time embarrassed, as it were,
by this wilful attempt to invade someone else's life.

I spent an evening with him at a wine bar shortly after he came back. If I had previously been able to suspect in my mind, already knowing the good-looking former nun by sight, that Dagoberto fully appreciated her charms, then his story over a glass of wine seriously undermined my suspicions. The question remained as to why he had taken a week out of the hectic period before his defense, but his reasons appeared unconnected with his feelings. No one returning from a "reconnaissance" dictated by the voice or merely the whisper of the heart reveals its results to a person who, though a friend, is after all a stranger. It was only later, thanks to an accident, that I discovered my mistake: At this time Dagoberto was already Sister Caterina's first Neapolitan lover.

The name of the Apulian village where she was born he had probably heard from her herself in their moments of intimacy: Monte Nevoso. Positioned at the entrance to a wooded ravine and overlooked by cartographers, containing as it did barely a few hundred souls, what did it have in common with mountains or with snow? Only the fact that in the harshest wintertime the sparse woods covering the slope of the entrance to the ravine were often dusted with the dry and loose whiteness of hoarfrost. With no one's help, Dagoberto found the cottage in which the Ongaro family had once lived; the still-visible name on the gatepost was a relic from past years. In fact, the old folks had died one after the other soon after the departure of their daughter; she was a pretty girl who was so devout that she always wore her black dress, was festooned with holy medallions and crosses, and every Sunday, regardless of the weather, would walk a considerable distance on foot across the fields to the church in the next village. Her older brother had emigrated to Australia. In fact, time had almost completely erased the memory of the Ongaro family; only a few inhabitants of Monte Nevoso remembered the name.

The convent in Tuscany (closer to Siena than to Volterra) extended comfortably across a deserted plateau, though it was well connected to Siena by a back road. Dagoberto was not even allowed inside; the gatekeeper looked at him with an angry snarl when he asked about Sister Caterina. "She's dead," the woman muttered eventually and slammed the half-open door. It was already growing dark, so he set off down the Siena road. In the first village he came to, he was given a bed in a squalid inn. And there the innkeeper told him what he had heard from some Carmelites who had once stayed there.

Sister Caterina's novitiate had been stormy because she had constantly striven through her own piety and zeal to show her peers up; she would reproach them for their "half-heartedness," mortify herself with an unhealthy delectation, recount her "visions" and anticipate her "miracles." At the same time she enjoyed impunity, being the sweet favorite of the still-attractive prioress. She was capable of lying prostrate for hours at the foot of the great crucifix that hung over the altar in the convent church.

A profound change took place when a new confessor came to the convent, a handsome young priest from Florence. The devout young woman turned into a "witch," predatory and impudent. In the convent they started to call her Suor Strega. She became pregnant, and she ran away from the convent along with the confessor, apparently to Sicily (where he was from). Here Dagoberto broke off his account; he simply did not know any more.

What (I repeat) did he need to find all this out for, even if one accepted that his relationship with the ex-nun was something deeper than a easy and short-lived romance? Yet who said that all questions concerning the intricacies and dark entanglements of human fate have to receive clear and unambiguous answers? There exist questions—perhaps they even constitute the majority—which lack reasonable answers. And my story, which stretches with large and frequent gaps from 1956—in other words almost from when I first moved to Naples—right until the last few days, is precisely one woven from questions that have no answers. The first was: Why would a lover want to know immediately at the outset exactly who his partner in his love adventure is? The second question should be formulated as follows: Why, virtually the moment his academic research was crowned with a doctorate in anthropology, did he leave Naples, without saying goodbye either to his friend (that is, to me) or to his lover? Why, to put it bluntly, did he flee Naples in panic? Never to return, though he was born in the city and had many relatives here.

Before his departure, or escape, came about, however, he took me to the Fontanelle Cemetery in the role of a learned guide. We spent a whole spring afternoon there, and at dusk he persuaded me to pay a visit to Sister Caterina, who lived close by. He referred to her by turns as Suor Caterina and Suor Strega.

In the thirties some Neapolitan bank robbers had dug a complicated tunnel that was supposed to lead them to the underground vaults of the Bank of the Holy Spirit (*Il Banco di Santo Spirito*). One is tempted to use the phrase *nomen omen*. Digging at night according to spurious makeshift maps, the thieves reached an area in which the Holy Spirit was at work; but it was not the same Holy Spirit that was "patron" of the Italian bank. For they found themselves in a long passageway whose ceiling beams were just strong enough to resist the pressure of the earth above them, though with the permanent danger of collapse. The passage was strewn, or rather filled to the brim, with human skulls, bones, and in places whole skeletons which had somehow avoided breaking up into their various parts. The failed robbers thus became archeological discoverers. The excavations that were begun immediately revealed an underground cemetery, the center of which was formed by a large circular plaza, with passages or shafts cut in the earth and the rock on the sides around its entire circumference. It was in these shafts that the skulls and bones were lying in disorderly piles. The plaza too was littered with human bones. There was no doubt that the inhabitants of the city were seeing the earthly remains of those who had died in the cholera epidemic of 1836. The cemetery was given the name of Fontanelle.

The spiritual essence of the cemetery was anonymity, for the remains that had been dug up were of unknown people who possessed neither family names nor given names. For this reason, their souls were adjudged still to be in purgatory—*anime in pena* or *anime di purgatorio*. Which in turn rendered it possible to make contact with them, to establish a dialogue with the dead. And by establishing a dialogue with the dead, with the other world, it was possible—through the mediation of the nameless skulls of souls dwelling in purgatory—to ask for intercession: for help in the adversities of life, in love, and with sufferings or ailments; for support for the infirm, for relief from the burden of old age, for miraculous cures for illnesses, for intervention in the daily struggles with fate, and even for small favors such as the smile of fortune in the lottery.

Even while it was still being excavated, Fontanelle became a cemetery of supplications—loud and dramatic implorations, and quiet and modest requests. In order to establish more vigorous and lasting contact with the dead, to oblige the other world to re-enter the present one more palpably, the Neapolitan pilgrims of hope began to adopt ownerless skulls and bones. In general everyone who entered the bounds of the cemetery knew where to find their chosen skull, the integument of a soul in purgatory, and they went straight to the place where they had previously left it. There were also those, however, who did not properly trust their visual memory, and who locked the skulls they had taken into permanent possession in glass cabinets brought from home, bearing the owner's name (and address!) and locked with a small key. The visits of both the former and the latter groups to Fontanelle Cemetery were transformed into long hours of communion with those who had died of cholera a hundred years before. They thoroughly cleaned the skull (and sometimes the bones too), kissing them at frequent intervals; and they spoke to them, enumerating their supplications. It was as if they believed—more, that they were certain—that the purgatorial soul of the deceased came alive during the time they bustled about the skull and talked to it. In the walls of some of the shafts the slow passage of a century had trapped entire skeletons, pinning them in so tightly that they could not be taken out without being damaged, broken, or shattered. It was these, the walled-in skeletons, that enjoyed special popularity amongst the girls, who probably thought that amatory spells, verbal love-potions, would be more easily received by the skeleton of a human figure than by a skull alone. Dagoberto led me to an underground passageway with a particularly abundant number of skeletons in the walls. Here, more than anywhere else, there were girls, often very young and pretty, who rose on tiptoe to deliver an almost passionate kiss as they whispered their secret request to the skull.

Dagoberto was writing his doctorate under the supervision of a well-known Neapolitan ethnologist, the author of a book (translated into many languages) about magic and witchcraft in southern Italy. He had chosen Fontanelle Cemetery as the subject of his doctorate, and he knew everything there was to know about it; his commentary accompanying our tour flowed like a well-memorized lesson. It would be beyond my capabilities to repeat faithfully everything he said. At certain points I could have consulted his little book, based on his dissertation; but alas, after so many years I have lost my copy, and have not been able to find another in the bookstores or the booksellers' stalls.

Dusk fell rapidly, and equally rapidly turned to evening. It was dark when, in accordance with our promise, we stood at the doorway of an apartment building in a back street; we began to climb the narrow, winding stairs, which had not been washed in a long time, up to the sixth and highest floor. A powerful stench, coming from the apartments on the stairwell, made it impossible to breathe easily or to stop on the landings to catch our breath. At last we rang the doorbell. Energetic steps could be heard coming from far away—though Sister Caterina's apartment was cramped, it gave onto a small terrace. She opened the door to us in her habit. And it was in her habit that people saw her till the end, in various circumstances that were not entirely appropriate for such attire—so it could not have always been the same one; either she had a supply in her wardrobe, or she ordered them as needed from a seamstress. Curiously enough, from the first moment I associated her habit with the armour of knights errant, of whom Cervantes writes that they regarded it as a weakness, to which they rarely succumbed, to "unarmor" themselves before going to bed.

She sat us side by side on a worn couch, while she herself took a seat on an uncomfortable wooden stool by a neatly made bed that looked somewhat spartan. That she was good-looking, I mentioned already having seen her from a distance. After seeing her close up, the phrase "good-looking" was not sufficiently accurate. She was beautiful. Her raven-black hair, falling onto her shoulders, framed an exceptionally expressive face, drawn as if in a portrait by one of the old masters, with huge, dark, penetrating eyes, a high forehead, and a fine nose. When she stood with her back to us at the little stove in the corner, and even more when she moved nimbly around the small room as she prepared something for us to eat, in spite of her habit, I was struck by her figure, shapely and at the same time muscular. But her greatest adornment were her eyes, piercing, deep, ostentatiously bold, boring into her interlocutor,

and at times lit with a cold flame; eyes that continually and deci-
sively had something to say. She wore her habit like an ancient
Greek chlamys or a kind of dressing-gown: One rarely sees the
breasts of nuns, whereas with her it was precisely there that her entire, almost provocative physicality was to be found.

We did not really have a conversation, but only exchanged isolated remarks about Fontanelle Cemetery, which could clearly be
seen from the terrace by the light of the moon and the street lamps
around the square. At one point Suor Strega, Sister Witch, speaking of the miraculous skulls and the souls in purgatory, seemed to
lose her calm and to yield to a sudden wave of vehemence. Staring
at her at this time, I could not resist an onslaught of images from
Michelet's *La sorcière*.

After an hour it became obvious that I was *di troppo*, as the Italians say—that "I was one too many." I stood up to leave. For a split
second I was tempted to hold onto her hand longer than usual.
Without suspecting it of course, I bid farewell to my friend forever.
I remember the hint of fear in his face.

Dagoberto's departure (or flight) put an end to my interest in
the Fontanelle Cemetery. To be completely honest, I found that
miraculous charnel house repellent, since in my own life I expected
no miracles and did not believe in contact with my own dead. Yet
after my visit to Fontanelle something unbearable happened to me.
I had seen my own dead fleetingly in dreams; but now they were
completely displaced by images from the Neapolitan cemetery. I
decided to put an end to this, and whenever I found myself passing
Fontanelle, I would automatically turn my head towards the street
on the opposite side. I do not think it was an accident that at these
times my gaze always rested on the apartment building in which
Suor Strega lived. Was I fascinated with her after that one meeting? Or was it that in some bizarre way, for me, the image of the
necropolis dug up before the war was concentrated in her person?

Both things were probably true, but three years later, that
is around 1960, the two—Suor Strega and the Neapolitan necropolis—had become so fused in reality that drawing a distinction in my imagination proved useless.

In a certain sense it could be said that the former nun, Sister
Witch, had assumed the throne in the kingdom of souls in purga-

tory, and of the traces of their existence on earth. And this was exactly what—using indirect language and circuitous hints, as if a superstitious caution were tempering or restraining his words— a certain journalist of our southern newspaper tried to suggest in a whole-page illustrated feature in the city life section entitled *Fontanelle e la sua Padrona*: its Sovereign, the Lady of the Cemetery. What was it all about? I read the article three times, my cheeks flushed, but it was still not entirely clear; one really did have the impression that the writer's hand was trembling as he wrote. In any case, it was just possible to extract the essence of the matter as described by the journalist.

Suor Strega—who was already known universally by that name, though in my view people took "Strega" to mean Sorceress rather than Witch—had taken up residence in the cemetery and had managed to convince its regular visitors that, first, only she knew how to choose appropriate skulls for those who wished to possess them; secondly, that only she was capable of establishing a dialogue with the world of the dead through the mediation of the purgatorial souls; and thirdly, that only she was able to convey the requests and wishes of the pilgrims of hope in such a way that the majority of them—*at least* the majority—were granted. The article did not even attempt to address the methods of the ex-nun (she still wore her habit, and in addition now tied a rope around it, from which hung a rosary); but there obviously existed evidence of her success on all three points, since the ranks of her devotees continued to grow, and efforts by the authorities to remove her from the cemetery provoked a virtual "rebellion of believers," during which a representative from the Office for the Conservation of Monuments and two policemen were hurt. Suor Strega had won herself the status of untouchable. And soon (and I think consciously) she pursued it to the point of fanatical veneration.

The phenomenon endured, and grew in strength day after day for two years. When it suddenly started to ebb—slowly at first, then with gathering speed—in our local paper there were debates regarding the cause of the reverse. Some supposed that her successes in sorcery were growing fewer, giving rise now to ill will, now to something worse among her followers. Others referred to a little known circumstance, namely the fact that at night, in a *cunicu-*

*lus* that was somewhat more comfortable than the others, Suor Strega slept with handsome men she had picked out during the day. She did not try to hide this; quite the contrary, which indicates to me that she was thinking more of her role as Witch (as we know it from Michelet's book) than as Sorceress. Whereas her votaries, gazing at her trustfully—no, devotedly—desired the opposite: They had faith in the Sorceress, and recoiled at the sight of the Witch.

In any case, her fame (not to say the special aura of saintliness that enveloped her, with its certain admixture of demonic elements)—her fame, then, faded away. It came about that she suffered abuse, that trash was thrown into her *cuniculus* of love, that one day she was driven out of the cemetery with rocks. And most important of all, that everyone stopped asking for her advice, her assistance, and her magic intercession. In other words, they took away the source of her income (which had once been considerable). She probably had savings from the fat years, and so was able to weather the first lean ones, wandering about in the neighborhood of Fontanelle, at times venturing to enter the cemetery gates, as if she counted on a sudden reversal of fate. She was written about less and less often in the city pages of our newspaper. Until the last mention, in small print, from which the readers learned that Suor Strega, had turned her apartment over to the owner of the building, and informed him that she was leaving for Sicily, where she apparently had a son.

Years passed, swallowing up the cemetery hag (for *strega* has that meaning too) like a high tide. In fact, the entire character of the neighborhood changed. Fontanelle was closed (the Office for the Conservation of Monuments had insisted on this): The public were allowed in only once a week, for a few hours in the afternoon. For the same reason, they closed the church of Santa Maria della Sanità, with its steps leading down to the catacombs, where there had been excavated other *teschi miracolosi*, miraculous skulls, belonging to people who had died of cholera in 1836. One of the most eminent historians of Naples had uttered a sentence that was later often heard on the lips of many of the more enlightened inhabitants of the city: "Let us at last leave the purgatorial souls and the bones of our ancestors in peace where they lie beneath the earth; let our own living souls and our living bodies lead the way to rebirth." The Cardinal Archbishop of Naples, asked to comment on this maxim, spurned it with a haughty silence.

Years of oblivion passed, then; popular pamphlets about Suor Strega were only infrequently found in the kiosks. But she had not died in Sicily as a mother, perhaps as a wife, perhaps as a grand-mother. In May of last year I saw her by the gate of Fontanelle, sitting on the ground with her head drooping between her knees, a torn habit on her shrunken, desiccated body; her face was wizened and crumpled, her eyes watery, while her open lips revealed a few yellow teeth. She raised her gray, tousled head for a moment only when the coins thrown by passers-by rattled against the bottom of her metal bowl. I may have been the only one who recognized her. I doubt, though, whether after so many years, almost forty, she recognized me. Something lit up and then was immediately extinguished in her barely seeing eyes; she raised her head for a little longer than usual, but she did not move a muscle when I greeted her loudly by the name of Suor Caterina, then more quietly as Suor Strega. I threw one more coin into the bowl. This time, without lifting her head from between her knees, she whispered: *Che Dio ti benedica*, may God bless you. After my summer vacation I took a special trip by metro to Fontanelle. A pair of beggars sat on either side of the gate, but despite a contribution they were unable (or un-willing) to say anything about their predecessor.

And yet I met the former nun one more time. A Neapolitan writer I knew, who was burdened with a large family and was on the verge of poverty, received from the city government a sinecure in the form of the director's position (along with an official apart-ment) in the St. January Home for the elderly poor. The home—by coincidence!—was situated halfway between Fontanelle and the apartment building in which Suor Strega had once lived. Before Christmas the zealous new director invited a series of professional groups from the city to the old people's home. At his request, I was included in the group of authors and journalists, though I am not a member of the Neapolitan writers' union. We toured numerous rooms on the top two floors of the home, rooms that resembled each other like peas in a pod: bare walls, ten beds to a room, stale air, and human figures wrapped up to the tops of their heads in dirty quilts or blankets. In each room, at the signal of a handclap

given by the director, the heads emerged slowly and reluctantly
from their covering. In some rooms the pensioners sat on chairs
around the walls, rocking ceaselessly like Jews at prayer, or stood
more or less upright facing the walls (despite an earlier prohibition
by the director). It was then that I saw Sister Witch for the last
time; she was lying on her bed with her head exposed. When she
noticed me not a hair on her head twitched; only her eyes opened
wider. Could it have been that she was lying amongst old men and
women who had once worshiped her in the old days in Fontanelle?
If so, the end of her life was not an easy one.

The director of the home asked us to write in the visitor's book.
When my turn came, without thinking twice I wrote a passage
from Cavafy's immortal poem:

> *How bored they are by the pathetic life they live.*
> *How they tremble for fear of losing that life, and how much*
> *they love it, those befuddled and contradictory souls,*
> *sitting — half comic and half tragic —*
> *inside their old, threadbare skins.*

After writing the Alexandrian poet's stanza in Italian in the visitor's book, I changed the title. Instead of "The Souls of Old Men,"
I wrote "The Purgatorial Souls *(Anime in Pena)* of Old Men."

*November 1995*

# A MADRIGAL
# OF MOURNING

## I

I MAY EVEN HAVE had something of a crush on Anna F. I was introduced to her years ago at a concert organized by the Scarlatti Society at the Naples Conservatoire, where she had recently become a teacher of musicology. She was Russian on her father's side, and Polish on her mother's. After the revolution, her parents succeeded in escaping to Rome. There her mother died giving birth to her; her father, born in St. Petersburg and educated there as an Italianist, found a job teaching some adjunct courses in Russian literature at the University of Rome. They lived in Trastevere on his earnings. Immediately after finishing secondary school the girl won a scholarship to study musicology in Naples. She herself was a rather competent pianist. For reasons unknown, her father would not come to Naples, and so his daughter faithfully and regularly spent every weekend in Rome.

When we met, we were still relatively young; we were both born in 1919. What attracted me to her, aside from her agreeable though by no means exceptional looks, was that special Russian femininity, whose first, sometimes rather exalted love is art (in her case, above all music, with painting and literature added on), while people have to make do with second place. Or, as I realized when I came to know more about the life and poetry of Marina Tsvetayeva, art and close friends in the end become united, existing like two organisms that have joined into one. Was Tsvetayeva in love with Rilke and Pasternak? Love of their poetry turned into "being in love" (though platonically) with its authors. When I met Anna, her boyfriend was a painter who, like her father, did not leave his native Rome (which in effect meant the artists' street of Via Margutta). So every week she traveled to Rome for the two men.

In the introduction to this story I said that I had "something of a crush" on Anna, because this expression, unknown in other languages, accurately conveys that state of part ordinary affection, and part delicate infatuation, which knows that it will never become anything more. And I think that Anna's feelings were the same from our first meetings (mostly at concerts, sometimes in the coffee house frequented by musicians). For it was clear that she was attracted to me too. For two reasons, I believe. Her Polish mother, whom she had never known other than from family photographs, stirred in her. And she liked knowing a writer. She had me read Polish poetry aloud to her (I am not much of a public reader). And I had to give her everything I had managed to have published in Italian. Naturally she also knew Russian, but at that time Russian did not know me as a writer.

It is quite possible that reading my books in Italian, which revealed to her my abilities as a writer, emboldened her to make what was for the moment only a vague proposition.

"Have you ever come across the name of Carlo Gesualdo, Prince of Venosa, the great Italian madrigalist? I dream of writing a monograph about him, a thick book about everything he composed. Of course it would be a work of musicology, though Gesualdo is something more than the 'Prince of Musicians,' as he's often called . . ."

I immediately recalled the piece by Aldous Huxley, which I had read long ago. Huxley knew music, though more as a music lover than a serious scholar. So I was struck that he devoted a whole essay to a madrigalist from the turn of the sixteenth and seventeenth centuries whom I had never heard of (though he had lived most of his life in Naples). Nor was this the relish of a collector of artistic curios. Huxley thought highly of the Prince of Venosa and created a little memorial to him.

This was new to Anna, as Huxley's volume of essays had not been translated into Italian.

"One good turn deserves another," she said with a laugh. "I'll get hold of the English essay and have someone translate it for me; in return for this information, which is important to me, I'll give

you some writings about the life of Carlo Gesualdo. For a writer
like you, they may provide inspiration."

I was all the more pleased because in only one, rather enigmatic
sentence Huxley had referred to the "personal tragedy" of his favorite madrigalist.

**II**

I RECEIVED THE PROMISED "writings" in a large package in the
mail. Soon after our conversation Anna had taken the vacant chair
of musicology in Lecce. She did not visit from there and I heard
nothing from her (it turned out later that she had had a hard time
during the breakup with her artist friend); she probably passed
Naples by on her weekly trips to see her father in Rome.

With the breaking off of our acquaintance, or rather our budding friendship, I lost interest in the contents of the packet. I threw
them on the shelf.

It was not until 1985 (the time of Gorbachev) that the news of
Anna's departure with her father to St. Petersburg—at that time
still Leningrad—galvanized me to "exhume" the Prince of Venosa.
Anna's letter, dashed off in Rome just before she left, informed me
that her old and ailing father wanted to die and to be buried in his
native city. She had tried to remind him that the two of them had
already bought a place for his eternal rest in the international
cemetery in Rome, next to his wife and her mother. "He insisted
with a vehemence that I had never seen or even suspected in him. I
had the unpleasant impression that he was 'leaving' my mother."
She had come to the conclusion that he could not be allowed to go
off alone at his age and in his condition to his distant homeland,
after so many years abroad. "Will we see each other again? Life
sometimes takes unexpected turns. My one consolation is a suitcase
of materials I'm bringing for my monograph. In the name of our
friendship, don't abandon the Prince of Venosa in your imagination." That request made me reach for the shelf. Over the space of
a few evenings I leafed through the meager "Gesualdiana" that was
available. The fruit of those evenings was the entry in my journal
dated February 10, 1985.

**III**

MANY PEOPLE HAVE taken an interest in the madrigalist prince. For musicologists and historians of music he was above all the "renewer of the genre" at the end of the sixteenth and beginning of the seventeenth century; out of a sense of duty they mentioned that he was also a murderer. For authors who enjoyed scandalous stories it was the opposite: They scarcely touched on his madrigals, concentrating their whole attention on the murders. Thus, there exists Carlo Gesualdo, the Prince of Venosa, as a marble bust in the pantheon of Italian music; and Carlo Gesualdo, the Prince of Venosa, as hero of a sixteenth-century "crime story," the murderer of his wife and her lover. In Brantôme's *Les dames galantes* he appears in the chapter entitled *Sur les dames qui font l'amour et leurs maris cocus* (On ladies who make love and their cuckolded husbands), of course in the role of cuckold. In England, in the 1920's a book about him came out under the title of *Musician and Murderer*, in which, apparently, the boundary between artist and criminal is deliberately blurred. Copies are not easy to come by today. (Note added in 1996: Werner Herzog recently made a film entitled *Gesualdo— Death For Five Voices*, which was not especially successful aside from the musical parts.)

Carlo Gesualdo came from an illustrious Neapolitan family whose princely title was associated with possessions and castles in the region of Venosa, on the border between Apulia and Lucania; the ancestral family estate was in the town of Gesualdo in Irpinia, to the east of Avellino. On his mother's side the prince was related to Pope Pius VI and to Saint Charles Borromeus. He married Maria d'Avalos, member of a no less eminent Neapolitan house. He was Maria's third husband. The previous two she had quickly dispatched to the next world, earning herself the appellation of "man-eater." She was considered the most beautiful woman in Naples; and also the embodiment of sensuality. She was twenty-two when she married the already famous madrigalist; she had first wed at the age of fifteen.

The Prince of Venosa was older than she. He had two passions, music and hunting. The chroniclers of the time particularly emphasize the former. He spent days and nights in his "musical workshop" in Naples, in the palace near San Domenico Maggiore, the Square of St. Dominic (famous because, rumor had it, St. Thomas Aquinas had proved his skill as a preacher from the still-preserved balcony of the former Dominican monastery). He composed many madrigals to the words of the poet Torquato Tasso, who was a friend of his. In the opinion of the chroniclers he had made a mistake in marrying such a beautiful and spirited woman, since in truth he was capable of only one love: that of Music. There were long periods when he did not even look into the marital bedchamber, while Maria, lonely and consumed by anger, listened to the sounds of instruments and the words of songs coming from his workshop. He treated her as an object for his infrequent "whims" and sexual distractions.

The most beautiful woman in Naples was said to be Maria d'Avalos; the most beautiful man, the "Archangel" Fabrizio Carafa, Prince of Andria. Their romance rapidly turned into a passion lacking any restraints. Whenever the madrigalist prince went on a hunting trip, the archangelic prince (who was married) spent whole nights in Maria's bedroom. Neither of them appeared to see the danger of the situation, especially Maria. This went on for a long time—as long as the prince was immersed in his madrigals, with his eyes closed. He opened them in 1590. On October 16th he pretended to be setting out to go hunting; then, a few hours after leaving, he returned to the palace at midnight. With his secretary and three servants he burst into Maria's bedroom. From the statements of the witnesses it emerged that after both lovers had been murdered by the prince and his escort, the deceived husband went back into the room from the threshold, and with a cry of *Non credo esser morta!*—"I don't believe that she's dead!"—he sliced the body of his faithless wife from crotch to neck with a short sword. The chroniclers speak of a double frenzy: the frenzy of a betrayed husband abusing the body of his wife; and the frenzy of the two lovers, who apparently knew that night with absolute certainty what awaited them, and prepared for death in an "embrace of love."

The court case was soon concluded. Carlo Gesualdo fled Naples for his castle in Gesualdo, out of fear of revenge by the d'Avalos family, and by the family of the Prince of Andria. After a year of solitude in the fortified castle—a year that was exceptionally rich in compositions—he left for the estate of the d'Este princes in Ferrara. There he married again; his new wife was Eleonora d'Este, a pious and submissive woman, whom he took back to his own Venosa. His grown son, from his first marriage with Maria d'Avalos, died in an accident; before that, an infant son from his second marriage with Eleonora d'Este had died soon after he was born. Despite remarrying, he continued to live a solitary life with his only true love, Music, and he was ever more prolific as a madrigalist. He died in 1613. Soon after his death, Eleonora entered a convent.

Three days after this entry in my journal, I wrote another. It will prove so fundamental in the continuation of my story that I must also include it here.

## IV

WHY SHOULD I hide it: It was as an admirer of Stendhal's *Italian Chronicles* that I thought about the Prince of Venosa. Did he know the story? Probably not, because if he had, his pen would not have been able to resist such a subject. Not because of the figure of the Prince of Venosa, who appealed to my imagination. Stendhal would have been fascinated by Maria d'Avalos: the bold, wild, reckless love of a woman; and the passion which tosses a challenge to death, growing even more wanton in its shadow. It is not so important whether the story described in the chronicles—about the pair of lovers awaiting their execution in an "embrace of love"—is true. One thing is certain: It was Fabrizio Carafa, the "Archangel," who had an instinctive urge to call it off when the lovers realized that the Prince of Venosa had found out about their affair; and it was Maria d'Avalos who accused him of "faint-hearted caution," as if in peril she perceived increased stimulation in love. The creator of Mathilde de la Mole, the man who (if my memory serves me correctly) once wrote that "love is the enemy of discretion," would have understood her—indeed, would have been entranced by her. Vanina Vanini, in the delightful novella of that name, cannot tolerate the thought that the Fatherland is her rival for the heart of a young carbonaro. In *San Francesco a Ripa* the Princess Campobasso has her circumspect and "overly calculating" French lover killed (so as later on, by the way, to become revered as the "model of all virtues"). As only he was able, Stendhal would in a few incomparably well-chosen sentences have shed all the light on "crazy" Maria d'Avalos, reducing the madrigalist prince to the role of a cruel and dull-witted cuckold, while assigning to the "archangelic" prince the part of lover of the *povero diavolo* type.

I wonder at the fact that over ten years ago, thanks to the counterpoint of Stendhal in my mind, I was able to perceive the heart of the Neapolitan tragedy with such a sense of measure and proportion. It was Carlo Gesualdo, the criminal, who "spoke to my imagination," to the detriment of the admittedly uncommon figure of Maria d'Avalos, the victim of his crime. To him I remained faithful to the end—I, a sworn Stendhalist. I saw the true victim of this crime as being the Prince of Venosa, while I charged Maria d'Avalos with killing him for twenty-three years of life devoid of life.

And it was in this vein that I wrote a long letter to St. Petersburg. Anna replied at once. How difficult it is for me to convey her joy, the trembling of her pen! I felt her almost physical closeness, and had no doubt that the hero of her monograph had forever tied us with the bonds of *amitié amoureuse* (at our age!). She defended the criminal furiously, even going so far as to assert that "someone had driven him to commit the crime," had thrust a sword into the hand of the composer, who was still in love—despite the betrayal, perhaps in defiance of it!—that reviver of the genre of madrigals of love and piety. He was regarded as a "musical Petrarch," and was one to his last breath (though with the mourning face of a mortally wounded killer). "I consider this spiritual brotherhood of ours, of yours and mine, this covenant of hearts," Anna concluded her letter, "to be a miracle. I longed for it but did not believe it would ever come."

## V

THUS BEGAN OUR correspondence, which became regular. Every month I received a letter from St. Petersburg. And the same day I

would write and send a reply. Since Anna was in constant contact
with her Neapolitan friends from the music world, I did not need
to refrain from writing about Naples in my letters. Her letters, on
the other hand, were a combination of a dialogue about the Prince
of Musicians, and long passages about St. Petersburg. I confess that
I looked forward especially to the latter. I wanted to know how she
was settling in with her father in his native city. And I was anxious
to learn about the new life in the Soviet Union after what was effectively the fall of communism, described by someone close to me,
and also—something that in spite of all the changes remained
important—in a language that was foreign to the censors; every
linguistic nuance that we both understood evaded their heavy-
handed control.

The beginnings were tough. Anna and her father lived in a
shabby little one-room apartment, using up the savings they had
brought from Italy. The situation was somewhat mitigated by her
father's state of mind: Though he was already very old, he gave the
impression of reliving anew, and in a state of permanent euphoria,
his entire life in St. Petersburg—from his childhood to his university studies and the revolution. Spared the torments of the "years
of transition," his memories were largely pleasant ones. True, he
could not fail to see the wounds inflicted on the city by the war, especially by the siege; but such things heal quickly. He was in constant motion with his old man's walking stick, and was able to seek
out old friends who had miraculously survived; vodka, by its nature, disposes people to wallow in their shared past. He even found
the brother of his wife Wanda; everyone else from her family had
died in the gulags. He was troubled only by the tiny apartment
which he had to share with his daughter. In Rome he had had his
own room, and everyone knows what it is to have your own room
*A Room of One's Own*: He would often longingly repeat the title of
Virginia Woolf's book, though without remembering what it was
about.

In any case Anna's father's mood was a great relief to her; she
realized too (and in her writing there was a hint of melancholy reflection) that he, who had come to St. Petersburg to die, seemed
gradually to be coming to life there. While she—though thanks to
her father she knew the language and to some extent the culture of

Russia (its music and literature)—was in essence a child of Italy. Even the time of fascism, which occurred in the years of her early youth, even *los desastros de la guerra* in the final period of the war, had not taken away from her that particular relish for life which was a part of Italian existence, even in misfortune. And which, by the way, in a curious and inexplicable way always infuriated her father. For him the only "serious" nation were the Russians.

A lucky turn of events came after a year, in mid-1986. Anna managed to publish an extensive article about the "madrigalist prince" in the musical quarterly published sporadically in St. Petersburg by the Academy of Music. Carlo Gesualdo was known to musicians in Russia (in 1960 Stravinsky had devoted a short work to him entitled *Monumentum ad Carolum Gesualdum*), but very superficially. She was given a poorly paid position at the Academy, along with a small unheated room in which to keep her madrigalist library. She regarded this as a dream come true. At the same time she took up with a high-school teacher who was a widower and the owner of a two-roomed apartment. Her father remained finally alone in the tiny old apartment. About herself and her companion (they did not marry) she wrote: "We are of the same age. In other words, the same age as you and I. Dmitry likes music." Enclosed in the letter was a photograph. His stern countenance with its lackluster gaze contrasted with her face, which was still handsome, animated, yet refined, resembling a little that of Akhmatova in her sixties.

## VI

OH, THE USED bookstores of Naples! A closed world, a kingdom of learned scholars that is enveloped in the smell of musty or bone-dry paper. Whoever loves ancient publications, whoever likes to hunt for manuscripts buried under piles of books, whoever believes secretly in their lucky star, should never leave a used bookstore muttering: "Once again, nothing." Bookstores of this kind, like grocery stores, exist on the basis of new stock coming in daily. Yesterday you went away empty-handed; today, amongst insignificant publications there shone, like a jewel, a work you had long been searching for, more disappointed and despondent with every day.

The street that splits Naples in two, the Spaccanapoli, is divided into many stretches, each with its own name. The section which for centuries has been watched over by the spirit of St. Blaise, the patron saint of booksellers, is the richest domain of used bookstores. When one knows the owners, one can count on information that is fresh, precious, even indispensable, given the indifferent state of the catalogues, which are rarely updated after they are published.

My bookseller (the "my" indicates a level of familiarity) had known for some time that I was on the trail of the Prince of Musicians. There was something intriguing and charming in the fact that his three rooms *en suite*, filled to the very ceiling with heaps of paper, were situated close to the Palazzo di Torre Maggiore, the palace of the Gesualdo princes next to the Piazza San Domenico. A person could imagine—and a bookworm without an imagination is half-dead, barely capable of a single movement—how the type of book called a *rara avis* made its way from the palace to the bookstore via underground passages through the cellars. And in fact, one day my bookseller telephoned me. He did not want to reveal to me over the phone what it was about, as if he were afraid to let out a secret to bank robbers tapping the line; but he asked me to come by in the evening, adding: "You won't regret it."

And indeed I did not. The dust-covered pamphlet of twenty pages, dated 1620—in other words seven years after Carlo Gesualdo's death—bore the title *La verità sul principe assassino*, "The Truth about the Murderer Prince." The author was given as Duca Federico Ignotus, obviously a pen-name. I paid the rather stiff price without haggling. And I carried the pamphlet home at my breast, beneath my shirt, even though I was well aware it was not the kind of valuable that aroused the appetite of street thieves.

It was not entirely clear whether the author had the right to call himself a duke and a friend of the Prince of Musicians (as he claimed, without ostentation incidentally), or whether the information he set out in print was first-hand, and not from the exuberant bush of "things heard from others." In the end, though, I decided to take him at face value. When it came down to it, I was not a his-

torian on the hunt, but someone from the outside who was involved in the whole business through a lady friend, a doctor of
music. I needed, then, to pass all my finds on to her, so she herself
could adjudicate what was and was not noteworthy. I sent a photocopy of the pamphlet to St. Petersburg.

## VII

YET I COULD NOT resist the temptation to add a letter with my
own commentary on the claims of Duke Frederick the Unknown.
After all, those claims concerned the social-psychological underpinnings of the crime, without embarking in even a single sentence
on the subject of the art of the madrigal (which, it appeared, was as
foreign to the writer as it was to me).

The greatest confidence was inspired by his connections to the
exclusive world of the Neapolitan aristocracy, whether it was
through direct family links, or only social ties. He wrote about the
highborn with such naturalness, such lack of deference, that it was
impossible to see it as dressing in borrowed clothes. At several
points he dropped subtle hints that the pseudonym of Duca Ignotus had immediately been deciphered by many people of his circle,
but that the author had retained it in subsequent editions of the
pamphlet for legal reasons (which I could not fully comprehend).
The theme of the Neapolitan nobility made me realize (and also
must have made Anna realize after she received my letter, if she had
not surmised it before) that the situation of the cuckolded madrigalist was public knowledge, and not only to those who were his
equals in rank: The common people around the Palazzo Gesualdo
also knew (probably from the palace servants) what was going on
with the love triangle of the Prince of Musicians, beautiful Maria
d'Avalos, and the Prince of Andria.

This statement by the author of the pamphlet led to another,
more sensational one. The aristocratic community expected the
deceived husband to avenge the disgrace. And this meant the entire
community, including the family of the lover. Such were the norms
of behavior amongst the upper classes at that time; while in fact
plebeian views did not greatly differ. The indignity to which Maria

d'Avalos and Fabrizio Carafa had subjected the Prince of Gesualdo and Venosa was a bloody affront; therefore it demanded blood in retribution. I repeat, that was the shared judgment of aristocrat and pauper. In his pamphlet Duca Ignotus particularly stressed this point, so that the reader should never forget that the Prince of Musicians had only one way out of the situation, whether he wished it or not. Did that mean he may not have wished it? Though Duca Ignotus was circumspect, he did not rule out such a possibility, especially considering that Carlo Gesualdo was regarded as more of a musician than a prince, and had a better grasp of sheet music than of ancestral traditions of honor.

In the Unknown Duke's exposition one thing was missing, which he raised and presented to the reader only on the last page of the pamphlet. It was a short, moving letter from the fugitive prince, written from inside the walls of the fortified castle in Gesualdo to the author of the pamphlet, seven years after the prince had fled Naples. Was it authentic? Fabricated? The text rather led me to be convinced of its authenticity. First, there was a dotted line, where probably there had been the real name and full title of the addressee. Then: "It is said that I loved music more than I loved Maria; and that this became the cause of the tragedy. I deny this with all the strength of my aching (*addolorato*) heart. I loved no one and nothing so much as I loved Maria from the first time I met her. Now I am not only the murderer of my wife and her lover. I am a widower condemned to an existence (which I hope will be short) as a living corpse. Everything that was in me died on October 16th, 1590 (the day of the murder). May God have at least a little mercy, at the entreaty of St. Charles Borromeus, upon the tormented soul of a man who (I confess it) wondered whether the terrible price of marital infidelity was not worth paying if it meant saving the life of the woman he loved above all else."

A short note in small print in the pamphlet explained why the Prince of Musicians waited in the castle of Gesualdo for a whole year for an attack by armed men and the bloody vengeance of the Princes of Andria from the family of the murdered Fabrizio Carafa, even though it was common knowledge that they too, like the rest of the Neapolitan aristocracy, considered that the exculpation of the criminal signed by the judges the next morning and initialed by the Spanish viceroy was just and in keeping with principles of chivalry. The point was, wrote the author of the pamphlet, that Carlo Gesualdo had not killed his wife and her lover on his own, but with the assistance of his servants. The sense of insult could have arisen from the blows that had fallen on the Prince of Andria by plebeian hands.

## VIII

ANNA'S TENDER REPLY from St. Petersburg was proof that she was pleased. Even more: that she was delighted. She thanked me profusely for the photocopy of the pamphlet by the Unknown Duke, expressing "absolute certainty" that it was authentic, and even trying to guess the identity of the author. She had already begun translating the pamphlet into Russian, for she had signed a contract with the Music Press in St. Petersburg for a simultaneous Russian edition of her own work about the great Italian madrigalist (the Neapolitan publishers had long been awaiting the original manuscript). The tone of her letter gave me pleasure. *Amitié amoureuse* is often born from the ties of a shared enterprise bringing two people together even more strongly and intimately. That appeared to be what was happening in our case, even though we were no longer young, and Anna had her life companion in St. Petersburg, while I was married in Naples.

Upon reading the letter through carefully a number of times, I realized what it was that had so delighted Anna. Writing a book about the Prince of Musicians and about his creative work (and she knew all the madrigals of Carlo Gesualdo), she naturally could not overlook his life, and above all his personal tragedy. She had come to her own conclusions about this at the beginning of her research, while she was still in Naples; but amongst her musicologist colleagues she had always encountered resistance and skepticism. Now this pamphlet, which I had dug up in a used bookstore, was a serious argument to tip her side of the scales, which up till now had been rather empty. For Anna had been claiming with an intuitive obstinacy that Carlo Gesualdo had murdered his perfidious wife and her lover *contre coeur*, that he was driven to the crime by those around him, in love despite everything with Maria d'Avalos. She had promised herself that she would demonstrate this cautiously through her musical analysis of the artist's madrigals, but it was understandable that she also sought confirmation in her study of his biography. The pamphlet of the Unknown Duke bore all the marks of such confirmation.

Yet she was avoiding the sore point in the crime, which for Anna was the principal impediment in her purely intuitive conjectures. If one accepted the position taken by Anna, and in part by the author of the pamphlet, then what was to be made of the murderer's attack of rage, his returning to the bedchamber with the cry of "I don't believe that she's dead,!" and cutting her so horribly from crotch to neck?

In her next letter, written a few days after the previous one, Anna informed me in a tone of triumph (rather premature, to my mind) that she had visited a friend of her father's from his university days, a retired professor of psychology called Litayev, who was considered a great specialist both in his native St. Petersburg and in many western universities. After a long conversation with the still lively and sharp-witted old man, who was most interested in the story of the sixteenth-century crime in Naples, Anna summarized the conclusion of his arguments. It could not be ruled out that Carlo Gesualdo was, as it were, killing himself; that he was "committing suicide" in his despair, as he ill-treated his dying or already dead wife in such a frenzy and with such cruelty. Though they were rare, there were comparable cases (asserted the St. Petersburg professor) in the tangled labyrinths of the human mind; cases which can be labeled "suicide by murder."

Anna was dazzled by this conclusion—or rather hypothesis (since it was a matter of a case so distant in space and time) —of the St. Petersburg luminary. Could I (she requested) pay a visit in Naples, to Marconi, on the Piazza Gesù? He was an acquaintance of hers who was a professor of psychology, and with whom she had often spoken about the ancient Neapolitan tragedy on the nearby Piazza San Domenico. Would I present to him the tentative diagnosis of his colleague in St. Petersburg? I could not refrain from smiling. Anna was well aware that I had little confidence in the mysterious science of psychology.

## IX

EVERYTHING TOOK PLACE within a radius of a few hundred yards. From the Piazza San Domenico, where the palace of the Gesualdo family had once been located, I passed along a short stretch of the Spaccanapoli (without stopping in on the way to my favorite Church of Santa Chiara) to the Piazza Gesù, the Square of Jesus; there I stepped rather unwillingly into the Chiesa Gesù, the Church of Jesus. Unwillingly, because the original façade of a former Renaissance palace concealed a ponderous, over-ornamented baroque interior. Nevertheless, I stood for a moment at the side altar dedicated to St. Ignatius Loyola. The Prince of Musicians had been buried at his feet immediately after his death in Gesualdo, without, oddly enough, encountering any objections from the church authorities. The great madrigalist was a criminal, it was true; but he was also related to cardinals, popes, and even a saint.

Right opposite the Chiesa Gesù, on the other side of the square beyond its central baroque column, stood an apartment building several stories high, its plaster peeling and riddled with holes; whenever I would cross the square to get to Santa Chiara, for some unknown reason I would always imagine that this building was a replica of the house in St. Petersburg in which Raskolnikov killed the money-lender and her sister. The crumbling façade did not alter the fact that inside there were fine, elegant apartments. In one of them lived Professor Marconi.

He had known Anna in earlier years, and so he listened with a patient and kindly smile to my account of the pamphlet by the Unknown Duke, the hypothesis of the St. Petersburg psychologist, and Anna's hopes that he would confirm it.

"I cannot do so," he laughed aloud, "because Professor Litayev, two or three of whose articles I have read in western psychology journals, and I belong to different research schools which are absolutely, diametrically opposed to one another. For me the idea of suicide in the form of murder—taking one's own life through the medium of a second, murdered person—is a preposterous notion. While Anna was still living in Naples, she would visit me sometimes; we would listen to music together (I'm something of a music

lover), and I would always advise her to leave her psychological inquiries alone and to confine herself to an analysis of the works. An
artist is above all his compositions; poking around in his biography
is nothing but a deception. The truth lies in his madrigals, not in
the murder of his wife and her lover. I don't doubt that Carlo
Gesualdo changed rather radically after that bloody business of his;
yet I'm certain the changes left their mark on his creativity, and
that is where they should be sought. There's no place for Anna's intuitions or Litayev's absurdly far-fetched hypothesis. Please, tell
her this openly in a letter."

I followed Professor Marconi's instructions. For a long time no
reply came; I suspected that she had been hurt. But the reasons for
her silence were different. Her old and yet still hale father had finally died (he had fallen down the stairs while drunk), and her life
companion had been obliged to take in his young son from his first
marriage from his parents in Kharkov. After being orphaned, Anna
had become a mother; her letter showed that a new and welcome
chord had sounded in her heart. At one time I had been convinced
that after her father's death she would return to Italy. That was no
longer a possibility, since she had even exchanged her Italian passport for a Russian one. Her father would have been pleased; but
her Polish mother now lay abandoned in the international cemetery in Rome.

In the same letter certain sentences testified to the fact that our
*amitié amoureuse* had grown even stronger. Anna accomplished this,
not without a certain poetic talent, as if she were imitating (though
I do not think she knew them) the letters of the eternally amorous
Marina Tsvetayeva, which were frequently written to men she had
met by chance and who were without a doubt more ordinary than
Pasternak or Rilke. (One such letter, to a very mediocre and dullish
Russian poet, I read a few years ago in Munich, thanks to the addressee's boastful courtesy.)

And lastly, the letter also contained the first part of a serious
lecture by the scholar about the development of the madrigals of
the Prince of Music; though she did not mention Professor Marconi, and did not say a word about my account of the visit I paid
him, it was clear that she was taking his advice.

# X

THROUGHOUT ALL THIS time—in other words, from the moment I met Anna and entered the realm of her interests—I had systematically been collecting recordings of the madrigals of the Prince of Musicians. Upon Anna's recommendation, I became a regular recipient of the disks of a German recording company in Cologne for whom Carlo Gesualdo was the object of a cult (and by all accounts, the source of considerable income as the master of the suddenly popular genre of the madrigal).

I am not a music specialist, only a music lover. And that was enough for me to succumb more and more to the charm of the madrigals as I listened in the evening to recordings from my by now extensive collection. Short pieces for five or six voices, ideally matched by the musical accompaniment (usually harp and lute), now pious, now about love, now dramatic, now light and almost gay, they entranced me ever more with their transposition of poetry into the language of music. It was not just that the words were provided by poets (Torquato Tasso, for example, was a regular supplier for the hero of our story); but that the art of the madrigal (as far as I remember, it was Huxley who made this observation) took on the character of musical, lyrical poems. Those who love poetry are aware that even the most beautiful lyric poem cannot transcend the barrier of the word, that it is the child and the slave of language: In the madrigals the music miraculously liberated it, without disturbing its linguistic roots. That was the first thing. And second, even poets are unable to avoid a certain lyric monotony, which in the madrigals blossoms into an unexpected variety. How much Carlo Gesualdo was able to extract from just one of Petrarch's poems!

Mood, modulation, and style make it possible to divide the work of any good madrigalist into distinct blocks or periods. Just as with poetry: We often speak of a great poet as "early" or "late," and occasionally we also introduce geographical periods (where such works were written). Anna's first lecture in her letter recommended that I read the relevant section of the *Breve storia della musica*, by the most eminent Italian musicologist, Massimo Mila. My purely amateur approach to music obliges me to quote the learned specialist's judg-

ment word for word: "The Neapolitan Carlo Gesualdo, Prince of
Venosa, the protagonist of a lugubrious marital tragedy and a murderer out of jealousy, seems to have brought the boundless chaos of
his passions into the insatiable chromatic feverishness of his music.
From Marienzio to Gesualdo there can be seen a transition from the
ordered harmony of the Renaissance to the convulsive interioriza-
tion of the Baroque. An excess of dissonances, an overuse of chro-
maticism, and harmonic caprices lead to complete tonal anarchy, the
mirror of spiritual torment, which directs the listener's mind to the
romanticism *avant la lettre* of Caravaggio."

Even without Anna's advice, with my musicological dilettantism,
I would have extracted from the quoted passage the ideas that were
most essential for me. Mila rightly noted the "feverishness" and
"convulsiveness" of Gesualdo's madrigals. This linked his music
with comparable qualities in Caravaggio's painting, an exceptionally
intelligent observation. But Anna categorically insisted I should remember that this description perfectly matched his Neapolitan
madrigals *before* the tragedy. Despite opinions to the contrary circu-
lating in the society of the time, Carlo Gesualdo was a man of
impetuous feelings who was easily subject to his passions. Like
Caravaggio. But the painter's "convulsive feverishness" continued to
grow, driving him towards crime, leading him to a wandering life,
and eventually bringing about his demise, with the help of malaria
and sunstroke. Whereas the Prince of Musicians reached the zenith
of his "convulsive feverishness," his impetuousness, on October
16th, 1590, the day on which his wife and her lover were murdered;
after this his emotions tended to subside, not to say more.

Although I was not a hundred percent convinced about this, I
accepted Anna's point of view. In Gesualdo's early madrigals there
could indeed be heard the play of the passions, resembling the constant tempest in Caravaggio's heart.

## XI

I WAS NOT A HUNDRED percent convinced, and Anna's point of
view seemed a little far-fetched. And yet listening frequently to
recordings of the murderer's madrigals, those composed in the

years of his widowerhood and even his second marriage—in other words from the second half of the life of the Prince of Musicians—disk after disk, madrigal after madrigal, this listening drew me in to an atmosphere which I had not previously perceived. At this point I have a wish, or rather a need, to make use of a metaphorical description. It was as if the voices and sounds were carried on the wind forcing its way in through the chinks in a window frame; as if these voices and sounds were echoing off the walls with a bizarre, barely audible moan; and, what was most important, with a chill, a terrible chill. I really did feel at last, perhaps not so powerfully as Anna, the difference between the man of hidden passions, from the period of his happy and impetuous youth, and the later man of solitude amongst people, searching in vain for a place for himself in a suddenly deserted world. Naturally (and especially as an amateur and dilettante) I do not presume to pass artistic judgment; I do not place the first period over the second or vice versa. Though I am a lover of the perpetual storm in the heart of Caravaggio—and thus according to Professor Mila's analogy I should rather incline to the early Carlo Gesualdo—I was on the contrary an admirer of his later madrigals. And at times, inspired by the musicologist's subtle juxtaposition, I tried to imagine a "quieted" Caravaggio. An artist who after all he had experienced in his youth, after his bloody adventures, passions and escapes, finally returned to his beloved Rome and gave his painting, once all atremble, the classical equilibrium of calm and solitude.

\* \* \*

IT WAS A TRULY extraordinary thing that, living so close, relatively speaking, to the castle in Gesualdo, I was informed by Anna in a letter from St. Petersburg that on October 16th, 1990, precisely on the four hundredth anniversary of the Neapolitan murders, the Prince of Musicians' ancestral town had decided to organize a festival. Scholars of the famous madrigalist from all over the world had been invited. It goes without saying that Anna's name was at the head of the guest list; in circles devoted to the musician of the sixteenth and seventeenth centuries it was widely known that for some time now Anna had been working on a weighty book about him. Anna's trip was funded jointly by the St. Petersburg Music Society and the *Società Carlo Gesualdo* in Avellino, a town situated close to the madrigalist's castle. Anna's letter informed me of the event and asked if I would attend; the request was so affectionate and kind that I did not hesitate for a moment.

Arriving around noon in the little town, which was filled with a colorful crowd, within a few minutes I ran across Anna at a table in a café near the Capuchin Church of Santa Maria delle Grazie. On the chair next to her lay a pile of Italian newspapers. I did not immediately see her face, which was hidden behind a paper, and I could observe only her figure: She was the same age as me, yet despite her seventy years she was still as slim and shapely as in the old times in Italy, and no one could have guessed how old she was by looking at her. Though that figure was dressed in wretched clothes, there was something aristocratic about her: the still-ripe fruit of the teachings of her father, who snobbishly emphasized their noble ancestry. She was engrossed in her reading; I stood so close to her that my knees touched hers. It was only then that she raised her head; her face, also still young and scarcely marked with wrinkles, was transformed into one great, joyful smile. She jumped up from her chair, and we fell into each other's arms and kissed like a married couple after a long parting. She now mixed languages— *dorogoy, caro*—and it seemed to me that she was more fluent in Russian, to the detriment of her somewhat rusty Italian. We made our way, not without difficulty, through the crowd to the church, which was also bursting at the seams and buzzing like a hive, though with a very unchurchlike casualness. Luckily Anna was spotted by a conservator from Naples who knew her. Thanks to his intercession, we were let in to see the Painting.

I write this word with a capital letter because it was the only visible or tangible legacy of the "musician and murderer," to use the title of the English book about him. It was hard to believe that Anna was seeing it for the first time (not counting its reproductions), let alone that this was her first visit to Gesualdo; it was mine too, though that was more understandable. Carlo Gesualdo had had the church and the adjacent monastery built in 1592. Sixteen years after his death church and monastery had been enlarged on the instructions of the brother-in-law of Pope Gregory XV, who had married the niece of the Prince of Musicians. The Painting is in effect the pearl for which the shell of the church was created. It is titled *Il perdono di Carlo Gesualdo*, and it is known that the Prince of Musicians commissioned it from a not especially outstanding Florentine artist by the name of Balducci; what is not known is when it was commissioned, or when the artist completed it. Nor is it known who is pardoning whom in the Painting. From the title it would appear that Carlo Gesualdo is doing the pardoning—that is, of his faithless wife and her lover. But certain details suggest that it is he who is asking for pardon for the murder of the two lovers. It may be that the ambiguity of the Painting was the madrigalist's intention. It should not be forgotten that his first madrigal, written in his youth, was entitled *Delicta nostra ne reminiscaris, Domine*— "Do not remind us of our sins (or crimes), O Lord."

Anna's eyes, which seemed to have suddenly clouded over or become dull, were fixed upon the bottom left-hand corner of the Painting. Carlo Gesualdo was on his knees, his hands folded together in prayer, wearing a black cloak with ruffed collar; standing next to him was his relative, Saint Charles Borromeus, with his right hand on his shoulder in a gesture of supplication to the Virgin Mary, the company of saints, and the Redeemer in the upper and middle parts of the Painting. In the lower right-hand corner was Eleonora d'Este dressed like her husband and in the same posture. Between them were the flames of purgatory, in which could be seen the naked pair of lovers and a group of angels bearing the figures of the sinners upwards. The Redeemer was on a cloud between the Virgin Mary and the Archangel Michael.

What a look it was that Anna fastened upon her Prince of Musicians! Am I exaggerating to call it "enamored"? His face, excessively elongated by the painter and too yellowed in color, was certainly not handsome. Yet it combined a manly nobility of expression with the delicacy of an artist offering his gift to God, while asking for forgiveness under the protective wing of a saint. So was it after all he who was asking for pardon, at the same time pardoning Maria d'Avalos and Fabrizio Carafa in the fires of what may have been passion, or the entrance to hell? When Anna finally rose from her knees and discreetly wiped her eyes with a handkerchief, her smile was meant for me.

We ate lunch in a restaurant whose windows overlooked the castle in Gesualdo. An earthquake in 1980, ten years before the festival, had damaged its façade and left cracks in the walls—especially in the belvedere in the tower, where could be found the musical workshop and apartment of the madrigalist, isolated from the rest of the castle. The whole area of the castle was surrounded front and back by a fence of narrow planks, and at a number of points in this barrier warning signs had been nailed up: *Pericolo! Ingresso severamente vietato.*

I could not hold it against Anna that she stared at the tower of the castle and paid no attention to my questions about her life in St. Petersburg. She may not even have heard them. Or perhaps she was giving me to understand in this way that she did not *want* to speak about what was supposedly her real homeland (though in fact she was forced to adopt it after her return from Italy). The latter version seemed more plausible to me. I was already rather familiar with the reactions of other Russian *vozvrashchentsy.*[1] These responses were not a matter of the legacy of the system, or difficulties with housing; the Soviet regime had created a different Russia, over which there hung a different air that was difficult for newcomers from the West to breathe.

In the meantime the anniversary festivities intensified their rhythms and gained in impetus and intensity, as all Italian celebrations do, moving steadily towards an evening climax. A procession was moving along the street from the Church of Santa Maria delle Grazie to the beat of a band and was drawing near to our restaurant, with the intention (it was explained to us) of circling the Castello Gesualdo. Beneath a red canopy the mayor of the little town led by the arm the Bishop of Avellino and the bursar of the Department of the Conservation of Monuments in Naples. The first rockets were going off; the real storm of fireworks and volleys from shotguns was planned for the hours between nightfall and midnight. When the band fell silent, school choirs began to sing. The Bishop of Avellino blessed spectators on both sides of the street. As he did so he did not hide his satisfaction, as if the festival were a commemoration of some triumph of the Church.

[1] Those returning (to Russia).

And yet—something that smacked of a kind of madness—this was a solemn celebration of the four hundredth anniversary of a murder, of blood spilt in a Neapolitan palace by a betrayed husband. Was it sufficient that he was a member of the aristocracy, a close relative of a saint, and many cardinals, considered *papabili*, protagonists of future conclaves?

## XII

THE OCTOBER WEATHER was favorable; the sun was as hot as in summer, and we wandered aimlessly around Gesualdo, holding hands, stopping at the stalls of the fair, and glancing every so often towards the always visible castle. The phrase "I had something of a crush on Anna" was still current; age was of no significance here. That "crush" meant an unbroken stream of tendernesses.

We ate dinner in the same restaurant. A dark night fell; the castle disappeared for a moment, but soon afterwards it was illuminated by the floodlights trained upon it. Anna went to the bathroom. She did not come back for such a long time that I knocked on the door. There was no response. Worried, I went to the parking lot behind the church and found the car with the diplomatic plates that the Russian embassy had lent her for the journey to Gesualdo. It was locked. Struck by a vague presentiment, I returned to the restaurant. I sat at the table till one in the morning, up to the moment when the floodlights lighting up the castle were turned off. The letting down of the window blinds in the restaurant gave me politely to understand that the servers were waiting to finally be relieved of my presence. I left and sat on the rim of the beautiful fountain that Carlo Gesualdo had had built in 1605. Night had swallowed up the town and its festival.

My vague premonition turned out not to be baseless. In the tower, in the window beneath the belvedere a light from a pocket flashlight or an ordinary match came on and was quickly extinguished again. The emptiness all around emboldened me; I tiptoed quietly up to the barrier of planks. It was easy to climb over it; the difficulties began further on, on the rubble-strewn flank of the castle. And yet, stepping cautiously and more than once stumbling to

my knees, I managed to make my way to the entrance of what
looked like some kind of corridor. It was indeed a corridor, which
was littered with rocks yet could be navigated slowly. At its far end
an exit through the cellar could be discerned. I tried to leave by it,
not without being startled by the sound of falling rocks; and saw
Anna above me. She leant down and gave me her hand.

The large chamber was dusty and cluttered with objects; there
was a rickety table, a three-legged chair, a cupboard full of waste
paper, and a broken bed, while the windows were covered with
sacking. It was in all likelihood the workshop and bedroom of the
Prince of Musicians. Anna had managed to light a small fire in an
alcove that resembled a fireplace. In front of it she laid her heavy
overcoat (which looked as if it had formerly been an army great-
coat), and told me to sit down beside her.

"Here," she said quietly, almost in a whisper, "he received the
blow, the mortal blow. There was really only one person left in the
world who was dear to him: Emanuele, his son from his first marriage with Maria d'Avalos. He could barely tolerate his second wife.
She had given him a son, Alfonsino, who died soon after he was
born; she irritated him with her meek and excessive piety. Emanuele
linked him to the only woman he had ever loved. He grew into an
energetic young man; he married in Bohemia, already had a small
daughter and was expecting another child. On August 20th, 1613,
on a hunting trip, he fell from a galloping horse and was killed on the
spot. His father summoned four people and drew up a new will, at-
tested by their signatures, after which he closed himself up in his
room. He refused to receive meals. He had decided to commit suicide in this way. During the last eighteen days before his death, he
wrote a last madrigal for five voices, which until recently was completely unknown. He gave it the title of 'Death: Longed For and
Blessèd.' He died on the evening of September 8th."

She broke off and turned her face to the wall. We sat like this
for some time in silence; I tried to keep up the fire in the alcove. In
the end Anna stood up and from the corner of the room brought a
traveling bag which she had probably taken from her car before she
set out to break into the tower. In the bag she had a small compact
disc player. She placed it carefully on the firmer end of the table,
and there came the sounds of the Prince of Music's last madrigal.

In the title of this story I called it a madrigal "of mourning." It was and was not one of mourning; in it, the breath of approaching death was interwoven with joy-filled callings. The word "welcome" was repeated many times in the lyrics. But it was always accompanied, like an icy gust of air, by a phrase including the words *delicta nostra*, our crimes. The madrigal was moving, and was after all one of mourning; I thought instinctively of Schubert's quintet written a few hours before he died. When one listens to such works, it is easier to believe in the existence of the next world; its aura only rarely, and yet sometimes with sufficient clarity, permeates the souls of the dying. Oh Lord, God of artists and of the faithful with pure souls, how magnificently You are able in the hour of death to reveal Your presence! And how tenaciously the artist must work to earn this privilege before departing our bitter and barren earth.

Anna was by now weeping unrestrainedly as she listened to the madrigal of mourning. I gazed into her glistening eyes and kept repeating one sentence in my mind: "You had a crush on a woman who from the beginning was in love with someone else." Was she in love with this madrigalist who had become a criminal exactly four hundred years ago today? Yes, that is how it was. Fate rarely allows us to witness (let alone to experience) a love of those who are dead. People are mortal, but our feelings for them are not. And did Marina Tsvetayeva, Anna's compatriot, not write once that from the time she was a young girl, through all her grown years and into old age she was in love with Pushkin both as a poet and as a man? She was unfaithful to him with the living, but only fleetingly.

In the gray light before dawn, with the aid of my flashlight we left the tower. It was still too early for the laborers working on the restoration of the castle. The town was deserted, except for a light that was on in a café on the corner. We drank a coffee there, then went to the parking lot. Anna was in a hurry to get back to Rome, where her flight to St. Petersburg (with a connection in Moscow) left at lunchtime. We hugged, and she whispered in my ear: "I'll never forget you," first in Italian, then in Russian. Which also meant that I would never see her again. I watched the red lights of her car as it disappeared round the corner. After which I began warming up the engine of my own car.

I am now holding in my hands the Italian edition of Anna Fedotova's book, a thick volume lavishly illustrated with pictures and musical scores. I am touched that in the epilogue she describes our shared descent from the castle hill. She called her book *The Prince of Musicians*, and under the title she placed an inscription in small print as an epigraph: *Nobilissimus Carolus Gesualdus, Princeps Venusinus, nostrae tempestatis Musicorum, ac Melopaeorum, Princeps.* The most noble Carlo Gesualdo, Prince of Venosa, in our age, Prince of Musicians and of Singers.

That was how he had been described in Blancanus's encyclopedia, published in Bologna in 1615, two years after his death.


*September–October 1996*

ACKNOWLEDGMENT is given to the Publishers of the following books from which quotes in these stories are used:

*The Devil: Perceptions of Evil from Antiquity to Primitive Christianity*, by Jeffrey Burton Russell (Ithaca: Cornell University Press, 1977).

*Barabbas*, by Pär Lagerkvist, tr. by Alan Blair (New York: Vintage Books, 1989).

*Pensées*, by Blaise Pascal, tr. by H. F. Stewart (New York: Pantheon, 1950).

*Poems*, by Paul Valery, tr. by David Paul (Princeton: Princeton University Press, 1971).

*Collected Poems*, by C. P. Cavafy, tr. by Edmund Keeley and Philip Sherrard (Princeton: Princeton University Press, 1992).

*The Master and Margarita*, by Mikhail Bulgakov, tr. by Diana Burgin and Katherine Tiernan O'Connor (Overlook, 1995).